DARK
HOMECOMING

This book is a work of fiction. Names, characters, places and incidents are products of the author's imagination or are used fictitiously. Any resemblance to actual events or locales or persons, living or dead, is entirely coincidental.

POCKET BOOKS, a division of Simon & Schuster Inc.
1230 Avenue of the Americas, New York, NY 10020

Library of Congress Cataloging-in-Publication Data

Lustbader, Eric
      Dark homecoming / Eric Lustbader
         p.   cm.
      ISBN 0-671-00329-1
      I. Title.
      PS3562.U752D37   1997
      813'.54—dc21   96-48909
                                                     CIP

First Pocket Books hardcover printing July 1997

10 9 8 7 6 5 4 3 2 1

POCKET and colophon are registered trademarks of
Simon & Schuster Inc.

Printed in the U.S.A.

DARK HOMECOMING

ERIC LUSTBADER

POCKET BOOKS

New York   London   Toronto   Sydney   Tokyo   Singapore

This is for Two Women:

My Wife, Victoria

and

Claire Zion

Both of whom shared this book
with me in the most intimate ways.

ACKNOWLEDGMENTS

The following medical personnel were extraordinarily helpful and patient:

Dr. Bertram J. Newman
Dr. Michael Baden, Chief Forensic Expert, NY State Police

Diane, Ken, Kimberly, Marilyn and Cynthia at the Dialysis Dept., Boca Raton Community Hospital

Candy Wilson, Transplant Coordinator, Palm Beach, Martin, St. Lucie Counties, South Florida Miami Organ Recovery Program, University of Miami

All the rivers run into the sea;
yet the sea is not full; unto the place
from whence the rivers come;
thither they return again.

    —*Ecclesiastes 1:7*

The Human body was designed
to walk, run or stop; it wasn't
built for coasting.

    —*Cullen Hightower*

DARK
HOMECOMING

PROLOGUE

"Last night I had a dream," Heitor Bonita said, "and this is what I dreamed—"

"*Madre de mentiras*, I beg you. Don't tell me your dreams," Antonio Bonita said. "I already know your dreams."

"This one's different," Heitor replied. "You don't know this one."

There ensued a small but ungainly pause while "Mope-itty Mope" by the Boss-Tones doo-wopped out of the speakers. Music of these old American groups from the 1950s was Heitor's idea. Antonio would have preferred Machito's hyper-hot Afro-Cubano jazz, but it seemed the kids who hung out in Miami's South Beach weren't very hip to Latino roots, and didn't much care to be. Their loss. But even Antonio had to admit it was the Boneyard's gain.

Ever since they'd opened this club, it had been packed. Antonio had been skeptical when he'd first heard the idea, but it had seemed so off the-wall that Heitor had glommed on to it right away. Not that they were directly involved; like always, they were far removed from official ownership. Deep in the shadows where nobody could see, they raked in the money. From the first moment they had set foot on American soil, they had made certain that all of their business dealings—from their main chemical and ore mining company to a fistful of import-export holding companies to their fledgling entertainment venture, which indirectly owned the Boneyard as well as other clubs throughout Florida and the Southeast—were strictly legitimate. Unlike in Latin America, where graft and wholesale corruption were among the main moneymakers of old-line family businesses and governments alike. These men were comfortable with politicians and bureaucrats. They knew their way around governments because they were able to sniff out the tiniest whiff of corruption and turn it to their own ends.

1

"I don't want to hear the dream." Looking around, Antonio could see that P. T. Barnum had vastly underestimated his market potential. There's *ten thousand* suckers born every minute. "I have an evil feeling about it."

When they looked at each other, it was like staring in the mirror. They both thought, simultaneously: *There is my brother, but there is also* me. That was because Heitor and Antonio were identical twins, even down to the extraordinary amber color of their eyes.

Heitor said: "An evil feeling, is it?" His face took on the aspect of a hungry fox nosing its way into a henhouse.

Tall and lean as serpents, they were handsome men, in their own way. Their hair, thick and curling, was tawny as copper, and the planes of their faces were sculpted hard over ridged bone. This attribute and many others they inherited from their mother. But another, mystic side to them they gained from someone outside their family circle. This was manifested in their auras, which were powerful and magnetic in the manner of a black widow. There was a remarkable stillness about them, the curled and damped energy one observes in liquid mercury. They were predators who did not have to move much in order to get what they wanted.

When "Hong Kong Jelly Wong" by the Royaltones came on, Heitor said, "This dream is important, and evil or not, it must be spoken of." He and his brother were dressed in shades of gray that most approximated the inside of an oyster shell: short-sleeved shirts, tight trousers from the 1960s, thin-soled Keds without socks. Both of them despised socks.

Antonio said nothing, knowing in his heart this moment would come.

Heitor said, "I dreamed I was a very devout Jew. And as this Jew I woke from a dream as if I was just born. Understand me, this dream was more like a holy vision." His arms, thrown wide, described a circle. "The holy vision told me that the Messiah was coming on Sunday. Good news, is it? The evil news was it was Super Bowl Sunday."

For a moment, the twins stared at each other. Then, as one, they exploded into laughter. The extraordinary thing was that even in such an unguarded moment, they seemed like mirror images. And, in truth, on the surface there was virtually nothing to differentiate them, save perhaps one liked doo-wop and the other liked Cu-bop.

"I spoke to the Weimaraner today." Heitor meant Senator Weiman.

"I told you not to do that," Antonio said. "It's too soon."

"He wants to take me hunting in Virginia."

2

Antonio sighed. "Wouldn't that be nice."

"The big firms in his state are beginning to make him understand the worth of our copper and lithium importing."

"Re-election," Antonio commented. "The American way, is it not?"

The twins stared at each other and grinned.

"I want to hunt in Virginia." There was an almost childlike wistfulness in Heitor's voice.

"Not now . . . not yet." Seeing the look on Heitor's face—*his* face, Antonio took his twin's hand and squeezed it. "I know how you live for the hunt."

"Both of us, my dear." Heitor's eyes were half-closed. "But it's for a very different kind of hunt." Quite abruptly, they'd left the pedestrian subject of the Weimaraner far behind.

Antonio's amber eyes appeared to glow. "Yes, I know you're burning to plunge the scalpel in yourself."

"I hate him," Heitor admitted. "He's arrogant and spiteful."

"He has what we covet," Antonio said, cutting to the heart of the matter. *"Paciencia."* Have patience. "Soon now it will all be ours. You know the plan and it's a good one."

"If we were in Asunción, my hands would be red with his blood."

"But you're not," Antonio admonished. "We have come up in the world. This is the big leagues. For the time being, our behavior is under a microscope."

"Civilization." Heitor grimaced. "It makes me chafe."

Antonio did not reply. Instead, he watched a blonde woman in her late sixties in wide red suspenders whiz by on in-line skates. All she wore under the suspenders was a pair of workout shorts and a tank top bathing suit. Just as she was passing the front window, they saw a small, dark-skinned man leap across her path. In one motion, he snatched her purse and pushed her violently off balance. Arms flailing, mouth opened wide in shock, she pinwheeled awkwardly onto the sidewalk as the dark-skinned man began to run.

The twins were up and out the door in an instant. Communication between them was instantaneous. Heitor sprinted very fast after the dark-skinned man. Like a cheetah he could run a quarter mile in record-setting time without breaking a sweat. He raced around a corner, lunged forward, and slammed his open hand into the small of the thief's back.

In one more stride, Heitor had him firmly in tow. Without a word he spun him around. The thief saw two fingers outstretched toward him. For one agonizing second he stared full bore into Heitor's amber eyes. What he saw there was impossible to say, but he gasped and took an involuntary step backward. Heitor, seeming to change his mind, reached out and, almost nonchalantly, slammed the back of his hand into the side of the thief's head. He did this with such force that the thief was hurled off his feet. In the air, the man gave a little surprised yip like a dog whose paw has been stepped on. Then his head cracked sickeningly into a concrete-block wall, and he collapsed in a tangle. Heitor bent, retrieved the skater's purse, and lost total interest in the man.

When he returned to the scene of the mugging, he found Antonio kneeling beside the woman. He'd gotten her sitting up, her back against the plate glass of the club front. Her right leg, apparently uninjured, was stretched straight out in front of her, but her left leg was bent at the knee.

"All right, is it?" Heitor asked.

"The dark stones know," Antonio replied, and this alerted Heitor. The palms of Antonio's hands were carefully pressed against the skater's left calf, the fingers gripping the muscle. The woman had the back of her head resting against the glass, her eyes closed.

"I need you," Antonio mouthed.

Heitor reached out and with his left hand cupped the woman's raised knee. Thus engaged, the two brothers stared into each other's eyes. Something passed between them, some spark or energy, transient as a flame quickly and covertly snuffed out.

In a moment, the woman gave a little sigh and opened gray eyes, filled with the memories of her years.

"I have your purse," Heitor said when her gaze alit on him. "I don't think anything is missing." His smile seemed to compel her to do likewise.

"Feeling better, perhaps?" Antonio asked her.

"Yes, much better." She wanted to get up, and they helped her. She looked from one of their faces to the other, clearly stunned. "The pain is gone. Not even an ache. It's as if nothing had happened."

"We have a saying where we come from." Heitor handed her the purse. " 'At sinrise, the night is only a shadow of itself.' "

"That's 'sunrise,' " Antonio corrected.

"Maybe it is." Heitor smiled.

As the skater looked from one twin to the other, Antonio lifted a beckoning arm. "*Escuchame, señora.* Come inside and have a drink. *Sientase.* Feel comfortable."

"That's extraordinarily kind of you." The woman allowed them

4

to guide her into the Boneyard and onto a sofa. "You both have been so wonderful. Genuine Good Samaritans."

As Heitor went to order her a *latte*, he heard her say to Antonio, "People like you restore one's faith in humanity."

"*Bueno, señora*. Being in the right place at the right time, there is no substitute for that, yes?"

A moment later, Antonio joined him at the bar. They were surrounded by bright, polished copper and fragrant steam.

"Our sainted mother knows we could be like that all the time," Heitor said.

"If we chose to." Antonio rested his elbows on the bar. He seemed relaxed, almost somnolent, like a crocodile in the afternoon sun.

Heitor watched the waitress deliver the *latte* and some chocolate and almond *biscotti* to the skater. "Why would we choose to?" he asked.

"Our sainted mother could not imagine," Antonio said. "And neither can I."

In a cloud of milky steam, Heitor said, "This puts me in mind of the time I was run over."

"Don't exaggerate," Antonio admonished. "It was only your arm that went under the wheel."

"That didn't stop you from hauling the driver out of his car."

"Honor bound me. He was careless with my brother," Antonio said. "Besides, I felt your pain and I was moved to great anger."

"Great anger, yes." Heitor said this with an almost wistful tone. In a peculiar way, he seemed more animated now than when he was bouncing the petty thief's head against the alley wall. It was as if he was vibrating to some inner rhythm. "You held his face quite, quite still."

"While you stared into his eyes."

"That was the good part," Heitor acknowledged. "Summoning the dark stones."

Antonio dragged in a deep lungful of percolating espresso and cinnamon chocolate. "Until the blood fountained out of his nose and mouth."

"Sped from his ears like horses under the whip," Heitor recalled rapturously.

"You remember the best part," Antonio prodded.

"But of course." The burst of memory was like a delicious taste in Heitor's mouth. "We came home covered in blood and leaped in the pool."

"Holding hands."

"Joined and energized, we could not stop shouting," Heitor said. "And Dona came out at the sounds of our raucous commotion."

"It was her birthday. *Perfecto.*" Antonio licked his lips with the tip of his tongue. "She saw the pool and thought we had filled it with pink champagne."

"We'd done that once."

"A truly shocking treat," Antonio affirmed.

"Not as truly shocking as this one," Heitor said.

Antonio nodded. "Not nearly. Dona squealed, stripped off her thong, and jumped in the bloody pool."

"Her hard, brown body in amidst the blood. Didn't *we* have a laugh."

"We certainly did," Antonio said. "Ah, brother, with everything that's falling into place, *la vida es muy buena.*" Life is good for us.

At that moment, as he canvassed Lincoln Road through the front window, Heitor mouthed, "I see him."

Without turning his head to look, Antonio said under his breath. "Leaving, is he?"

Heitor, looking beyond the gray-eyed woman enjoying her *latte* and *biscotti,* kept the man in the periphery of his vision. "As predicted. Your information was prescient."

"Now he's a dangerous man."

"Others, as well," Heitor said.

Antonio's amber eyes seemed to brighten, as if he were shaking off a dream.

"All work and no play is making us acutely dull."

Heitor said, *"Madre de mentiras,* when you speak in oxymorons, something is not right with the order of the world."

Antonio laughed. "My thought exactly."

The twins turned and removed themselves from the Boneyard like wraiths.

Having purloined and stored the Boneyard's computer data on a floppy disk he carried on his person, Robin Garner walked with an unhurried gait down Lincoln Road. Garner, a federal agent, had insinuated himself into the Bonita twins' sphere of influence with the extreme care of a probe navigating the outer rim of a dark star. That had been eighteen months ago. With sufficient difficulty and hazard, he had gotten his entrée and, as per instructions, had crouched like a drone at the edge of their intricate web. *Do nothing,* his handler had cautioned him, *and the Bonitas can suspect nothing Wait and, above all else, watch.*

Garner had the eyes of an expert watcher. It was what the ACTF had trained him to do. The Anti-Cartel Task Force was the semi-official entity within the Justice Department for whom he toiled in darkness and filth. The ACTF had been created to interdict the alarming rise of the exportation of criminal activities from country to country. Governmental studies had established this as a world-wide trend. As such, it was as much a symbol of the new order in world eco-politics as it was a threat to the United States. Instantaneous access to information made every government's—as well as every criminal organization's—actions interrelated. But on a personal level, the ACTF gave him work he could sink his teeth into, work that mattered.

So Garner had waited and watched, becoming a spider just like the Bonitas. It wasn't all that difficult. Why would it be? He was a natural at penetration and camouflage. From an early age, Garner had become proficient at hiding his true nature. When, at twelve, he'd realized that he was profoundly different from the boys around him, he knew he was better off waiting. Two years later, when he'd had it confirmed to him by a sexual incident that he was gay, he knew he'd have to learn even more patience. His parents were not the kind of people to be supportive of alternative lifestyles, and he was no rebel to declare himself and let the chips fall where they might. Family was important to him; at that time, more important than his sexual orientation. If that made him a coward in certain people's eyes, so be it.

Being gay in SoBe provided distinct advantages. For one thing, Garner blended in just fine. Here, you'd better be either gay or bi or you didn't really belong. For another, it made him seem less of a threat to the macho Bonitas. Also, his years as a mole inside his own family that sensitized him to the subtle vibes to which others were blind. This talent, especially, served him well in the warren of offices behind the Boneyard, where he had worked ten hours a day since the day it had opened. Being tuned in to those vibes had allowed him to crack the case he'd been working on.

The worst part of being gay for Garner was the feeling it gave him of being helpless and ineffectual in a straight society. All he wanted to do was make a difference. And bringing the Bonita twins to justice would make a helluva difference. Even if others took the official glory, which they inevitably would, Garner, deep in the Washington shadows, would have his satisfaction.

Slowly, inexorably, through chinks so minute only he could have sensed them, he'd caught quickening glimpses of the Bonita's clandestine operations, suspected but never provable. Only now, having leaped through a sudden crack in their defenses, did he have enough to put them away for multiple lifetimes—if only he could get the data to the safe house where his handler awaited, patient in his own way.

Garner slipped into a side alley that reeked of urine and dried fish. Using a key he had been given, he opened a side door to the White House. This hard-core gay club, which had taken over a long-abandoned movie theater from the 1940s, was named not for the American presidential residence but the similarly named Russian senate building.

In truth, Garner did not know what to make of his handler. Of course, he trusted him with his life, but the disadvantage of Garner's sexual orientation arose when they met.

"They don't fully trust you." His handler always opened their debriefings in this unsettling manner. *"Yes, mea culpa, I'm harder on you than I am on my straight agents. That's because when it comes to you, they're harder on me."*

But they trusted Garner enough to embed him within the Bonitas' sphere of influence. That was the paradox of federal bureaucracy that remained, like time, a constant.

Since Garner had joined the ACTF, it had been rocked by turmoil. Most of what he knew came from rumors he had gleaned in the dimness of company bars, of hidden agendas woven deep within the bureaucratic quagmire that was part and parcel of any federal agency. He might have discounted these rumors as simply part of the paranoia that went with the boggy territory. But even he, in those restive periods when he waited to be dangled at the end of a penetration line, had noticed the altered vibrations, as if, down in the center of things, quickened drumbeats could ever so faintly be heard. Nothing definitive, mind you, just echoes of verbal charges: an altered directive here, a change in personnel there, cuts in field teams in Southeast Asia, a beefing up of others in Latin America. That was before Spaulding Gunn was installed as new director of the ACTF three years ago. Quite quickly after that the subrosa drumbeats faded into obscurity and the gossip mongers of Foggy Bottom turned to fresher, juicier items to slice and dice in their mean-spirited way.

What it all meant Garner could not say, except that eighteen months ago his handler had given him the Bonitas as high priority subjects for an undercover operation. Why were the Bonitas suddenly at the top of the ACTF enemies list? Up until last week, Garner had had no idea. Certainly, his handler wasn't going to tell him. Quite frankly, Garner had no business speculating. Hand to his heart, wrapped in the flag, he was required only to soldier on; to follow orders and, hopefully, to win the day.

Garner made his careful way through dark and deserted corridors smelling of old age and new sex. The partying that went on here all through the night and early morning was often inconceivable to him. Like religious sects, there were all kinds of gays. Long ago, Garner had decided that, though gay, he wanted to make his way in the so-called straight world. This required an entire set of attitudes that the gays who inhabited this place found repugnant. The naming of the club was no happenstance, but a form of quasipolitical statement. Here was new territory, as far from the auspices of mainstream USA as was Russia. This was the United Nation of Queers, long may it wave!

He found the old, rickety staircase hidden behind one end of the long sweeping bar on the ground floor and went silently and steadily up it.

But try as he might, he could not be the good soldier, running full tilt into unquestioning battle. He was too good at using his brain. The trouble was, Garner sometimes thought of himself as cannon fodder—clever but eminently dispensable. If this turned out to be a suicide mission, *they* would not blink an eye, let alone feel the remotest twinge of remorse. He wondered whether his handler would think of him after he'd turned away from Garner's newly turned grave.

Dark thoughts for a straightforward undercover operation. But it was one thing to gather enough evidence to bring charges against subjects for a well-oiled drug operation cleverly hidden within the cracks of an oh-so-legit business, quite another when these men were Antonio and Heitor Bonita. *They* had no idea how dangerous the Bonitas could be. The twins were fanatically secretive; a sure and unquiet death lay in wait for anyone who they discovered penetrating those secrets.

Coming to the head of the stairs, he shook off such morbid thoughts. He was used to them; they cropped up near the end of missions, when the nerves were rubbed raw, the danger level at its highest, and holding on to patience was his most valuable resource.

He was close to the rendezvous point. Close to bringing to a successful conclusion the most important mission of his career. He could not rid himself of the fantasy that at long last even his handler's handler would recognize his contribution. That, after this triumph, his handler would never again open a debriefing with the words, *They don't fully trust you.*

Garner's handler thought it ironic to set up a safe house in a place that personally made him want to puke. Garner could not afford to be offended; he could see the logic in it. When in Rome . . . The old saw still made the most sense.

As prearranged, Garner entered the back office without knocking. It was an anteroom, actually part of the star's dressing room when this place had hosted vaudeville acts between film showings. On the old wooden desk near the door to the back room was an imitation Tiffany lamp that no longer worked, a dried-up blotter, and a pile of out-of-date *People* magazines. Frosted windows, painted shut long ago, allowed a feeble seepage of light.

Garner went through the gloom and counted the number of *People* magazines in the stack. There were seven, all aligned. That meant Garner's handler was in the next room and everything was secure. This was part of the handler's job: to keep the safe houses sterile, the rendezvous points secure, the agents-in-place from being terminated.

Garner opened the door to the inner room and was swallowed by darkness. Three paces inside, he slipped on something slick. He almost fell, but a strong hand grasped his elbow and steadied him.

"*Cuidado*, you could hurt yourself."

"Thanks," he said, automatically. But he stiffened. What was that smell?

"It's a shame," the familiar voice said, "but we no longer trust you."

"What?" Garner turned his head so violently he heard a vertebra crack.

"Such a shame," another, similar voice said, "because we liked you."

More than a smell, it was a stench. A closely held beam snapped on and Garner blinked.

"*Madre de mentiras*, look what you stepped into."

Garner stared down and his heart almost slammed into his rib cage. Blood and intestines lay on the floor in an almost perfect circle.

"*Muy hermosa*," said the second voice. Very beautiful.

Garner's gaze followed the beam of light as if it were a magnet. Its uncompromising glare marched across the small room. Garner gave a little groan as he recognized the face of his handler. That was about all he could recognize of him. He tried to look away, but as he did so, a hand of iron seized the back of his neck and he was forced nearer and nearer to the object of their desire. In the uncertain light the human head, floating as if on a sea of silken darkness, had an almost surreal look, like an evil omen in a dream.

Lights blazed. Garner, caught like a deer in headlights, looked up, blinking into the glare. Four metal-shell photographer's floods, clipped to shelves, drenched the bloody scene in light so bright it was obscene.

"*¡Ay, fantastico!*" It was Heitor Bonita's voice, crowing. "*¡Que dulce!*" How sweet! Now that the initial shock had dissipated, Garner was certain.

"*Señor, por favor*, this way."

Garner felt a powerful tug on his elbow from Antonio Bonita. They knew everything, Garner thought. How had they found out? Who had given him away?

But there was no time to pursue these deeply disturbing thoughts. He saw that the homey ex-dressing room had been tricked out in frightening fashion. The walls on either side of him contained markings drawn in blood—the handler's blood, Garner had no doubt. These symbols seemed vaguely familiar to Garner: a triangle within a circle; a single spot, red and ominous, within a square; a cross within three concentric circles. Though he could not place them, they sent a certain thrill of dread through the core of him. Some primitive part of his brain instinctively recognized a mortal enemy.

And there, on either side of him, were the Bonita twins. Long and lean, their amber eyes reflecting the awful glare, they stood in a concentration of energy Garner felt in a frisson along his exposed flesh.

"You tricked us," Heitor said in a hearty gust of disillusionment.

"Traduced us," Antonio echoed, his grip like an iron band.

"I haven't traduced you," Garner said, feeling a foolish and clearly hopeless desire to defend himself.

Garner's gaze was drawn by light coruscating off the blade of a scalpel Heitor held in one hand.

"I've made no false statements against you." This was not a court of law Garner had entered, but an execution chamber.

"No?" Heitor grinned wolfishly. "What were you going to tell your handler in your debriefing?"

Antonio spun him roughly around, struck him again and again in strategic parts of his body until the damning floppy disk was exhumed from his person.

Garner, crumpled on the slick floor, tasted his own blood. His head lolled uncontrollably with his pain. He sucked in a ragged breath and gasped. The heat of the lamps caused the reek of human offal to rise from the floor like spirits from the grave.

Antonio raised the stolen floppy disk on high. "*This* contains all the answers, names, dates, et cetera, et cetera," he said in the ringing vengeful tones of a hanging judge hell-bent for blood. "Are your eyes blind that you cannot see?"

"We know what you were going to do with this highly inflammatory information," Heitor said. The scalpel moved, and having moved, pointed to the disembodied head of Garner's handler. "We were provided with confirmation."

Briefly, absurdly, Garner wondered where the rest of him was.

"Without cross-checking," Antonio admonished with considerable irony. "Without independent corroboration."

"We were to be condemned out of hand." Heitor crouched down in Garner's face. Antonio hunkered down beside him.

"Like common criminals," Antonio, pitched forward on the toes of his Keds, whispered in Garner's ear.

Heitor must have heard this because he said, "Listen to me. There is nothing common about us."

Garner had begun to sweat, and sweating, he prayed.

"*Oye*, Heitor," Antonio said, "he's beginning to stink."

Heitor pushed his head forward and sniffed. "*Madre de mentiras*, it is not a good stink."

"Not like blood," Antonio affirmed. "Not like the dying."

Now Heitor said something in a singsong kind of voice. It was not a language immediately known to Garner, whose fascination with arcane dialects had led him to become a linguistics expert. But, as Heitor continued, impressions came: of poverty-stricken hovels and packed-dirt streets, of roosters crowing and mangy dogs prowling the edges of an emerald jungle beyond which rose a modern industrial skyline. This was a Paraguayan Indian dialect, Garner thought. Guarani.

And, suddenly, the dripping designs on the walls came into sharp focus, and Garner felt a sick, panicky feeling in the pit of his stomach. He knew something of this obscure dialect. Linking it up to the bloody symbols, he understood what the twins had been trying to tell him: death was the least of what was to come.

"I want you to understand this," Heitor said with the touch of his amber gaze heavy and knowing on Garner. "The stones. You have heard of the dark stones, haven't you?"

"We can see the answer in your eyes," Antonio said. "The dark stones know."

His hand snaked out, gripping Garner's bicep like a pincer. Without seeming effort he shot to his feet, dragging Garner with him. Now he moved very fast, hauling Garner across the room like a sack of wheat. The toe of Garner's shoe caught in a glistening fold of intestine, dragging it with him like an unwilling pup.

Antonio spun Garner, slamming him so hard against the back wall that all the breath went out of him, and Antonio was obliged to hold him upright. Garner was surrounded by the largest of the three concentric circles of blood. He imagined the bloody cross converged between his shoulder blades. He shook his head to try to clear it.

Looking past the Bonita twins, he saw the bloody symbol on the fourth wall. It had not been visible before because it had been behind him. He saw two curving lines that met to form what appeared to be the outline of an eye. But it was unlike any Garner had seen before because it had two pupils. It was eerie, like the orb of God, imagined but forbidden to look upon.

Heitor, moving slowly as a crocodile in the full heat of the day, fingered the shining scalpel. "This is pure instinct now. You've left reason outside in the night."

"Here's the meat of it." Antonio's glistening teeth clacked beside Garner's ear. "We will reveal to you the sole Law of the Universe: the further a creature gets from pure instinct, the more flaws it possesses."

"Take man, for instance," Heitor said. "*¡Madre de mentiras!*"

"Flatulent with flaws," Antonio whispered. "His capacity to reason—his *obsession* with it—has wiped out the instinct that made him what he was."

"Once," Heitor said, advancing.

"No more," Antonio said.

"*Comprende, señor.*" Heitor stood squarely in front of Garner. "For us, this is the game."

Antonio, up on his toes, the backs of his legs taut, wedged Garner in. "The *only* game in existence."

Heitor smiled. "*The one thing that means something to us,*" he said in the peculiar dialect of the Guarani.

"The rest," Antonio said, "does not exist."

Now Heitor's lambent gaze pinioned him, and Garner screamed. He didn't want to, but he couldn't help himself. The stifling air in the tiny room seemed to have gained a charge of electricity as the symbols on the walls came to life. They appeared to pulse and shine, eclipsing even the fierce glare of the photo floods. Was it hypnosis or magic? Garner, raised and trained in the world of man's technological marvels, was inclined toward skepticism. He had discovered in the course of previous investigations that Haitians died of voodoo curses simply because they believed in them. There was no more mystery to it than that.

As if Heitor could read Garner's thoughts, he put two fingers on the side of Garner's neck where his carotid artery pulsed, and Garner felt an involuntary shudder go through him. It was as if an enormous boa constrictor had settled on his shoulders, and a certain fear he could neither understand nor control began to pulse like a drumbeat in his lower belly.

Heitor was summoning the dark stones.

Garner began to fight, but it was far too late. Antonio's grip held him fast even though he twisted and struck out with fisted hands and scrabbling feet. Strangely, frighteningly, it dawned on him that the harder he fought, the longer he held on, the better they loved it.

His heart seemed to freeze in his chest. What was happening to him? It was as if something he felt but could not define was boring through the backs of his eyes into his brain. He felt as if he were on fire, and involuntarily, his body began to dance a manic jig. He tried to pull his gaze away but he couldn't. Horrified, he stared into those amber eyes and found himself being subsumed by another presence. He felt himself plummeting down like a parachutist through layers of ever thickening cloud. And it was as if the airplane he left behind was his own body, dwindling in size, grown dim and indistinct until it was thoroughly obscured by those clouds. Still, Garner fought with every ounce of strength left him.

They could have kissed him for his heroic efforts. It was hours and hours later that Heitor used the scalpel. Before that—for a long and ecstatic time—there was simply no need.

DAY ONE

1

Rachel Duke undressed slowly and languorously. As she let her clothes fall to the floor, she thought of Gideon's body. Gideon, who was just a cubicle away and very soon would be closer than that. Her mind filled with images of Gideon's long, lean musculature: sinuous biceps, sleek flanks, hot butt. She was so in love with Gideon, she couldn't see straight. It might have been a yucky cliché, but the truth was she never knew what intimacy meant until she met Gideon. Rachel's parents weren't exactly big on intimacy; God alone knew how they had had her.

But she was not in her parents' world now; she was in Gideon's. Gideon was eighteen—three years older than Rachel. Not that the age thing mattered to either of them. Gideon's world was terrifying and intoxicating and exhilarating all at once, and Rachel couldn't get enough of it. She glanced at her watch: just past 2 A.M. and their day was just beginning. The last bit of clothing slithered to her ankles. She reached out, and as she pressed her palm to the bare wall that separated her from the next cubicle, a tremor of intent went through her. Gideon.

As she readied her body, so she readied her mind.

Soon, Rachel, at the Boneyard, was plugged in and turned on. She sat in the tiny cubicle. Dim illumination played like sunlight cascading through densely forested foliage. The drowsy sounds of birds and bees, the soft burble of a nearby stream wafted on air perfumed with a combination of cypress, juniper, and a hint of lime.

Rachel liked the dirty-sexy-free feeling that came from being in heat outdoors with the animals watching and *knowing* what you were doing. So she had dialed up all this synthetic light and sound and smell through the computer interface to which she was hooked up. The tangle of humid odors came to her through a hopped-up network that spewed aromatherapy essential oils into the cubicle.

She was naked, save for odd-looking garments of black rubber strapped across her breasts, over her groin, and around her thighs. Electrical leads ran from points on these garments to the computer terminal, and a flexible penislike projection rose up inside her.

The Boneyard was a virtual sex parlor, one of the first of its kind. Gideon had turned her on to it. It was a way to explore fantasies, to make real—or virtually real—what was in your head without fear of AIDS or other sexually transmitted diseases. It was, in short, the ultimate analgesic for the new, severely anxious generation.

Rachel sat back, legs spread, and watched through eyes slitted with a surfeit of drugs and lust, the electronic image of Gideon. With the computer interface, you could, of course, pick out anything to look at from the data bank images. But she and Gideon preferred their own images, as least when making virtual love to each other. When, on occasion, they interfaced sexually with like-minded individuals a half-continent away, they appeared on the monitor as all sorts of strange and wonderful people.

Rachel's right forefinger moved the trackball mouse pointer higher up Gideon's virtual inner thigh. At almost the same moment, jolts of pleasure were transmitted through the leads in her garments to one erogenous zone after another. With a little scream, Rachel came. Gideon, knowing her so well, kept her at the peak for so long, her feet lifted off the floor and her thighs began to shake uncontrollably until her head lolled to one side.

Afterward, in the sweaty interim between bouts, she snorted more coke. Gideon, in the next cubicle, was doing the same, she knew. Somewhere in the dim recesses of her mind Rachel knew it was too much, but she didn't care. She wanted more, needed that much in order not to think about her father, the flaming pyre of his death.

That particular thought caught like a thorn in her throat. She wanted to dissolve in tears but instead did more coke.

Was it true you never stopped loving your daddy no matter what? Even after he was dead? What part of him lived on in your heart like a dark seed, growing?

Part of her desperately wanted her mother to burst in and rip her from the sexual net, but her mother would never do it. For one thing, her mother would never believe the kind of secret life she was living. For another, she wouldn't know how to tackle it. Though she demanded to know where Rachel was going at night, every night, coming home at five, six in the morning, Rachel wouldn't tell her.

And still she let her go. That was her way. See something nasty, something incomprehensible and do the ostrich dance—stick your head in the sand. *Why the hell didn't she stop us?* Rachel thought. *Because the time when she could is long past, and now it's far too late.* Then the feeling—that peculiar burning that began in her thighs and crept upward took hold of her and felt *too good.* She thought: *Maybe once I wanted her to come and save me; but what if I didn't?* Because she was feeling that thorn in her throat again, she did more coke. Because if she didn't surely she'd set herself on fire. She'd tried, once, and Gideon had saved her. Had Gideon done a good or a bad thing?

The conundrum made her thirsty, and she gulped down some of the black lemonade she had purchased in the parlor outside.

This so-called parlor, the large common room of the Boneyard, was strewn with a hodgepodge of comfy Art Deco furniture. There you could just chill, rap a little while drinking a variety of coffees, cappuccinos, *lattes,* or, as was becoming increasingly popular with the kids who found their way here by word of mouth, a collection of sodas, dark and thick with herbal tinctures, featuring names like DOA, Skullcrusher, and BaddAss Brew. It was all loose-limbed, informal, low-tech out front. But back here in the CyberCubes, the surroundings were high-tech city.

She felt Gideon suffusing her with pleasure again and she forgot about her father's ghost. Groaning, she dropped her black lemonade to the countertop. She used her mouse to give as good as she got, and soon enough, panting, her breasts heaving, she came again.

Sweat sheened her and she grabbed for the rest of her black lemonade.

She was in the midst of her third orgasm when the last coke hit brought back layers of the acid trip that had been hovering in the corners of her mind. She felt as if Death had come into the room and scythed apart reality. She saw herself from above, slumped and damp, glassy-eyed in the aftermath of cyber-sex; she was also that person, dimly aware of a presence like an angel hovering above her shoulder.

And the angel that was Rachel left the room, as it always did, on its personal search to find her uncle. He had been a cop when he and her mom had been so pissed at each other they stopped talking. But Rachel had seen pictures of him; she even had one hidden in her room. When she stared at that photo she imagined what he might be like: strong, tough, big as a bear, and smiling at her always. That she was conjuring up the perfect father, who would love and protect her unconditionally, never occurred to her.

She only knew that she hated her mother for refusing to tell her where her uncle was. Her mother actually seemed frightened that Rachel had become more and more curious about him as Rachel had grown into a teenager. All Rachel knew was if *she* had a brother she'd never treat him like her mother treated hers.

Reality kept slipping out of focus like a lighthouse in the fog. Now the cyber-stimulation came again, but this time it felt like a hive full of wasps had gotten under her skin.

When Rachel screamed it sounded like a jet airplane revving its engines. She jumped up, popping cables. Those that did not break, slewed her off balance, and she fell into a bog of quicksand. She screamed again but her mouth was full of sand. Her arms were a mile long, her legs like the wobbly piers of a suspension bridge in an earthquake. Nothing seemed right or good or . . .

A frightful bout of nausea caught her like a steamshovel in the gut and she doubled over. She retched so hard that she vomited blood. She blinked back tears and found she couldn't see. Then she was doubled over again in an agony so profound it all but paralyzed her. When it felt as if it couldn't get any worse, pain exploded in the small of her back and she spasmed into a fetal position.

The door to the cubicle burst inward and sixteen images of Gideon followed themselves inside. Rachel's mouth worked spastically and she tried to reach out, but she'd lost all control of her limbs.

Then the world shattered into a hundred-thousand razor-sharp fragments, taking her with it into an oblivion where even her insupportable pain could not be felt.

2

When the wahoo took the line, Bennie Milagros cursed under his breath. "Shit," he said as the line spun out across the blue and gold sea, "I wanted a sailfish."

Lew Croaker, his steady gaze already on the dancing fish, cut engine speed and got ready to maneuver. "Watch it," he said. "This is no pussycat." The wahoo was a powerful fish that could move at such astonishing speeds its first run often burned out the fisherman's reel.

"You an' me, we chow down on this wahoo at dusk." Bennie Milagros was braced tensely near the stern of the boat. A tall man in his thirties, slim as a flamenco dancer, he had a high domed forehead and long hair down to his shoulders. He wore a white short-sleeve linen shirt, a pair of red-and-black shorts that reached almost to his very hairy knees, and reed huaraches. Tufts of wiry black hair waved from the knuckles of his toes. The shorts were held up over his skinny hips by a belt with an enormous oval silver buckle gaudily engraved with gold steer horns. A Smith & Wesson .38 was tucked into his waistband. Bennie was one of those rich Paraguayans who had come to South Florida to spend money and be seen. If he also did a little business here and there, so much the better. "Fighting fish like this reminds me. There was this *guapa*, she was special. God hears me, I would a married her if I could, but that woulda spoiled her, you know?"

"You mean it would've spoiled *you*."

"You know, Lewis, you are a very hard-hearted man." Bennie was grinning. "But, no, listen to me. This *guapa* she was like a magnificent wild animal, you break its spirit, it's a sin, you know? I mean, you gotta treat a woman with respect. I look darkly upon men who disrespect women." What, exactly, Bennie Milagros's business might be wasn't known to any official entity of the United States. Croaker suspected that was just as well.

"So this *guapa*, what could I do? I respected her, kept her spirit alive *here*." He thumped his chest with his free hand. "But God hears me, I am the poorer for being without her." He flicked the rod. "Now, magnanimous man that I am, I am willing to share with you this piece of philosophy. I swear on the soul of my dead mother, your cock'll grow feathers the minute you meet a *guapa* like this one. Pearl in a fuckin' oyster, believe me." Bennie grunted as the wahoo struck outward and the reel began to spin madly. The eight-foot rod flexed severely as the fish took off, and Croaker turned the wheel over hard, heading *Captain Sumo* away from Alligator Reef. The reef dropped off sharply, and they were soon in about three hundred feet of water, three miles out from Islamorada, one of the middle Florida Keys.

The ocean stretched blue and green, the white-gold sparkle of the sun lacing the wave crests. It was cool and clean out here, and Croaker loved it; the rime of salt borne on breeze and spray coated human skin and boat lacquer alike.

Bennie worked the fiberglass rod—glass, in fisherman's parlance. "But, shit, I wanted that fuckin' sailfish."

19

"You already landed one today," Croaker pointed out. "Relax. You're only allowed one billfish a day."

"I feel a need for it in my soul, understand? Maybe you don't." Bennie risked turning his flat face toward Croaker. "You Anglos, you have some weird fuckin' ideas 'bout spirituality. See, it's all, like, televangelists caught with their pants down an' after-death experiences an', like, alien abductions. An' you see all that shit in the *National Enquirer* so much that's what defines *spirituality* for you. You gents just don't get it, an' that's why you're all crawling over each other to find it." He reeled out some line. His coffee-colored eyes flashed with salacious good humor. He was a handsome man, his pockmarked cheeks making him seem all the more powerful.

Croaker slowed some more and turned to starboard. This fish was going to get away unless they were both very careful. "Don't lump me into your great Anglo stew."

"Oh, yeah." Bennie flicked his wrist, began to reel in line. "I forgot myself for a minute. You're an ex-cop. NYPD detective lieutenant." He shook his head. "Dirty business."

"More than you could imagine," Croaker said. Fifteen years prowling the filthy underbelly of the city's streets had made Croaker immune to life. Even little pleasures had dissolved like wet snow in the city's acid gutters. He'd spent early mornings washing the blood of murder victims and violent perps off his hands until he'd scrubbed his fingertips raw. And when he had come in out of the slime, he'd been met with a cynical web of Police Plaza corruption between politicos and penthouse residents, played like a game of squash where no one worked up a sweat. Soon he'd been driven back onto the streets again, trying to wash away what would never come off.

"He's doubled back!" Bennie tensed, reeling in line like a madman. Croaker whipped the wheel around. Bennie was a fine fisherman; Croaker never had to baby-sit him as he did with many of his well-heeled clients who, jaded by afternoons cell-phoning from the golf course, had decided sport fishing made for a power experience.

"Here he comes!"

Croaker could see the wahoo's narrow wake, knew Bennie was right—the fish was making a run at the boat. "Make sure you take up every inch of slack!" he shouted as he goosed the engines to life, moving *Captain Sumo* out of the way of the wahoo's charge.

Bennie was reeling like crazy, his eyes following the wahoo's silver wake, sharp as a knife. At the last instant Croaker could see that the wahoo was going to try to go under the boat, and turned again. The wahoo jumped instead, and then ran. Bennie's reel spun madly.

"Oh, good one!" Bennie cried. "Yeah, well, you an' I, we got something in common besides loving South Florida and fishing." He took one hand off the rod for an instant, struck himself in the midsection.

"Yeah? What's that?"

The wahoo chose that moment for a spectacular leap, then began another run. Bennie was almost jerked off his feet. He took one lurching step, fetched his hip bone against the rail. With a powerful sweeping motion, he lifted the tip of the rod as the line spun out. "Lotta life yet in this one," he grunted.

Croaker once again altered the boat's speed, coming to port.

With the wahoo more or less under control for the moment, Bennie said, "We both know what it's like to have enemies."

"You've got to be joking." Croaker laughed. "I'm like the manatee. I've got no natural enemies."

"Really? You, an ex-cop, work now and again when the mood prevails with the elite Feds, what're they called, the Anti-Cartel Task Force. Anyone official inquires, they don't know you, you don't know them. Your name ain't on their books, so who's to say who's lyin'."

"You know that for a fact?"

"It's a guess, what d'you think?" Bennie grinned as he worked his rod. "Also, word is you did some mighty fancy footwork with the mob. You got friends—and enemies—in high places, Lewis, don't lead me to believe otherwise." Bennie shrugged. "I know what I need to 'bout you," he said.

"Where'd you hear all this nasty stuff?" Croaker asked.

"Guys I play mah-jongg with." Bennie had a laugh like a macaw's startled screech. He flashed a quick glance at Croaker.

The wahoo was tiring, no doubt about it. Its runs were shorter and less powerful. Bennie definitely had him under control. It wouldn't be long before they could gaff him aboard. "I know something about that mechanical left hand of yours. I know it ain't no handicap. Far fuckin' from it. Also, I know how you came to South Florida baby-sitting a *guapa* witness to multiple murder, and when the case was over, you threw in your shield prematurely and settled down with the *guapa*. What was her name?"

"You tell me."

Bennie shrugged. "She was a model, right? Now she's off in Paris, Milan, fuck knows where. An' who cares, anyways? She sure as shit ain't here. Her idea of life was different than yours. Just like your Mafia princess back on Long Island. She was beyond the law *and* she was married. Ooo, I like the size of your *cojones, señor!"* He shook his head. "God hears me, the *guapas* can be cruel when they want to be."

"They weren't cruel," Croaker said, despite himself. "Like you said, they were not for me."

Bennie ignored Croaker's comment. He flicked the glass rod, hurting the fish more, weakening it further. "So you came back to this forty-foot Hatteras and the sport fishing charter company you'd started years ago, after you realized the obvious: that the thing with the Mafia princess was, like, unworkable."

"Very impressive."

"Didn't do it to impress you," Bennie said, reeling in the wahoo. "Did it to make a point 'bout the kind of man you are an' the kind of man I am."

The wahoo's wake was wide now. Exhausted from the fight, it was almost on its side. Croaker threw the boat into neutral, then climbed out of the cockpit and went to fetch the short, stout gaff.

As Croaker came up beside him, Bennie's coffee-colored eyes slid his way. "You an' me we're the same, deep down inside, is what I think."

Croaker held the gaff vertically, as if it were a medieval halberd. Next to Bennie's slender frame his bearlike bulk seemed overpowering. He had the handsome weather-beaten face of a cowboy; Robert Mitchum tall in the saddle. Sunlight flared in his gray eyes. His artificial left hand, made of black polycarbonate, stainless-steel, iridescent blue titanium, and matte-gray boron components, looked like a knight's mailed fist. "And what kind of man is that?"

"Very fuckin' careful." Bennie grinned fiercely as he handed off the rod to Croaker while he took possession of the gaff. It was his fish to land all the way into the boat; that was one of Croaker's rules of the sea. "Like, here's a for instance. You come down here your rep precedes you. You begin to do work for the Feds, helping the Coast Guard out now an' then, wrapping up drug smugglers they can't get a handle on. Did a lotta tracking in the 'glades." He meant the Everglades. "Nasty kinds of stuff in there, gators, crocs, snakes, I mean to tell you. But you, very careful, you learned your way around. Like a fuckin' native. Like—what's the name of those Indians, not the Seminoles, who came down later on from somewhere north, right?"

"Georgia. They came in the eighteenth century."

"Yeah," Bennie said. "So anyway, not them. I mean the original

Florida gents, got whacked like the Indians in Mexico and Peru by the fuckin' Anglos hornin' in, taking whatever the hell they wanted."

"The Calusas."

"Right. You hit the 'glades like, you know, a fuckin' Calusa. *Careful.*" Bennie stretched over the side, swinging the gaff down. He was trying to find the gill slit to hook into. "Lots of evil happenin' in South Florida, I don't have to enumerate to you. Pays t'be 'specially careful down here."

"And you'd know about being careful, Bennie."

"Sure I would. What I do in life—" Bennie paused as he made another pass at the wahoo's elusive gill slit. "When it comes right down to it I don't really do anything at all. I'm a fixer. People have problems an' I fix 'em. Business problems, personal problems—I fix 'em all. An' not like you think—I see that look on your cop face. You seen I'm carrying, I know what's on your mind. But you're wrong. The piece is for protection only." He spread his hands. "I negotiate. I find a way to make a settlement." He hunched forward, his voice lower, more throaty. "See, my experience has been that people—no matter how stupid, stubborn, or prideful—are motivated by the same thing: they don't want to lose. I show 'em how they won't lose."

Bennie wiped salt spray out of his eyes with the back of his arm. He was concentrating on the movements of the wounded wahoo. Hurling itself against the boat hull, it still had a bit of life left in it. Finding the gill slit at last, he bent over farther, grunting.

"Ah, shit!" The wahoo had flicked one last time and the gaff's hook ripped through skin and flesh. "I'll never get this part clean." Ribbons of blood darkened the water.

"You want help," Croaker said, holding tight rein on the line, "just say the word."

Bennie was balanced precariously on the top rail. "The day I need help landing a fuckin' wahoo—"

The rest of his sentence was lost in a guttural scream. The water around the wahoo, already dark with uncoiling blood, turned black, then a sickening white. With a great roar, the water purled upward and, foaming madly, revealed the head of a tiger shark.

"What th' fuck?" Bennie shouted.

It was huge—over a thousand pounds for sure, Croaker estimated. The jaws gaped open inches from Bennie's hands. The cavity looked as big as the Lincoln Tunnel. As the massive jaws clashed shut, the gaff snapped in two and part of the wahoo disappeared in a bright maelstrom of flying blood and churning water.

Bennie tried to scramble back, but his belt buckle got hung up on the rail. For a moment he hung there, his upper torso suspended out over the water.

Croaker extruded stainless-steel nails from the tips of the polycarbonate and titanium fingers of his left hand, slashed them horizontally, snapping the monofilament line. He dropped the glass rod to the pitching deck as, with a sickening lurch, the tiger shark surfaced again, coming right at Bennie.

"Madre de Dios!" Bennie's white face was flecked with fish gore. Scales refracted miniature rainbows off his cheekbones, nose, and eyebrows. His wide, staring eyes reflected the ugly gray-brown snout of the shark.

Bennie's head was directly above the gaping jaws, and still the shark rose, gripped by a frenzy of blood lust. Croaker used his right hand to grab Bennie by the back of his shirt collar, hauling backward. But that damn silver buckle was caught beneath the top rail.

In desperation, Croaker shouldered in beside Bennie. Bending over the rail, he swung his left hand down in a flat arc. Sunlight glittered off the back of his artificial hand. The extruded stainless-steel nail of his thumb pierced the shark's right eye, while the other four buried themselves in its snout. It was the only part of the shark's anatomy that seemed sensitive. Croaker remembered stories of divers who claimed they'd fended off attacks by slamming its nose. He prayed they were true.

The tiger shark thrashed, its powerful tail churning the water, the flailing of its thick body rocking the boat. Its sandpaper hide scraped against the hull, stripping off layers of paint and wood. Half-blinded and blood-maddened it rose vertically a third time, then crashed downward. Croaker's nails were embedded deep within monstrous flesh and cartilage. In reflex, he'd curled them and now couldn't extract them. The shark's abrupt downward rush threatened to take him with it.

Bennie, who had been struggling with his buckle, lurched free and, taking hold of Croaker's sweat-soaked shirt with one hand, drew the .38 Smith & Wesson from his waistband and pumped six rounds into the shark's head. He was aiming for the brain, but it was so small and so well armored he couldn't be sure he'd hit it.

Either by malevolent design or by simple reflex, the shark leaped out of the water again. Could Bennie have been such a poor shot, even at point-blank range or was the prehistoric beast's body unaware as yet that it was dead? No matter. The ruined snout burst upward in an eruption of pink spume. The leading edge of its double-rowed teeth grazed the inside of Bennie's right forearm and he gasped. He was so startled he dropped the .38 as if it were a hot iron. It disappeared down the shark's throat. Then Croaker, bunching his fingers, tore his steel nails clear through cartilage and flesh, ripping open the shark's snout in a long, bloody rent that went from end to end.

It was dead. For sure it was dead, with six .38 bullets in it and blood pumping out of it like a fountain. But Croaker had seen too many landed sharks presumed dead come to life with tragic results. The beast continued its psychotic thrashing, lashing out with tail and mouth, more dangerous than ever. Croaker turned and, grabbing a boat hook, proceeded to jam the brass end of it through the shark's good eye.

The boiling water slowly subsided. Blood spread like an oil slick from a damaged tanker. Turning slowly on its side, spinning like a dying sun in space, the shark gradually sank beneath the ocean, leaving nothing in its wake. To the very end its jaws were working spastically.

"Goddamnit," Bennie said, leaning against the railing. The color was already returning to his pockmarked cheeks. "The sonuvabitch took my wahoo *and* my gun."

As soon as they docked, Croaker drove Bennie to the Fisherman's Hospital to get the shark wound tended to. It wasn't much more than a shallow gash, but you never knew. It was on the inside of Bennie's right arm and had come very close to the large median vein.

On their way to dinner, Croaker and Bennie drove through a late afternoon chewy with brine and the iodine of dried seaweed. They were in Croaker's 1969 flamingo and white T-bird, which, Bennie loved to say, wallowed like a pig but rode at top speed like a magic carpet. Bennie, his right arm resplendent with yellow disinfectant and squooshy gauze, used his cellular phone to call a woman named Maria. Croaker heard him making plans for her to meet him at ten that night. Bennie gave her a Mile Marker number, which was as much of an address as you were going to get in the Keys. "It's right off U.S. One, Maria. On the left. You can't miss it. An' about Sonia, she's cool with it? Good."

He turned to Croaker as he hung up. "Now when the *guapas* show up don't, like, get your head turned around."

Croaker laughed. "Hey, Bennie, since when do I care who you go out with?"

Bennie grinned. "Maria's my date. Sonia's for you, bright boy."

Croaker shook his head. "No go. You know I'm not into that scene."

"What scene? What?" Bennie spread his hands expressively. "*Jesus Christo*, Lewis, this girl's no whore." He gestured with his chin. "You recall that story I told you 'bout the *guapa* stole my heart?"

"I remember everything you tell me, Bennie." He grinned. "Pearl in the oyster."

"Hey, don't laugh, man." Bennie settled himself in his seat. "You think I introduce you to just any woman? No fuckin' way." He sniffed the yellow disinfectant on his injured arm and wrinkled his nose in distaste. "Sonia's someone's pearl, let me tell you. Could be she's yours."

A formation of pelicans, long beaks tucked close to their gray chests, swooped low across the water toward their nests among the mangroves. Croaker followed their flight, looking out over the pale turquoise shallows of Florida Bay that led to Everglades National Park. Locals called it the backcountry, in this area alone, a six-hundred-square-mile warren of waterways, basins, and inlets between mangrove islets, and rookeries for tropical birds, that were too small and numerous to be counted or fully mapped. He'd fished many times for trout and snook and bonefish in the purling waterways where, at the dawning of the century, the Calusa and Tequesta silently paddled their buttonwood canoes. It was there that he'd met Stone Tree, a Seminole who had become his guide in the Everglades.

Stone Tree, tall as a Calusa, thin as a length of whittled wood, slowly brought into focus for Croaker the moments of sublime backcountry beauty that few people ever saw or understood. *Things here can keep you alive and healthy for decades,* Stone Tree told him as they stalked strange flora and fauna through hardwood hammocks and coastal prairies. *Things here can kill you in a matter of minutes. It's all a matter of knowledge.* In that self-contained environment a man could lose himself to the rest of the world until the day he died.

Not ten minutes later, Croaker and Bennie were tucked away in Papa Joe's Tiki Bar, a second-floor crow's nest overlooking the western expanse of the mangrove-woven bay. Papa Joe's was an Islamorada institution, part bar, part restaurant, part fishing marina, and all hangout.

"It was like looking into infinity." Bennie's hand clasped a tall beer glass beaded with moisture. "Like understanding for the first time that there are forces beyond your control, forces so primitive and urgent they're, like, incomprehensible."

He was talking about the tiger shark. The bar, crowded with

garrulous regulars, was like a color-drenched reef behind them. In front, the oblate sun was setting over the water. It was that gorgeous Keys color, neither orange nor red, but part of both. A few clouds, ungainly as a clown's whiskers, floated by overhead, and a couple of motorboats slashed their way across the luminescent skin of the bay. A handful of laughing gulls set up shop behind the restaurant on the dock below, where the small fishing skimmers rocked gently at their moorings.

The sky near the horizon was turning that peculiar shade of green found nowhere else but in the tropics. Everyone was standing, staring at the sunset. Down here, it was more than a ritual; it was a basic part of life, like drinking and fishing.

As the last curve of the sun dropped below the horizon there was a burst of spontaneous applause. Then everyone got back to drinking and socializing. The Keys were the great equalizer. Status was nonexistent here. It didn't matter worth a damn whether you had money or not, whether in some other part of the world you counseled presidents or commanded a seven-figure salary. Here, you were no better or worse than the next person.

Bennie, dressed in dark raw silk shorts and a blindingly bright aloha shirt, was in a serious mood. "That fuckin' shark was, like, *symbolic*, right? Symbolic of what the world is and what we never can be. See what I mean?" He made horns of his forefingers, pointed them at his temples. "We got all these smarts, we got opposable thumbs." He wiggled his thumbs as an exhibit. "We invented weapons that can level cities, weapons that can kill people but not buildings. We got E equals M C fuckin' squared." This was not the street-smart cocky businessman most people got to see, but the other Bennie Milagros, a deep thinker, a kind of philosopher who questioned everything in life. Croaker knew instinctively that he was privileged to be seeing this side of the man, just as he knew some unspoken bond was being woven between the two of them.

"What I mean is, all these things they don't mean shit to the shark." Bennie finished his beer in one long gulp. "I swear, Lewis, we almost got our asses chewed to meat out there today."

Croaker got more beers as the waitress came with plates of whole grilled pompano from the restaurant below. He said, "It was a force of nature, like a storm or a tidal wave, nothing, more nothing less."

Bennie stared at the fish made fragrant with fresh rosemary and thyme and Croaker could see the look on his face. He was reminded, as Croaker was, that if not for this particular force of nature they'd be eating wahoo now.

"See, you're wrong, Lewis. That fuckin' *thing*—that was our future. That's what's gonna take us all down one day—a force of fuckin' nature, unknown, unannounced, unstoppable."

Croaker pulled Bennie's glass over, peered into the bottom. "Whoa! I think I'd better drop some mighty Prozac in here."

Bennie laughed sourly, but he was watching the spectral outlines of the brown pelicans on their perches atop the pier pilings. The frightening encounter with the shark had set off something inside him. "I tell you, Lewis, there's something out there waiting for us."

Just after ten o'clock, Maria appeared with Sonia right behind her. Maria was a willowy South American with a massive swirl of black hair, black eyes, and the manner of a woman born to money. Sonia, also Latina, was tall, very slender with thick layers of dark brown hair, and startling hazel eyes. She moved with a certain energy and an unselfconsciousness that was immediately endearing. It was Croaker's experience that women who used their beauty like a bank account soon proved dull or self-involved or both.

At Croaker's suggestion, they went to the Shark Bar, a place both he and Bennie knew. It was a fairly new club on Islamorada, a funky but hip place. It featured salsa bands, a tropical setting, and, best of all, it catered to the Latin American crowd down from South Beach for sport fishing. Which was good for Croaker's business. But he had another reason for hanging out there and he saw that reason standing head and shoulders above the crowd.

"Hey, Rafe!" he called.

Rafe Roubinnet, owner of the Shark Bar, waved and grinned like a man spotting an old college roommate.

"How you been?" Roubinnet thundered. "Must be grand, 'cause I hear you've been out on *Captain Sumo* almost nonstop for a month." His laughter was infectious. "Been reeling in the charismatic mega-vertebrates?"

Croaker, with Sonia's hand in his, maneuvered through the crowd toward the restaurateur. "You bet. The big fish are running and my client list keeps getting longer. I can't complain."

Roubinnet was very tall, lean, and lined from tropical sun and wind, his skin dark as mahogany. He wore white jeans and a midnight blue T-shirt on which was printed in large white Gothic letters: NO RECREATIONAL WHINING. With his dark, thick hair, bright blue eyes, and rugged good looks, Croaker supposed he could have been a model. But Roubinnet seemed too addicted to the slow and easy pace of the Keys.

"*Ai de mi,* who's the beautiful lady?" Roubinnet cried. "Bring her on over here, *compadre!*"

Croaker and Roubinnet had a special relationship. Croaker had gotten a lot of business from the Shark Bar ever since he had relocated from Marco Island on the Gulf Coast. It was his home away from home; he was known there, and well liked, not to mention much admired. Not long ago, he'd ended a spate of death threats against Roubinnet by tracking down a local wise guy who'd been hired by a couple of Miami mobsters wanting a piece of Roubinnet's lucrative action.

Roubinnet, grinning hugely, kissed Sonia's hand, then clasped Croaker's right hand in his, and gave it a squeeze that was as professional as it was powerful. You could tell many things about a man from the way he shook your hand. Before his incarnation as a restaurateur, Roubinnet had been mayor of Miami for a term. Being half-Hispanic hadn't done him any harm, and having Bennie backing him with money and influence hadn't either.

"It's good to see you," Roubinnet said in that special way of his that made you believe that you were the center of his attention. "Spending too much time on that boat of yours. You've got to kick back a little. Relax. Like now."

Someone called to him and he waved. "Minute!" He clapped Croaker on the shoulder. "Don't be such a stranger, *compadre*. Take advantage of the hospitality of the house. Your *dinero*'s no good here." Then he was striding through the crowd, shaking hands, laughing as he listened to bits of gossip delivered up by his best customers.

"He's some character," Sonia said.

"Comes on strong but he's a good guy. Big heart and a straight shooter." Croaker smiled. "Drink?"

"Right now I'd rather dance."

"It will be my pleasure," he said, as he led her out onto the dance floor. "So. Sonia. Is that your first and last name, like Madonna?"

"Madonna's over," Sonia said. "So is having one name." They swung to a sensuous merengue beat. "My last name's Villa-Lobos. Like the music composer." She smiled. "I like the way you dance. Very, you know, liquid. Reminds me of my brother, Carlito. I used to dance with him like this when we were little."

"I learned from the best," Croaker said. "I hung around Spanish Harlem up in New York so much the Latinos finally got used to me."

He watched her move to the music's insistent beat. "Why did you come tonight?"

She looked at him curiously, her arms hooked around his shoulders as their bodies carved out patterns on the floor. "Because Bennie asked."

29

Now he was curious. "Just like that?"

Sonia looked at him as if he ought to know. Then she laughed. "Bennie, Maria, and I all come from Asunción. We know each other a long time."

The band took a break and the dance floor emptied toward the bar, the front of which was fiberglass molded and realistically painted to look like a giant shark. A set of jaws from a real great white shark, its wicked teeth intact, jutted from the wood-paneled wall behind the bar. It was replicated in the mirrors, which reflected the exuberant, casually dressed crowd. Everything was *muy* casual in the Keys.

"Would you like a drink?" Croaker asked.

Sonia nodded. "But afterward I want to dance some more." Her eyes sparkled. "It's not every night I get to be with an Anglo who knows how to merengue."

"You like to merengue."

"It's a very sexy dance," she said.

He took her hand, threading through the raucous throng. Recorded music came on. Jimmy Buffett, and then a succession of well-known salsa artists. Elbowing his way to the bar, he shouted his order to Frank, one of the three bartenders working that night. He got a frozen margarita for Sonia, another mescal for himself. What the hell, he thought.

They headed away from the bar, across the packed room and out of the glass doors onto a wide wooden patio. In true South Florida tradition the frigid air inside became an instant memory as the humidity hit them with a moist slap. They could smell the mangrove hanging rank and heavy in the spangled night. A bed of stars arched overhead. The soft lap of the waves was everywhere, the frenetic scene behind them seemed a million miles away. You didn't even have to close your eyes to believe you were walking on the far edge of the universe.

They looked up. The stars seemed to burn more brightly in the velvet sky. In the distance the lights of the Keys glowed like pearls around a beautiful neck.

"Are you going to ask me to have sex with you?" Sonia asked.

Croaker laughed, taken aback. "I hadn't quite gotten around to thinking about it."

"That's a relief," she said. "Because I don't do that kind of thing, even for Bennie."

"I think he knows that," Croaker said, recalling Bennie's description of Sonia as a pearl in an oyster.

Her eyes danced in amusement. "Don't get me wrong. I mean I

like sex. But I prefer to choose my partners. And, anyway, these days, well, there's a dark side to it and I worry about . . . things." She took a breath, let it out very slowly.

"Like AIDS," he said.

She stared out at the ocean; tears glittered in her eyes. "A friend of mine is very ill."

That's all she needed to say. Suddenly, it seemed very important to be at her side. "I was eighteen when my father died," he said. "He was a cop; I became one because of him. It seemed right to follow his example because he was so moral. All the evil in the world, it seemed, tried to get to him, and he resisted it all. He knew what it meant to be a defender of the law." Croaker, holding her hand, imagined his father sitting beside him, laughing with his eyes crinkling and his hat pushed back to the crown of his head.

He looked into Sonia's beautiful eyes and said, "He died violently, shot in the back in an alley not three blocks from where we lived. He was killed by someone he knew and trusted. In the end, that was the only way his enemies could get to him, by corrupting someone close to him."

He took the point of Sonia's chin gently in the crook of his finger. "He was a good man; he didn't deserve to die before his time. He didn't deserve to die like that." He searched her eyes. "I think maybe it's the same with your friend, isn't it?"

She nodded, tears spilling from her eyes. When he wiped them away, she laughed, and the soft, musical sound sluiced away the dark rustle of anxiety that had built up around them. She stood very close to him, her eyes and lips glittering in explosions of refracted light from the interior of the club. "I don't know what I expected tonight, but . . . maybe I wasn't really expecting to find someone."

She put her drink on the wooden railing, cupped his left hand in hers, turning the blue metal over in the light. "Tell me about this."

"It's actually a biomechanical contraption," he said. He'd long since gotten over being self-conscious about it. "My hand got sliced off in a fight when I was in Japan and a team of microengineers put together this prototype. It runs on a pair of lithium batteries, but believe it or not there's a lot of me inside it. There are boron bones, titanium joints, and stainless-steel nails, but my own artificially regenerated nerves, tendons, and sinews are in there as well. But they're so well protected, I could literally put the hand in fire without feeling any more than a pleasant warmth."

Her fingers glided over the matte-gray polycarbonate palm, the titanium fingers with uncommon delicacy. "Does it need repairs, like a car?"

"Periodically, I'm supposed to go back to Tokyo to let the surgical team make adjustments, but I haven't the inclination. I just change the batteries once every six months." He looked at her rapt face, and hoped she wasn't one of those women who got hung up on the thing. It'd happened before. "It's been seven years and I suspect they want to replace it with a newer model." He shrugged. "One of these days I'll get around to it."

"Or maybe you'll just keep what you have," Sonia said. "Maybe you're content just the way you are."

With a start Croaker realized there was more than a grain of truth to that, and he nodded, grateful at this moment to be with her.

He was aware of the intensity in her eyes as she touched the tip of each finger of his flesh-and-blood right hand. "I like hands," she said. "Hands tell you a lot. They can't lie." She traced the lines on his palm, felt the thick calluses. "You have worker's hands. Strong and capable."

"That comes from being brought up in Hell's Kitchen," he said. "That's a real rough part of Manhattan's West Side. You had to be hard as nails or the hoods would take you apart."

"I know what that's like." Her thumb pressed against his. "I was raised in the roughest part of Asunción." Her eyes got dark. "I learned two things there: to be thick-skinned and to be patient. Being patient is hardest of all, don't you think? It doesn't seem to be an innate human trait, that's why it's so hard to learn."

Suddenly, he seemed as tongue-tied as a kid on his first date. He remembered being with Stone Tree. They were standing in still backcountry water, the sun perched on the edge of the horizon like a demure girl. Without seeming to have moved at all Stone Tree reached into the water and pulled up a perch. He gutted it, spit it on a green branch. The morning was filled with pearly light and the perfect smell of roasting fish. A roseate spoonbill flew by, its unearthly pink haloed by the sun. Stone Tree said, *Life, at its best, is pure and sweet. Moments like this, caught in your hand, stored in your heart, is all a man needs.* And before Croaker knew what he was doing, he was kissing Sonia. An instant after he felt her lips opening under his, he pulled guiltily away. "I didn't mean to do that."

Her eyes were huge, the irises very pale. "But I mean to do *this.*" Putting one hand at the nape of his neck she drew him gently but forcefully until their lips touched. Then she melted against him, her lips opening and her tongue wrapped around his. As if she were a night-blooming flower, he was filled with her scent. It was a heady sensation and he breathed deeply. A quick surge of music made his heart pump all the harder.

"Lew?" A light, female voice.

Not now, he thought. *Can I be unlucky enough to run into an old girlfriend just at this moment?* With extreme reluctance, he broke away from Sonia. Keeping a firm hold on her hand, he turned to face the woman who had come through the glass doors from the interior of the Shark Bar.

"Hello, Lew."

Croaker stared at the woman, his mind refusing to work. "Matty." It was as if it were encased in a block of ice. He felt his stomach give a quick flip-flop.

Matty, beautiful, regal as a princess, was looking from him to Sonia and back again. She wore a very expensive dress in matte black jersey and a string of diamonds at her throat. She was so impeccably made-up she looked as if she'd just emerged from a beauty salon. In her formal designer splendor she looked totally out of place. "I know this must come as something of a shock—"

"Christ, you can say that again."

Matty's gaze flicked quickly to Sonia and, as if she were embarrassed, whipped back to his stunned face. "I'm sorry to intrude but I've got to talk to you. I didn't want to leave a message at the marina and they said you'd probably be here some time tonight." Clearly nervous, her words came out in a tangled rush.

"You said you never wanted to speak to me again." Croaker was aware he was gripping Sonia's hand as if it were a life preserver in high seas. He could hardly hear the conversation over the pounding of his heart. "That was, what? Twelve years ago?"

"Fourteen," Matty said. "Fourteen years, one month, seventeen days." She tried to smile but failed miserably. She took a deep breath. "It was at Rachel's christening."

"How could I forget," he said bleakly.

"She's fifteen now."

"And not a word from either of you in all this time."

"I'm not aware that you ever tried to contact us."

"After what you told me I had no reason to think you'd want to see me."

"Okay. I deserved that."

He stared at her stonily.

"Lew—"

"What is it? You made your bed. You married Donald Duke. That life's everything you wanted, or so you took the trouble to tell me over and over."

33

Matty's eyes were full of tears. "That was a long time ago."

"Lew," Sonia broke in. "What's going on?"

"Everything's changed," Matty went on, as if she hadn't heard Sonia. "Donald walked out on me."

Watching her expression, he said, "What do you want from me, Matty? Am I supposed to be surprised or even sympathetic?" He was painfully aware that he was roiled with emotion as the past came rushing back. He had to turn it aside. "Oh, yes, how thoughtless. The introductions. Sonia Villa-Lobos, this is Matty Duke. My sister."

In the stunned silence, he let go of Sonia's hand. "Eighteen years ago she met a man named Donald Duke."

"Lew, don't—" Matty pleaded.

"He was a corporate raider, a shark who fed off other people's misfortunes. He plundered one company after another, selling off the divisions, firing people."

"Christ," Matty said, "you talk about him like he was some kind of criminal."

Croaker concentrated on Sonia's face as his anger once again bound up his heart. "He maneuvered people he didn't like out of boardrooms, hounded them out of New York, maybe even taking pleasure in doing so."

"What proof?" Matty said. "There wasn't any."

His eyes blazed. "Nevertheless, my sister married him. She was dazzled by the lifestyle, isn't that right, Matty?" Matty bit her lip and looked away. "Of course it is. She wouldn't listen to my warnings; in fact, they incensed her. I told her what kind of man she was marrying. But she turned everything around. She accused me of being jealous of Donald's wealth and position. She made fun of me because I was a cop and I saw the world through a cop's pea-brained eyes." He cocked his head. "Wasn't that the word you used, Matty? And then you said, what was it? You're pathetic, Lew. You'll end up like Pop, lying dead facedown in an alley." He shook his head. "The lifestyle, the money and power were all more important than her own family. She met Duke and she was suddenly embarrassed by her family, by where she had been brought up."

"That isn't true!" Matty protested.

"Which part isn't true, Matty? Tell me." He watched her face. "At the wedding you gushed over Donald's wealthy friends while we sat alone and isolated. You never brought him home. Mama only wanted to cook for him, but you never gave her the chance."

"Stop it!" Matty cried in anguish. "You don't understand anything."

34

Croaker was not to be deterred. "Worse, you kept Rachel from us as punishment and Ma died without ever having a chance to get to know her granddaughter. You cut us out and it broke Mama's heart. Not to mention mine!"

He turned to Sonia. "At Rachel's christening, I'd finally had it, and I told her what I thought of her husband and her new life."

"Damnit, Lew, you threatened Donald. In church!" Matty was trembling. "In front of everyone."

"And I meant every word of it." A kind of crazy pulse was beating in his head as remembrance flooded back. "That's when she told me she never wanted to speak to me again," he said to Sonia. Then he rounded on Matty. "Now aren't you glad you came back?"

Without another word to either woman, he opened the glass door, strode through the crowded club, past Bennie and Maria, clamped in fiery embrace on the dance floor, and out into the sea of cars in the asphalt parking lot.

It wasn't long before Bennie Milagros came dancing down the Shark Bar's front steps. Above the entrance, the front half of a gargantuan fierce-looking molded plastic shark thrust skyward in a plume of fake foam. It was tacky, but Rafe Roubinnet said it made him laugh every time he looked at it.

Bennie moved aside to allow a couple of South American businessmen and their women to get by, then went purposefully across the lot to where Croaker sat behind the wheel of the T-bird.

He climbed into the car beside Croaker and handed him a drink.

"Here, I thought you could use this."

Croaker accepted it without comment.

Bennie extracted a long Cuban cigar from his breast pocket, took some time with the ritual of lighting it. He smelled of mescal and male sweat. A hint of Maria's perfume clung to him like pink clouds cling to cherubim. Pretty soon the cigar smoke masked it all.

"Regarding you, I think that, you know, a bat outta hell woulda left the club in better shape." He puffed on his cigar, not looking at Croaker, not looking at anything. "Sonia is steely-eyed, so you must've somehow gotten to her; she's upset for you. Maria's kibitzing with her, and me, I'm out my ecstatic dancing partner, maybe for the rest of the evening." Another languorous puff. "Oh, yeah, I almost forgot. There's this juicy *guapa* askin' everyone in there where you went. God hears me, she's got some kinda figure on her."

"She's my sister, Bennie."

"Well, shit." Bennie frowned darkly, clamped the cigar between his lips.

Above their heads, the palm fronds clattered like an unruly chorus in concert with the high chirps of the tree frogs.

Someone bursting out of the club caught their attention. "Here she comes," Bennie said softly. He waited until he had Croaker's gaze. "This sucks, man, this bad feelin'. It's like poison, you know?"

"I'm sorry I screwed up your evening, Bennie."

"Don't be dim." Bennie waved his cigar in the air. "This here's bigger than an evening with Maria." He blew out a cloud of aromatic smoke. "You know what I thought about in that moment when the shark came up, Lewis? It wasn't my whole life flashing like a line of tarot cards. What I thought 'bout was my sister. Not my father, not my brothers. *Mi hermana.*"

Bennie turned to face Croaker. "Rosa died five years ago. And what I was thinking was this: my father, he always sort of dismissed her accomplishments, even when she went to graduate school in Bogotá, earned her master's in economics and got a job at the World Bank. Not that he didn't love her, not that he wasn't proud of her in his way. He just never showed it."

Bennie's eyes were clouded with memory and regret. "So in that moment I thought of Rosa. I saw her being wounded by my father's indifference, by my brothers' inattention, by my own benign neglect." He looked at Croaker. "See, something's changed now. The fuckin' shark did that to me, an' I'll never forget it. I miss her an' I'll never get a chance to tell her that."

Then, he leaned over, took Croaker's right hand, pointed to the tracery of blue veins along the back of it. "What's this?" he hissed. "It's fuckin' *blood*, Lewis." He nodded his head, as if he'd just solved the riddle of the Sphinx. "Just remember, whatever your sister is or isn't, whatever she's done, whatever hurt lies between you, you two're joined. She's blood."

Matty had spotted them and was walking over. She gave Bennie a hesitant look. Bennie slid out of the car. He chivalrously left the door open for her, went around to the driver's side, stood at Croaker's shoulder as Matty came up to the T-bird. He gave her his best silken smile, then leaned over, whispered in Croaker's ear: "God hear me, women can find more ways to be cruel. But, you know what? Sometimes their brothers can be worse."

Croaker watched him saunter slowly back to the club entrance, smoking contentedly. What an enigma Bennie Milagros was. Every time you thought you had a handle on him, he showed you another facet of his personality. He was mercurial, crass, *muy simpatico*, improbably spiritual—and endlessly puzzling.

A moment later Matty stood beside the T-bird, saying nothing. She'd darkened her curly, wild hair to the color of toffee. It suited her coloring better than when she'd had her hair dyed blonde. She was tall and willowy with the long legs and curvy figure a man like Donald Duke would have coveted—until someone taller and leggier came along.

About to say something she started, as car doors slammed and an old Buick fired up. Headlights swung across her face as the Buick rolled out of the parking lot. Then she took a step toward him. Her tension was palpable. "You know you have a habit of embarrassing the hell out of me in public."

"Maybe now you know a little of how Mama and I felt."

Her expression was bleak, her lips thinned by anxiety. "Christ, this isn't easy."

"Why should it be? You sure as hell made it hard on us."

She took a deep breath, then compulsively opened her purse, slipped something out of her wallet, passed it over to him.

It was a recent color snapshot of Rachel. She had Matty's thick, curly hair and her intense expression, but Donald's ice blue eyes and fair coloring. Whoever had taken the photo had caught her in an unguarded moment of concentration. She seemed as carefree as a person could get.

"She's beautiful," he said with a painful pang. He'd just realized how much he'd been cheated in the last fifteen years. He'd never had a chance to watch her grow up.

"Thanks." But she forgot to smile. She shook her head when he tried to hand back the snapshot. "That's for you."

Croaker's gaze lingered over it. "I can see both of you in her face."

"The thing is . . ." She hesitated. "Donald had been gone for two years. Six months ago he died. He was killed when his private jet got caught in a thunderstorm and crashed into a mountainside outside San Francisco."

Croaker wanted to say he was sorry, but the word stuck in his throat. Instead, he could not help saying, "That must have made you rich."

"Not really." She seemed resigned to his barbs. "A year ago, Donald remarried. A young oil heiress from Texas with impeccable family credentials which, I suppose, he'd longed for all the time. She gave birth to their son a week before he died. Donald stipulated that the estate will eventually go to him."

"Tough luck." He held the photo up. "But you still have Rachel."

Matty's face seemed abruptly pale. She looked like she was about to say something, then at the last minute changed her mind. "Lew, I . . ." Her gaze twisted away. "I have a confession to make. I know you didn't say anything when I said you'd hadn't tried to contact us."

His jaw clenched involuntarily.

"You see, I know you tried to keep in touch with Rachel." She took a long, shuddering breath. "I know because I made sure she didn't get the letters."

"Sonuvabitch!" His hands slammed the wheel, and she winced.

"It was terribly wrong of me, I know." She shook her head. "But I thought I was doing the right thing, shielding Rachie from someone I didn't want her to see."

He looked at her and said, "Why didn't you want her to see me?"

"Goddamnit." Matty's eyes were wet and she tried to look everywhere but at his face. "The truth is . . ." Her lip was trembling and she licked a tear that had slid down her cheek. Her gaze finally found his. "You see, she's so *damn* much like you."

Voices came, laughing and high-spirited, as a group came out of the club. Another engine started up and headlights lit the parking area for a moment before swinging out onto the road.

"Well, hell, what d'you know?" Croaker said in some wonderment. He looked at the photo of Rachel again before sliding it away.

Matty settled herself silently beside him. He smelled a waft of Giorgio perfume. They lapsed into an uneasy silence. Old wounds, surfacing, were proving difficult to deal with. Matty's anxiety had increased; he could feel it like an itching in his bones. The salsa band had returned, its rhythms insistent and alluring. He longed to be inside, dancing hip to hip with Sonia. He wanted very much to apologize to her.

As if she could read his mind, Matty said in her best brittle tone, "You look like you can't spare much time. Go ahead, then. Your girlfriend's waiting for you. But I must say I don't know why you waste your time."

"Oh, for Christ's sake." He'd been expecting something like this.

"You can do so much better than that."

"Like I could do better than being a cop," he said.

"I always had such high hopes for you."

"But they were *your* hopes, Matty. Not mine." He turned to her. "Tell me something. How come you never asked what it was *I* wanted out of life? How come you assumed you knew."

She seemed on the verge of tears. She was trembling slightly, and

Croaker had the distinct impression she was keeping the tears back by sheer force of will. "But I *did* know," she said in a small voice. "We both wanted more for ourselves than Mama and Pop had. I know that; we used to talk about it when we were young."

"Sure I wanted better than what had been," he said. "But I didn't want to turn my back on it. That's what you set out to do, Matty."

She squeezed her eyes shut. Slowly, tears formed at the corners, welled, and dropped into her lap. "I wish I could make you understand."

"Try."

She shook her head from side to side. "That would mean . . ." Her eyes flew open and she glared hotly at him for a moment. "All right." But she couldn't sustain it, and she tilted her head back and stared up into the clattering fronds of the coconut palms. "See, for you it was different. You were a boy and the streets of Hell's Kitchen were made for boys."

"That's no reason—"

"Please be still," she said. "It's hard enough . . ." Her eyes squeezed shut again, and when she spoke her voice was as quiet as the breeze drifting through the palms. "Just let me tell it, okay?" She licked her lips as if they were dry, and he could see that she was terribly frightened. Of a memory? "There was this boy. Richie Paglia."

Croaker remembered him: dark hair, hot eyes—a hunk. He'd gone out with Matty for a while; then she dropped him cold and disappeared into the world beyond Hell's Kitchen. She'd turned her back on her neighborhood and her family. Not long after, she'd married Donald. It had pissed Croaker off, the way she'd tossed aside a local kid who'd cared for her, treating him like dirt. He had seen in that gesture an intimation of a larger betrayal to come. All for Donald and his glittering world. Croaker bit back an acid comment.

"Richie," Matty was saying. "He was so sweet on me." She put her fingertips to her lips, as if she had to flog herself to continue. "See, the thing of it was, Ritchie got me pregnant."

"*What?*"

Into the stunned silence, she forced more words: "He offered to marry me but I said no; I didn't love him and he didn't know what he wanted. There wasn't anything between us but sex. We'd had fun, that's all. It happens, Lew."

"Not to my sister."

"I knew you'd say that." She sighed. "But it *did* happen." Her voice trailed away. She put a hand up, pressed it against her forehead for a moment. "I couldn't go to you. I was, what, nineteen?

I'd finished college in three years, made dean's list. I wanted a career, but what did any of that matter to you? I knew you'd make us get married and we'd be miserable. Either that, or you'd beat the crap out of Richie, which he didn't deserve. Besides, Catholic that I am, I was ashamed. You remember how strict Mama was about religion."

She stared down at her hands. "I was in a panic. I felt I was inside a box that was closing in on me. Richie and I decided the best thing was for him to disappear from the neighborhood. That was the easy part. He'd gotten a job across the river in Hoboken and he said he'd move there. As for me . . ." Her restless gaze roved the treetops. "As for me, I had to find a place outside of Hell's Kitchen. A clinic, a doctor."

Croaker could scarcely catch his breath. How could his reading of their shared past have been so flawed? The truth had a cruel habit of surprising just about everyone. "So you had the abortion."

Matty nodded. "It was a decision that almost tore my heart out. For a long time I felt unclean, wrapped in a sinner's ashes. I couldn't bring myself to set foot in church. I felt I had turned my face away from God. But I had no other choice."

She buried her head in her hands, and he waited, his heart beating very fast.

"Afterward, I found that I couldn't go home. I couldn't face the inevitable interrogation you'd put me through. I knew you, Lew. You'd take one look at my face and know something was wrong."

"I tried to look for you."

She nodded. "But you couldn't find me. I had just enough graduation money to stay in a hotel for a couple of weeks. When the money ran out I got a job as a copywriter at an ad agency. And for the first time I was happy. I felt free."

"Free of us," Croaker said. "Your family."

Matty shook her head. "Free of that apartment. It was so dark and depressing. My God, Lew, how could you stand living there for so long?"

"Mom and Pop were there," he said. "It was home."

Matty turned her head away. "The agency is where I met Donald." Her tone turned wistful. "I worked long hours and didn't mind. I was trying to stare down my conscience in the mirror, but after a while I found I was so happy I was no longer racked by guilt." She ran her hand along the T-bird's chrome work. "Six months after I started work Donald bought the agency. I'd moved up by then. I had a group of midlevel accounts I was handling. Anyway, the day the papers were signed Donald fired all the high-priced executives, along with their triple-martini lunches, then put together a transition team from those remaining to evaluate the company and the staff for him. I was part of the team. I worked alongside him for three months. Every day. I never thought he noticed, but I was wrong. He told me later he'd been watching me from day one."

She turned to him, her face full of tears. "Without even knowing it, I'd slipped into a whole new life. So you see, after everything that had happened, everything I wanted to forget, I couldn't face the family—especially you, Lew. Mr. Detective. Even after months and months had gone by I was terrified you'd see the truth in my eyes every time I tried to lie."

Croaker, stunned and ashamed, heard Bennie's words coming back to haunt him: *God hears me, women can find more ways to be cruel. But, you know what? Sometimes their brothers can be worse.*

Something hard and ugly broke apart inside him. "Matty—"

Just the soft, conciliatory tone of his voice caused her to break down. She was sobbing as he reached for her, her shoulders shaking, her head pressed against the crook of his shoulder. He held her close to him, and wonder of wonders, his eyes were wet, as well. Bennie was right. No matter who she was, no matter what had gone on between them, they were blood. It was odd to realize that what he had mistaken for anger was simply mischance and misunderstanding.

"I couldn't face you," she whispered. "I couldn't bear the recriminations, the look on your face when you found out, your contempt for me for being so stupid, for doing all the wrong things. So I took the coward's way out; after I'd married Donald it was easier to cut the family out. But I swear it was your unwavering sense of morality that stared at me in the mirror every morning."

He held her closer, said, "What's done is done, Matty. It's all in the past. We can start over again."

"Really? Oh, my God, Lew, that would be so wonderful, a dream come true, but—"

She was rigid with tension, and he drew her gently away from him so he could see her face. "But what?"

Her eyes were wide and staring in mortal fear, and instinctively he knew that the stark terror he saw in her eyes was what had driven her to seek him out after all this time.

"Matty, what is it?"

"Oh, dear God," she whispered through her sobs, "Rachel's dying. Lew, my little girl is slipping away and I don't know what to do."

41

DAY TWO

1

Royal Poinciana Hospital was a twelve-story pale gold brick edifice that rose at the east end of Eucalyptus Street. Though it was a stone's throw from the Flagler Memorial Bridge and within walking distance of Royal Poinciana Way and the Breakers Hotel on Palm Beach, its immediate surroundings were dark, bleak, and not a little dangerous.

Across the moat of the Intracoastal, women with big hair emerged from gleaming Rolls-Royces without a care in the world. Here, you were obliged to lock your car doors the moment you slid behind the wheel. It was more than symbolic that the hospital, facing the light-spangled Intracoastal, had turned its back on North Dixie Highway and, beyond, Broadway. That area, filled with broken-down cement-block houses and floodlit fifty-cent coin laundries, was the mean province of the black community that lapped precipitously at Palm Beach's outer edge. It was no wonder that the Palm Beach concierges urged their charges to avoid the immediate northwest territory.

Be that as it may, Matty seemed entirely unperturbed as she got out of her black Lexus. They hurried across the blacktop parking lot and up the stairs into the hospital. A faint smell of bandages and antiseptic floated in the close-to-freezing air. A security guard showed them where to check in and pick up day tags.

Matty turned back to Croaker. This morning she looked exhausted, as if she had paced the floor all night, waiting for dawn to arrive. She'd tried to do something with the dark circles under her eyes, but when she took off her Donna Karan sunglasses Croaker could see she'd failed.

At the end of the hall on the sixth floor they went through the double doors marked DIALYSIS UNIT. They entered an area that looked for all the world like the waiting room of hell. Old people, bent and haggard as last year's saw grass, were lined up in the hallway. They were supported by walkers, wheelchairs, and crutches. The occasional nurse marched down the line inspecting them like the guard outside a disco who decides which people will be allowed to enter. The place reeked of medication and resignation. As Croaker passed this rank of the infirm, he could hear thick and ragged breathing, tiny moans and disturbed grunts, as if he had come upon a watering hole in the African veld.

"Diabetics waiting for their dialysis," Matty murmured.

Beyond another set of doors was CCD, the Critical Care Dialysis. It was a warren of claustrophobic cubicles built around a central nurses' station. Surrounding patients in beds were crash carts, IV stands, monitors, arcane medical paraphernalia, and, in some cases, dialysis machines.

Of the eight people in the unit only Rachel was young. The rest seemed to have been plucked from those unfortunates who had been on the dialysis line too long.

Croaker approached Rachel tentatively, as though he might wake her with an incautious step. But she was beyond such concerns. According to what Matty had told him Rachel's condition was critical. She had been in a coma at the time she had been admitted to the hospital and had not come out of it. She was so pale it looked as if every drop of blood had been drained from her. Blue veins throbbed beneath the thin skin of her temples. A tangled mass of hair spread lankly on the pillowcase. A gold nose ring had been pushed aside by a plastic tube. Croaker tried to imagine her as the child she had been at her christening, when he'd held her in his arms, but the memory eluded him. All he saw was the fifteen-year-old who lay before him. His heart was caught in a viselike grip. He was struck all over again by how beautiful she was, but her face looked like a death mask.

She was catheterized and tubed, hooked up to monitors that showed her pulse, heart rate, and blood pressure. IV drips punctured her veins. A computerized dialysis machine, perhaps four-and-a-half feet high, clad in beige plastic, pumped dutifully at her side, cleansing her blood, doing the work her damaged kidneys apparently could not.

At last, his heart broke and he turned back to Matty. "What's going on? What the hell happened to her?" There was more than a little anger inside him.

Matty stood mutely, staring dully at the dialysis machine, which had taken on an odd and vaguely unsettling presence, as if it were a large and loyal dog that would not leave its master's side.

"Simply put, she's suffering from nephro-toxic poisoning brought on by an overdose of cocaine and amphetamines."

Croaker turned to see a female doctor in her midthirties, fit as an amateur athlete, pretty in a tough, no-nonsense way. Her reddish hair was pulled back from her catlike face.

She stuck out her hand and Croaker took it. "I'm Dr. Marsh. Jenny Marsh." She cocked an eyebrow. "And you are?"

"Lew Croaker. I'm Matty's—

"Ah, the prodigal brother returneth." Dr. Marsh smiled. "From all Mrs. Duke has told me, I'm glad she was able to locate you. Excuse me a moment." She turned to Matty. "We'd like to take some more blood and urine, Mrs. Duke, if that's all right."

Matty nodded mutely and Dr. Marsh signed for a lab tech to come in.

"Doctor, I'd appreciate some details on my niece's condition," Croaker said as the tech began to draw blood from Rachel's arm.

The cubicle had gotten uncomfortably cramped, and Dr. Marsh said, "Why don't we continue this conversation outside." She and Croaker stepped out into the center area, but Matty stayed behind.

"My sister—"

"Personally I'm relieved you're here," Dr. Marsh said. "Mrs. Duke is having difficulty assimilating everything that's happened to Rachel. That's perfectly understandable, given the nature of the situation. However, she tells me you're an ex-cop, is that right?"

Croaker nodded.

"Then I assume you've had experience with teenagers on drugs."

"Too much."

Jenny Marsh nodded as she led him out of the Dialysis Unit and through a frosted glass door with a cardboard sign taped onto it that read: PALM BEACH COUNTY DRUG ABUSE RESEARCH STUDY—GRANT AUTHORIZED PERSONNEL ONLY.

Croaker found himself in one of two windowless rooms, crammed with zinc-topped lab tables covered with Bunsen burners, banks of autoclaves and centrifuges, and microscopes. Behind these were neat rows of test tubes, retorts, pipettes, glass slides, eyedroppers, and precisely tagged glass bottles of chemical reagents. A single electron microscope hulked in one corner. This paraphernalia made him vaguely uneasy. It could not help but remind him of morgues he had been in, escorting relatives or close friends of murder victims making painful and traumatic identification while he stood by stoic and, for the moment, helpless.

Against one wall was a row of stainless-steel cabinets, along with an outmoded refrigerator and a small table laden with a hot plate, coffeemaker, paper cups, jars of Cremora, and the like.

"There's a drug abuse research study going on," Jenny Marsh said. "It's county funded, but because the hospital's involved, I volunteered to oversee it."

"Don't you already have enough on your plate, Doctor?"

Jenny Marsh smiled. It was a nice smile that caused her physician's cool mask to slip just a fraction. "Yes, I do. But this study's important. Frankly, I'd rather be a part of it than sleep."

Croaker watched the lab assistant he'd seen in Rachel's cubicle come in, presumably with her blood, and go into the other room. While there was activity here, it was far calmer than in the CCD.

"As soon as Rachel was diagnosed as a drug O.D. blood and urine samples were taken for the study," Dr. Marsh said. "It's being done twice a day. Her contribution to the study is very helpful, and I promise you the amounts of blood withdrawn will not affect her in any way."

"Matty said okay?"

"Once the value of the program was explained to her," Dr. Marsh said.

Croaker nodded. "It's fine by me then."

"Okay, first things first." Jenny Marsh went to the table with the coffeepot. "Rachel was brought in through Emergency. She was exhibiting all the classic signs of drug overdose."

Croaker said, "What? She was confused, highly agitated, hallucinating?"

Dr. Marsh nodded as she poured coffee for them both. "All of the above. Plus, she was having seizures with severe vomiting in between. In the attending physician's opinion she was clearly in shock." She looked at him. "Black? Cream?"

"Black's fine," he said.

She methodically put four packs of sugar into the dark and unreadable waters of her coffee. Then she handed him a paper cup. "Dr. Niguel, the attending, tried to revive Rachel without success. At this point, he dispatched one of the nurses to talk to your sister—who had brought Rachel in—to see if she could tell him what sort of drugs Rachel was into." Dr. Marsh's gaze turned sympathetic. "I'm afraid that's when Mrs. Duke freaked out."

Croaker put his cup down. "What do you mean, she freaked out?"

Dr. Marsh perched on the edge of a backless lab stool. "She went into hysterics, said she wanted her daughter back, that she'd sue us up and down for malpractice, that her daughter had never taken drugs in her life, and we were a bunch of incompetents to insinuate otherwise."

"But she was wrong."

"She was wrong." Dr. Marsh crossed her arms over her breasts. "At the tender age of fifteen your niece is a habitual drug user."

"How bad? Was she shooting?"

"That's the good news. The *only* good news, I'm afraid." Dr. Marsh sipped her coffee. "We found no evidence of needle tracks. Coke, uppers, pot were her thing. Blood work confirmed this." She sighed. "Then, according to Dr. Niguel, her kidneys started to shut down. In Emergency they were looking for signs of bacterial endocarditis, which is an infection you find in needle drug users."

"Right. Infection of the heart valves. Causes blood clots that can break off and go to the brain—or the kidneys." He put aside the coffee. The acid was doing unpleasant things to the lining of his stomach. Or maybe it was the subject of their conversation. This was his niece they were talking about, not someone off the inner city streets. "But Rachel didn't have bacterial endocarditis."

"No." Dr. Marsh got up, rummaged through the old refrigerator. She sniffed at an open container of yogurt, then used a forefinger to taste it. "You want anything?"

"A million dollars, the ability to leap tall buildings in a single bound." When she gave him a wry look, he said, "But nothing from in there."

"Smart man. You have to be a doctor who hasn't eaten in thirty-odd hours to be desperate enough to ingest this stuff." Jenny Marsh closed the refrigerator door. "A renal ultrasound revealed no trace of polycystic kidneys, the most typical problem for young people. It's hereditary."

She took some more yogurt with a plastic spoon. "But the ultrasound did reveal something interesting. At this time Dr. Niguel called me in. I determined her blood pressure was dangerously low and there was a serious lack of oxygen in her kidney."

"Nephro-toxic poisoning."

"Bingo."

"But you said kidney, as in singular."

Dr. Marsh ate her yogurt slowly and methodically, savoring it as if it were manna from heaven. "That's the anomaly the renal ultrasound showed us. Your niece was born with only one functioning kidney. The other is shriveled, nonfunctional."

"Did you get her medical history?"

Dr. Marsh nodded. "After I got her started on dialysis I asked

Mrs. Duke for Rachel's family doctor. His name's Ronald Stansky—
he's in West Palm. While you're here you'll surely run into him.
He seems genuinely concerned." She swiped her fingers around the
inside of the container, gathering the last of the yogurt. "Anyway,
Dr. Stansky knew nothing about the one kidney. But that's hardly
surprising. Unless Rachel had had renal trouble in the past, there's
no way he would have known or had cause to check."

"And she hadn't."

"No."

Croaker thought this sequence of events over in his mind until
he could picture everything that had happened, step by step. The
process served to settle him down. His emotions were so roiled
they threatened to impair his reasoning. That wouldn't do anyone
any good, especially Rachel.

In the other room, a phone began to ring. "I want to know what
I can do," he said. "You've made it clear her condition's very bad
and I . . ." He paused to take a breath as a painful image of Rachel
lying unconscious and helpless not twenty yards away blazed in
his mind. "Jesus, I just found her again and . . ."

"Take your time," Dr. Marsh said softly. For the first time, he
noticed her eyes seemed to change color with the light, from green
to hazel. "This is a large dose of emotion to deal with at once, I
know." A lab tech stuck her head in, told her there was a phone
call, and Dr. Marsh mouthed, "Not now." To Croaker, she said, "I
want to be sure you're with me completely for this."

Croaker nodded. "I'm okay. It's just that her life's just beginning.
The thought of her spending the rest of it on dialysis—well, it's
going to take some getting used to."

"If only it were that simple."

Croaker felt as if he were in free fall. "What do you mean?"

Jenny Marsh leaned forward. "The kidney needs to be replaced
pronto."

A cold pool was forming in the pit of Croaker's stomach. "Why?"

"Normally, dialysis would work. But, in Rachel's case, there are
complications."

Her face grew grim and determined and Croaker had the terrible
suspicion that they'd entered the final phase of this nightmarish
conversation. "Like what?"

"She's developed sepsis. An infection."

"From the catheter?"

"Not in this hospital and definitely not in my section," she said.
"When she passed out she fell. I suspect the sepsis developed from

the wound. The attending in Emergency was quite rightly concentrating on the renal failure. The wound was treated later."

She put the empty yogurt container aside. "This is why I wanted to get you away from your niece and your sister. Mrs. Duke is going to need your cool head in the days and weeks to come. You see, I've tried several times to fully explain Rachel's situation to her, but she just won't listen."

"Tell me, then," Croaker said with a certain sense of dread.

She took a quick breath. "The dialysis machine is washing her blood, doing the work of her kidney, that's true enough. *If* we can stabilize her. But the hard truth is she's far from stabilized now. In the meantime, we're having difficulty controlling the sepsis. It's sapping her last reserves of strength."

Croaker stared at her. "Bottom line."

Jenny Marsh was not one to flinch from hard truths. "Without an immediate kidney transplant, she'll die."

"Immediate." The cold pool spread up into his abdomen and chest. "How long?"

Dr. Marsh shrugged. "Now that becomes a matter of medical interpretation. This medical professional says two weeks, maybe three, no more." She said this in a clear, steady voice while looking him straight in the eye. He appreciated that.

"Doctor, tell me something. How good are you?"

"I'm the best." She said it flatly, as a statement of fact. There seemed no ego involved at all. "My advice to your sister was to get a second—even a third opinion—if she desired. She did and both doctors concurred with my prognosis. You can speak to them if you wish, but the bottom line is Rachel has got to have a new kidney."

"Would you be the one to put it in her?"

Dr. Marsh nodded. "Most assuredly."

"Okay. Then we get her one."

Jenny Marsh sighed ruefully. "Yes, the ideal scenario is for a sister—preferably a twin—to donate his or her kidney. There are no other siblings in this family. I've tested Mrs. Duke. She isn't compatible."

"You'll test me, of course."

Jenny Marsh nodded. "ASAP. But I have to be honest, the chances of a match aren't good. Your sister's already been screened and rejected."

"Okay. Say she can't use one of mine. Give me another alternative."

"Every kidney that becomes available for transplant in this country is typed. The report is then put on-line at the National Computer Center of UNOS in Richmond, Virginia. The United Network of Organ Sharing registers each and every organ. There are no exceptions. Organs are harvested, but there are never enough for the growing list of recipients. If anyone's to blame it's our fellow man. People just don't want to donate. It's tragic. I'll give you one example close to home. Last year we had thirty-five thousand deaths in Palm Beach county alone. If all those people had been organ donors, Rachel and others in dire need like her all across the country wouldn't have a problem."

"But we do have a problem," Croaker said.

"Yes." Dr. Marsh nodded. "And it's an insoluble one, I'm afraid. There's a waiting list for a kidney of about thirty-six thousand people nationally. Also, there's a case for need. Rachel's young, which is in her favor, but she's a drug user, which is definitely not. In terms of time, we're looking at between sixteen and twenty-four months at the earliest."

Croaker rocked backward, as if he had been slapped across the face. "Christ, this can't be happening. It isn't possible."

"I'm afraid it is," Dr. Marsh said. "In one way, we've become lucky with kidneys. They're the only major organ we are able to keep alive outside the host body. With a perfusion machine you chill it to thirty-two degrees centigrade and pump Belzer solution through it. Believe it or not, it's a potato starch compound. It's a real medical breakthrough. You can even do it on a brain-dead body. Just pump the chilled solution into the abdominal cavity. That way, you've got seventy-two hours before the kidney becomes compromised."

"But in Rachel's case this breakthrough does us no good at all." Croaker tried not to sound bitter.

"Unless you can pull strings I don't know about and get her a kidney."

He leaned forward. "Doc, can't you, you know, pull strings?"

She looked at him for a minute, and he thought he saw a flicker of pity in her eyes. "This isn't city hall. You don't pull strings to get a new kidney; not unless you have a hundred million dollars to donate to renal research, and even then it's more a matter of luck than anything else. As I told you, each kidney is registered. If I—or any other doctor in this country—is caught putting an unregistered organ into a patient it's not only our license that's forfeit, it's our freedom. The act's illegal."

Croaker's biomechanical hand curled into a powerful fist. "But there's got to be a way," he said.

Jenny Marsh silently regarded that curious and singular weapon with the respect it merited. "Unless you can come up with a donor who's willing and whose blood type and HLA—human lymphocitic antigens—are compatible with Rachel's, I'm afraid there isn't."

"Did Matty tell you I was a detective in the NYPD?" Croaker said.

"Yes, she did."

"I'll find Rachie a donor." Then the look on her face registered. "What're my odds?"

"I can tell you from experience there aren't many people around willing to give up a kidney. At least, a kidney in decent shape. But even if you did find someone, their blood type and three of six of their HLAs would have to match Rachel's body chemistry."

Croaker was shaken all over again. "Christ, I'd have as much chance of winning the Florida lottery."

She shook her head sorrowfully. "Mr. Croaker, if it weren't for bad odds, you'd have no odds at all."

Speaking of which, Sonia Villa-Lobos was having a very bad day indeed. When she got up that morning, she discovered that the power was off. It flickered on just long enough for her to take a shower before it died again. In the morning's light, she carefully made the bed, smoothing down corners and edges that were ruffled. She was forced to break out her emergency equipment: a battery-powered hair drier. She did her makeup sitting in her car with the door open. The sun streaming through the tinted windows would have otherwise destroyed her color sense.

Mrs. Leyes emerged from the house next door, and Sonia leaned out the car door to complain about the power outage. Estrella Leyes, a Paraguayan from the hill country, stopped to hand over a casserole covered with aluminum foil.

"For Nestor." She kissed Sonia warmly on both cheeks. With her only daughter long moved away she had come to look on Sonia as a surrogate. "He's better?" she asked hopefully.

"Unfortunately he's not." Sonia put away her hair drier.

"You should have him come see me," Mrs. Leyes said.

Sonia smiled and patted the older woman's arm. "I would, but he's gotten to the point where he can't get out of the house."

"*Ay, pobre!* Then I should come see him."

"That would be nice," Sonia said. "But I don't know what good it would do. Nestor's dying."

From where Sonia lived in El Portal it was not more than twelve minutes due south to work. However, three days a week she made a detour off NE Second Avenue to look in on her friend. Nestor had been a professional dancer, a young man with a beautiful, sinuous body. His work had been ethereal, so it was doubly a crime that he was dying of AIDS. She often brought him food she made or, when too busy, that she bought at the Thai restaurant down the road. Nestor loved Thai food. He didn't care much for Estrella's goat casseroles, but Sonia had the good sense never to tell the older woman that.

Today, she discovered Nestor lying in bed, facing the wall. The sheets were an unholy mess, and she spent forty minutes cleaning him up. He was in one of his unresponsive moods, so while she worked she recited poems by Rudyard Kipling. She'd read them to him so many times they were committed to memory. He loved the precise cadences of Kipling's nineteenth-century mind, and he responded to the profound sense of mystery Kipling must surely have felt for the exotic places to which he traveled.

Her heart broke to leave Nestor alone, but in truth there was nothing more she could do for him and she was already late for work.

Lord Constantine Fine Imports on NE Fortieth Street in the Design District of Miami was a two-story persimmon-colored building with a gated courtyard filled with palms and hibiscus trees.

She got into the office and hit her desk running. As one of three partners, she was in charge of buying from the South American and Mexican export companies, which accounted for three-quarters of Lord Constantine's high-end furniture and accessories business. Consequently, there were an alarming number of urgent calls she had to make. She was so busy she didn't have time to brief her assistant on the afternoon's appointments. Sonia liked to have just the right furnishings displayed for her best decorator clients.

At twelve-thirty, just as her stomach was starting to growl like a lion at feeding time, Carol, her assistant, stuck her head in the door.

"Sorry," she said, "but I just got a call from Florida Power and Light. You were having power outages?"

Sonia nodded. She was still wondering whether to show Ellen Wright, her first appointment, the pre-Columbian head that had just arrived. "This morning."

"Well, they've got to get into your place."

"Okay, make an appointment for—"

"They say now." Her assistant's freckled face held an expression of regret. "There seems to be some kind of royal screwup that has to do with the gas lines and they say it can't wait."

Sonia cursed under her breath. There went her afternoon. "Okay.

51

Tell them I'll be right there. Oh, and Carol, please cancel Mrs. Wright, then take a look at my calendar. I'll phone you with an update as soon as I get a handle on how long I'm going to be. Hopefully you won't have to cancel anyone else."

It had begun to rain as Sonia drove home. Not just rain, but a South Florida torrent dropping out of a roiling charcoal sky. The rank smell of tropical vegetation turned the air to soup. Thunder boomed and rolled and the lines of cars on the road threw off thick sprays of water.

Instead of work she found herself thinking about Lew Croaker. She longed to call him, promised herself she would as soon as she had a spare moment. She liked him a lot, which surprised her. First of all, she hardly knew him; wary at heart, it usually took her a while to warm up to a man. Second of all, he was Anglo. Oh, but not just any Anglo, she reminded herself. He knew Latinos, appreciated their culture. Plus, he wasn't a *muy macho* pig, like so many men she'd met.

She was surprised that even though the power was still out in her house, she heard the TV from Estrella's next door. Mr. Leyes had been a lineman for Bell South. He'd been paralyzed falling off a pole, and now he stayed home all day and watched ESPN.

She'd forgotten to return the umbrella to the car where she usually kept it, so she got soaked running from the side carport to her front door. Her house was neat and freshly painted, a white one-story with tile roof and stucco facade dating back to the 1950s. Its trim was a shade of very pale blue that seemed indigenous to El Portal. She ran past the cement seahorses holding up a cracked fountain that no longer worked, past a dripping lemon tree and thick night-blooming jasmine, now whipped by the wind and bent by the rain. She went up the steps to the covered porch, then took a look around. Where the hell was FPL? Just like the utilities to cry emergency then be late showing up. She decided to wait for them inside.

The warm, vivid, tropical colors with which she'd decorated were muted in the gloom. Rain pelted the windowpanes, sheeting down the glass. Another roll of thunder boomed and echoed outside.

She went through the living room and into the small kitchen. Out of habit, she opened the refrigerator, but she saw nothing appealing inside.

She went into her bedroom and turned on the battery-powered bedside radio. Gloria Estefan crooned in Spanish, which was followed by a very sexy Afro-Cuban number by Machito. The Cu-bop was in two-four time, and she merengued into the bathroom. A plastic bubble skylight lent what little illumination there was, and she leaned over the sink, peering at herself in the mirror.

She started. What was that? Her gaze flicked to a corner of the mirror. What had she seen there? A shadow moving? Must have been a car passing outside, she thought, her gaze returning to her own reflection.

In the bedroom the music had stopped. An announcer was reading an ad for a Latin party jam in South Beach this Saturday. It sounded cool. She wondered whether Croaker would go with her if she asked him. She hoped he would. Getting hot and sweaty with him would be a treat. The more she thought about him the more she wanted to see him. He was awfully sexy. Her thoughts drifted to them dancing the merengue at the Shark Bar before his poor sister had popped up out of nowhere. Sonia remembered how he held her, how he moved with her, and her breath grew hot in her throat.

She started; she saw it again. Now she was sure. There was movement behind her—either in the bedroom, or beyond, in the living room.

For a long time, she did not move. Her gaze flicked from one side of the mirror to the other, scrutinizing the wedge of the interior she could see in reflection. She did not want to turn around yet, did not want to give any overt sign that she had seen something amiss. She was not frightened, but she was wary. She'd had a gym-freak boyfriend about a year ago who was paranoid about urban violence. He'd shown her a trick or two about self-defense, and after that she hadn't been afraid of getting into her car at night or even driving to the nearby 7-Eleven at three in the morning for milk or sugar. The night crawlers who hung out there didn't bother her.

But this was her home.

Was someone in the living room?

She turned and, as calmly as she was able, went back into the bedroom. She stood there for a long, breathless moment, scanning the gloom. *Hello,* she thought. *Anybody there?* She felt herself give a little shiver. A male voice was spewing out the news in rapid-fire Spanish. None of it was good.

She stared at the telephone, which was on a nightstand on the far side of the bed. Her knees felt suddenly weak, and she sank to the bed. As she did so, she glanced into the living room. At this new angle, she saw something that made her heart leap into her throat. There was a darkly glistening puddle on the wood floor of the dining alcove. Rainwater. But she hadn't been near the dining alcove. From this position a wall protruded out, blocking off most of that small space. Someone could be standing there, waiting.

Could it be one of the electrical linemen? But then why didn't he say something?

There was more urgency inside her now, and she sprawled across the bed, reaching for the phone. The bitter taste of fear was in her mouth and now her only thought was to call 911. She felt the shock wave of air coming her way even as she lifted the receiver. Darkness, like a great shadow, bloomed on her right side, and the bed rocked as someone hit her full force.

She screamed as she went flying. The receiver bounced on the bed, spun away from her as she hit the floor on her back. A weight like a six-hundred-pound gorilla pressed painfully onto her breasts and rib cage, immobilizing her. At the same time, something soft and perfumed and very familiar enveloped her face. It pushed down, making breathing difficult, then impossible. It was her pillow. Someone was trying to smother her.

She opened her mouth to scream but cotton-covered down filled it. Her jaws were thrust wide open by the terrible pressure and she began to choke. Something dark and primitive went off in her brain like a Roman candle and she began to thrash wildly with arms and legs. It was too little too late.

Breath caught in her throat and she began to gag. But she did not give up. Her clawed hands raked and scraped flesh until a powerful grip pinioned her wrists against the floor.

She heard a voice hiss: *"Cuidado!* Be careful! You know this! She must not be damaged in any way!"

It was a Spanish dialect that seemed awfully familiar to her. Where had she heard it before? Then she had it: Bennie's grandfather, that strange and sometimes frightening man, had used it on occasion. It was curious the minutia the mind could latch onto at such moments. She recalled Bennie's grandfather—a tall, stoop-shouldered man with craggy brows and a thick pure white mustache—with a preternatural clarity. Smoking one of his aromatic hand-rolled cigars, he seemed to hover in the air. He was whispering to her in his dialect, and she knew he was trying to tell her something vital. She cried out in her desperation to hear him, but she could not.

Life was escaping her with each beat of her heart. She tried to take a ragged breath through the wadding that filled her mouth, but to no avail. Her lungs were on fire and when she gagged again, acidic vomit filled her throat and she spiraled downward.

Bennie's grandfather had disappeared. On the Shark Bar's dance floor, she merengued with Lew Croaker. The sensual beat throbbed through her, insinuating itself into her very bones. She looked into his eyes and melted. She was weeping for joy.

I want you, she said in her mind as she died.

2

By late afternoon Croaker felt drained. He'd given blood to Dr. Marsh for HLA typing, he'd interviewed Dr. Niguel, to see if he had any further insight into Rachel's condition when she was admitted to Emergency, and he'd spent more time with Matty and Rachel.

At last, he took a breather outside in the hospital's parking lot and used his cell phone to call his charter office at the marina. He had them cancel his appointments for the next several weeks. Between the money he had been paid by the Feds for his work after he'd left the NYPD and the successful investments he'd made over the years, he didn't need the income from the fishing charter in order to live. He did it because it gave him pleasure.

He'd just hung up when the cell phone chirped.

"Hello?"

Silence. No, not quite. He could hear a quick catch of breath.

"Lew?"

"Yes."

"This is Maria."

Maria. It took him a moment to orient himself. Bennie's Maria.

"Hola, Maria. *Como estas?"*

"Do you know where Sonia lives?"

"El Portal. Yes, she told me."

"We need you here."

We? "Maria, what's the matter?" His throat seemed to fill up with alarm. "What's happened?"

Croaker heard a muffled sound. She was sobbing. "Maria, are you in El Portal? Are you at Sonia's?" He realized he was shouting.

"Please." It was a kind of moan. *"Now."*

Croaker was already running toward his T-bird.

Croaker made the ninety-minute trip from Palm Beach to the upper reaches of Miami in sixty-five minutes. He was lucky, in that what obviously had been a torrential downpour here had petered out to a fine drizzle.

He whipped down I-95 at such speed that he missed the Ninety-fifth Street exit. Cursing under his breath, he got off at Seventy-ninth Street, went east to NE Second Avenue and turned left through the northern end of Little Haiti. Just past Jacky Jackson's Relax Barber Shop he crossed over the Little River Canal into the peaceful, pretty enclave of El Portal. By that time the rain had stopped altogether and sparks of bright late afternoon sunlight were piercing swiftly scudding clouds. He drove down streets lined with small, neat one-family houses of stucco or brick face over cement block, painted the soothing tones of the Caribbean. Banyans vied with citrus trees for curbside space, and here and there, vivid sprays of bougainvillea and tree hibiscus seemed newly scrubbed in dazzling sunlight.

Bennie's black Humvee was easy to spot, and Croaker pulled in beside it. For almost anyone else outside Hollywood the Hummer would have been a kind of absurd overkill. Not for Bennie. The U.S. Army vehicle was armor plated with bullet-proof glass and special door locks that could not be jimmied. In his line of work it was something of a necessity.

When Croaker got out of his T-bird, he saw someone sitting in the Hummer's front passenger's seat. The windows were rolled down and he walked over. Maria was sitting stiff-backed in the seat. She must have heard the scrape of his shoe soles against the cement of the sidewalk because her head jerked around. Her eyes were wide and staring.

Croaker stopped beside the open window. "Maria. I'm here."

For an eerie instant, she did not move or even blink. "I called Bennie. He's here, too." She spoke as if she were oblivious to the fact that she was sitting in his vehicle.

He put his hands on the window frame. "Maria. *Digame.* What's happened? Is Sonia all right?"

She gave no reply.

"Lewis."

At the sound of Bennie's voice, Croaker looked up. He saw Bennie coming around the side of a white house with pale blue trim. He recognized it from Sonia's description: it was her house. Bennie slapped his palms together, getting rid of dirt and leaf debris. In a pale linen suit, he looked overdressed for rooting around on the ground. There was a peculiar look on his face as he came up to where Croaker stood. Somehow that look sent a chill down Croaker's spine.

"Listen to me," Bennie said quietly. "Turn around and get out of here. She shouldn't have called you."

"This is bullshit, Bennie. What's going on?"

"Go home," Bennie said. "I don't want you involved."

"I'm already involved," Croaker said. "You saw to that yourself when you introduced me to Sonia. Pearl in the oyster, remember?"

"*Yo recuerdo,* Lewis." Bennie's gaze searched his face.

"*Digame.* What's this all about?"

"Nothing good." Bennie gestured and they moved away from Maria and the Humvee. "At approximately three this afternoon Maria gets a call from Sonia's assistant at Lord Constantine Fine Imports. This woman is kinda, you know, freaked. Someone from FPL calls the office saying they need access to Sonia's house and she leaves the office just past twelve-thirty. By, like, three she's missed an appointment, hasn't phoned in as promised. The assistant tries numerous times to call here but can't get through."

Bennie's gaze flicked past Croaker to check on Maria, sitting still as a statue in the Hummer. He looked back to Croaker. "That's when she calls FPL. Get this. They have no record of a problem, calling the office, or dispatching a crew. That's when the assistant phones Maria."

With a sinking feeling in his stomach, Croaker said, "You check the power?"

Bennie nodded. "I just came from there." He jerked his head. "Someone cut the lines into the house. One clip; very clean. Professional job."

"You see anything else? Footprints, any other kinds of impressions? The ground looks kind of marshy from the downpour."

"I didn't notice."

Croaker lifted his chin toward the Hummer. "You got any electrician's tape in there?"

Bennie looked at him for a moment, then went loping back to the Hummer. He checked on Maria while he rummaged under the driver's seat. In a moment, he was back with a roll of black tape.

They took a quick reconnoiter around the house. Croaker could see no sign of footprints, but at one point he got down on one knee to show Bennie what appeared to be a run of parallel lines bruising the wet and glistening grass.

"These mean anything to you?"

Bennie shook his head.

They came upon the cut line. "I don't feature sticking my head into a dark oven without knowing whose hand is on the pilot light," Croaker said. Using the polycarbonate part of his biomechanical hand to ground the live ends, he spliced the line with electrician's tape.

When he rose, he took a deep breath. "I think we'd better try to get inside. Front door?"

"It's locked, but that's no problem." Bennie dangled a set of keys on a chain from one finger. "Maria brought the spare set Sonia gave her."

"Okay then." Croaker turned toward the front of the house. "Let's go."

Bennie's hand on his arm stopped him in his tracks.

Bennie's eyes were dark and very sad. "Lewis, we may be heading into a crime scene. I can't, I *won't* ask this of you."

"You won't have to. We're friends. There's nothing more to say."

"One thing, only." Shadows from the lowering sun shrouded Bennie, making him seem part of the coming darkness. "Remember when I told you I sensed something out there waiting?"

Croaker nodded. "But if this is it," he said, "I recall you saying it was waiting for *us*."

Bennie gave a sharp jerk of his head. *"Bueno."*

Together, they went swiftly across the lawn, past the fountain held aloft by stone seahorses, up the steps and onto the porch. In front of the door, Croaker said, "You get that thirty-eight replaced yet?"

Bennie drew a Smith & Wesson from a shoulder holster and dropped the keys into Croaker's palm.

With a constriction in his throat, Croaker opened the door. Immediately, Bennie pushed past him into the gloom of the small house. He could hear Bennie's soft footfalls hurrying across the Mexican tiles of the foyer. Croaker went in after him and switched on the lights. The bright tropical colors of the living room seemed to leap at them. The room was neat and clean and inviting. Nothing out of place here.

Croaker paused at the edge of the dining alcove, staring down at what the flashlight beam illuminated. "Bennie, look at this. See the last residue of water shining? Someone had to stand here for this much rainwater to accumulate. Either Sonia or someone else."

Bennie was breathing softly but energetically, like a powerful engine at idle.

They turned on the lights as they went methodically through the house. They checked the only closed door in the hall on the way into the bedroom, found linens and towels neatly stacked by color and pattern. Next came a bathroom, the guest bedroom. Then they went into Sonia's bedroom. Bennie stepped into the master bathroom, quickly emerged, shaking his head. *"Nada."*

Croaker swung around, took a hard second look at the bedspread. At first glance it appeared as if it had been neatly made. But then as he noticed the repeat on the pattern he could see that it was rucked in one direction. It was like an arrow pointing to the phone on its night table. Looking at the bedspread again it seemed to him as if someone lying on it had reached for the phone, wriggling their body in the process—or else been dragged across it.

Croaker walked around the foot of the bed to the far side.

Bennie peered over his shoulder. "What're you looking for?"

"I don't know," Croaker admitted as he carefully examined the carpet. Kneeling by the side of the bed, he plucked a small clump of hairs that had been embedded in the fibers of the carpet as if by a grinding motion. They were the right color and length to be Sonia's. Judging by the roots, they'd been ripped from her head.

He rose and, reaching out with his biomechanical hand, plucked a stainless-steel nail at a place where the pillow was exposed, as if the bed had been hurriedly remade. "Sonia was a neat freak, wasn't she?"

Bennie nodded wordlessly. He seemed fascinated by Croaker's examination.

Using one stainless-steel nail Croaker gingerly lifted the bedspread away from the pillows. The one on his side was slightly askew. He saw lipstick smears over its center.

"What the hell?" Bennie said.

Looking closer, Croaker spotted a couple of eyelashes sticking to the pillowcase. He let the pillow fall back as he looked around the bedroom.

"So where is she?" Bennie whispered.

Croaker pointed to the closet.

Bennie had replaced the lost .38 with a .22. With the gun at the ready, he flipped the door open. Nothing but clothes on racks and shoes neatly lined in rows on the floor.

Croaker looked out the window. "Her car?"

"Still in the carport," Bennie said. "I checked it out."

Croaker, looking down at the small answering machine, hit the Messages button with a stainless-steel fingernail. The tape began to play. Two hang ups, then a male voice said, "Sweetheart, it's Nestor. So looking forward to seeing you in the morning. Love you for it, but you might as well eat the food yourself. This boy isn't feeling any better. But, hey, what the fuck, I've got to make the best of it, right? Love you. 'Bye for now."

"This would be before the power went off," Bennie said.

"Right. Sounds like sometime last night." Croaker looked at Bennie. "Who's Nestor? This was the last call before the power was cut."

"Nestor's a dancer," Bennie said. "Or at least he was until he got AIDS. Now he's dying slowly an' Sonia's made him, like, her pet project."

Noting Bennie's tone, Croaker looked up. "You disapprove?"

"It's, like, the proximity issue." Bennie made a face. "You know, man, it's not a pretty thing."

"No kidding," Croaker said. "Think how Nestor feels." He tapped the top of the answering machine. "You know where this guy lives?"

"Nah, but try Sonia's speed-dialer. He's on there; you can ask him yourself."

Sure enough, Bennie was right. Croaker wrote down Nestor's number, then they retraced their steps through the house. The kitchen was the only room they hadn't been in yet. Croaker stopped in the open doorway, flipped the switch. Cold fluorescent light flickered on, and he stared, wide-eyed. It appeared as if the entire contents of the refrigerator were lined up in neat rows along the countertops. Cartons of milk and orange juice, bottles of jam and ketchup and mustard, plastic containers holding leftovers, a tub of butter. The rows were arranged in ascending height. Every edge was perfectly aligned.

"What the hell is this?" Bennie said.

Croaker was afraid he might already know.

Bennie shook his head. "All this stuff from inside the refrigerator. Why was it taken out? You think Sonia did this?"

For a very long time, Croaker did nothing. He stared at the refrigerator door.

Bennie, seeing where he was looking, said, "Jesus." He passed a hand briefly across his eyes. "Go on, *amigo*. We've come this far."

It didn't pay to think too much, not at this juncture. Croaker closed his titanium and steel fingers around the old-fashioned handle and pulled.

The door swung open and he saw an interior totally devoid of food. The side walls had been smeared with blood. On one was painted a triangle inside a circle; on the other a dot within a square.

The shelves themselves had been rearranged to make room for the one item which sat inside. An item about the size of a twenty-pound turkey but one not normally found in anyone's refrigerator.

Croaker tried to close his ears to the slow drip-drip-drip of blood. A good size pool had already formed on the bottom shelf.

It came from Sonia's head and neck, which had been very neatly severed from the rest of her, pale hazel eyes opened wide in a fixed expression of full-blown terror.

Back in the bedroom, Croaker walked slowly around until he stood in the open doorway to the bathroom. "Someone standing in that spot in the alcove where the rainwater is, you couldn't see him from here." He walked along the side of the bed as Sonia had done hours earlier. "Not from here, either."

Bennie looked at him. "If that's where the killer stood, he chose the perfect spot to watch her."

Croaker ignored the sudden chill that went through him. "Smart, too. He didn't leave any footprints. He must have left his shoes outside."

He pointed to the pillowcase with Sonia's lipstick smears and eyelashes. "This is how she was killed."

Bennie came over for a closer look. "Smothered, you mean?"

Croaker nodded. "That pillow over her face, pushed down hard. Sonia was no weakling. It had to be someone with a great deal of strength."

"Or more than one someone," Bennie added.

"Right," Croaker said.

He pointed to the spot between them, where he had plucked the clump of Sonia's hairs from the carpet. He could picture her as she lay there, helpless, the back of her head being ground into the carpet, dying. He felt what he always felt at the scene of a murder, as if a vise were squeezing something vital out of his heart.

"She died right here," he said.

Bennie's right hand curled into a fist. Blood seemed to have surged into his neck and cheeks. He gave an inarticulate cry, then lurched out of the bedroom.

"Bennie!"

Croaker caught up with him in the kitchen. Bennie was reaching into the refrigerator.

Croaker's blood ran cold. "Just what the hell d'you think you're doing?"

"I apologize but I have no intention of leaving her head here for strangers to find." Bennie was taking the head out of the refrigerator. As he did so, he averted his gaze. From Sonia's head or the bloody symbols? Croaker wondered. Bennie began to wrap the head with extreme tenderness in the first of the three towels he'd taken from the linen closet in the hall. "I won't allow Sonia to suffer that indignity."

Croaker curled his biomechanical fingers around Bennie's wrist. Bennie's head came around, and he glared at Croaker with eyes suddenly the color of flame. "*Escuchame, señor.* Men have perished for that."

"What about friends?"

"*Amigos* know better."

"Then you have friends without backbones." Croaker took a step forward. "Tell me, Bennie, is this really about Sonia's dignity?"

"Yes." But Croaker would not back down and he would not be bluffed. Perhaps it was just this toughness that appealed so profoundly to Bennie.

At length, his mouth twisted in a parody of a smile. "Let me go, Lewis, and we will speak of it."

He watched as Croaker slowly and very deliberately unfurled his fingers one by one. "With so little effort you could have ground to powder every bone in my wrist." His voice had about it a disarming lassitude, as if he were speaking of inconsequential matters while basking in the sun. "You would have caused me great pain and no little inconvenience." Now he did smile, and as he did so he revealed the .22 he had drawn. "But I would have shot you in the belly. Then I could have done anything to you, Lewis. Anything at all."

There was a terrible stillness in the air, as if all at once the oxygen had been sucked from the room by some monstrous creature that had appeared out of nowhere.

Bennie shrugged. "But this is no way for friends to talk—or even to think."

"Maybe you're right," Croaker said. "Or maybe you have a screwed-up idea of friendship."

Bennie, jamming the gun back into its holster, threw his hands wide. "What, are you pissed, Lewis? Now we are no longer friends?"

Croaker stared at him.

Bennie nodded. "Okay, okay, you made your fuckin' point. God hears me, you got the *cojones* of a Latino." He stuck out his hand. "Let no bad blood begin here." When Croaker took it, he squeezed it with obvious affection. "I wasn't lying. I got this thing 'bout death—it's got to be treated with a certain degree of respect, otherwise"—he shrugged—"the spirit that lives on is clouded with uncertainty." He waved a hand. "But, you're right, that's not the whole story." He shook his head. "No way I'm gonna let the police get clued in 'bout this, Lewis. Their interference I cannot allow. Unequivocally. This is why I told you to leave, why I didn't want you to become involved."

"Hey, Bennie, wake the hell up. This is the scene of a major crime you're messing with," Croaker said. "You'd better have a damn fine explanation."

Bennie gave him an evil grin. "The electrical line, the pillow, the answering machine, I seem to remember you doing your share of tampering." He calmly resumed folding the towels over Sonia's head. "But to be less argumentative, my fuckin' business is explanations." Beneath the razzle-dazzle ripostes, he seemed immensely relieved that Croaker made no move to stop him this time.

"Give me one, then."

"I never do anything without just cause, remember that." He opened several kitchen drawers in turn, rummaging through them. At length, he came up with a roll of twine you use to truss up chickens or turkeys for roasting. "As sure as we're *amigos* I know who killed her." He began to bind the package with the twine. "That's why Sonia's murder must be kept between the two of us." He looked up at Croaker. "An' when you hear the history of it, I religiously believe you'll agree with me."

Maria freaked out when Bennie told her about Sonia. They took her back to Bennie's place, a nineteen-room extravaganza built in the Venetian palazzo style overlooking the Intracoastal on Forty-ninth Street in Miami Beach, not two blocks from the Eden Roc Hotel across the water on Collins Avenue. The place was exhausting. There were seven bedrooms—one presumably for each night of the week—all with open-air whirlpools. There was a European-style library, a billiards room, a fully automated film screening theater, a stone-encased wine cellar, even a louvered cigar patio off the formal dining room. It had water frontage with a landing stage guarded by ornate stone winged lions that appeared flown whole from the Grand Canal in Venice. Tied up to it was a sleek midnight blue cigarette, one of those sexy boats built for speed and nothing else.

Croaker and Bennie walked out onto the dock. The lush, Deco colors of sunset dappled the Intracoastal. Far out, over the southern ocean, the last remnants of the afternoon's thunderstorm hung against the horizon like a black and impenetrable curtain. A soft breeze ruffled their hair, washed their faces with sea salt. All across South Florida, it was a time for easy drinking and, if you were a fisherman, talk of the day's exploits.

Though he had an ice-cold Corona in his hand, Croaker did not feel like drinking. The day's events gnawed at his heart. Bennie deposited the large round package under his arm into the cigarette. The doctor he had summoned, a small balding Colombian with a thin mustache that did not quite cover a harelip, ministered to Maria behind the closed doors of one of the many upstairs bedrooms.

Croaker stared at the carefully wrapped package rolling with the waves of the Intracoastal. Now Sonia's head was here, and with Bennie's call to her partners at Lord Constantine that she was attending to a family emergency, there was no reason for anyone to suspect foul play.

"There was something even weirder than finding the decapitated head," Croaker said at length.

Deep aquamarine water could be glimpsed through the carved stanchions of the stone balustrade. It seemed a symbol of purity in which the cigarette's cargo had been unceremoniously dropped.

Bennie took out a cigar and went through the ritual of lighting up. "Yeah? Then I missed it."

" 'Cause it wasn't there. No blood, Bennie. How come? She was smothered by a pillow in her bedroom." A flash of Sonia's long legs spun through Croaker's consciousness like a shining lure that's just been struck by a game fish. He felt a wave of intense sadness mixed with anger at how her life had been cut short. "We find her head in the 'fridge and the only blood's dripping from it. There's not a speck inside the house."

Bennie continued to smoke, staring out at the light of day slowly being extinguished.

"The killer didn't have a lot of time," Croaker continued. "So what did he do after he smothered her? We know he didn't decapitate her inside the house."

"But there were those two parallel marks," Bennie said. "Suppose he dragged her outside an' did her there?"

Croaker shook his head. "Uh-uh. We checked the outside. Except for those two parallel marks there was nothing. No blood, no viscera, no bits of skin or bone. Besides, doing it outside's too risky. A neighbor or a passerby could see him."

"So what the hell happened?" Bennie asked.

"I have no idea."

Croaker was abruptly overwhelmed by an image of Sonia's surprised and happy face as he merengued with her across the dance floor at the Shark Bar. Part of him marveled at the calm with which he was dissecting the last few hours' events. Another part of him was ashamed.

Bennie must have had some inkling of what was happening. He kept his own counsel as Croaker turned away. Taking a deep breath, Croaker leaned against the balustrade and watched a white fishing boat plying the dark, purling waters of the Intracoastal. As it passed, its wake sent wavelets sloshing against the wooden pylons so that the cigarette rolled at its berth.

He could see Stone Tree, limned against the kind of lime and orange sunsets you got only in the Keys. The Seminole was aft in the small boat as he navigated it through the mangrove islets. *"Do you see it?"* he said. Croaker thought he was going to point but he didn't. *"I don't see anything,"* Croaker replied. *"It's getting dark."* Stone Tree had said, *"Not for me,"* telling Croaker as much as he needed to know.

The doctor emerged from Bennie's house, came down the marble stairs to join them. "Maria's resting easily now," he said in Spanish. "She's obviously had a difficult time." He knew better than to ask the cause of her shock. "With what I gave her she'll sleep deeply, and chances are when she wakes up she'll be fine. If not—" A card appeared between his fingers, and Bennie took it. "This is the name of a friend of mine. He's a counselor. If your friend is in need . . ." He tapped his mustache, as if it had tilted out of place. "You have my assurance that he is the soul of discretion."

Bennie showed the doctor out to the part of the carpark where his emerald BMW stood beside the Hummer and Croaker's T-bird. Croaker saw no money change hands. That was not how Bennie did business. Debt was amassed and discharged in intangible ways. Favors, influence, accommodations, were the invisible but potent coin of his realm. Bennie disappeared into the house, presumably to look in on Maria.

Watching the lights coming on along the strand of Collins Avenue Croaker wondered just what his friendship with Bennie and Sonia had gotten him into. Suddenly, shockingly, he felt that the moment he had crossed over the Little River Canal this afternoon he had become part of Bennie's shadowy world, and he did not yet know what that might entail. He only had the unsettling presentiment that everything in his life had changed.

Shaking off this evil feeling, he used his cell phone to place three calls to friends in different sectors of the federal government. Two were unavailable, and he left detailed messages on their voice mail. The third answered and, after hearing about the desperate plight Rachel was in, transferred the call to a doctor pal of his at Walter Reed Hospital. The doctor pretty much reiterated what Jenny Marsh had told Croaker.

"Major organs are in hellishly short supply," he said. "And because she's a user I'm afraid her chances of jumping the line are nil." He paused. "The one good thing is she's in very capable hands. I know Dr. Marsh by reputation, and she's first-rate. If there's a way to save your niece you can be sure she'll find it. But if the situation is as you have described it . . ." He sighed. "I wish I had better news for you, Mr. Croaker. Right now, I don't think there's anything anyone can do except pray for a miracle."

Croaker thanked the doctor and hung up. He immediately dialed a local number, then entered his Anti-Cartel Task Force access code. As a freelance without official ties to the ACTF, he was given a temporary code each time he was hired. Apparently the last code still worked because he received clearance. He punched in Wade Forrest's extension. Croaker had worked with Forrest before in ACTF. He was fairly high up in the organization and rising. Unlike Croaker, who was a sporadically used freelancer, Forrest was a career man to the core. Though he'd come to Miami from Washington for a specific mission, he'd opted to stay on. Croaker didn't necessarily like Forrest—he was loud, overbearing, and something of a bully. But Croaker respected him; he was loyal. The first rule that Croaker's father had taught him in law enforcement was that loyalty was the one commodity you couldn't buy, borrow, or steal.

Forrest wasn't answering his line, which was not surprising. Out in the field, most likely. What was surprising, however, was that no human voice came on the line. As far as Croaker knew, the ACTF field offices were manned twenty-four hours hours a day. In fact, Croaker thought he heard the distant clicks and whirs he associated with an automatic call switching device. Perhaps it was just his imagination because a moment later Wade Forrest's recorded voice led him through the standard voice mail menu. He left a Most Urgent message. Maybe, just maybe, Forrest had connections with UNOS. But he'd have to speak to him to find out.

He disconnected just as Bennie returned. His friend was carrying a small zippered flight bag.

"Okay, Bennie. It's time for a little show-and-tell."

Bennie nodded. *"Bueno."* He rolled the cigar meditatively between his lips. "Time an' place, Lewis. In my business they are everything." Bending over, he stowed the flight bag in the cigarette then deftly slipped the aft line, jumped down into the boat. *"Andale, muchacho,"* he said. "We have important business on the Atlantic."

As Croaker stepped into the boat, Bennie scrambled to let go the bow line. Then, back in the shallow cockpit, he fired the powerful engines. The cigarette gave a throaty roar and a puff of blue diesel smoke as Bennie turned her out into the Intracoastal.

The party lights of Miami Beach swept by. On their left, Croaker could see a long line of white limos disgorging a festive wedding party into the gargantuan lobby of the Eden Roc Hotel. Flashbulbs popped like sunspots, and there was a burst of wild applause as the bride pirouetted around the grinning groom for the kneeling photographers.

The bride, who looked like a model, sleek in fitted white satin and organza, reminded him of Sonia. He had a terrible flash of the model's head bouncing like a gaily striped beachball down the staircase of the Eden Roc while flashbulbs fired like cannons. Taking a deep breath, he wrenched his attention away.

Bennie veered off to starboard, heading at low speed for the outlet into Biscayne Bay. This far south, you needed to take the bay to pick up the channel between the tip of Miami Beach and Fisher Island in order to get to the Atlantic Ocean.

Croaker clambered over to Bennie's side. " 'There's something out there waiting for us,' " he said over the heavy thrum of the diesels. "Isn't that what you said, Bennie?"

Bennie nodded. "Close enough." Water, churned to white froth, plumed from the rear of the cigarette. "You know, Lewis, there's a certain, what?, *inevitability* 'bout life. Like with me being in the line of work I'm in. I've made enemies, I've been up-front 'bout that. Okay, that goes with the territory, but there are enemies and then there are *enemies.*"

Croaker could smell something like fish entrails surfacing in the Intracoastal. It was sharp and immediate, like a hit of ammonia; it made his pulse pound.

"God hears me," Bennie was saying, "I've made enemies like that. Case in point. There are, like, these two brothers. Antonio an' Heitor: the Bonitas. An', shit, not jus' brothers. Identical twins. I mean to tell you, Lewis, these *cabrones* are some bad motherfucking sonsofbitches." Bennie's hands made complex patterns in the air. "It's like, how can I put it? It's like these *bastardos* popped outta their mother's womb pissed off at the world, know what I mean? They're malicious as shit and, what's worse, they get off on it."

Croaker eyed him. "What do these Bonita twins have to do with Sonia's death?"

A subtle change had come over Bennie, and Croaker was struggling to figure out just what it was. "Everything," Bennie said. "They whacked her cold. I know it"—he smacked the left side of his chest with the heel of his hand—"here."

"That's a mighty big assumption to make." But, in truth, Croaker did not immediately disbelieve him. On the contrary. He had a suspicion that another piece of the enigma that was Bennie Milagros was about to reveal itself. "What're you going on—besides pure instinct, I mean."

"Spoken like a true detective." Bennie was chomping so hard on his cigar he was slowly making a mess of it. "About the Bonitas, God hears me, I got a lot more than hunches." Bennie maneuvered out into Biscayne Bay. House lights on either side lent the sky a soft magenta glow. All around them the water was dark, mysterious with man-made reflections. "This is why I can't have the cops involved. It was Antonio an' Heitor all right. They whacked Sonia as, like, some kinda warning to me."

"What makes you so sure?"

Bennie's eyes caught a cusp of the starboard running light, and for one brief instant, copper spun in their depths. "It's happened before."

Croaker didn't want to say anything at all. It was like having a dangerous fish on the line—sometimes all that was required of you was to let the line pay out.

Bennie had the kind of look on his face someone would have if he was about to lie down on a bed of nails. "I mentioned my sister Rosa, didn't I?"

Croaker nodded. "In the parking lot of the Shark Bar. You said she died five years ago."

Bennie's hands worked the controls and the cigarette lurched forward, up on plane. "Didn't tell you, though, *how* she died."

Croaker grabbed a handrail as he felt the slap of the salt spray on his face. Bennie's eyes were slitted by the wind, which was quartering out of the west. He broke out a pair of heavy windbreakers, threw one to Croaker. Out on the open water at night, moving at speed, the chill was instantly penetrating, and it would only get colder once they hit the Atlantic. As they bounced over the calm of the bay, a double line of cormorants swooped overhead like the soft flutter of a ribbon. He tilted his head back, watching them for a moment, inscrutable black runes against an indigo sky.

"Time an' place," he murmured as if to himself. "The Bonitas an' I go way back, Lewis. We grew up in the same neighborhood in Asunción. Just like Sonia an' her brother. An' because of this, how you say, affiliation, they are people with whom I made a grave mistake."

"What was that?"

"I took them on as clients." Bennie shook his head. "That was eight years ago. God hears me, that was the blackest day of my life." He shrugged. "But, see, I was very young. An', you know, when you're young you're, like, convinced you know all the secrets of the universe. Wisdom equates with enthusiasm; it seems so simple, what life can be reduced to."

The cigarette juddered and hummed happily as it gathered speed across the bay. The expanse was dotted with islands, ablaze with light. In the distance, Croaker could see the MacArthur Causeway that ran from Twelfth Street in Miami to Fifth Street in Miami Beach.

"So you took the Bonitas on as clients," he said.

Bennie adjusted their course to starboard at the approach of a boat from the opposite direction. "Antonio an' Heitor are in the misery business, and let me tell you they're quite fuckin' adept at it. Drugs, white slavery, arms shipments, these are their true businesses in South America, although they make *mucho dinero* in the minerals company left to them by their mother. Copper, tin, lithium, beryllium, they're market movers in these ores and they do an increasing trade with the U.S. So much so, in fact, that in the past two years they've opened subsidiary offices in Miami, New York, and Washington."

"D.C.?"

Bennie nodded. "Part of their business comes from selling directly to the U.S. government." He readjusted their course to the southeast. "But the minerals business bores them. These twins live for their fun. In South America, elements within the governments call on them from time to time to disappear people—rivals, political enemies, intellectuals amassing too much of a following."

"Did you know what they did when you took them on as clients?"

"No, but I learned very fuckin' fast."

"So what you discovered was they're in effect assassins for hire."

Bennie spat over the side. "If only that's all they were." They were heading directly for the MacArthur Causeway. South of that, they'd round the tip of Miami Beach and head out into the Atlantic. "See, here's the thing, Lewis. Antonio an' Heitor, they have, how should I put it?, very specialized tastes. They don't just, like, kill someone; that wouldn't be fun at all. They disappear 'em; they warehouse them. Then, at their leisure, they spend a great deal of time having their bit of fun. When it's over, they harvest the organs an' sell 'em to the highest bidder—usually that's a minister in the South American government or a member of a minister's family or a close personal friend or a political ally. You get the picture." Bennie looked at Croaker. "In this unholy fashion, the Bonitas have amassed something far more valuable than mere capital—they possess the kind of power you an' I merely dream about." He bared his teeth in a sour grin. "They own people, heart and soul. Whatever they want in South America is theirs for the taking, no questions asked. Down there, they are revered as gods. Except gods could never be half as evil as these two."

Bennie swept the cigarette around a marker buoy. "Now they've moved their operation here, Lewis. You see? They killed Sonia and took her body. Why do you think they did that?"

Croaker, staring out at the glittering lights along the bay, did not have to answer. If Bennie was right in all his suppositions, the Bonitas were harvesting her organs. What if it were true? For a moment, he was overcome by a terrifying emotion. He couldn't help but think that they must have a healthy kidney that could save Rachel's life. Could it be that somewhere in Florida there was a black market in human organs? Then reality struck him with the force of a hammer blow and he realized what he had been thinking. The stench of his own desperation disgusted him. What had his father told him? Desperation could so easily lead to corruption. What Antonio and Heitor had done to Sonia was horror enough, but his momentary response to it cut so close to the bone it laid bare his marrow. It made him feel unclean, unworthy to be Rachel's champion. In that instant, he felt an enmity to the Bonitas so profound it wrenched his heart. They had touched him deeply and personally, made him for an instant vulnerable, and that he could not allow.

Croaker and Bennie in the cigarette passed beneath the causeway in uneasy silence. The specter of the Bonitas, who seemed from Bennie's description to be imbued with an unnatural potency, hung in the night like a malevolent spirit.

"Bennie," Croaker said almost gently, "what happened with your sister? What happened with Rosa?"

"Ah!" It was almost a cry of anguish, ripped from Bennie's heart. "Five years ago, there was a particularly difficult negotiation with an American company whose market share in ores and metals would give the Bonitas, like, lickety-quick entrée into the States. They told me to get it for them at all costs. That I tried to do, but this bastard, he knew how much they wanted his business an' he wouldn't go for the deals I proposed. One night he ran into them at a club an' he laughed in their faces. God hears me, that pissed them off something fierce."

Bennie took the cigarette in a breathtakingly fast arc around the tip of Miami Beach. Pale spray fountained up like the tail of a peacock. "They couldn't whack him 'cause then they'd lose what they wanted most. But, like I said, they were born pissed at the world an' now they were royally pissed. They had to blame someone for the affront, so they blamed me." He was looking out at the inky darkness of the sea. His shoulders and neck were lost within the billowing folds of the windbreaker, giving him the aspect of a wary softshell turtle.

"I hadn't done my job. If I had, the affront would never have taken place. So they told me. I was their employee but I didn't understand the true meaning of working for them. So they told me." His eyes squeezed shut for a moment, and when they opened they were glossy with incipient tears. His knuckles were white around the steering wheel. "They took my Rosa, Lewis, *mi hermana linda*. They disappeared her, had their ungodly fun with her. An' then, to make sure I'd learned my lesson, they delivered her head to my office."

Croaker, standing very close to Bennie, could tell he was shaking. "What happened then?" he asked softly.

Bennie barked out a laugh as he came to a new heading. They were in the Atlantic now, cutting through rolling swells as the wind picked up. "What d'you think happened? I made the fuckin' deal for them. It was unholy. I abased myself for them an' got the job done. Like I shoulda done in the first place. So they told me." He shook his head ruefully. "So then, three weeks after the deal is signed, they drag this guy out of his bed an' work on him for, what?, thirty-six hours, must have been, at least. His heart's in the president of Argentina an' his liver's in the brother of the finance minster of Brazil. He paid for his affront. God hears me, we all fuckin' paid."

"But that was five years ago, Bennie." Croaker, bracing himself more firmly, jammed his freezing hands into the pockets of his windbreaker. "Why would they start again with Sonia?"

"They have long memories, you know? I thought they were through with me, but I was wrong." Bennie put the cigarette full out and they thundered across the water with teeth-jarring bumps as they sliced through rolling wave crests. He turned to Croaker briefly. "An' you know the worst part, Lewis, the part that eats at my heart like a demon? They were right about me, Antonio an' Heitor. Deep in my soul I didn't want to make that deal five years ago. I didn't do my best. I wanted out from under them. I wanted the deal to fail. But I didn't consider the, like, consequences. I was sure I could outwit them when no one else could." He thumped his chest with his fist. "*I killed Rosa. As much as them, I am to blame*

71

for her death." His head whipped away. "You see now how life can be when you're young and know all the answers? You find out quick enough, Lewis, that you not only don't know the answers, you're clueless 'bout which fuckin' questions to ask."

His left hand jerked back on the throttle and the cigarette came off plane, slowing. The engine burbled as they rocked in the swells.

"We're here," Bennie said. He gave Croaker the wheel, then pulled out the flight bag and opened it. "Kill the engine," he said.

All hard sound ceased. In its place crept the soft susurrus of the sea. They were alone on the ocean. Land was a thin strand of light far off on the western horizon, a glow like the time-altered radiance from a distant star.

"Now this is important," Bennie said, "so pay attention." He leaned forward, dipped his hand in a small clay pot, daubed something black across Croaker's forehead, cheeks, and chin. Then he did the same to himself.

"Bennie, what the hell are we doing?"

"Shh." Bennie put his forefinger to his lips. "We are saying good-bye to Sonia."

"This"—Croaker threw his arms wide—"is your idea of a funeral?"

"Not my idea," Bennie said. "My grandfather's." He took up the towel-wrapped package that was Sonia's head. "We can proceed now. With the soot hiding our features, no spirit will be able to recognize us and pull us down as we set Sonia's spirit on its journey to the other side."

"Bennie—"

"No! Be still!" he hissed. "This is something sacred I got from my grandfather. He was a healer an' he, like, knew things. *Escuchame.* Until we set Sonia's spirit on its path we're vulnerable now to forces we can't control or understand." His eyes bored into Croaker's. "*Es verdad,* Lewis." It's the truth. "You ready to let the world in?"

Croaker nodded. "I'm ready."

Covered with lines of black soot, Bennie's face seemed strange, as if his features had undergone some metamorphosis. Croaker put the fingertips of his right hand to his face, wondering if the same thing had happened to him.

From out of the flight bag, Bennie had produced a small iron brazier. "Listen to me, Lewis. Our world consists of three things, okay? Natural law, which has nothing to do with man-made law; energy; and consciousness. Now, consciousness is what defines you an' me—human beings, I mean. We can reason; animals can't.

They're bound solely by instinct. I mean, we have instinct, too, but we've also got consciousness. Sometimes that's good; you know, we invent, we strive—our progress comes mainly from our consciousness. But, lots of times, consciousness gets in the way of instinct, an' that, *amigo,* is no good at all."

"You know," Croaker said, "you have a spiritual side that's both charming and surprising."

Bennie snorted good-naturedly. "I suppose that's your idea of a compliment."

As they spoke Bennie was mixing powders poured from plastic phials. He added what appeared to be dried leaves and small twigs, ground them together in the bottom of the brazier. Out of the wind, he lit the material and silently beckoned for Croaker to crouch down beside him. The brazier was between them. Croaker saw Bennie's nostrils dilate as he drank in the smoke, and he did the same. Immediately, he was pierced with the scents of peppermint, cedar, and orange, as well as other odors, unfamiliar, pungent and earthy as chilies. He drank them in like food and, almost automatically, his eyes closed. Gradually, as he continued to breathe in the aromatic smoke, he felt his body growing heavier and heavier, as if he were becoming more sensitive to the earth's gravity. Then, there came a brief wave of dizziness, and he felt as if an umbilical had been cut. He was adrift, as if his body had taken flight and, like the cormorants high above, floated on the thermals.

In the darkness he heard Bennie's voice: "Boats are vessels for the spirits an' for the dead. My grandfather told me that boats had three uses for his Guarani ancestors. He said they all could be traced back to the migrations across the oceans the ancient peoples made. The migrations were, you know, harder than we could ever imagine an' sometimes they, like, took a lifetime. The first use is to exorcise sickness an' evil spirits; the second use is to find the lost soul of a patient near death; the third is to ferry the soul of the dead to the shores of the next life."

Silence, save for the lapping of the waves against the fiberglass hull of the cigarette. But, as in a dream, the boat seemed to rock far below them, part of another realm. He and Bennie existed as spirits around the heat of a blazing sun.

"The sea," Bennie said, "is the realm of the dead. It's vast and it's wide and it's depthless. Here begins Sonia's path; here begins her journey."

Through closed eyes and drug-heightened senses, Croaker saw Bennie rise and, leaning out over the ocean, gently deposit Sonia's remains into the water. Through closed eyes he saw the towel-wrapped package bobbing on a wave crest. Over it spun a shape he could not define. Then it resolved itself into what looked like an outline of a human eye with a double iris. At that instant, Sonia's head was sucked down into a midnight black trough never to reappear. Croaker opened his eyes, blinking. Bennie was sitting across from him as if he had never moved. But, looking around the cigarette, Croaker could find no trace of the towel-wrapped package. In a last sharp inhalation of commingled scents, an image appeared in his mind for the space of a heartbeat and then winked out. It was of Sonia plummeting like a stone into the fastness of dark waters, running with currents and certain mystery.

Croaker slept like a dead man all the way back to Bennie's. He dreamed of dancing with Sonia. They were in the dark but he knew it was the Shark Bar. He swept her around the dance floor in long, exhilarating arcs, feeling her body warm and strong as an athlete's coming close to him, then pushed apart by the dictates of the dance steps. She returned again and again to his arms, and each time she did it was like a renewal, another life being built from scratch. Her breath was warm and fragrant on his cheek, and her laughter reverberated like sweet bells on a mountainside. When they passed through a beam of diamond-bright light, it sizzled the red highlights in her hair, picked out the green motes in her eyes. And all at once he knew it wasn't Sonia he was dancing with but Jenny Marsh, Rachel's doctor. She lifted a hand and made a sign that shimmered the air with gold dust: an outline of a human eye with a double iris. A sudden movement caught his attention, and he turned to find Sonia's bloody head rolling down the steps of the Eden Roc Hotel in a welter of green sea grape and translucent jellyfish. Out of the watery depths at the bottom of the stairs rose a mammoth tiger shark. Opening its jaws, it engulfed all that remained of her. Croaker had one terrifying look into its unfathomable eye before it vanished beneath the black waves.

He awoke in a sweat to find the midnight blue cigarette already tied up at Bennie's private dock. Scrubbing his hands across his face, he rose. He wondered if he'd dreamed Sonia's entire funeral. For a moment he watched his friend hose down the cigarette.

"Bennie, what exactly do the Bonita twins want?"

Bennie wiped his hands on his trousers. "Huh, they're mad as hatters. Who can say what's in the minds of madmen? Their hearts have been, like, burned to fuckin' ash by their insanity. In that event, they are beyond understanding."

"Sometimes, yes," Croaker said. "But sometimes madness has a purpose. It used to be my job to find it."

"They, maybe, want me dead." Bennie waved a hand. "Forget maybe—*definitely*. But they're like gods, you see? *Those whom the gods destroy they first make mad.* They want to drive me mad."

"*Are* they mad, Bennie?"

Bennie took up his flight bag and climbed out of the cigarette. He lit a cigar while Croaker followed. "You know, in the old days, when the world was less, like, complicated, hat makers were slowly poisoned by the mercury used in making hatbands. It, like, seeped into their fingertips while they were hand-working the satin an' felt, an' eventually they went, like, nutso, insane." He blew out a cloud of aromatic smoke. "I religiously believe something of that nature happened to the Bonita twins. They were poisoned in their mother's womb by evil spirits, who the fuck knows what."

He turned away abruptly and went up the marble stairs toward the house.

In Bennie's huge dining room they shared a charbroiled three-inch-thick porterhouse Bennie ordered from a place in Miami. With it came cottage fries that Croaker knew even as he was eating them would give him indigestion. Ravenous, he ate them anyway. Afterward, Bennie brought out the mescal, but by that time Croaker had had more than enough altered awareness.

Coffee he could deal with, and as Bennie went about fixing espresso from scratch, Croaker said, "I'd like to know something."

Bennie was grinding the dark, rich beans. "Shoot."

Croaker took a breath, exhaled it slowly. "When the Bonitas delivered your sister's head, were there symbols like the ones we found in Sonia's refrigerator?"

Bennie's hand slipped and he had to fumble with the Off button. "Why d'you ask?" He was facing the kitchen cabinets and Croaker could not see his face.

"Because when you took Sonia's head to wrap it you wouldn't look at those symbols." Croaker stood next to his friend. "I took that to mean they had some significance for you."

"Amateur shrink." Bennie dumped the ground beans into the top of the espresso maker.

"I know you well enough to see that you don't ever necessarily say what's in the back of your mind."

Bennie turned the espresso maker on. Then he stood quite still. Even so, Croaker could feel emotion emanating from him in waves.

"Okay, well . . ." Bennie broke off, took up a paring knife, and began to deftly peel away the rind of a lemon in thin strips. "See, the thing is . . . those symbols . . ." He bit his lip. "Those symbols, they are, like, the cornerstones of my grandfather's world." The scars on Bennie's face shone livid in the light. "I mean they're central to his beliefs, the magic he . . . the magic he taught the Bonitas."

For a long moment, there was only stark silence in the vast house. The sudden hiss of the espresso maker made them both start.

"The Bonitas were pupils of your grandfather's?" Croaker said.

Bennie nodded unhappily as he got out tiny cups, dropped a curl of lemon rind into each. "He initiated them in the Guarani healing arts of the indigenous people of my country. It is called by the Guarani *Hetá I,* which in loose translation means Many Waters." Bennie's eyes were wide and staring, as if his sight extended through the fixed past into the unknowable future. "But what they did, Lewis, was unforgivable. They took the healing arts and in their madness perverted *Hetá I* into a terrible force for evil."

Croaker thought about this chilling new strand to what was fast becoming a far-reaching web as Bennie poured the espresso. He said, "What do the symbols mean?"

"They're power gatherers. There's one for each cardinal point in the compass. When you have them all together there is a summoning of the spirits, a nexus of power."

Croaker accepted a cup. "But there were only two in Sonia's refrigerator."

Bennie nodded. "The third is a cross within three concentric circles; the fourth is the outline of a human eye with two irises." He took up his cup but he didn't drink. "See, each initiate takes a symbol as his or her own. The two-irised eye was my grandfather's symbol."

Croaker felt a small chill creep down his spine. He told Bennie about seeing that symbol in his vision and in his dream.

Bennie slowly put down his cup and walked out of the kitchen. Curious, Croaker went after him. Bennie opened a slider and went out onto the side porch. When Croaker came up beside him, he saw that his friend had gone pale.

"Bennie, you okay?"

Bennie seemed to think about this a long time. At last, he said, "To be truthful, Lewis, I'm not at all sure." He gripped the railing and stared out at the reflections of lights swimming like electric eels in the water. "When my grandfather died, it rained for ten days without a break. I was fifteen an' I can remember sitting in that rain. It was a cold rain. My grandfather died on the coldest day of winter. He was pulled from the Paraguay River by fishermen. He lived by the river. He was very old by then, past ninety, and everyone said, he must've, you know, lost his balance in the dark and fallen in, hit his head on the rocks. I never believed that, though. My grandfather was so surefooted he could, like, catch fish with his feet. I saw him do it many times. It always made me laugh."

Bennie's arms were like steel beams as he leaned against the railing, and he hadn't yet regained his color. "Anyway, my grandfather, being a healer, had to be burned. We built a funeral pyre and placed him on top of it. We slaughtered his favorite horse, cooked its flesh, and ate it to honor him while the pyre burned. The wood burned despite the rain. Everyone said it was a miracle."

Bennie put his head down. His chest was heaving as if he were having an asthmatic attack. Croaker heard the crickets and the tree frogs as if from far away. "I sat in a tree," Bennie said, "an' watched the body burn. My grandfather, he always told me he was part animal. Once, when I asked him which one, he smiled an' said, 'When I die you watch me closely. You'll find out.' "

Bennie shook his head. "You have to understand something, Lewis. When my grandfather died, I was terrified. See, he wanted to initiate me—he wanted me to keep the traditional Guarani ways alive. I refused. I don't know why. Maybe I didn't want the responsibility that would, like him, tie me forever to Asunción. He had so many people who depended on his healing. I already had money on my mind, and an unquenchable itch to see the world." Bennie took out a cigar, stared at it. "Better to admit to that than the alternative: that maybe, deep down, I didn't really believe."

Bennie looked away and shrugged. "So my grandfather, he turned to Antonio an' Heitor. God hears me, they needed a strong hand. Their father died when they were young an' their mother, well, the best that was ever said of her was that she was highborn. That she was, but she was also some kind of witch. My grandfather, I think he, like, felt sorry for them. He passed the traditions on to them, tried to give them some kind of sense of family."

"Why were you afraid when he died?" Croaker asked.

Bennie stared at his cigar for some time. "Oh, well, you know . . ." He tried to smile, but when he looked up he had a kind of haunted look in his eyes. "I was pissed at him—for, you know, making me feel guilty, for being who he was, I guess. I don't know. Anyway, shit, I stopped talking to him. So when he died . . . Jesus, I was beside myself."

"So what happened?"

Bennie lit his cigar. The ritualistic motions seemed to calm him somewhat. When he'd got it going to his satisfaction, he said, "I sat in the tree, you know, watching the flames defy the rain. I was scared and, like, entranced at the same time. I kept my eyes on that charred body because I was sure I'd see his spirit emerging as, like, a bird or something. I mean, birds were sacred to us."

"But you didn't."

Bennie blew out a cloud of smoke. His voice had taken on an odd inflection, rising in pitch as if he were again that teenager in Asunción. "See, there needed to be a lot of water. That's why it rained for ten days without letup."

"Why, Bennie?"

"Because when my grandfather's spirit finally did emerge it wasn't as a bird or a horse or an ocelot." He turned to look into Croaker's eyes and the light from inside the house made his face shine like the moon. "What he had become, Lewis, was a shark."

"Bennie—"

"No, no. I saw what I saw." Bennie waved a hand. "That beast rose from the flames, from the white-hot ashes an' it, like, swam into the torrent of rain. Like smoke, it vanished into the black clouds." He took the cigar out of his mouth. "That tiger shark that took my wahoo yesterday, the symbols—my grandfather's symbol—that came to you during Sonia's funeral . . . I told you we were vulnerable to spirits." He put his hand on Croaker's shoulder. "You killed the shark, Lewis, an' now, God hears me, my grandfather's spirit, he's here." Bennie pressed the fingertips of his other hand into the muscle above Croaker's heart. "That tiger shark was no coincidence. Of all the fishermen on the ocean he found us." Bennie leaned into Croaker as he whispered, "Lewis, my grandfather's, like, trying to tell us something."

"Such as?" Croaker said.

Bennie squeezed Croaker's shoulder. "Like, maybe, who killed him. He can't pass fully into the netherworld until his murderer's found an', like, brought to justice."

Croaker stared at Bennie. The truly curious thing, he thought, was that in the aftermath of everything that had happened this evening, the profound spirituality of Bennie's grandfather's world seemed perfectly believable. He shook his head. Maybe it was the residue of whatever he'd inhaled on the cigarette or maybe he was just going nuts. In any case, it was getting late. He glanced at his watch.

"You gotta split?" Bennie asked.

Croaker nodded. "Yeah. I've got to get to the hospital, check up on Rachel."

They walked slowly back inside the house.

" 'Bout that . . ." Bennie paused as they came to the front door. "I've been thinking 'bout your niece." He took Croaker's hand in his, laid something in it.

It was a dark green stone, perfectly oval, worn smooth in the way only centuries of water could accomplish.

Croaker looked up at him. "What's this?"

Bennie took Croaker by the arm, led him out the front door into the gentle night. Crickets and tree frogs made a soft susurrus that was almost hypnotic.

Bennie said, "Once, as a little boy, I saw my grandfather heal a woman's arm shriveled by disease. How is this possible, you ask." He pointed above their heads. "Like that tree frog who doesn't have a clue about our conversation, you haven't got a clue 'bout this healing process. You don't have the healer's consciousness, so you don't get that. 'Bout this, you're like that tree frog up there. To him, this conversation can't, like, exist 'cause he doesn't have the ability to get it. But that doesn't mean it doesn't exist, see?"

Croaker nodded

"This spirit-stone, it belonged to my grandfather." Bennie's voice was as quiet as if he were in church. "It's very powerful. I want you to put it on Rachel's chest." He put his hand over Croaker's fingers, making him grasp the stone. "It's a healer's stone. But I'm not a healer, Lewis, and neither are you. So the energy in it's, like, limited. Still, who knows, it may help in some way."

Croaker thought he felt a kind of warmth emanating from it, but perhaps it was just his imagination. "I'll take good care of it."

Bennie looked at it almost wistfully. "You know what they say about Guarani healers, Lewis. They never die. Their power, like, remains."

Bennie walked Croaker to the car. Silence enveloped them. As Croaker opened the T-bird's door, Bennie said, "*Esuchame,* Lewis. I have a favor to ask of you."

"Anything, buddy."

Bennie nodded. "Two days from now I want to charter your boat."

Croaker laughed. "You're giving me more business? What kind of favor is that?"

"It's not for fishing, Lewis. I need it, like, for the night."

Croaker frowned. "This isn't for anything illegal, is it, Bennie?"

"No, nothin' like that. But—" He looked around, as if the rustling palms might be studded with directional microphones. "But this is strictly between us. You can't tell anyone—not even the people in

79

your office. Far as they know, you're using the boat for yourself. Okay?"

"Sure, but you have your own boat."

"Cigarette's no good for this run." Bennie clapped him on the shoulder. "Thanks, buddy. This is, like, super important. I don't know anyone else I can trust." He held the T-bird's door open wide for Croaker. "Remember. In two days."

"What time?"

"Gotta midnight appointment. We'll need to leave Islamorada at eight."

"Where the hell are we going, Bennie? Miami or Cuba?"

Bennie said nothing, put his forefinger across his lips.

He sure was being damn secretive, Croaker thought. Then he shrugged mentally. What the hell. What were friends for, anyway?

"Bennie." On impulse, he embraced his friend. "Whether it helps Rachie or not, thanks for your grandfather's spirit-stone."

3

It was after nine; it had taken him an hour and a half to get back to Royal Poinciana Hospital in Palm Beach.

Matty was asleep when he arrived. The nurses in the Dialysis Unit had let his sister sleep on a bed in one of the empty cubicles. Croaker tiptoed past her on the way to see his niece. He asked the duty nurse about Rachel's condition. When she told him it hadn't changed, he wondered whether that was good or bad. Perhaps it was a little of both. Barring a miracle, it was the best they could hope for at the moment.

Rachel lay as he had left her, on her back, unconscious, hooked up to so many hoses she looked like some postmodern mythic creature, part human, part machine. Shadows still as death lay across her like shrouds, and Croaker felt an unspent shout of denial welling up inside him. He could not let her drift away into oblivion. He had to find some way to get her a healthy kidney.

When he sat down beside her, he found that he was trembling. He slipped his right hand into hers, trying to warm it. It seemed to him that memories of Sonia, brief but poignant, mingled with his awareness of Rachel, almost as if their two souls shared a space on another plane of existence. Linked in a cosmic and unknowable manner. Perhaps this sense was his way of feeling closer to a niece he had longed to know, or, perhaps, tonight of all nights was special and what he felt had some basis in truth. In any case, he would not laugh at himself for harboring such odd and spiritual thoughts.

He dug out the spirit-stone Bennie had given him. Its dark green color seemed dull, muted by the fluorescent lights. Croaker turned it over a couple of times between his fingers. It looked to him no different from any of a thousand such wave-washed stones one might pick up along a seashore.

Nevertheless, he set it carefully between Rachel's breasts. It lay there, dark and seemingly heavy, creasing the sheet with which she was covered. He looked at her face, willing her back to life, but of course nothing happened.

He waited for what seemed an extraordinarily long time while the many machines ticked over, the fluids dripped into her, and she continued to drift deep inside her coma.

At last, he reached out to pluck the spirit-stone from atop her chest. His fingers closed over it, and he felt a kind of warmth that almost burned him.

"Who's there?"

He started just as if someone had jabbed him with a needle.

He leaned over her bed. "Rachel?"

Now that she was awake, he could see her ice blue eyes for himself, so vivid they were riveting.

"Who are you?"

"I'm your uncle Lew. Mommy's brother." He moved into the light so she could see him better. "She's right outside. I'll go get her."

"No!"

It was just a whisper but it held him as immobile as if it had been a shout. He could feel her grip on his right hand, as if she were using all the strength she had left to keep him at her side.

"My God, Uncle Lew. I was . . . I think I was dreaming about you." She tried to smile, failed. "You were on a white horse and your armor shone like the sun."

He smiled both at the image and to encourage her. "This is Florida, honey. I think its much too hot for armor. But it's me. I'm here now."

She squeezed his hand. "I know it's you, Uncle Lew."

"Rachel, honey, let me get Mom. She's so worried about you. I know she'd want to talk to you."

"But I don't want to talk to her." Those eyes stared up at him.

"The doctor, then. Honey, you've been asleep for some time. I've got to tell them you're awake."

"Please, Uncle Lew. I can't bear to be poked and prodded. In a minute you can call them. But now just stay here with me."

It was wrong and he knew it. Dr. Marsh should be notified at the very least. But he seemed helpless before her or, more accurately, his feelings. He was bound to adore her, he had known that. His only niece, he would accept her unconditionally, and, to be brutally honest, her intense desire to be with him mirrored his own fondest wish. He could not find it in himself to deny her. Besides, the detective inside him fervently wished for answers.

"Rachie, what happened to you?"

"All these tubes," she whispered.

"You're in a hospital. You took some bad shit, is all."

Her expression was curious. "You're nothing like Matty. She doesn't have a clue I'm into drugs."

Her expression changed abruptly and her mouth began to tremble. He could feel a vibration coming through her fingers where he gripped them tightly. Her eyes fluttered closed.

"Rachel—?" He pressed the spirit-stone down against her breastbone.

When he looked at her, he met her placid gaze. "I'm okay." The monitors confirmed her heartbeat and blood pressure were stable. The tip of her tongue moved over her cracked lips. "Could you get me something to drink? Like a diet Coke? I'm so thirsty."

"You're getting fluids through some tubes, honey. I don't think it's a good idea to give you anything else right now. Maybe later, after the doctor takes a look at you."

Those ice blue eyes stared up at him with a naked hunger for knowledge. "What happened between you and Matty?"

The cop in him could not resist. "I'll tell you if you'll tell me where you got the shit that's rotted out your system."

She seemed intrigued. "I've played this game before."

"What game?"

"I'll show you mine if you show me yours."

He wondered how sexually active she was. She was only fifteen, but these days that was no barrier to having sex. He stifled the desire to ask her; that was a Matty question, definitely to be avoided.

He smiled down at her. "Yeah. I've played the game once or twice myself."

"You good at it?"

What kind of question was that from a fifteen-year-old, he asked himself.

"I don't know," he said. "You'll have to tell me."

"Okay. You go first."

Keeping her hand in his, he stood by her bed. "Your mother and I . . ." He paused, unsure how to continue. "We're like, I don't know, oil and water, sometimes. She sees black, I see white, and so we butt heads over just about everything."

"You're bullshitting me," Rachel said. "Please don't do that, Uncle Lew."

So he told her as much about her father's nefarious history as he thought she could digest, how Donald managed to drive a wedge between the family. It wasn't even half of the story, but he knew it had to be enough to satisfy her.

"Parents are so like cats," Rachel said, "you never know what's on their minds. When Matty deals with me, she's so, I don't know, transparent. But when it comes to her and my father, God only knows the real story."

"Maybe the answer is that parents aren't really as transparent as they seem," he said. "They just jump when you press their buttons."

With an adolescent's disarming way of posing questions that cut to the quick, Rachel said, "Here's the thing that drives me nuts: did my father leave Matty or did I drive him away?"

Croaker leaned toward her. "Honey, what makes you even think that? The breakup had nothing to do with you."

"In this family people are always leaving—you, my father. The one constant is me."

"That's just not true."

Pain filled her eyes. "Really? After the divorce my father never came to see me. Why would he do that unless he blamed me?"

Oh, Donald, I hope you're rotting in whatever hell you've gone to, Croaker thought.

"And Matty—she talks to me *too* much."

Something in her tone alerted him. "About you and Matty. What's the problem?"

"It's more like what *isn't* the problem."

"Meaning?"

"Because she wants certain answers, she asks all the wrong questions. She hasn't a clue what's happening."

"Rachel, what *has* happened—to you, I mean?"

She clamped her jaws shut. The look in her ice blue eyes chilled him to the bone. Croaker could see that she had an ability to tune people out, even people who were close to her, who loved her. That was dangerous, maybe even self-destructive. Could be this dark streak was what had gotten her into this mess in the first place? he wondered.

"Okay, I told you what you wanted to know," he said. "Now it's your turn. Where did you get the bad shit?"

Rachel turned her head toward the wall.

"Honey—"

Her hand squirmed free of his.

He'd seen this attitude before. Who was she protecting? "Rachel, you promised."

"Did not."

"But the game . . ."

"You don't know shit about the game." Her voice was so filled with spiteful venom he was taken aback. "I didn't cut a loogie."

"What the hell is that?"

"It means spit. If I don't cut a loogie when I agree to play, I don't have to answer my part. Every dork knows that."

"Not this dork," he said. "Besides, you're in no condition to spit."

That got a reaction. She either laughed darkly or sobbed. But in any case she kept her face to the wall.

He began to feel a kind of desperation, as if something ugly and unknown was slipping like jelly through his fingers. He had to find a handle, some way to get through this thorny facade she had suddenly created.

"Rachel, listen, I'm not the enemy. Just a minute ago I was the only one you wanted to be with. Now you're shutting me out. What happened?"

For a very long time there was no sound in the room save the monotonous beeping of the monitors, the soft, pliant soughing of the machines. "You wouldn't understand," she whispered at last. "No one does." And when she rolled her head back toward him he could see that she was crying. "I'm messed up." She almost choked on her tears. "I'm so fucking messed up." She stared up at him as he dabbed her face with the edge of his sleeve. "Uncle Lew, am I going to die?"

"No, honey."

"Because if I am I want to know."

He kissed her damp forehead. "You're not going to die."

"Because if I am I have to prepare."

He kissed her cheeks. "Honey, I told you—"

Her hand sought his, gripping it tightly. "Because if I am I have to see Gideon."

"Who's Gideon?"

Rachel's ice blue eyes went wide as she spasmed up off the bed. The monitors were going blooey and Croaker was howling for the duty nurse.

"Uncle Lew, Oh God—!"

For one brief instant, he stared into eyes so filled with terror he felt utterly and irretrievably lost. Her expression, her emotion, flooded through him like shards of broken glass.

He clutched her to him, as if by this act alone he could keep her safe. "Hold on, Rachie! Hold on!" He picked up the spirit-stone, squeezed it, placed it back on her, then took it inside his fist.

Rachel's eyes rolled up in their sockets and her hand felt like ice. There was no grip left in it.

He was still howling when three nurses and the doctor on call hurried in with a crash cart. One of the nurses had to hold on to Matty, who was trying to shove her way into the crowded cubicle.

"My girl!" she screamed. "What's happening to my little girl?"

The doctor, a dark-skinned Latino, looked up at Croaker and said in a very civil voice given the circumstances, "Would you mind leaving us to it, sir?"

"Dr. Marsh," Croaker said.

"Already been paged." The Latino doctor's hands were filled with a vial and a hypodermic. He barked orders to one of the nurses, then pulled off the syringe's plastic cap with his teeth. He had no more time for anything but his patient, and for that Croaker was profoundly grateful.

Croaker realized he was still gripping his niece's hand. He stared at the monitors, which looked like they were giving readings for an extraterrestrial. Then, he let go, pushed passed doctor and nurses, and, grabbing hold of his sister, carried her bodily out of the cubicle.

Croaker dragged Matty to the lavatory and, spinning open the cold water tap, pressed her head down into the spray. The water wasn't icy—tap water never was in Florida—but the force of it got her attention. She stopped screaming and kicking, but he caught a sharp elbow in the ribs. He grunted and pushed her face farther down into the sink.

He heard her try to say something and bent down. "What?"

Another jumble of words and he let up on the pressure enough so her head could turn sideways.

"I can't breathe, you bastard," she gasped.

"Now there's a familiar epithet." He reached up for a roll o paper towels that stood atop the empty stainless-steel dispense

Then he released his grip on her and she came up coughing and sputtering.

He unrolled the towels, handed a wad to her. She stood, staring down at it as if she did not know what it was. Then a moan welled up from her gut and she began to sob.

"Oh, God, Lew! Oh, my dear, sweet God!"

He took her in his arms, holding her tightly, stroking her damp, disheveled hair. He felt the spasms rack her, felt all the strength go out of her, and he thought back to the time he'd felt this before, when, wet with melting sleet and his father's blood, he'd held his mother. Limp with grief and despair, she had clung to him, her lifeline at the moment of life's severing. Donald Duke was gone, but Matty still had her daughter.

Matty began to shiver and shake uncontrollably. She looked up at him, tears streaming down her face, clearly terrified.

"Lew," she whispered hoarsely, "I can't stop." Her teeth rattled together. "What's the matter with me?"

"Shock," Croaker said. "Honey, it's just shock and exhaustion." He passed a hand over her forehead, smoothing away stray wisps of wet hair. "I'm going to take you home now."

Her eyes had the terrified, haunted look of a doe suddenly caught in the beams of a car's headlights. "But my baby . . . What about Rachel?"

Her expression told him clearly that if there was bad news she was in no shape now to hear it.

He led her to a toilet, sat her down on it. "Wait here," he said. "I'll be right back."

Critical Care Dialysis, always quiet, seemed preternaturally still. Terror gripped his heart as he hurried past the central nurses's station. He saw Jenny Marsh with a couple of nurses just outside the drawn privacy curtain of Rachel's cubicle. She was deep in conversation and he tried to slow his headlong rush. He paused for a moment at the briefly deserted nurses' station.

"She's okay, for now," Dr. Marsh said as he came up. She was scribbling something on Rachel's chart. "Dr. Cortinez is in with her."

"What the hell happened?"

"I was hoping you'd tell me. You were with her when she woke up, I understand." Her tone held a certain rebuke. She handed the chart to one of the nurses, nodded to her before turning her full attention on him. "You should've called a nurse, Mr. Croaker."

"I wanted to, but Rachel was adamant. She didn't want me to

leave her. I'm sorry. I know it was wrong but I didn't see that I had much choice."

Jenny Marsh appraised him coolly. "Rachel emerges from a coma—which, given her condition, I must say defies medical logic. Even so, I doubt very much whether she could be lucid, let alone adamant."

"That's where you're wrong, Doctor. She was perfectly lucid. We had a conversation." He'd made an initial decision not to mention the spirit-stone, and he knew he had to stand by it. Dr. Marsh's training would never allow her to accept such an arcane explanation. Croaker barely knew whether he did; maybe it was just a coincidence. The only problem with that was he didn't believe in coincidence.

Jenny Marsh looked at him as if he'd just grown wings. "My initial prognosis still applies, Mr. Croaker. She needs that kidney. Without it, she won't make it."

He ran a hand through his hair. "Okay. I get it. How'd my tests come out?"

"You're not compatible." She relented and gave him a rueful smile. "I'm sorry."

Croaker sighed. How the hell was he going to find Rachel a kidney when there wasn't one to be had anywhere? He could not help thinking again of the Bonitas who, according to Bennie, harvested human organs in South America, and now possibly here, for the select few who could pay their no doubt exorbitant price. There must be a way. He couldn't give up hope.

"What can I tell my sister about Rachel?" he asked.

"As I said, she appears stable, but I'm afraid she's lapsed back into a coma," Dr. Marsh said. "We're doing tests now to try to determine what happened to her. It'll be a while—the morning at the earliest. Why don't you take your sister home, Mr. Croaker? There's nothing either of you can do. And we'll call the moment there's any news."

Dr. Marsh was about to turn away when he said, "Lew. My name's Lew." His gaze held hers. "Doctor, about that kidney. There must be a source, something I don't know about." Could she know about the Bonitas? Could they really, as Bennie had claimed, be harvesting organs in this country? "Is there?"

She looked at him. "I've made calls, tried to pull strings. I've pleaded and cajoled and, frankly, once or twice, I've made myself look like a fool. There's nothing more I can do."

But she was not quite done and he knew it. He felt rather than saw her hesitation, and he quickly stepped into the breach. "Doctor, if there is another way, I need to know about it. Please." Like his father, he'd seen enough rich men, predators, corruptors, and thieves to recognize when conscience was warring with convention. Not to say that Jenny Marsh was any of these; it was a truism of the street that matters of conscience happened more often to people of good character and kind heart.

Jenny Marsh looked into his eyes for what seemed a very long time. Then she lifted an arm in silent invitation and he followed her across the Dialysis Unit, through a door marked DOCTOR'S LOUNGE. It was a medium-size room filled with cast-off furniture, no doubt donated, and a window that overlooked the Intracoastal. It was empty.

Jenny Marsh shook her head. "I must be out of my mind." She jammed her hands into the pockets of her lab coat. "Look, you have to understand something. All of us in the organ transplant area are scrupulous—and I underline that word—about ethics. We will *not* be caught alive or dead with an unregistered organ. For us, that it's illegal to deal in stolen organs is almost beside the point. It's *morally* wrong and we'll have none of it."

Like a strange beast happened upon along a forest path, transforming a peaceful stroll into a tense encounter, Croaker knew their conversation had taken on a new and precarious dimension.

"I'm still listening."

Jenny Marsh drew her shoulders square, seeming to steel herself. "From time to time, I've heard that unregistered organs do surface."

Croaker, trained to elicit confessions from reluctant witnesses and suspects, was adept at reading between the lines. "Are you telling me you know that here, in this country, there's an underground commerce in selling stolen organs?"

She gave an abrupt nod. "You didn't hear it from me. If you dare tell anyone I mentioned such a thing I'll deny it." Fear had turned her eyes muddy. Only a glint of green now and again marked the hazel of her irises.

He discovered that his right hand was tightly clutching the back of a sofa. He thought of Sonia's head sitting in her refrigerator like an offering. What had Antonio and Heitor done with the organs in her body? This was the question Bennie and he had asked of each other. Now, abruptly, a confirmation of their worst suspicions had presented itself as startlingly as a graven image in a jungle glade. Croaker felt a tremor roll through him, and again he felt that peculiar vulnerability, as if his very marrow had been exposed. "Who's doing the trafficking?"

"We've known for years the Arabs, the Chinese, and the Pakistanis trade in stolen organs. They're notorious for it."

"The South Americans, too, from what I understand. When they disappear people—dissidents, rebels, political enemies, whoever—they like to get some monetary gain from it."

Jenny Marsh nodded. "I've heard that."

"What about here?"

Jenny shrugged."

He continued to press her. Could the Bonitas have moved their organ harvesting here to the States? "Does that mean you don't know or you won't say?"

"I don't know. Nobody does."

"Somebody must." Croaker thought for a moment. "Tell me something. If everyone in your field's so morally incorruptible, who's buying these organs?"

"Everyone *I* know is ethical."

"Come on," Croaker said.

Jenny looked around them, as if she was afraid she'd be overheard. Then she beckoned him to follow her. There went out of the lab, past the Dialysis Unit and down a short corridor ending in door which read: CAUTION: OPERATING THEATER. There, she led him into a small operating room. She switched on the lights. Against one wall was a stainless-steel and porcelain object no larger than a portable writing table with flexible tubes running from its casing. It was oblong in shape, with legs and rubber-clad casters. She went over to it. "This is a perfusion machine." She put her hand on its sleek top. "It's what keeps a kidney alive long enough for us to perform the transplant."

Croaker examined the perfusion machine, but nothing about it seemed odd or unusual. It looked like another bit of surgical apparatus, mysterious and, therefore, vaguely menacing.

"Let me give you a hypothetical situation," she said. "There's an accident on I-Ninety-five. Multiple deaths. These days, things are so backed up these bodies aren't even carted off to the hospital. The M.E. takes them until they're identified, then they go to a mortuary." She plucked some stray hairs back behind her ears. "Now say, in this hypothetical scenario, this M.E.'s unscrupulous. He's in debt or just wants to make a little more money. Whatever, he's in business for himself. He ices the abdominal cavities of the corpses to thirty-two degrees centigrade until he can get the body onto the perfusion machine. Then he floods it with Belzer solution. Remember, with a kidney he's got seventy-two hours. Anyway, probably he's already got buyers lined up. He does his antigen typing. That typically takes six to eight hours. Bingo! He matches the kidney to his list and sells it. No one knows because accident victims are typically in such bad shape a surgical incision by the M.E. will go unnoticed by the mortician."

He cocked his head. "Is this scenario hypothetical or typical?"

She looked at him unhappily. "It's been known to happen."

"Okay. But then what? Whoever buys the kidney isn't coming to you or someone like you to sew it in."

"No." Jenny used long, slender fingers to smooth the front of her lab coat. "But no doubt there are others who would."

"With your specific knowledge?"

Her expression was bleak. "You'd be surprised at how easy it is to do a kidney transplant. Any private clinic has the facilities—even one doing out-patient procedures. And, bare bones, all you really need are three competent professionals: a surgeon, an anesthesiologist, and an OR tech."

Croaker searched her face. "So you're saying, what?, this happens?"

"Form your own conclusions," Jenny said softly.

"Why have you told me about this?" Croaker asked. "Even if I were able to procure a kidney you wouldn't put it in Rachel—even to save her life."

Jenny Marsh put a hand to her temple. "I don't know. I told you I must be out of my mind." She turned away to stare blankly at the operating table, empty now, gleaming in the overhead lights. "Maybe it's that . . . you're a cop. Cops are like priests in a way. Sometime it feels good to confess to them."

"But you haven't done anything wrong."

She turned back to him, the green of her eyes piercing. "No, but in Rachel's case I seem to be thinking about it."

"And that scares you."

"More than you could know."

"Meet me tomorrow night for dinner," he said. He had to know more about this Stateside organ harvesting. Perhaps it might provide a lead to Antonio and Heitor. And besides, wasn't she offering a slender ray of hope, glimmering fitfully in the darkness? If she knew someone who could get a healthy kidney—registered or not—for Rachel . . . Harvesting an organ from an accident victim was nothing like what Antonio and Heitor were doing. But still. The thought that he might have to make such a decision scared him as much as it obviously did her. "Right now I've got to get my sister home, but we'll talk more about it then."

"I'm busy."

"No, you're not," he said. "I stole a look at your schedule when I went by the duty station. You're off at ten."

That cool appraisal again. "How do you know I don't have a date?"

"Do you?"

Jenny's gaze flickered and she looked abruptly drained. "It doesn't matter. There's nothing to talk about."

"Maybe not, but there's no harm in having dinner with me." He smiled. "Call it a thank-you on Rachie's behalf. You've gone above and beyond for her, and she—we're all grateful."

"Even if I wanted to . . ." She shook her head. "I make it a policy not to socialize with the family of my patients."

"That's sensible, I know." He gave her an ironic look. "But there are times when it's best to throw caution to the wind."

"And you think this is one of those times, Mr. Croaker?"

"Lew," he corrected her. "Yes, I do. How many cases like Rachel's have you had, doctor?"

"None."

She hadn't hesitated; he thought that was a good sign.

"Well, then, let's go to hell with ourselves and break *all* the rules."

Jenny Marsh studied him for a long moment, then nodded reluctantly.

"That's great," he said. "I'll pick you up here."

Again, she gave him that rueful smile. "Why do I think I'm going to live to regret this?"

"Because you're a woman who plays by the rules."

"Isn't it nice," she said, her smile broadening just a bit, "to have all the answers?"

4

Matty lived in the Palm Beach apartment that Donald Duke had bought five years ago and became hers as part of the divorce settlement. It was on the twelfth floor of Harbour Pointe, one of those glitzy high-rises that dotted South Florida's Gold Coast. It was a place that boasted views of both the Atlantic Ocean and the Intracoastal and, in best South Florida tradition, pointlessly added letters to its name. It was within walking distance of the Breakers Hotel and the high-profile restaurants of Royal Poinciana Way, and was coveted by anyone who wore diamonds at the beach. Besides awesome views, three-thousand-foot-plus floor plans, lavish marble and gold-plate baths, and a state-of-the-art rooftop cardiovascular fitness center, Harbour Pointe also boasted both a doorman and a concierge.

The lobby was typical of places that used the word *residences* for apartments that began at one million dollars. With its four massive crystal chandeliers, its custom Missoni carpets, and its pink suede and brushed bronze furniture, flamboyant was a woefully inadequate adjective to describe it.

Up on the twelfth floor, he turned on all the lights in the apartment, as if banishing the dark could dispel Matty's sudden and crushing depression. To his report of Rachel's stable condition she had said not a word during the short drive over the Flagler Memorial Bridge, down Royal Poinciana Way to Palm Beach proper.

He put her on one of the two facing oversize sofas in the living room. The entire place was furnished grandly in a decorator's idea of the European style: period furniture, upholstered in sweeps of pale moiré fabric and French provincial patterns, antique Oriental carpets in Iranian reds and blues muted by time and sunlight. This was all set off by eclectic accent pieces: statuary, paintings of the French countryside, mincing side tables, swags on lush curtains, massive cut-glass bowls, and ornamental knickknacks in profusion. The walls were partially paneled with the ubiquitous Floridian mirrors, which reflected the two bodies of water in dizzying and unexpected angles.

All this highly conspicuous artifice provided a brittle surface of culture. That hardly surprised him, given what he knew of Donald Duke, but something else did. In all this wonderland of overpriced junk, Croaker discovered no photographs, no personal possessions or mementos of the last fifteen years, no sense of individuality. Where was Matty amid this anonymous chic and glitter?

Matty sat with her bare feet on the carpet, looking undone by terror at the center of this perfect, hollow splendor. She was like a projectile in transit: in a limbo defined not by stasis but by velocity.

"When was the last time you ate?" She made him prompt her out of silence. "Matty . . . ?"

"I don't remember."

He headed for the kitchen. "I'll fix you something."

"You'll have to be some kind of magician," she called after him. "I haven't shopped in a week."

She wasn't kidding. In the comparatively small kitchen he discovered a refrigerator with nothing in it but three white paper containers from Chinese takeout, half a carton of spoiled skim milk, an empty box of shredded wheat, a head of garlic, half a head of spoiled iceberg lettuce, some semiwilted scallions, and a jar of Reese's peanut butter. The freezer held foil-wrapped packages of cake, a bag of gourmet coffee beans, and two unopened pints of Häagen-Dazs ice cream.

"Jesus," he muttered, peering into the containers of Chinese takeout. One held rice hard as ice, the second a shrimp dish whose ammoniac smell made him wince. The third had once contained an order of ginger beef. All that remained, however, were long slivers of ginger embedded like wooden splinters in a congealed brown sauce.

He rummaged through the cupboards, found pasta and a third of a bottle of Scotch. All in all, with the plastic packet of soy sauce from the takeout, it was enough. He dug out a large pot, filled it halfway with water, and set it to boil. In a bowl with some warm water he spooned out the peanut butter, thinned it to the proper consistency. Then he chopped up the garlic and scallions, added the slivers of ginger and the soy sauce, then the garlic, and got that mixture going in a saucepan. He slopped in a generous dollop of Scotch. By that time the water was boiling in the pot. He measured out the pasta and dumped it in.

When, fifteen minutes later, he called Matty to the table, her eyes got big as saucers. "What the hell is that?" she asked, pointing to the pasta in a pale brown sauce.

"Sit down and eat," he ordered, sprinkling the scallions over the top.

Matty sighed, ran her hands through her hair, and sank into a chair. By this time, she had scrubbed her runny makeup off her face and he could see all over again the beautiful young girl he remembered. Once she started to eat, she couldn't stop. After her fifth or sixth forkful, she looked up. "You *are* some kind of magician. This is fantastic!"

"Thanks." He sat down opposite her, took a small portion onto his plate. It was mainly for show; the steak he'd eaten at Bennie's was sitting on his stomach like a leprechaun digging for a potful of gold.

Matty wiped her lips. "Where'd you learn to cook like this?"

"In Japan," Croaker said. "Actually, it was something of a necessity. I hate raw fish, so wherever I was I ferreted out the best Chinese restaurant. And let me tell you there are some great ones there." He spiraled some pasta on the tines of his fork. "Somehow I always managed to get friendly with the chef." He laughed, remembering. "It wasn't so surprising." He extruded the nails from his biomechanical hand. "Once I gave 'em a demonstration of my own brand of slicing and dicing food, they were always asking me back into their kitchens. You should have seen 'em crowd around."

Matty shook her head as she helped herself to more pasta. "You really are full of surprises."

"So are you." He looked at her pointedly, and when her gaze met his, he said, "Matty, d'you think you can tell me why Rachie thinks she drove Donald away?"

She frowned. "She said that?"

"Uh-huh. She also said that her father didn't come to see her after the breakup."

"That part's true enough." She put her fork down, frowned. "Let me tell you, we had some screaming fights on the phone about that."

"Not in person?"

She shook her head. "Donald was adamant about that. He'd cut the ties and as far as he was concerned that was that. For him the divorce was like an operation; he couldn't understand why anyone would want to go back and revisit their gallbladder."

"But Rachel was his daughter—"

She raised her eyebrows. "In his eyes, Rachel was mine; she was part of the life he once had and had gotten bored with."

"You say that so calmly."

She pushed her plate away; she'd had enough of her food. "Donald was a driven man. He had furies in his head. He was always restless, always tearing down and building, never satisfied with what he'd created. I understood him. That was something you never bothered to do."

Despite himself, Croaker was incensed. "You're defending this bastard—still?"

Matty sighed, raked scarlet nails through her thick hair. "I can see where this will lead and I have no desire to go down that road again." She put a hand over his. "Not when we've found each other again." She smiled at him. "But, truly, Lew, there was a side to him you never quite got. You were too busy hating his guts."

"He gave me good reason."

Her eyes turned hard for just an instant, and Croaker clenched his biomechanical hand beneath the table. "The truth now, Matty.

The whole truth and nothing but. At Rachie's christening I was so happy for you, despite how you'd treated us. Then Donald came up to me and put his arm around me. I swear he almost kissed me on the cheek."

"I remember that."

"But you don't know the rest," Croaker said. "He told me how great it was to have a cop as part of the family, what great buddies we were going to be—how we'd do things together, you know, guy to guy. Like flying out on his private jet to go hunting and fishing. 'The whole country is our preserve,' he told me. 'And when we go, I want you to feel free to bring your cop pals. You know, the big shots from downtown, the high-steppers from City Hall.' He hugged me to him. 'My marrying your sister is the best thing that ever happened to you,' he said. 'Trust me. Together, we'll make more money than you've ever dreamed of. *If* you get your buddies to play along.'"

"What do you mean?"

He saw the dismayed look in her eyes and he held on to her hand. "Before I go on . . . This is the last of him, Matty. He's spent too many years standing between us. I won't allow that to happen anymore. It's all in the past. Agreed?"

She nodded. "Yes, Lew," she said breathlessly. "As far as I'm concerned, Donald's history. But I want the *true* history now."

"All right. Donald wanted to be hooked into all the right people in New York. That meant politicians, cops, and union leaders. He wanted me to make the introductions, twist arms here and there if need be. All so he could make his dirty deals." He leaned forward over the table. "Honey, that's when I blew up and threatened him."

"You never told me," she whispered.

"Because I was so stone cold angry," he said. "But also maybe you weren't ready to hear it."

Croaker's heart broke at the look of desolation on his sister's face. Now she knew that there was more to Donald than she had known. The funny thing was, he'd dreamed of this moment, of setting her free from her self-induced fantasy about Donald. But now that it had happened, he tasted only ashes in his mouth.

"Jesus, I fucked up my life."

"No, honey. You fell in love."

She laughed harshly. "Is that what it's called these days?" She shook her head, but she continued to grasp his hand as if it were a lifeline. "I was smart, beautiful—and vulnerable. And Donald saw it all in a flash, spread out in front of him like a four-course feast."

She tried to smile. "This is the way it was, Lew. All his friends—

95

no, strike that—all his *associates*—young millionaires and clever entrepreneurs—had married for status. They moved in on women of certain pedigree whose families' status would ensure them entrée to circles beyond even their money. Okay, but Donald was different. Maybe that was too easy a game for him. He wanted something more. To tear down and build something almost from scratch like he did in business. He wanted to play Henry Higgins to my Eliza Doolittle. He wanted to *create* a lady of culture and breeding out of this waif from Hell's Kitchen."

She waved a hand. "Oh, he made no bones about it. For my part, I was thrilled. Who in my position wouldn't be? The attention and grooming he lavished on me was my dream come true. Tutors in diction, manners, foreign languages—my God, he even hired a famous coach of the Met's opera divas! I had private lessons in ballet, tennis, horsemanship, polo, exercise, sailing. When he judged me ready, I came out. We went on fox hunts in England, played polo in Argentina, crewed in Newport. It blinded me to everything else."

She held on to her elbows as a drowning woman will clutch onto a spar. "This is my Walpurgisnacht." Her gaze struck Croaker's face with full force "Donald's dead now, my daughter's on the point of death, and everything I admired in him is turned to dust. At last, the truth is staring me in the face like a death's head. And if I can't face up to what he was now, I never will."

Matty reached out and placed the palm of her hand on the crown of his head as if in benediction. Then she ruffled his hair, as she used to do when they were young.

"It's okay." Her voice, with the depth and timbre of a coloratura, filled the room. "At last I understand just how angry we've been with each other."

She rose and took his chin and turned his face so that she stared into his eyes. Then she kissed both his cheeks. "But now everything's been said and we'll forget about it, because we've found each other. After all this time."

Then she busied herself with clearing the table and washing the dishes. She did it all with clean, economical movements, and by her straight-ahead efficiency, he knew that she had adjusted to being alone, if not to the tragedy that had befallen Rachel.

When she heard him come into the kitchen, she turned and he slid his arms around her, holding her close. He could hear her heart beating fast and he ached for her, and for himself. At last, they broke away, and returning to her washing, she said, "Lew, what else did Rachel say to you when she was awake?"

"Your daughter is angry."

Matty, her hands encased in yellow rubber gloves, nodded sadly as she rinsed off a plate. "Aren't ninety-nine percent of the teenagers in the world?" She said it as if she needed to convince herself. Rinsing off a plate, she gave him an anxious glance over her shoulder. "What's the matter? You too old to remember what it's like?"

"Despite what you see on TV, they aren't all taking drugs," he said. "Also, they're not all hiding a secret like Rachel is."

Matty whirled around, her face suddenly pinched with new concern. "What kind of a secret?"

"I don't know," he admitted. "I was hoping you'd tell me. She wouldn't."

Matty went back to washing dishes, but he could see she was shaken.

He took a plate out of the drain board and began to dry it. "Have you noticed a difference in Rachel over the past, say, three or four months?"

She shook her head. "Not really. She's been uncommunicative, reclusive since Donald died. When he was killed six months ago something seemed to snap inside Rachel. I don't know what it was, except maybe then her hope that he would one day welcome her back into his life was shattered."

"Have you talked with her about it?"

"Many times. But I don't get anything about her world. Try as I might, I can't understand Green Day or any of these other rock bands that spew out noise. It all sounds like a hissy fit to me." She put another plate on the drain board and began scrubbing a pot. "And to be brutally honest, Rachie would rather I *don't* get it. Any attempt at contact with her world she takes as an intrusion."

"Matty, the amount of drugs she's been doing—something's seriously wrong. Can you remember anything at all?"

"As you can imagine, the breakup didn't help." Then she shrugged. "There's nothing else, really. I mean, six months ago she went to Dr. Stansky for her annual school physical and everything was okay." She frowned. "I'll tell you one thing, Stansky didn't say anything to me about her taking drugs."

"No surprise there," Croaker said. "Chronic drug users know all the tricks to pass physicals." He leaned forward. "Are you sure there's nothing? No erratic behavior, failing grades in school, no chronic lying, no money missing out of your purse, that sort of thing?"

"Absolutely not. She gets straight As in school. As to the rest, I brought Rachel up with better values than that."

"Drugs can change people, Matty." He waited for her to respond.

When she didn't, he said, "I'd like to take a look at Rachel's room. Is that okay?"

Instead of answering, she said, "I wish I'd had a chance to talk to her."

"Do you know someone named Gideon?"

She turned around. "A boyfriend is my guess. I know she saw someone named Gideon. I never met him, though. She wouldn't talk about him."

"You let her see him without knowing anything about him?"

"Lew, Rachel is fifteen going on twenty-two." When she saw the look on his face, she said, "What would you have me do, put a leash on her? I can't ground her every night of the year. She seems to hate me enough as it is. These days, she says it often enough."

"And her father? How did she feel about him?"

Matty sighed. "There isn't a bigger mystery in my life. I've told you that Donald never seemed to care much about her. Of course Rachel was aware of it, but it never seemed to faze her. When he was away she used to hang on every call he made, waiting to talk to him. And even though he'd disappoint her every time, her hope seemed undiminished. Just the opposite, in fact. Oh, how that used to infuriate me!" Her voice rose harshly as she continued to amass a pile of clean pots and plates.

He had been tuning into her wavelength for some time, and he was struck by this discordant note. "Matty, what is it?"

"Nothing."

"You've come this far," he said gently. "Take the next step."

She shook her head. "Don't read into anything." She shrugged. "It's just that, you know . . ." He could see her take a deep breath. "Well, sometimes it seemed to me that Rachel and Donald . . . that this thing between them was some kind of sick game." She gave off an embarrassed laugh that was almost a sob. "Stupid of me."

"No, it's not," Croaker said. "Tell me what you mean."

Matty washed dishes as she did everything else, with a meticulous attention to detail. No wonder Donald's Henry Higgins routine worked so well with her. As she had proved in school and again at the ad agency she had unlimited aptitude. "It's just that this approach-avoidance thing with them while Rachel was growing up . . ."

"Before the divorce, you mean?"

Matty nodded. "Yes. There was something about it, an edge. Sometimes it seemed to me they fed off it, that it was their way of dealing with each other. Rachel would approach him, Donald

would fend her off, and it would escalate like that until they were both at some kind of fever pitch."

"And then what would happen?"

"I don't know." Matty's eyes were bleak at the remembrance. "Like a bubble it would suddenly burst. One moment it would be there and the next . . . their emotions were back to normal."

"Did he finally consent to see her? Was that how the tension resolved itself?"

"Sometimes, yes; at others, I don't think so. At least, I wasn't aware of them being together." It was clear Matty was struggling with this mystery. "In either case, Donald was back to his routine and Rachel would be sunny and somehow calm. Until the cycle started all over again."

Croaker said gently, "Matty, I have to ask this. Was Donald in any way abusive to Rachel?"

"Absolutely not." Her eyes were clear and he could see no reason to doubt her. "You know me better than that, Lew. I never would have allowed it. But the issue never arose; Donald was not that kind of man. He was too confident in himself and in everything he did. He knew so many subtle ways to exert his power he'd never even consider the physical one."

For a time, she seemed lost in thought. She was through washing. Pulling off her gloves, she put a hand gently on his arm. Her eyes glittered with tears. "Go see her den of iniquity."

He went down the hall, his footsteps muffled by the thick carpet. At the far end of the hall, he took a step into Rachel's room. It looked like a typical teenager's bedroom. It was painted clear white with trim black as funeral bunting. There were posters on the wall of Kurt Cobain, the late lead singer of Nirvana, along with posters of other rock bands: Stone Temple Pilots, Live, and REM.

The bedspread was black-and-white in a pattern that reminded Croaker of those old dinettes from the 1950s. He sat on the bed and looked around. He wanted to get a sense of the room from Rachel's point of view. When she got up each morning, this is what she saw. It had been his experience that people liked to wake up looking at their favorite possessions. He saw Kurt Cobain on the wall; he saw the window with the lights of Palm Beach strung like jewels around a dowager's crepey neck; he saw a photograph on her dresser. Inside the black wood frame was a black-and-white shot of a striking young woman with dark, chin-length hair. She was dressed in a see-through vinyl raincoat and was clutching a white, long-haired cat to her chest. Beneath the vinyl raincoat, the woman wore a thick black belt covered in metal studs. Croaker got

up and went over to it. The photo was not personal, but a page cut out of a magazine. The young woman was a model. He turned the frame around and opened it, but the back of the page held nothing more informative than part of an ad for Buffalo jeans. The name of the magazine or the date did not appear.

He replaced the photo in its frame, took up another, smaller photo that had been hidden behind the first one. This one was of Rachel. She had on an aquamarine satin dress with a sweetheart neckline. She was made up and there was a string of pearls—perhaps a loan from Matty—around her neck. She looked beautiful and very grown up. About to go to a prom, Croaker guessed. The only thing was she didn't seem at all happy. He slid out the photo of her his sister had given him and compared the two shots. In his, Rachel had been caught in an unguarded moment. In this other, posed shot, her intensity dominated to the point where she appeared brooding, almost sullen.

He put down the prom photo, but as he looked at it, something bothered him. It had moved slightly and there seemed to be something behind it. He slid it out of its frame, and to his utter surprise found a picture of himself. For a moment he could not remember when or where it had been taken. Then the memory came flooding back. It had been at their cousin's wedding in Forest Hills. But hadn't this photo originally been of him and Matty? He held the photo up to the lamplight, saw that the left side had been carefully cut away. Looking this closely, he recognized part of his sister's arm and hip.

After he returned the photos he went methodically through Rachel's drawers, checking in corners, through piles of black T-shirts and cotton blouses, underpants, and bras. He was looking for two things: any sign of drugs and her diary. Girls her age almost always wrote in diaries. Diaries were for secrets, and he suspected his niece had more than her share of those. Like who was Gideon? Someone she saw at night. Matty thought a boyfriend; to that Croaker would add drug connection. He found nothing except a large sachet of lilac potpourri in the bottom drawer.

Her walk-in closet was more empty than full. There were some clothes—mostly all black, three pairs of jeans, a couple of pairs of thick-soled Dr. Marten's boots, the ones that laced high up like U.S. Army combat boots, one pair of black-and-white retro-looking Airwalk sneakers. A cluster of black belts larded with metal studs of different shapes and sizes hung from a wire hanger. He thought of the photo of the model in her see-through vinyl raincoat and black studded belt. In a corner he found a black leather jacket.

Across the back someone had handwritten the word MANMAN in white permanent paint.

Directly below, heaped on the floor, was the aquamarine satin prom dress. He stooped, picking up the dress to hang it, when he saw something lying on the floor. He couldn't have seen it before because the dress had covered it. He used his stainless-steel nail to bring it out into the light.

It was a red rubber ball with silk cords attached to either side. Croaker had seen such items before. This was a ball gag, part of the ominous, ritualistic paraphernalia used by people into S-M. The ball went into the mouth, the cords tied at the back of the head to hold it in place. For a long time, he crouched there, staring. A vein pulsed in one temple as he contemplated the growing enigma that was Rachel. When it came to sex, his attitude had always been live and let live, but this discovery shook him. This was his niece, not some hooker on the Tamiami Trail.

Into his mind came Matty's face, her confusion painful to witness. She had been talking of Rachel's relationship with her father. To Croaker, there was more than a hint of S-M to it, even if it was only expressed on an emotional level. Matty was smart enough to suspect this. But what if, in Rachel, it was more? What if her sexual relationship with Gideon involved a true acting out of these perverse emotions?

At length, he reached out, put the ball gag into his pocket. He had no intention of letting his sister find it. She'd had more than enough shocks for the time being. Before he did anything else, he carefully hung up the prom dress, smoothing the bodice. It seemed important to get rid of all the wrinkles, as if by this act alone he could restore his image of Rachel to what it had been before he'd found the red rubber ball fraught with so many dark implications.

He went methodically through the pockets of the leather jacket. He discovered half a roll of Life Savers, a couple of wadded-up tissues, thirteen cents in change, a small ball of aluminum foil. It was tightly packed. He extruded a stainless-steel nail and opened it carefully with the razor sharp tip. There was nothing inside except a whitish residue. He put this up to his nose, then licked it tentatively. Could be coke, he thought, but there was too little to be sure.

He was putting back the Life Savers in the left-hand pocket when something fell against the back of his knuckles. He felt around but couldn't get to it. Curious, he took the jacket off its hanger and turned it inside out. He checked the seams. They were solidly stitched except for a four-inch length on the left side, which had been hastily basted. He snagged the loose thread and, with a sudden sense of foreboding, pulled. Then he stuck his fingers inside.

He extracted an ounce plastic bag filled with white powder. Opening it, he gave it a taste on the tip of his tongue.

He cursed mightily under his breath. The taste was unmistakable. It was cocaine.

Matty was working steadily in the kitchen. She'd brewed coffee and she was slicing a slab of what looked like a rich Russian coffee cake she'd taken from the freezer. "Emergency rations," she said when he came in. "If this isn't an emergency I don't know what is."

She gave him a tentative smile as she popped the pastry into the microwave, turned it on. "Find anything interesting?"

"There's something about Gideon and Rachel," he said softly.

Fear harrowed Matty's face as he took out the one-ounce bag of coke.

She put her hand to her mouth. "Oh, Christ. Is it . . . ?"

He nodded "Cocaine. I found it in Rachel's closet."

Croaker watched her beautiful, haunted eyes. The microwave beeped and automatically she opened the door. The kitchen smelled of cinnamon and walnuts and coffee. She stood staring blankly into the interior. At last, she said, "What in God's name is she doing to herself, Lew?"

"I don't know." He watched as she slid the coffee cake onto plates then, licking her fingertips, poured coffee into pale green mugs. But her frayed nerves betrayed her at last and she spilled some before Croaker, coming quickly up behind her, steadied her hand.

"Oh, Christ. Oh, Jesus." She leaned back against his solid strength, rocking a little. "My daughter and I haven't had much of a relationship. The sad truth is I don't know who she is."

Croaker held her tenderly while she gathered herself.

"I'll take the food in," he said.

But she shook her head and slowly disengaged herself. "No, I need to do this. I can do this."

She carefully finished pouring the coffee and Croaker could see that her hands no longer shook. Then she put their plates and mugs on the tray, and led him into the dining room. She sat down, swept her hair back from the side of her face, sighing. "My God, I feel as if I married a stranger."

He took a bite of the coffee cake. "Not so long ago I was involved with a woman—a married woman." When Matty raised her eyebrows, he added: "An *unhappily* married woman, but that didn't make it right." He took another bite of the pastry, washed it down with the rich coffee. "Anyway," he went on, "this woman had a daughter. She was a beautiful girl, and smart. But she was sick. Bulimic. She got sick because of her parents. They had a terrible, almost adversarial relationship and the girl was aware of it all."

Matty, who had been stirring cream into her coffee, paused. "You see a parallel?"

"This girl felt she was unloved."

He could see his sister stiffen. Color flushed to her cheeks and she began to tremble. "I love my daughter," she whispered.

"I know you do. I said the girl *felt* she was unloved. That's not the same as her *being* unloved. In fact, her mother loved her desperately."

"I love Rachel desperately." She looked at him imploringly. "Besides you, she's the only important thing in my life, Lew. But now I think, What if I've come to that realization too late?"

"Tell me something, where was Rachel when you and Donald were riding to hounds in England, playing polo in Argentina, and crewing in Newport?" He waited a moment. "She needed you then; she must have. Girls need their mommies."

Matty used a nail to slowly and methodically extract the walnuts from the cake. She did this until she had made a hole clear through the pastry. At last, she said, "In those days, I tried to be there for her. But Donald was so insistent. He needed me, too. He'd given me so much, opened up so many doors for me. So I went with him and left Rachel with the nanny." Matty gripped her mug with both hands, as if trying to warm herself beside a fire. Her knuckles were white and her eyes seemed bleak and lifeless. At last, she said, "What's happened to our lives—what's happened to *her* when I wasn't looking?" She was shaking in terror. "Do you think that when Rachel says she hates me she really means it?"

"What I think doesn't matter; I'm only a newcomer here," he said. "What do *you* think?"

"Lew, she's taking drugs, she's seeing people I know nothing about. At night, she goes . . . I don't know where she goes. And when she woke up it was you she wanted to talk to, not me." Her face was stricken. "And now all I want is to make it up to her. I want to hold her close and tell her how much I love her, but what if it's too late."

She trailed off and Croaker squeezed her hand in his. He wanted to tell her that it wasn't too late, but the words felt hollow in his mind. In a week, maybe two, Rachel could be dead. "Don't give up hope. I'm using all my resources to try and find her a kidney."

She bit her lip. "My God, Lew, do you think you can? It would be a miracle."

"Hold on, Matty. Just hold on."

Tears rolled silently down his sister's cheeks, dropping one by one on the tabletop. When she could trust herself to speak, she said, "Donald gave me everything I ever wanted. In return for making me into a fairytale princess, I did everything to please him, which was maybe the problem. Somewhere along the way I got lost."

"No, honey," he said, "you were already lost when you met him."

Croaker, staring at the photo of the model in the clear vinyl raincoat, fell asleep on Rachel's bed. Afterward, Matty tiptoed in and covered him with a light cotton blanket. Before she tucked the left side all the way around him she took a long look at his biomechanical hand. She didn't have to wonder what it must be like to be so seriously maimed. The first two months after Donald walked out on her she'd felt as if her legs had been amputated. Dead though the marriage might be, it had become her life-support system. Without it she was certain she was going to die. That she hadn't had come as a minor revelation to her.

As she covered her brother with the blanket she realized that she had never asked him the details of what had happened to his left hand. Typical, she thought. It was not her way to confide or ask confidences. Any form of intimacy other than the strictly physical kind was painful for her. It had been this way for so many years that it had become the norm. But she saw now what a terrible failing that was. It probably had been with Donald; it certainly had been with Rachel.

Matty wished with all her heart that she had been able to fully embrace Rachel after the breakup, to take her daughter into her confidence so that neither of them would have had to feel so alone. But she just couldn't. So many terrible emotions . . .

In misery, she realized now she'd suspected for some time that Rachel was having a hard time. She just couldn't admit it to herself. But now the full extent of her daughter's emotional pain hit her with the force of a freight train. For a moment, she doubled over just as if all the wind had been taken out of her. Her legs gave way and she found herself kneeling on the floor of Rachel's room. The carpet felt rough against her burning cheek and with each shuddering breath she took she drank in the smell of her daughter as if it were lifeblood that could sustain her.

What else could she do except pray? *Dear God,* she whispered. *Don't take my baby away before I have a chance to get to know her.*

DAY THREE

1

Croaker arose before dawn. He had a kind of internal alarm clock that never failed him. He showered, dressed in his same clothes, and slipped out the front door all without waking Matty. It would be hours before she got up—God knew she needed her sleep—and by then she could make her own way to the hospital.

Outside, glimmers of security lights skittered like fugitive spirits along the sidewalk. He listened for the crash of the surf, heard hungry gulls calling instead, and the peaceful lapping of the Intracoastal.

He decided to walk to the hospital, not more than fifteen minutes on foot. By the time he got there, daylight would have broken, and he wouldn't have to bother returning Matty's Lexus. His T-bird was still in the hospital parking lot—hopefully. If it hadn't been stolen or vandalized.

On the way, he stopped at a rank of newspaper vending machines, got a copy of the *Sun-Sentinel*. It was the Broward County daily and would list all the current events scheduled for the area. He riffled through local news, looking for the right section.

It hadn't been happenstance that he had fallen asleep in his niece's bedroom. He'd wanted to breathe her in, to give his unconscious time to work on the significance of what he had seen. Some things in Rachel's room just hadn't added up to the mental picture he was forming of her. Out-of-place elements usually meant one thing: the picture you'd formed was in some way false.

I once went out to fish, Stone Tree had told him. *I was hungry, and the hunger drove me outside into the rain. But the moment I put my hands on the boat I knew. If I went out in it, I would not return. So I went back inside and screwed my door and windows shut. Within the hour, the wind was so high it drove sand through the cracks in my house boards. So now I remember: if a thought doesn't feel right, put it aside.*

Croaker had fallen asleep with the image of the model in his head, but that image didn't feel right. He had awakened seeing in his mind the strange word handpainted on the back of the black leather jacket—the coke jacket. Thoughts, images, or impressions he had just before going to sleep or as he was waking up were often the purest and, therefore, truest, even if at first they made no sense. Eventually, when enough other pieces fell into place, they always did. They always led him to the truth.

MANMAN was what the jacket back had said. What in the world was Manman? He hadn't had a clue last night, didn't even know whether it was significant. But this morning intuition had quickly bloomed into a suspicion. He'd got up and stared from one poster of a rock group to another.

He was more or less in the middle of the Flagler Bridge when he found the club listings in the *Sun-Sentinel*. On the surface, it seemed like a very long shot that he'd find it here, but he kept scanning the listings and the ads, thinking of the leather jacket and when Rachel would wear it. On rainy days, maybe, though leather was not waterproof. The handful of really cool days in the winter? Okay. When else? At night, when she went out to clubs.

And here he was looking for clubs with live music because—

Almost all the way across the bridge, he stopped. Calmly, he folded back the page, folded it again until the small, square ad in the center was made more prominent. Somewhere not far distant a motorboat engine began to gurgle, curdling the placid water of the Intracoastal. The sweetish tang of marine diesel came to him briefly, before being borne aloft by the morning breeze. Salmon-colored light tinged the lateral cloud bank just above the eastern horizon. Soon, the parade of fishing boats and pleasure yachts would lift anchor, coming through here on their way to the Atlantic. He smelled the ocean, heard the gulls and frigate birds calling, but only distantly, as if they were part of another world.

At a club called the Lightning Tube on Washington Avenue in South Beach a band named ManMan was currently playing. He checked the dates and the show times. As he walked toward the hospital, he imagined Rachel at the Lightning Tube. She was wearing her MANMAN jacket and she was talking to one of the members of the band. Maybe a tall, lean guitarist named Gideon, who covered her hand with his, transferring a one-ounce packet of coke. It seemed logical; better, it felt right. While he'd slept in Rachel's room his unconscious had drunk in the scent of her. In his mind, he could see her as she had been before the renal failure. He walked at her side, silent as a ghost, but alive as a spirit. He felt the nettles of her rancorous rebellion, fueled by her father's rejection and her need to disengage herself from her mother. It seemed clear to him that Gideon must somehow have a hand in that rebellion. Tonight, he'd find out.

On the other side of the Intracoastal, Croaker walked the three blocks north on Olive Avenue to Eucalyptus Street. A police patrol car passed him, slowing slightly as the driver checked him out, before driving on. Not surprisingly, Croaker saw no pedestrians at all. At the end of the street, he went into the hospital parking lot and checked on the T-bird. Miraculously, it was untouched. He was just about to enter the hospital when he heard a car door slam behind him and footfalls crunching the grit of the parking lot blacktop.

"Mr. Croaker?"

He turned. A tall, cadaverously thin man was walking toward him. He was neither sauntering nor hurrying, nevertheless there was a quality about him that gave Croaker pause.

He was dressed in a stylish café-au-lait tropical-weight suit. His hair, slicked back off his wide, gleaming forehead was the color of freshly oiled gunmetal. His face was almost all jaw. For the rest, a slash of a mouth, a knife-thin, knobbed nose, and eyes the color of undiluted coffee set beneath bony brows sufficed to define him as a man with both confidence and means. The two did not often go together, as Croaker had some time ago discovered, and he'd learned to mark men who possessed them.

The man came up to him. His skin was the color of polished teak, and his face had a slightly Latin cast. He was carrying an attaché so sleek and thin it seemed impractical. He wore black loafers of ostrich skin, a slim Patek Philippe wristwatch, and a simple gold wedding band on his left hand. Very elegant.

"You are Lew Croaker." He smelled faintly of sandalwood and lime.

"And you are?"

The cadaverous man smiled, showing teeth yellowed by years of tobacco smoke. "Marcellus Rojas Diego Majeur." A business card was proffered between his fingers.

Croaker gave it a quick read. Mr. Marcellus Rojas Diego Majeur was an attorney-at-law. It figured.

Croaker looked up. "Mr. Majeur, it's what, a little after six in the morning?"

Majeur crooked his left arm, glanced at his Patek Philippe. "Seven minutes past the hour, sir, to be exact."

Croaker frowned. "How long have you been waiting for me?"

"Since three." Majeur said it as if sitting in parking lots in the dead of night was routine.

"You look fresh as a daisy."

"Thank you." Majeur gave a little bow. "Mr. Croaker, I wonder if I could have a few moments of your time."

"Not right now," Croaker said. "I've got to get upstairs."

"Yes, I understand." Majeur nodded sorrowfully and, tongue against the roof of his mouth, made a clucking sound. All that was missing was for him to exclaim Oh, dear! like a beloved aged uncle.

"Some other time, maybe." Croaker nodded. "Give me a call. I'm in the book."

Another, darker look appeared on Majeur's face. "I'm afraid another time won't do, sir. Not at all. It's now or never."

"Then it'll be never."

Croaker was about to turn away when he saw the gleam of a small .25 caliber gun in Majeur's hand. It was pointing at Croaker's stomach.

"No," Majeur said with no emotion at all. "It will be now."

Croaker looked from the muzzle of the almost toylike gun to Majeur's face. "Do you expect me to believe you'll shoot me here on the steps of the hospital?"

Majeur shrugged. "It's been done before." A quick smile cut across his face like lightning in a nighttime storm. "But not by me." His dark and enigmatic gaze held Croaker's for some time. "I'm licensed to be armed, by the way."

"I'm sure you are, but I very much doubt you'd put yourself in that kind of jeopardy for any client."

Majeur's bland expression never wavered. "That would presuppose you knew something about me. You don't."

Staring into those coffee-colored eyes, Croaker took a gamble, cobbling together a thumbnail sketch from quick observation, intuition, and past experience. "I know what I need to know. You're the kind of man for whom clients are money. The larger the retainer the more you'll risk, the equation's as simple as that. If the pay is up to your standard, you're detached, professional, committed to the end. Tell me, how wide off the mark am I?"

A wry smile was creasing Majeur's face. "I can tell you that whoever said money isn't everything is not living my life." As swiftly as the .25 had appeared, it was gone. "I apologize for alarming you. I am not by nature a violent man, unless severely provoked. But I needed to gain your full attention, Mr. Croaker, because the nature of my errand is urgent. For my client—and for your niece."

Croaker felt a small shock wave go through him. "What are you talking about?"

"Don't play games with me, sir, it is an unproductive endeavor." He jerked his head toward the hospital entrance. "I've been up to visit her, you see."

"You?" Croaker took a menacing step toward him.

"*Calmate, señor*," he said. "I mean your niece no harm. Quite the contrary."

"The nurses have no business—"

"I handed them my card." Majeur's mouth smiled. "You'd be surprised the liberties one can exercise as an attorney. I told them I represented a potential donor, which is, more or less, the truth."

Croaker suddenly felt chilled, then feverish. "Donor?"

Majeur leaned forward even as he lowered his voice to a stage whisper. "*Kidney* donor, *señor*. I mean to say, that's what your niece is in need of, yes?"

The sky was a pellucid blue. High above, clouds were lit up with sunlight as if they were neon signs. The early morning air felt hot against Croaker's skin, and all of a sudden he was acutely aware of where they were standing. An ambulance was pulling up outside the adjacent Emergency entrance, and people—mostly doctors and nurses changing shifts—were drifting in and out.

He looked at Majeur, who was waiting patient as a buddha. "Is there anywhere we can go and talk?"

Majeur's eyes seemed to sparkle in the newly reborn sunlight. "I think my car will suffice." He lifted an arm to indicate the way.

Marcellus Rojas Diego Majeur's car turned out to be a pristine 1967 turquoise Mustang. He smiled as he unlocked it and opened the long door, which was one of the beautiful signatures of this automobile. "You see, right off the bat we have something important in common."

So he knew Croaker drove the vintage T-bird. How much else did he know? Croaker wondered as he peered into the interior. Inside, as outside, it was buffed and polished to perfection. This man loved his car.

"So what do you think?" Majeur stroked the chrome. "It is a beauty, no?"

"It's beauty, yes."

Majeur gave a strange laugh, a little girl's high tee-hee. "Want to take it for a spin?" He nodded as Croaker looked at him. "Sure as a verdict you do." He dropped the keys into Croaker's hand, went around to the passenger's side, and got in.

Croaker hesitated for just a moment, then slid behind the wheel and fired up the ignition. The engine thrummed happily.

"Make a right when you get to Dixie Highway," Majeur directed as they pulled out of the lot.

Had this been his plan all along? Croaker wondered. Had he been that sure of himself? He went north on Dixie, made the jog left, then right as it became Broadway. No man's land, dangerous for a white man. Stopped at a light, he risked a glance over at Majeur. He looked and spoke like a litigator. Croaker could imagine him in the courtroom, fiery with indignation as he addressed the jury. Croaker imagined him winning far more cases than he lost.

Majeur provided more directions, and they ended up cruising slowly down a deserted street called Rosemary Avenue. Croaker had never been here before. Up ahead, he could see the black wrought-iron fence of a cemetery.

"Park at the end of the street, would you," Majeur said.

It was a No Standing zone, but that didn't seem to bother the attorney any. When they got out, Croaker saw that Majeur had exchanged his attaché for what looked like an old-fashioned lunch box with a domed lid. Majeur saw the direction of Croaker's look and said almost apologetically, "Breakfast. With my schedule, it pays to be prepared twenty-four hours a day." He shrugged. "Tomorrow never knows."

He led Croaker across the pavement to the locked gates of the cemetery. He produced a key and unlocked the gates. They slipped through and he carefully relocked it.

Sun shone and birds twittered, flitting from tree to tree. They strolled, seemingly aimlessly, down moss-strewn paths, past granite headstones scrubbed dull by wind and torrential rain. Occasionally, they passed the tattered remains of an offering: the stems of flowers long dried to dust, burned-down votive candles in red glass cups.

"Hungry?" Majeur placed the lunch box atop a headstone and snapped it open. This grave had a bouquet of fresh flowers atop it, tightly wrapped in green florist's paper, as if someone had just placed it there. But Croaker, scanning the vicinity, determined they were alone in the cemetery.

"Breakfast for two." Majeur pulled out a pair of big Cuban sandwiches of roast pork and fried onions wrapped in waxed paper. He also had a thermos of rich, dark Cuban coffee and Cuban sweet rolls.

"I think I'll pass, for the moment," Croaker said.

"Pity. I waited for you." Majeur was already unwrapping waxed paper from around a sandwich.

You could tell a lot about someone by the way they ate and the way they made love, Croaker had found. Not surprising. Both stemmed from a primitive place, animal instincts that existed in all human beings. But it was in the way in which those instincts manifested themselves that spoke of how a personality had been shaped, twisted, and bent, what was important to it and what was not. In eating and making love, artifice ended and the true person began to emerge.

Majeur was fastidious. He manipulated the awkward sandwich the way Croaker imagined a surgeon handled a living heart. Firmly, delicately, precisely, Majeur took dainty, even bites out of the monstrous thing, reducing it by stages to smaller and smaller squares until it was entirely consumed. When he had chewed and swallowed the last bite, he spun off the top of the thermos and poured coffee into the plastic top. The smell of it was instantly overpowering. He did not touch the sweet rolls.

When he was finished, he did not even have to wipe his lips. He rubbed his hands together and got down to business. "Mr. Croaker, my offer is a simple one. My client has access to a healthy human kidney. It is compatible with your niece's blood type and body chemistry. We would, of course, provide all the necessary documentation for the doctor—I believe her name is Jennifer Marsh."

The thought that Rachel had a shot at life made Croaker feel woozy with elation, as if he'd had too much of Bennie's mescal. But he needed to calm himself, to get some assurances, to make certain this wasn't some kind of scam. "If you have any shred of human compassion, Mr. Majeur, you'll tell me the truth. Does your client really have a compatible kidney? I mean if this is bullshit . . . well, a young girl's life is nothing to fuck with, I can tell you."

"I assure you it exists, Mr. Croaker, and that it is available to my client." From an inside breast pocket he slipped Croaker a set of folded papers.

"Is this a registered kidney?"

Majeur smiled. "As far as UNOS is concerned it's strictly kosher."

Croaker had seen papers like these before; Jenny Marsh had shown them to him just before she'd administered the compatibility tests. They were certificates of specification—blood type compatibility, HLA typing, so forth. Because Jenny Marsh had shown them to him, he knew Rachel's blood type and HLA levels. A match of six out of six human lymphocitic antigens would be perfect; the risk of organ rejection that much less. Also, it would be too good to be true.

Croaker's pulse rate accelerated as he saw that five out of six of the donor's antigens matched Rachel's. Good God, this was no joke.

Majeur had the one thing that would save Rachel's life It was like a gift from God.

Majeur bent forward from the waist and whispered as he had done at the hospital entrance. "So easily it will be available to your niece."

Croaker ruffled the pages. "I'll want to hold on to these."

Majeur spread his hands wide. "By all means. Show them to your Dr. Marsh. Check everything out. My client wants you to feel secure in his promise." He waited only a moment. "But do not take too long. As I am certain Dr. Marsh has made clear your niece has very little time remaining before even a compatible kidney will do her no good." Croaker scarcely heard Majeur. His heart was beating so fast he could hardly hear himself think. The kidney was real, it existed. It was Rachel's only chance at life. He could not let it slip through his fingers. But what did this joker and his client have up their sleeves? "How does your client know about my niece's situation?"

"From Dr. Marsh, I believe." Majeur held out one hand, palm up. "Indirectly. She's made quite a number of phone calls on your niece's behalf. Renal pathology is a kind of closed community, so the word spread quite rapidly. He has many physician friends."

"And your client is . . . ?"

Majeur smiled. "For reasons that will shortly become apparent, he wishes to remain anonymous."

"Sorry," Croaker said. "I don't do business with anyone by that name."

"Oh, come now, sir." Majeur spread his arms. "Back north in New York City you dealt with many an anonymous source."

"Criminals."

Majeur stroked his temple with a forefinger. "Not all of them, surely."

Croaker stared at him, silent.

Majeur was unperturbed. "In any case, I don't believe you have any choice in this matter." He waited an appropriate moment, and Croaker had another flash of him dramatically addressing a jury in closing arguments. "Not, that is, unless you want Rachel to die." His first use of Rachel's name was as shocking as a splash of cold water in Croaker's face. "And she *will* die, sir, without that kidney. Dr. Marsh—and others, I have no doubt—have confirmed that."

Croaker said nothing for a very long time. Dimly, like a background wash, he could hear the traffic picking up on Broadway. Rap music, raw and searing, on a boom box, waxed and waned, drifting away on the sunshine. Here, in the cemetery, it was unnaturally still. And getting hotter by the minute.

Croaker stirred. "Okay. Say your client does have access to a kidney that's compatible. How much does he want for it? I'm not a millionaire, though my sister's got access to money."

"Oh, it's not money," Majeur said. "No, no, nothing like that. In fact, my client would like you to keep the keys to the Mustang."

"I don't think so."

"Tangible evidence of his sincerity and good will." Majeur carefully stuffed the used waxed paper back into the lunch box. "There are no strings attached, I assure you." He poured himself more coffee. "Ownership papers are in the glove compartment; you'll find them in order, I assure you. The car is yours no matter what may eventuate."

Then he looked up at Croaker and smiled his most benign smile, the one he reserved for the members of the jury, the one they'd undoubtedly take back with them to their deliberations. "Take it, sir. I know my client. It would be an offense if you refused his gift."

By that one simple statement Majeur was telling Croaker all he needed to know about the mysterious client: he was rich, he was powerful, he had considerable influence. He was generous, probably honorable, quite possibly without scruples.

"What's the quid pro quo for the kidney?"

Majeur nodded, as if he approved of the decision Croaker had made. "Before I begin, my client wants you to know that it was his wish to donate this kidney to your niece free and clear. Unfortunately, circumstances make that largesse impossible." His forefinger tapped the front of the headstone. "You see this?"

Croaker looked at the granite marker. It said: THERESA MARQUESA BARBACENA 1970–1996. MAY GRACE AND MERCY FOLLOW HER FOREVER.

"As you can see, Theresa was twenty-six when she died." Majeur closed the lunch box slowly and silently. "When she was murdered." His hands were clasped loosely atop the lunch box, like attendants awaiting further instructions.

"What relationship was the girl to your client?"

It was Majeur's turn to keep his own silent counsel.

Croaker took a deep breath. "So in return for the kidney your client wants me to find out who murdered her."

"Oh, no, sir." Majeur had clearly reached the climax of his summation. "My client already knows who killed her. Her husband, one Juan Garcia Barbacena. He killed her by beating her insensate, then tying an electrical cord around her neck and squeezing until her tongue popped out of her mouth and blood leaked from her eyes."

Majeur was a master. He waited just long enough for Croaker to have digested the grisly details of the murder before he went on.

"And do you know why he killed her, sir?" He shook his head. "It was for the most banal of reasons. He had a mistress, and Theresa found out about it. Instead of going to someone who could help her—someone such as my client—and allowing him to act on it in his own time and manner, she confronted Juan Garcia. She threatened him—verbally, not physically, I assure you. She was not that kind of person. And, in response, he promptly killed her."

"Sounds like an open-and-shut case," Croaker said. "If what you say is true—"

"It is true."

Croaker continued on relentlessly. "If you have sufficient evidence, you or your client should go to the police."

Majeur sighed. "Mr. Croaker, in the best of all possible worlds that would already have happened. Juan Garcia Barbacena would already be incarcerated." That pause again; Croaker was getting to know this man's persuasive style. "But this is not the best of all possible worlds. It is reality. And the reality of this situation is that no matter Juan Garcia's evil, no matter his culpability in this crime, he will never be charged, let alone arraigned."

Majeur's fingers curled around the smooth granite headstone of Theresa Marquesa Barbacena, as if by that gesture he could somehow gentle her restless spirit. "This man is protected, even from the direct force of my client. There is a wall around him none can penetrate." He held up a finger. "*Almost* none."

A slow creeping had begun along Croaker's spine, as premonition began inexorably to align itself with reality.

In a voice that raised the hairs on Croaker's forearms, Majeur concluded his summation: "*You*, sir, can get to him. My client is convinced of it. Here, in a nutshell, is his proposal: in return for the kidney that will save Rachel's life, you will penetrate Juan Garcia Barbacena's defenses and you will kill him."

2

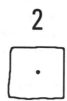

"**I**'m not going to kill," Croaker said, "for you or anyone else." Majeur's offer wasn't a gift from God, he thought. It was a deal with the Devil.

"I see." Majeur put his hand on the front fender of the turquoise Mustang with the same force of feeling he might fondle a naked woman's thigh. They were standing outside the gates to the cemetery, which the attorney had relocked. From this vantage point they could just make out the bright spray of color of the fresh flowers laid at the grave of Theresa Marquesa Barbacena. "That sentiment will come as a shock to the family of Ajucar Martinez."

With a tremor of achy recognition, Croaker's mind flew back a decade. "Martinez was a monster. He'd killed five hookers by the time I caught up to him. Slashed their foreheads and cheeks, cut off their breasts before he slit their throats."

"You shot him dead," Majeur said coolly.

"Yes, I did." Croaker was no longer surprised at the depth of information Majeur had unearthed about him, even though much of it was classified and so extremely difficult to obtain. Majeur's first contact with Croaker was part of a major operation. These people were clearly not fooling around. "He came after me with his straight razor."

"Blew his face right off."

"I shot him in the knee first," Croaker said. "It wasn't enough."

Majeur threw the dome-lidded lunch box into the Mustang's backseat. "Then there was Dunston McGriff."

"Another psycho," Croaker recalled. "Raped his stepsister after he had ripped out her heart and ate it. Then he went on a killing spree. Four dead, six injured. Thirty-ought-eight shotgun was his weapon of choice."

Majeur settled himself against the fender of the Mustang. Sunlight spun dizzyingly off its highly polished surface. "One bullet through the temple, another through his neck. A crack marksman's kill. You iced him clean."

"Had to. He was about to take out my partner."

Majeur folded his arms across his chest, closed his eyes, and put his face up into the sun. "And now we come to Rodrigo Impremata."

Croaker looked at Majeur. The attorney had been ever so successful in resurrecting the old days. Events that Croaker had buried deep in his psyche strode through his conscious mind like a host, jackbooted and bristling with the weaponry of war. "What is this, a laundry list?"

"An accounting of the dead," Majeur said. "If my sources are correct, Don Rodrigo ran the coke cartel in New York's Barrio for many years. Also, it seems, he ordered your father killed. Any discrepancies so far?"

"None that I know of." Croaker waited for the other shoe to

drop: surely Majeur must know about his freelance career with the feds.

Majeur nodded. "In this age of prevarication and shifting culpability I appreciate your candor, sir, surely I do." He tilted his face more fully into the sunshine. "The Don was the worst kind of egomaniac, wasn't he? As he amassed power, he brought reckless danger to everyone around him. Even his colleagues wished him dead. But the Don was too clever for them; he kept them weak and warring among themselves." Majeur's eyes snapped open, catching sight of Croaker staring at him. "Which is where you came in. Some bright spark who knew—or suspected—that the Don had had your father wiped, leaked you some key information—a hole in the Don's formidable defenses through which a man of your abilities and determination could slip." Majeur cocked his head to one side. "How am I doing?"

Croaker shrugged noncommittally, but inside he was roiling. He thought he was over the bitter feelings the Don had awakened in him. He thought he had come out the other side of that particular maelstrom.

"That's sort of the semiofficial story." Majeur's gaze drifted off through the iron bars to Theresa's grave. "On the other hand, there are those—and I must confess to belonging to this camp—who believe you already knew who had your father whacked. I mean to say you certainly did enough investigating on your own time."

Majeur's gaze snapped back to Croaker. He was looking for confirmation. When he got none, he went on. "Anyway, as this version goes, it was you who went to the Don's bitterest rival and cut a deal: he rolls over on the Don and you take the sonuvabitch out. Neat, clean, everybody's interests are served."

Now Croaker could see that Majeur had done so much more than resurrect his past. He had evoked not merely remote events pressed into the pages of a scrapbook, he had also managed to conjure up the emotions Croaker had painstakingly interred in the dark recesses of his mind. Croaker was reliving the red rage of revenge that had gripped him like a hurricane-driven tide. He would have done anything to bring his father's killer to justice—and had.

Majeur levered himself off the car. "Tell me, how old were you when this incident occurred?"

"Twenty," Croaker said. "If it happened like you said."

"Oh, it happened just as I related it." Majeur opened the Mustang's door. "You know it and I know it." He gave Croaker a thin smile. "So let's save ourselves some time here. You have the essential qualities: you are both skilled and resourceful."

"Hey, tell you what, when I need a job reference, I'll call you."

Majeur gave him a wry look. He was still in summation; no sarcastic bit of business was going to derail him from his appointed task. "You know what they say about killing a human being—either you can do it or you can't. Period. I believe you have amply demonstrated that you know how to kill a man. In fact, one could say that you are an expert at it."

"My abilities are not at issue," Croaker said. "If I killed in the past there were damn good reasons for it. A, those perps deserved it. And, two, I had no other choice."

"With Martinez and McGriff, you may have a point," Majeur said. "But not with the Don."

"There you're wrong," Croaker told him. "We never could get anything on the Don. No matter how hard we tried he kept slipping through our fingers like an eel, as if he knew what we were up to before we knew ourselves." He nodded. "And you're right. I did a shitload of detective work on the Don. He had my father killed, no doubt of it. But the people who spoke to me were too scared to go to the cops and testify. And even if I had the proof, the Don would walk. He was wired into the NYPD all the way downtown. He was an untouchable. And in the meantime kids were dying from the shit he was selling. There was no other way."

Majeur stood very close to him. In the growing heat of the morning, the smells of masculine cologne and sweat were suddenly rife. "There was no other way. He was an untouchable." Majeur whispered the echo. "In other words, he was protected on all sides."

And in just that way, Croaker felt the trap snap shut on him. He looked into Majeur's coffee brown eyes and felt the full brunt of the attorney's intensity.

"Just like Juan Garcia Barbacena is an untouchable, protected on all sides." Majeur's hands lifted and fell. "*Madre de Dios,* the filthy pig killed his wife in cold blood in the full flower of her life. You think he didn't know just what he was doing, you don't know Juan Garcia Barbacena worth a shit. He is Don Rodrigo Impremata all over again."

Blood had risen into Majeur's face, darkening his skin to the color of stained mahogany. Whether or not Barbacena committed the crime, Croaker saw quite clearly that Majeur believed he was guilty. Maybe Croaker had gained an insight into the attorney. Maybe he wasn't just a cold and clever mercenary, working the anatomy of the bigger buck. He wasn't perfect, either. He hadn't uttered one word about Croaker's ties to the ACTF. This had to mean he didn't know.

"I have only your say-so for that," Croaker said. He was aware how with each exchange Majeur was leading him deeper and deeper down this particular path. But he didn't see that he had much choice. Rachel had to have that kidney. And if Majeur was telling him the truth about Barbacena . . . Treading morally suspect ground was new to him, despite Majeur's magical mystery tour of his NYPD past. On one point Croaker was clear: he had been justified in each homicide he had committed. This situation with Juan Garcia Barbacena was another matter altogether. He needed some time to check things out and to think. But time was the one commodity he couldn't afford. Rachel's condition wouldn't wait for every *i* to be dotted, every *t* to be crossed.

"Some things one must take on good faith," Majeur said. "Believe me, sir, we have not lost sight of your niece's welfare."

"I need some time, talk to Dr. Marsh, let her check out your documentation."

"You have twenty-four hours," Majeur said. "At that time, we trust you will be prepared to move forward."

"Dr. Marsh will want to be sure this organ exists."

Majeur smiled. "Can and will be done." He nodded. "On the back of my business card you will find a handwritten number. You may reach me anytime, anywhere, within the next twenty-four hours. That is a guarantee, sir. A tangible example of *our* good faith."

Majeur gave Croaker a stern look. "Twenty-four hours, this is all the grace period my client is prepared to give you."

This piqued the detective in Croaker. "In something of a rush, isn't he?"

"As is your Rachel." Majeur shrugged. "As it happens, my client does have a most pressing deadline." He stepped closer to Croaker and lowered his voice, though who he was afraid could hear him but the dead souls and the seagulls that guarded them was anyone's guess. "At midnight tomorrow, Juan Garcia Barbacena arrives in Miami under a massive security blackout. He stays for twelve hours only while he holds high-level business meetings. When and where are closely held secrets. It is during this period you must terminate him."

Croaker felt the sweat break out along his spine. "You're giving me next-to-impossible odds. I wouldn't have nearly enough time—"

"Calm yourself, Mr. Croaker. The moment you give me your assent, you will receive a veritable torrent of details on Barbacena's itinerary, the number of his bodyguards, the extent of their weapons, as well as a complete workup of his preferences for food, clothing, shelter, and sex. You see, we have no intention of throwing you to the crocodiles, Mr. Croaker."

"Sure of yourself, aren't you?'

"Certain events in a man's life are inevitable." Majeur stuck out his hand. When Croaker took it, he said with a surprising amount of genuine feeling, "I entrust the Mustang into your hands without reservations. Enjoy it fully, sir."

Back at the hospital parking lot, Croaker dropped the lawyer off, watched him climb into a new Lincoln Continental in the metallic grape color so popular in Florida. He jotted down the license plate number before parking the Mustang.

He unlocked the glove compartment. Inside, he found papers of ownership and registration for the Mustang. Both were already made out in his name, including his address and Social Security number. What didn't these people know about him? The transfer of ownership form listed Marcellus Rojas Diego Majeur as the previous owner. No mention anywhere of any other name, such as Majeur's mysterious client.

Upstairs, in the CCD, he checked on Rachel. Matty was in the cubicle and she shook her head: no change. He could see the terror lurking in his sister's eyes, and his stomach turned over.

Croaker went to the nurses' station in search of Jenny Marsh. But she was in the OR and was expected to be there most of the day with four succeeding procedures. He'd have to wait to see her until their dinner date at ten that night.

He stuck his head back into the cubicle to take a long look at Rachel, lying peaceful and half-dead, her mother tense and tight-lipped beside her. There was also a distinguished-looking man with gray hair and an old-fashioned pencil mustache. He turned and gave Croaker a brief nod. Matty introduced him as Dr. Ronald Stansky. Rachel's personal physician.

The two men shook hands.

"I was just telling Mrs. Duke that I have a certain amount of pull at the United Network of Organ Sharing." He murmured in a hushed voice, as if he might wake the patient. "Perhaps there is something I can do."

"That would be great," Croaker said, "but I was under the impression that UNOS was sacrosanct."

"Yes. Of course." Dr. Stansky wore a tropical-weight sharkskin suit, a neatly pressed white shirt, a dark, conservative tie, and the oily mien of an undertaker. "I didn't mean to suggest I could just ring up and have them pluck out a kidney, dear me, no." Disturbed, he traced the line of his mustache with the tip of a long, elegant forefinger. Then, he brightened. "But friends are friends, and I have no doubt they will make their best efforts on our behalf."

He squeezed Matty's hand. "Don't you lose hope," he whispered to her.

Croaker tapped Stansky on the arm. "Could I see you outside, Doctor?"

"Of course," Dr. Stansky said.

Croaker gave Matty an encouraging smile as he held the curtain back for the doctor. Outside, he said, "Dr. Stansky, my sister tells me you examined Rachel six months ago."

"That's true." Away from Matty, Dr. Stansky's almost obsequious demeanor dissolved like ice in sunlight. Revealed beneath was a flintlike intransigence most often brandished like a weapon by wary people in unfamiliar circumstance.

"And?"

Dr. Stansky looked aggrieved at this obvious waste of his valuable time. "She came because the school she is attending required it. She was not ill."

This was like wrenching water from a rock. "Go on."

Dr. Stansky spread his elegantly manicured hands. "The test results were normal in every way."

Croaker shook his head. "Doctor, I'm curious about something. How is it that your tests didn't discover that Rachel was smoking pot and cocaine and dropping psychedelics?"

"I understand that you were once a detective on the New York City Police Force." Dr. Stansky's eyes were like hollow pits into which all genuine human emotion vanished like a stone in a well. Croaker harbored a strong suspicion this was a trait taught in medical school along with Anatomy and Cytology. "Why ask a question to which you already know the answer?"

"I wanted to hear what you had to say."

Dr. Stansky was bristling now. "It is child's play to pass a physical." He waggled a finger in warning, as if he were a professor before an abruptly unruly class. "It happens every day of the week in every city in the country. It's outrageous but that's the reality of it."

"But you understand she's drug dependent now." Croaker had not meant it as a question and he was met with stony silence. Getting a physician to admit a mistake was tantamount to cajoling God into conceding somewhere along the line in man's creation He'd erred. "Thank you, Doctor. I appreciate your candor."

Dr. Stansky, misinterpreting irony for apology, pursed his lips in what may have been stiff acceptance.

Croaker spoke to Matty briefly. He longed to tell her about his interview with the mysterious lawyer Majeur, but he didn't have the heart. How cruel to get her hopes up if he couldn't go through with the deal or if Majeur was running a scam. But he did tell her he was continuing to work with his government contacts to try to secure a kidney. Not exactly the truth yet, but not a lie, either.

As he left the hospital, Croaker considered where he would sleep that night. It was too far to drive back to his house in Islamorada, and the idea of staying with Matty in Harbour Pointe gave him the willies. Overbred high-rises like that were no place for him. He dug in his pocket and discovered he still had the keys to Sonia's house. He'd neglected to give them back to Bennie.

He went through the parking lot to the T-bird, turning over the notion of staying in El Portal. He opened the trunk, punched in a number on a small keypad he'd installed himself. A hidden door opened and he extracted a padded briefcase. Inside was a small laptop computer. He hooked it up to his cell phone, used the internal modem to dial up the State Motor Vehicle database. The software asked for an access code and he typed in a number Rocky Saguas, a detective lieutenant buddy on the Metro-Dade Police Force, had given him. He got in and punched in the license number he'd copied off Majeur's Lincoln Continental. The system was jammed up. Typical. He switched to Bell South and, using the same code, gave them the phone number of Sonia's dying friend, Nestor. A moment later, Nestor's full name and address popped onto the screen; it was not far from Sonia's, in El Portal. He disconnected and got rolling.

The Town Center Mall was on Glades Road, one of the two major east-west arteries that ran from one end of Boca Raton to the other. The mall itself was between Butts Road and St. Andrews Boulevard, one of those vast complexes that virtually defined the east coast of Florida.

Despite his morning shower, Croaker had been in the same clothes two days straight, and he was about to project a halo of body odor like the rings of Saturn. He went shopping at the Gap for underwear, a couple of pairs of lightweight trousers that needed no alterations, and a half-dozen assorted polos and short-sleeved shirts. He felt neat and clean by the time he strolled back into the mall and ran right into Rafe Roubinnet, the owner of the Shark Bar.

"Hey, *compadre!*" As usual, heads turned at the rolling thunder of his voice. It seemed to Croaker that Rafe was still, at heart, a politician. From what he understood, Rafe had done a more than creditable job as mayor of Miami. There were many who'd wanted him to run for re-election, but he'd declined, never giving a reason. Like being a cop, politics took its own toll; you never knew when you'd burn out.

"Just the man I wanted to see!" Roubinnet, his blue eyes flashing, pulled Croaker out of the mainstream of the mall's pedestrian traffic. He wore white jeans, a blue-and-white striped short-sleeved shirt, and Docksides without socks. He had the kind of muscles—well cut, not as big as your head—that made most women's eyes cross, but he was totally unself-conscious about them.

"I heard a good one the other day," Roubinnet went on. Restaurateurs and politicans, Croaker thought, they both love a good joke, preferably dirty. And Rafe was at the top of the list. Jokes were his major sideline; he seemed to have a warehouse of them. Maybe he got them from his customers. "There was this Eskimo, see? One day he gets into his snowmobile and heads into town. Just as he gets to the outskirts, the snowmobile develops engine trouble, so the Eskimo glides into a nearby service station. The mechanic comes out, takes a long look at the snowmobile, then looks at the Eskimo and says, 'Blew a seal.' And the Eskimo says, 'Nah. That's frost on my mustache.'"

Croaker laughed. "Good one, Rafe." He was always aware of how Rafe's head and shoulders stuck out as he maneuvered through the crowds. He must have been murder to guard when he was mayor. Croaker clapped the tall man on the back. "It's really good to see you away from the bar. What're you doing off the Keys?"

"Provisioning myself." Roubinnet laughed. "Ah well, every once in a while I like to come north and see how the other half of the world's living." To Roubinnet, *up north* meant Boca Raton. "But with the fishing so good I'm surprised to find you here."

"I'm tending to personal business. My niece is very ill."

"My condolences, *compadre*." Roubinnet put a hand on Croaker's shoulder. "Anything I can do?"

"Not unless you can find me a kidney for transplant that matches my niece's antigens."

"I was known as something of a magician when I was mayor," Roubinnet said, "but this is a bit out of my league. Sorry."

"Forget it. It's not your worry."

"But where are you staying up here?"

"I'm not sure yet." His hand slid around the set of keys Bennie had given to him. All of a sudden, he found he'd made up his mind. "No, I'll stay at a friend's house in El Portal."

Roubinnet's face split in a smile. "Ah, now there's a district with history and style—with *soul*." He shook his head sadly. "The nineties has no style—no soul. Instead, there's this big gaping pit into which has fallen all of the musty crap from the fifties, sixties, seventies, and eighties, recycled like a bad dream. Do you take my meaning? Clothes, music, the new hip phrases—even recreation. Video games are back, and so is pinball—very low-tech. Beat poetry's returned to its status as being tragically hip, and coffeehouses are cool again. Which reminds me, I'd better get out all my old Kerouac." He laughed. Roubinnet had the kind of laugh that made you want to laugh along with him, a natural politician's innate gift.

His mood quickly sobered. "There's worse, though. Drug-wise, heroin's in again." He gave Croaker a rueful shake of his head. "All in all, consider this. I'm telling you it's the invasion of the cultural body-snatchers."

They walked out of the mall. Heat, humidity, and brilliant sunshine hit them like a fist. They began to stroll toward their cars. Croaker spent a bad couple of moments debating with himself. He did not want to involve anyone in this deal with Majeur, but he desperately needed information. And when it came to the scoop on people in southern Florida, Rafe Roubinnet was the man. His stint as mayor of Miami had made him privy to the inner workings of the city and, indeed, the state as a whole that few people got to glimpse, let alone master. And consensus was that Roubinnet had mastered them. That meant he knew the dirt on everyone who mattered in Florida—and probably all of Central and South America as well.

When they got past the jostle of people, Croaker said, "I've got something to ask you."

"Shoot."

"You know an attorney named Marcellus Rojas Diego Majeur?"

Roubinnet's clear blue eyes looked startled. "Lew, *mi compadre*, is this a casual inquiry or something of a more substantive nature?"

Croaker met Roubinnet's gaze. "The latter."

The restaurateur pursed his lips. "In that case, may I ask what kind of deep water you have ventured into?" His gaze was as intense as it was curious.

"I'm not sure yet," Croaker admitted. "What's the deal with Majeur?"

Roubinnet looked off into the distance, where valets for T.G.I. Friday's were busily parking cars. "This counselor is hardwired into the Colombian drug lords—not the ones who've been taken down recently with all the fanfare and press coverage. No, no. Majeur's clientele is so discreet, they don't seem to exist. I mean, even the professional vultures at *Hard Copy* don't have a clue these boys are on the face of the planet."

"Meaning?"

"Meaning," Roubinnet said, "that his clients are protected at such a high level, you get up there and right away you get a helluva nose bleed. If you're stupid enough to ask too many questions about them, they cart you away on a stretcher and chances are rich you're never heard from again."

Croaker thought about this for a moment. "What about a man named Juan Garcia Barbacena?"

"Doesn't ring a bell," Roubinnet said. But something in his eyes didn't quite match his studied nonchalance.

"If you'd heard of him, you'd tell me, wouldn't you?"

The blue eyes held steady; that was the politician in him. "Certainly, *compadre.*"

Croaker shook his head impatiently. "Rafe, this is me. It's okay for you to turn off the bullshit machine."

"I resent that," Roubinnet said.

"I don't know why," Croaker replied. "The machine's got your name on it."

"Hey, *compadre,* back off a pace, okay?"

"Sorry, Rafe. But I'm in a helluva bind and—"

"What kind of bind?" There was genuine concern on Roubinnet's face now. "Look, Lew, you went to bat for me. I don't forget things like that. Whatever I can do to get you out of this situation, just say the word."

"Barbacena."

Those blue eyes showed a snarl of unknown emotion. "Take it from me, Lew, you don't want to know about this man."

"I'm afraid I don't have a choice."

"Is this true?"

"I'm very much afraid it is."

Roubinnet waited while a pack of Q-Tips—retirees with white hair and white shoes—made their agonizingly slow way to their car. Abruptly impatient, he took Croaker aside, into the shade of a stand of trees that divided the parking lot. "Do you know what you're doing, *compadre?*"

Croaker didn't want to think about dire warnings now, even from Roubinnet. The truth was he couldn't afford to. Not when Rachel's life was hanging in the balance. If taking down Juan Garcia Barbacena was the only way he could save Rachel's life, he'd do it. Maybe Jenny Marsh would present another alternative at dinner; or one of Dr. Stansky's colleagues would come through with a suitable kidney. But Croaker knew these were long shots without real odds. Like it or not, reality was resolving itself down a single path: if, at his dinner with Jenny Marsh, she okayed the paperwork on the kidney Majeur had given him, he'd call the lawyer and accept his deal. Rachel was running out of time.

"Rafe," he said softly, "just do me a favor and tell me what you know about this man."

Roubinnet looked around him at the brilliant sunshine flooding the tree-lined parking lot. "This is not making me happy, Lew. And I have to say I'm doing you no favor."

"Granted and noted."

Roubinnet pulled him deeper into the shade of the trees. Beyond, in the drenching sunshine, cars rolled up and down the aisles like sharks along a reef. "Listen to me, Lew," Roubinnet said in a low voice. "Barbacena is a devil. He's a man who controls many things. Drugs are just one of them. Remember I said that heroin was the new drug of the moment? That's his good fortune. He's got ties into the Far East, opium factories that turn out high-grade heroin. He's so low profile he's positively invisible, one of those few people no one can get to."

"You mean he's protected."

"Precisely so."

"Okay. By whom?"

"Politicians. Government. They use him to keep control on rebellions, revolutions, that kind of shit, throughout all of Latin America. Anyone down there needs arms, they call Barbacena."

"He's the man, huh?"

"Lew, I've come to know that look. It's the one you had when you went after those goons who were putting the squeeze on me. Hell, man, you've got to take this seriously. This guy's the real thing." Roubinnet lowered his voice. "Barbacena is tight with all the rebel leaders, all the dissident commanders, all the wannabe-rulers, generals, tin-pot dictators. They kowtow to him because he's their supply line. And whatever secrets they tell him, whatever plans they have, he passes on to his contacts in the South American governments. In return, the government protects him unconditionally. He does whatever the hell he pleases and they turn a blind eye. Get this. They even sell him arms and take a kickback percentage of his profits. Why not? They get fabulously rich off each other. It's the way the world works."

Croaker waited a very long time. A line of sweat rolled down the back of his neck. "Rafe, someone wants this man dead. Badly."

He grunted. "I'm not surprised. From what I hear, Barbacena's made so many enemies they could form their own country. The whole power trip has gone to his head. He believes in the illusion of his own invulnerability. No one is invulnerable in this day and age."

Croaker waited while another group of Q-Tips went slowly by. "Rafe, do you know who has ordered his death?"

"I don't know, *compadre*. But I could fill a whole legal pad with suspects. Whatever, I don't think we'll have to wait long to see if they make good on their order. Word is Barbacena's arriving here in Miami tomorrow at midnight."

"About that. I may need to get close enough to Barbacena to do some sniffing around," Croaker said. "If so, I'll need all the help you can give me."

Surprise was not a word in Roubinnet's lexicon. He nodded. "Just say the word. Barbacena is no friend of mine." He grasped Croaker's hand in his firm, politician's grip. "For you, *compadre*, anything."

On the way down to El Portal, Croaker used the computer to dial into the Motor Vehicle database again. This time he got through. The grape-colored Lincoln was a rental from a local company. Croaker didn't know whether or not to be surprised. He got the company's address and closed down. Since he was just north and east of the location, he decided to go there now. He exited the highway at Atlantic Boulevard and took it west to 441.

Margate was an old, basically working-class area west of Ft. Lauderdale. He turned into a strip mall on the east side of 441. In front of him were, in succession, a Cuban restaurant, a place that sold graveyard monuments, and a shopfront with blacked-out windows called the Margate Gun & Racquet Club. He had to laugh. The name was a wicked jab in the ribs at those condo complexes in more precious areas like Boca that used Yacht & Racquet Club in their names, though they were, in fact, neither. At the southern end of the strip mall was Gold Coast Exotic Auto Rentals.

When he went in, there was a young woman behind the counter. She was chewing gum while leafing through a recent copy of *Allure*. Otherwise, the place was deserted. Fly-specked and sun-bleached posters of Porsches, Ferraris, Lamborghinis, Lincolns, and the like were tacked to the walls, which were panels of plastic with a wood-grain finish. A couple of cheap, swaybacked couches and an old-fashioned metal ashtray stand were what passed for furniture. A plastic ficus tree, drooping in accumulated dust, stood like an arthritic pensioner by the front window. The place had the unmistakable air of quiet desperation.

The young woman looked up at his approach. She was no more than twenty, with permed blonde hair, bright eyes, and pink fingernails as long as knife blades.

"Hi, I'm Vonda." She pointed to a tag that gave her name: VONDA SHEPHERD.

Croaker introduced himself. "I'd like some info on a late-model grape-colored Lincoln Continental."

Vonda's head bobbed like one of those little dogs on the back shelf of a car. "Let me check inventory."

"No, no," he told her. "I'm not interested in renting. I want to know who's rented one from you recently."

"Why?" Her voice had turned wary. "Was it in an accident?"

"Not to my knowledge."

She popped her gum. "Then I guess you're outta luck."

He showed her a badge and her eyes widened. "Oh, wow!"

"Vonda, this is very important. And I can guarantee your boss'll never find out."

"Gee, I'd like to help you."

"Then by all means."

"You don't know my boss. See, the girl who was here before me, she didn't follow the rules and she got shit-canned." She shook her head of bright curls. "I can't show you anything without that court order." She laughed nervously as she pulled at her pink short-sleeved blouse. "I'm sorry."

She looked so wistful standing there. Croaker felt sorry for her pent up in this rat trap of a job. He could read her face because he'd seen so many like her. Right now, she wanted nothing more than to get in her car and drive off. Wherever she might end up, she wouldn't care. All she wanted was to feel the wind in her face and to be away from this drag of a strip mall.

"You come back with a court order, it'll be out of my hands," she said. "I'll show you whatever you want to see."

"Court order," he mused. "Sounds like this's happened to you before."

"Not to me," she said.

"Tell me something, Vonda." He rested his elbows on the countertop. "Would you know one if you saw one?"

"I sure would." She dug out three sheets of coffee-stained paper stapled together, tapped them with her clawlike fingernail. "My boss gave me this copy of one. If it doesn't look just like this, he told me, it's a fake."

He nodded, showing her he was impressed. "Your boss sure seems to have covered all the bases." He also seemed inordinately concerned about court orders. "What's his name?"

"Trey Merli." She spelled it for him automatically, as if she was used to doing it. With a name like that he wasn't surprised.

"Thanks for your help." He paused on his way to the door, as if just remembering something. "By the way, what time do you close?"

"Six-thirty, sharp."

Back outside, he climbed into the T-bird and slipped in an Everly Brothers tape. As the music played, he went east to I-95, got on heading south. He dug out Majeur's business card and, on a hunch, used the computer to hook into Bell South. He spent some time getting access, then gave the software the number where Majeur assured Croaker he could be reached night or day.

He glanced at the "Processing" message. It was clearly going to take some time to run down the number. He put the computer on standby mode.

By the time he got to El Portal, he'd replaced the Everly Brothers with Jay and the Americans. Jay Black started to sing, "Only in America."

Sonia's five-year-old Camaro still sat in her carport. It had a green and blue SAVE THE MANATEE sticker on its rear window. He sat for a moment listening to the T-bird's engine tick over. Every so often the shouts of kids on bicycles floated on the gentle breeze. Down the block, cars on NE Second Avenue passed with uneventful sighs. He stared at the house with its pale blue trim and its cement sea-horses out on the front lawn. The fountain they were holding up seemed to represent Sonia's life. It was cracked and empty, a void waiting to be repaired and filled; waiting for the bright flicker of wings, the soft cheep of songbirds perched on its beautifully curved rim. How little it would have taken to repair that fountain; and how little it would have taken to make Sonia happy. Now, neither would happen. The mossy seahorses and their cracked fountain seemed the very embodiment of the melancholy that hung sus-pended over the place, as if Sonia's restless spirit were still here, waiting to be set free. Maybe, like Bennie's grandfather, she could not make the journey to the nether world until whoever had mur-dered her had been brought to justice.

The Bonita twins.

When it got so hot that the sweat began to roll down Croaker's back, he got out of the car and went up onto the porch. From there, he could see past Sonia's bedroom awning to the side of the house next door. It was pink stucco with a three-foot-high layer of bricks set in. A grapefruit tree in dire need of pruning overhung its near corner.

He put the key in the lock, turned it over. Inside, he could still smell her scent, stronger now, as if the haunting were real and not a romantic figment of his imagination.

"Sonia?"

He said it softly, gently, and knowing that she would not answer did not make his voicing her name any less imperative.

"I'm here," he said, feeling not in the least bit foolish. "I've come back."

The pent air seemed thick and cloying, as if Sonia had used the last of its oxygen during her violent death. Croaker passed the vividly colored furniture on his way to unlock and throw open every window in the house.

In Sonia's bedroom, he kicked off his shoes and threw himself on the bed. The soft afternoon breeze floated in through the open windows, and the awning on the front window deflected enough of the early afternoon sun to keep the room deliciously cool.

The recognition of the bright Caribbean colors in Sonia's bedroom sent a pang of sadness and loss through him. He turned. Through the open side window, he heard an announcer's voice busily describing in detail a video replay of an accident in a NASCAR auto race.

Curious, he got off the bed and pressed his nose to the screen. He found himself looking through the overgrown grapefruit tree into the side of the pink stucco and brick house next door. Someone was listening to ESPN. Croaker glanced at his watch and something clicked in his mind.

He padded around the bed and went out of the house. As he knocked on the front door of the pink stucco and brick house he felt his pulse quicken. This was, more or less, the time of the afternoon when Sonia had been killed. If someone was home and watching TV today, chances were they'd have been doing the same yesterday—the day of the murder. He shook his head as he knocked on the door again.

It finally opened and Croaker found himself looking at a moon-faced man in a wheelchair. He looked to be in his mid-fifties, dark-skinned and balding, with nubby gray tufts of hair over his ears and down the back of his neck. His eyes were watery, possibly from staring at the TV all day. His shoulders were well developed and the hands that lay in his lap were huge and thick-fingered.

He looked up at Croaker expectantly. "What can I do for you?" From behind him, the ESPN announcer was talking excitedly about ambulances, yellow caution flags, and totaled cars.

"Sorry to take you away from your show." Croaker stuck out his right hand. "My name's Lew Croaker. I'm a friend of Sonia Villa-Lobos. You know, your next-door neighbor."

"Oh, sure. My wife knows her better than I do." The man in the wheelchair stuck out his hand. "My name's Leyes. Pablo Leyes. Come on in, if you like. I could do with the company." Then his gaze strayed to Croaker's biomechanical hand and he nodded again. "I've got a little something cool to drink."

Where Sonia's house was bright and sunny, this place was dominated by shadowed gloom. Heavy brown-and-white batik drapes stood guard alongside windows overhung by aluminum awnings. All the colors were shades of brown. The rooms were neat and clean, everything arranged just so, but the furniture dated back to the late 1950s and early 1960s and seemed nearly as neglected as the grapefruit tree outside. Without refinishing and professional repair, most of it would have shown its age a decade ago. Now the brown tweed sofas were tattered and worn on seat cushions and arms, a couple of chairs had poorly mended armrests, and the dining room table had legs so scratched the unstained wood was exposed white as bone.

Leyes had wheeled himself adroitly across floors bared to accommodate his disability. Carpets and rugs would have slowed him down. He emerged from the kitchen with a tray on his lap. It contained a large plastic pitcher of what appeared to be lemonade, and a pair of cheap glasses with little pastel-colored flowers on them. He nodded toward the scarred wooden coffee table. "Would you mind?"

Croaker took the portable computer off the table. It was on, set to an Internet web site.

"When ESPN gets dull, I like to surf the Internet." Leyes slid the tray onto the table and, taking up the remote, killed the sound on the TV. "All kinds of fascinating stuff to learn." Apparently, he didn't want to miss a minute of the car crash's aftermath. "Can't take the place of going out and doing, though. I was always a doer, y'know?"

He poured the chilled liquid and handed Croaker a glass. "Looks like Key limeade, smells like it, too." He winked. "But I'm here to tell you it packs a mighty wallop."

Croaker took a long, thirsty pull and dropped to one of the sofas, as if impelled by the eye-watering strength of the drink. He thought he ought to get the recipe for Bennie.

"That's homemade rum you're drinking, son. One-ten proof, the real stuff." Leyes laughed as he stroked the meat of one arm. "My Estrella makes it, believe it or not." He waved a hand. "Well, my wife's more than capable. Anytime you're sick in body or in spirit, Estrella's the one to see. She's got quite a reputation. Justified as hell, too, I might say, You just ask anyone at Jiffy Tyme Cleaners. Go on. Everyone on Biscayne Boulevard knows her."

Leyes had drained his glass, and taking up the pitcher, he topped off Croaker's glass, then refilled his own. He leaned forward in his wheelchair and pointed at Croaker's biomechanical hand. "Is it true what they say?"

Croaker knew what he meant. "I still feel my real fingers, sometimes. And in my dreams my hand is whole and beautiful as an opened rose."

Leyes nodded. "Worked as a lineman for Bell South. Fell off a damn pole. Stupid filthy accident." He slammed meaty fists into his thighs. "I was supervisor for a while, but it wasn't the same. You know what I mean. They meant well, I guess, but it was a bullshit job all the same. Pushing papers, staring at computer screens. Christ, like to blow your brains out stay at that 'til you retire." He returned to stroking his arm, to comfort himself, Croaker supposed. "I keep asking Estrella if she like go back to Paraguay. She doesn't, though. I would. Never been there, but I've heard so many of her stories I feel like I have." His expression turned wistful. "Asunción's a lot less dangerous than it is around here." He shook his head and slurped his drink. "Think it's not a worry? Pretty dangerous down by Biscayne Boulevard. I wouldn't let Estrella out after dark over there, I can assure you. They say in the fifties 'n' sixties you could hang out at Eighty-sixth and Biscayne all night. At the 8600 Club." His colorless eyes focused on Croaker. "That place was something. Famous as hell. Open all the damn night. But come seven in the morning, they'd throw everybody out into the parking lot for a half hour so they could sweep the joint. That's where the phrase 'eighty-six this guy' came from." He laughed. "No damn fiction."

"I'd like to ask you a question, Mr. Leyes. It's about yesterday. Were you here all afternoon?"

"Sure was. Right here watching ESPN." He smiled. "Always the same, my days. It's okay. That way, I know what to expect."

"You were alone?"

"Yep. Estrella works. Nine to five."

Croaker leaned forward. "Did you see or hear anything?"

"Well, I *thought* I heard something."

"Like . . . ?"

Leyes's moon face screwed up in concentration so badly he looked like he wanted to swallow his nose. "Dunno, really. I thought maybe an engine, then I figured it was coming from the TV. Races, you know." He worried his lower lip. "Later on, maybe that night, I thought, No, it was more like a generator."

"A generator. Could you tell where it was coming from?"

"Seems to me it was from outside Miss Villa-Lobos's house."

"The front?"

Mr. Leyes shook his head. "Nah. That was the odd thing. It was this side. Between her house and mine."

That was the area, Croaker thought, where he and Bennie had found the parallel drag marks on the soft, wet ground.

"What do you think was making this sound, Mr. Leyes?"

Leyes put the cold glass against the meat of his arm. "Maybe it was coming from the panel truck."

Croaker's heart seemed to skip a beat. "What panel truck?"

Leyes shook his head. "The white one. It was pulled up on the concrete path at the side of her house."

"What time was this?"

"Let me see . . ." That scrunched-up face again. "I'd make it after one and before two-thirty. I remember what races was on, that's how I keep track of the time."

Croaker said slowly and carefully, "Did you notice anything about the panel truck other than its color? It's year, make, or model? The license plate?"

"It was white, like I said," Leyes said. "Had a Florida tag, for sure. I remember the colors. Don't know what kinda truck it was, though, except it was American, not one of those Japanese brands."

"How about any writing on it?" Croaker asked. "Was it municipal? Did it have a company name?"

Leyes shook his head. "No. No writing at all that I could see."

"Anything else? Anything at all."

"Yeah," Leyes said. "Come to think of it, there was this little decal on the back. It was the outline of a triangle inside a circle."

Croaker did not go immediately back to Sonia's. Instead, he took the T-bird across El Portal to the address Bell South had given him for Nestor, Sonia's dancer friend. As he drove, he was all but deaf to the music coming out of his speakers. He was thinking of what

Mr. Leyes had seen on the back of the white van—the triangle within a circle, one of the two symbols that had been written in blood inside Sonia's refrigerator; one of the four magic signs Guarani healers took when they were initiated into *Hetá I.* The Bonita twins had been taken in and trained in ritual and magic by Bennie's grandfather; yet, clearly, they were no healers. They were reavers.

Unlike the vast majority of the houses in El Portal, which were neat and trim and freshly painted, Nestor's was in gross need of repair. A handyman's special, if it had been listed for sale.

The original stucco was crumbling, revealing here and there the underpinnings of the concrete block skeleton. Hard to discern just what the color had once been; now it had been reduced to the dull pallor of oatmeal.

A mahogany-skinned woman opened the door to his insistent knock.

"Like to wake the dead, with a hand like that," she said by way of admonition. "And you are?"

"Lew Croaker. I'm a friend of Sonia Villa-Lobos."

Still she hesitated until a watery voice from the interior said, "It's all right, Mrs. Leyes. Let him in."

She was a handsome woman, looking a decade younger than her husband, with huge coffee-colored eyes, high cheekbones, and a generous mouth. A thick crop of hair was tied at the nape of her neck with a hand-worked silver pin. It was black, save for a white streak like nighttime lightning down the center.

An odd assortment of smells assailed him: the sickly sour odor of the infirm, mingled with the cleansing scents of cedar, peppermint, and rosemary. These last rose in slender tendrils from the center of a bronze brazier on a side table.

Estrella Leyes stood aside, a small woman with a fiery countenance. But she was as quick to smile as to defend. "I'm sorry," she said as she closed the door behind him, "but Nestor has trouble with his bills. *Pobrecito.*"

A phlegmy laugh erupted from the corner of the room. "What she means is I'm broke. I haven't enough money left even to pay my rent. But that's okay; I don't have much life left, either."

The voice belonged to a man who, like the house, was in a shocking stage of disrepair. His affliction, however, was irreversible. Skeletal, white as a corpse, he reclined on a dusty rattan chaise lounge that had been overlaid with dingy sheets and rucked cotton blankets. A network of blue veins could be seen pulsing slowly just beneath the tissue-thin veneer of his skin.

"Hush, now," Estrella Leyes said. "Where will that kind of talk get you?"

Nestor swiveled a head around on a stalklike neck. "One step ahead of the process servers."

Once, not so long ago, he must have been an exceptionally handsome man. He had a high, wide forehead and an aquiline nose. But prolonged high fevers had robbed his wide-apart eyes of most of their color. And when he'd danced, surely he'd not been afflicted with the rubicund sores that pocked his cheeks and lips. He was as scabbed over as a chronic drunkard who can't keep his balance.

"I think you should be in a hospital," Croaker said. "If you don't have insurance, I could speak to some—"

"Oh, I could get hooked up to tubes," Nestor said. "I could engage life support with all the fervor of a Baptist to water." He smiled and raised one enervated hand. "But why trust to blind science when I have Mrs. Leyes to heal me?"

"Now I do insist you keep still." Estrella Leyes threw a cautionary look over her shoulder at Croaker as she admonished Nestor: "You need to husband all your strength."

"An odd phrase to apply to me, but I take your meaning nonetheless." Nestor's head dropped back to striped pillows damp with sweat. "What Mrs. Leyes means to say, Mr. Croaker, is that she doesn't trust you to observe the secrets of her healing arts." No doubt because of the advanced nature of his infirmity, he had developed the disconcerting habit of speaking with his eyes closed. In this manner, he seemed no more than a bizarre puppet being manipulated by an unseen force.

"Nonsense!" Estrella Leyes exclaimed, though she took a protective step toward a large reed basket that sat atop a round table.

"Mrs. Leyes," Croaker said gently, "if it will put your mind at ease, I just spoke with your husband. He told me rather proudly of your reputation as a healer."

A shy smile spread across Estrella Leyes's face. "*Si*. That's Pablo."

As she began to unload items from her reed basket, Nestor said, "I haven't seen Sonia today. How is she?"

"Fine," Croaker said. "But since she was called away on business, she asked me to stop by."

"That's most kind of you," Nestor said.

Out of the corner of his eye, Croaker could see that Estrella Leyes had turned to give him a dark and penetrating look. He wanted to smile, to reassure her, but was disconcerted to find that he could not. He seemed drawn in by her mesmerizing gaze until her eyes welled up with tears and she gave a stifled sob.

Nestor turned his head and his pale eyes opened. "Mrs. Leyes?"

"Nothing, *pobre*." She shook her head, not trusting herself to look at him. "I dropped a powder, that's all."

Nestor sighed and his eyes slid closed, as if he no longer had the strength to keep the lids open. As Mrs. Leyes prepared her herbs and powders he dropped into a deep sleep.

"The diseases exhaust him utterly," Estrella Leyes said in sorrow.

Croaker came over to the table to watch her.

Without turning around, she said, "She's dead, isn't she? My little Sonia."

Croaker nodded wordlessly and Estrella Leyes bowed her head. "I could hear her ending in your voice. It was a violent and terrible death."

"How do you know that?"

She lifted hands dark with the stains of her herbs and medicines and moved them around him as if in outline. "A disturbance here . . . and here. You carry around the memory like an overcoat."

He was not even aware he had taken hold of the spirit-stone in his pocket until he felt its unnatural warmth against his palm. He took it out and displayed it for Estrella Leyes.

"I'd like to use this on Nestor," he said softly. "Maybe it will help."

"*Dios*." Her eyes opened wide, and quick as the wind, she curled his fingers around the smooth stone and held them there, clasped tightly.

"Do you know what this is?" she whispered. Her gaze searched his face.

"I pressed this against my niece's chest and she awoke temporarily from a coma, even though the doctors swore it was medically impossible."

Estrella looked fearfully at the dark green stone he held. "It is not wise, *señor*, for you to be carrying such a thing."

"I disagree. Do you know what I found inside Sonia's house?" He dipped his forefinger in a dark powder and, on the tabletop, traced out a triangle inside a circle, a dot within a square.

With a sharply indrawn breath, Estrella Leyes swept away the symbols. In their place, she drew the outline of a human eye, inside which were two irises. Her eyes narrowed as she looked at him. "You know what you should not know. You are no healer."

"Nor am I a reaver," he said. "But the people who made those signs are. And I want them."

"Why?" Though said softly, there was a sharpness to the tone that warned him of the importance of his answer.

"These people murdered Sonia. As you said, her death was violent and terrible." He took a breath, knowing he was about to embark on uncharted waters. "Also, I can feel her restless spirit inside her house."

"You think she cries out for vengeance from beyond the grave?"

This woman was almost better at interrogation than he was, Croaker thought. "No. It wasn't Sonia's way to seek revenge. She hated the thought of violence."

"*Es verdad.*" Estrella Leyes's coffee-colored eyes appeared depthless. Something in her expression softened like the stone cold winter ground at spring's first thaw. He seemed to have passed some kind of test. "Then what are you proposing?"

"Rest," Croaker said. "Eternal rest for her spirit."

Estrella Leyes came closer and, in a hoarse whisper, said, "Who has been teaching you about *Hetá I?*"

"Bennie Milagros. When we covered our faces in soot and buried Sonia. Do you know him?"

"I was acquainted with Humaitá Milagros, his grandfather." Estrella Leyes turned abruptly away. "Everyone for five hundred miles around Asunción knew Humaitá. He was a great and revered Guarani healer."

"Did you go to his funeral?" Croaker asked. "Bennie told me it rained for ten days. He was there for the whole time."

"That's true enough." Estrella Leyes was busying herself with her potions. "He and Bennie had a difficult relationship. But there was an unbreakable bond between them; special among all the grandchildren. Humaitá had a secret name for Bennie he always used when they were together. Sero, he called him. Sero, the mountain. That's how he thought of him. 'The mountain keeps its own counsel,' he told me one day. 'The mountain has its own concept of time and place.' I knew he was speaking about Bennie."

"I also heard that Humaitá drowned in the Paraguay River."

There was a muffled sound as the canister she had been holding fell to the tabletop. Croaker caught her as her knees began to buckle.

"Mrs. Leyes—"

She was so light he could imagine she had the hollow bones of a bird. But she had not fainted. Peering down at her face as he held her, Croaker could see that her eyes had rolled partially up and her eyelids were spasming like someone in REM sleep. She might have been dreaming while awake.

Without conscious thought, he pressed the spirit-stone into the hollow of her throat. Almost immediately, he heard her voice. It was soft, as echoey as if it were coming not from her throat but from somewhere very far away. "I come from a family of Guarani fisherfolk," she said. "And on that terrible day twenty years ago, I was with my father and brothers on the Paraguay. I was twenty-two, already married once and widowed and I was back to working the family trade as I had when I was a child. The sun had not yet risen above the mountains, but the misty air had about it the color of the inside of a pearl shell. I loved that time of the morning. So lovely, the riot of tropical colors muted. And so perfectly still you could hear the fish swimming beneath the water."

Croaker crouched down, Estrella Leyes clasped firmly in his arms. He was afraid. He wanted to wake her from her trance, but he wanted more to hear the oral history she was reciting.

"We found Humaitá's body," she went on. "At first, we thought it had become entangled in the roots of a mass of mangrove that stretched out red and black into the river. The shoulders, chest, and arms were all red. At first, we thought it was the detritus borne on the current, dyed red by the tannin leached from the mangroves. But then we noticed that it was not prone, floating, as it would have been if he'd stumbled and fell.

"He was sitting up, rootlets beneath his armpits. And he was covered in blood. It was clear he had been placed in that spot. Because he was a healer, no animal or bird had touched him. Even the primitive crocodiles kept their respectful distance.

"No one moved except my father. He scrambled off the boat and pulled the body out of its nest of roots. And I remember this so clearly it might have happened this morning: he rolled Humaitá over, belly down in the river, and scrubbed at his face. He scrubbed and scrubbed and all the while he was sobbing like a child in need. I'd never before seen my father weep, and it terrified me. Soon after, on my father's direction, we helped him drag Humaitá onto the boat. His face was so clean that it was impossible to believe I'd seen what I had: when we'd found him, each cheek was painted in blood. On his left cheek was a triangle in a circle; on his right cheek was a dot within a square."

Estrella Leyes's eyelids ceased to spasm and her body went limp in Croaker's arms. A moment later, she stared up at him out of her dark eyes. She seemed calm and serene, as if waking from a long, rejuvenating slumber.

Croaker palmed the spirit-stone. "Mrs. Leyes, are you okay?"

She lifted a hand and slowly traced something on his forehead with the tip of a slender forefinger: an oval with two dots inside—the double-irised eye. "He wasn't destroyed. I can feel Humaitá's spirit in you." She looked up at Croaker in wonder. "All these years

I held my peace about his death because my father swore us to secrecy. He made us swear by the story we all gave as testimony: that we'd found Humaitá's body floating facedown in the river."

"Why did your father do that, Mrs. Leyes?" Croaker asked. "Why did he lie and make you give false testimony?"

"Because he'd seen the symbols and he was afraid."

"Afraid of what?"

"He knew the boys who had taken those symbols as their own. Everyone did: they'd become almost like Humaitá's adopted grandsons. And they'd killed him. They'd left their symbols on his flesh to prove it."

"Antonio and Heitor," Croaker said. "The Bonita twins."

She nodded.

"He was their mentor; he loved them like a father. Didn't they love him in kind?"

"What do those two know of love?" Estrella Leyes said. "They have been severed from the Family of Man; and God has turned His face from their countenance."

Despite his First World upbringing and education, Croaker felt a chill lance through him. "But why did they kill him?"

"After Humaitá had taught them everything they needed to know, they had no more use for him." Estrella Leyes seemed to shudder in his arms. "You see, I believe Humaitá knew how evil they were. His hubris was in believing he could deliver them from this overriding evil. His lasting greatness was that he believed in the goodness in all people. But I think this is what destroyed him. The Bonitas were beyond change. And, the tragedy is, in trying to change them, all Humaitá managed to do was to give them more power. Terrible power." She clutched at him. "You called them reavers and you are right."

She made a sign and he lifted her back onto her feet. "This spirit-stone you carry, it belonged to Humaitá, didn't it?"

Croaker nodded.

She put both hands over his right hand. "Keep it safe. Keep it close to you." Her gaze raked his face and her voice turned urgent. "Promise me this because you will find the reavers—or they will find you."

"I promise."

Estrella Leyes looked deep into his eyes. Whatever she saw there must have satisfied her because she nodded and went back to her herbs and potions.

As she worked, Croaker said, "Tell me about the four symbols."

Once, Croaker had seen a troupe of Cambodian dancers perform.

138

Estrella Leyes had extraordinarily long fingers, and she used them as these dancers had, giving distinct expression and a sense of presence to the most mundane gestures.

"The triangle within a circle is the sign of man; fire; death." Her fingertips blackened as she broke dried fungi into spore dust. "The dot within the square, the sign of woman; water; resurrection." She combined the black spores with a yellow powder that smelled vaguely of cacao. "A cross within three concentric circles denotes a bird; flight; journeys; the heart of the universe."

"And the fourth?" Croaker asked. "The sign Humaitá took as his own?"

Her features were creased in concentration as she poured a brown liquid into the paste she had made. "The double-irised eye represents the dreams we see with our inner eye"—she broke off long enough to point to a spot in the center of her forehead"—our Third Eye." Her fingers were like a pair of fans as she spread them in an arc. "Always, the dreams guide us. This is what *Hetá I* means. The Many Waters are the paths of the Innermind. The Innermind is revealed to healers by dreams." She broke open a small, withered branch and extracted the white, cottony material from its pith, added it to the tangy brew. It smelled of the rich humus along the banks of the Paraguay. "These are reckonings of the past, paintings of the present, and portents of the future."

"I've dreamed of the double-irised eye," Croaker told her.

She seemed unsurprised. "And you will dream of it again," she promised.

"Whatever you're doing here," he said from over her shoulder, "will it work?"

Estrella Leyes shrugged. "There are some things God has determined are fixed." She shook her head. "I am foolish, perhaps. Like Humaitá, I attempt the impossible." She turned with a vessel filled with a brackish liquid clasped between her hands. "This is something you should remember when you come face-to-face with the Bonitas. Their place in the universe is fixed. It cannot be changed, by you or anyone else. Humaitá tried. He thought he recognized the spark of humanity in them and they killed him. Do not make the same mistake."

She went to where Nestor lay slack and grimly pallid, and gently woke him. Croaker held him upright while she put the vessel to his lips and made him drink. But neither her carefully mixed potion nor Humaitá's spirit-stone pressed to his bony chest could stem the voracious tide of the opportunistic viruses eating him alive.

3

When Croaker returned to Sonia's house, there was someone waiting for him on the front porch.

"You the boyfriend?"

He was a handsome man in his thirties, with clean, smooth features. His hair, gelled and slicked back into a ponytail, was the color of burnt caramel. He was slim and agile, which said to Croaker that he was athletic. He wore a mushroom-colored silk suit of expensive manufacture and, incongruously, a pair of Keds. Beneath the suit was a cream Versace polo shirt with two large gold-and-black enamel buttons. He was imposing, in the manner in which he seemed to confront head-on whatever life put before him. What was most startling about him, however, was his amber-colored eyes.

"Who wants to know?" Croaker responded as he reached the porch.

The slim man hit him so hard and so fast Croaker was stumbling backward before he even felt the blow. His ears rang as he gripped the porch rail, and there was a growing numbness on the left side of his jaw.

"Next time I'll put you all the way down."

Croaker could see that the amber-eyed man was both surprised and pissed off that the punch hadn't decked him. "I ask the questions here. This's my sister's house."

"You're Sonia's brother?"

"Carlito." Raw hostility oozed out of him like poison from a snake bite. "I see it didn't take you long to move in, Anglo."

Croaker came off the porch railing like it was the top rope in a boxing ring. "My name's Lew Croaker. And this was the most convenient place to stay . . . for the time being." How to handle the delicate matter of Sonia's death? As far as Croaker knew, only he, Bennie, and Maria knew the score. "Maybe we should talk inside."

The slim man had about him the predatory aspect of a fox. *"Madre de mentiras,* what could we have to talk about?"

Croaker shrugged as he opened the door with his key. "Come on in," he called.

The amber-eyed man walked with a minimum of effort, as if he were an expert diver arrowing through water. Inside, he craned his neck. "My sister here?"

Croaker shut the door behind them. "Carlito, when was the last time you saw Sonia?"

The slim man stared at him with his amber eyes. He had about him an uncanny stillness.

"Or spoke to her?"

"What is this, the Spanish Inquisition? You have no business asking me these questions."

Croaker gestured to one of a pair of couches covered in tropical cotton. "Why don't you have a seat?"

Amber eyes seemed to glow in the last of the late afternoon light. "What the hell is this all about?"

Seeing no easy way into this, Croaker said, "I'm afraid your sister is dead."

The other man seemed to unwind in stages until he was sitting bent over on the rolled arm of the sofa. "When?"

"Sometime yesterday afternoon." Croaker took a breath. "She was murdered."

The handsome head snapped up. "Murdered? *¡Madre de mentiras!* How? By whom?"

"She was decapitated. I don't know yet by whom."

"What're you, a detective?"

"As a matter of fact I am." Croaker showed him one of the official badges.

Tears glittered in the amber eyes as he nodded. "What happened to her body?"

Croaker thought of the white van with the symbol painted on back and the parallel tracks he'd found around the side of the house. That's where Antonio and Heitor had sliced off Sonia's head. There was no reason to tell her brother, who was already on a short fuse, what had happened to her and every reason not to.

"I have no idea," Croaker said without inflection.

The slim man grunted. "Some detective!"

Carlito's reactions came into focus. Something about them seemed the slightest bit off, Croaker thought. What was he missing? Had Sonia and her brother been estranged?

"What is it you want here?" The amber eyes blazed with naked enmity. "What's in it for you?"

"Keep quiet a moment," Croaker said.

As the amber-eyed man came off the sofa arm and took a threatening step toward him, Croaker put up his hand. "Just listen," he admonished. This gave the other pause, and in that moment, Croaker said, "Can you feel her?"

The amber-eyed man spread his hands, frowning.

"It's your sister's spirit." Croaker turned slowly in a circle. "She's still here, she's still waiting."

"For what?" Maybe mysticism wasn't his thing. On the other hand, he wasn't laughing.

"For a way home," Croaker said. "She's held here, without peace. Until I find out who murdered her." He looked into Carlito's face, saw eyes hard as chipped stone. "To answer your first question, yeah, I was the boyfriend, or I would have been if she hadn't been murdered." He took a breath. "She was a beautiful woman in every way."

"So, what is it, *maricone*, you were fucking her brains out?"

Croaker took the other man totally off guard. With titanium and polycarbonate fingers Croaker crushed his suit lapels and expensively woven cotton polo as he rammed him across the room until his back fetched up with an explosive bang against the far wall.

Croaker was so close he could faintly smell the steak and grilled onions Carlito had eaten for lunch. "A man who doesn't respect women is a pig," Croaker said in idiomatic Spanish. "But a man who doesn't respect his own sister is no man at all."

A weird pale light flared in Carlito's eyes and just as quickly fled.

"And don't call me *maricone*." Croaker kept to the idiomatic Spanish.

A slow, crafty smile spread across the slim man's face. "You don't talk like an Anglo. And you surely don't think like one, either."

Maybe that was as close as a man like Carlito—hostile, arrogant, *muy macho*—could get to an apology.

Croaker let him go and stepped back. Carlito stared down at the front of his jacket, which looked like it had been run over by a mountain bike.

"You know," he said slowly and evenly, "I've killed men for less than this." A gravity knife bloomed in his left hand. The stiletto blade flicked upward into dead air, not a threat in any way. They'd been through their macho phase, these two men, and it had ended, more or less, in a draw. The tilted blade was just an illustration to a story he was telling. "I slit their throats from one end to the other and watched the blood pump out in a slow, sensual rhythm."

Croaker was getting the measure of him. He was like a child, really, in the way in which he studied Croaker's reactions to his outrageous behavior. Croaker could imagine a young Caligula reciting a list of his egregious sins, greedy for reaction from those older and more easily shocked than he. But, like Caligula, this lightning rod of a man was a daft and dangerous child, never to be taken lightly or underestimated.

"Then, when their brothers and sons came after me," he went on, "I'd do the same to them. I'd lie awake at night, creating a shining path, willing them to come over the wall like evil dreams, to invade my house." He smiled that sly smile. "You see, I made them sin. I never invaded their house, I never laid a hand on their property as they did mine." The knife point flicked upward, sent spinning in a blur a ray of vagrant sunlight. "I made them sin and then I punished them for it until my blade ran red with their blood."

Croaker went into the kitchen, as much to take a break from the overpowering personality as to slake his thirst. There was half a six-pack of Corona beer in a cupboard, but he was reluctant to put it on ice. The interior of the refrigerator was still painted with Sonia's blood. He found an open bottle of Cuervo Gold tequila, and he poured double shots into a pair of glasses. He came back into the living room, handed one to Sonia's brother.

When the two of them had drunk some, he said, "I'd like your permission to stay here." It was the formal construction he would have used if he'd asked Carlito for his sister's hand in marriage.

The slim man had put away the gravity knife. "This is not a small thing you ask." He stared into the depths of the pale liquor. "But it is not a small thing you are doing for Sonia—and for me."

"I understand, and I appreciate your kindness." Croaker switched topics and tones. "What I'm trying to follow up on is a possibility Heitor and Antonio Bonita might have murdered Sonia. You know them?"

"You have already begun your investigation, I see." The slim man sat down on the couch. A lozenge of late afternoon sunlight struck him across the face, firing his burnt caramel hair. "What makes you suspect them?"

"The manner of your sister's murder. Decapitation seems to be their specialty."

Amber eyes regarded Croaker evenly. "How much do you know about Heitor and Antonio?"

Croaker sat in a facing chair. "Not enough."

"I was in business with them once—about five years ago."

"Five years—then you must know Bennie Milagros."

The amber-eyed man was so still it was possible to see the pulse in the side of his neck just above the collar of his sleek Versace shirt. "Oh, yes," he said at last. "Benito is well known to me." His

143

head swiveled and the amber eyes flashed briefly. "You are friendly with him?"

"Perhaps so."

"You are a cautious man. That is all to the good." He nodded. "With a man such as he all due caution is warranted."

"What do you mean?" Croaker said.

The slim man seemed not to hear him as he took a contemplative sip of his tequila. He switched to idiomatic Spanish. "You must understand, these men—Heitor and Antonio, the Bonitas—make it their business to be in anything that's dangerous enough to give them big profit margins: drugs, war matériel, black-market telecommunication and computer components, semiconductor chips, girls, murder-for-hire, white slavery—yes, even that in this day and age. But what makes their operation unique is that they're never connected directly with any of these industries." He waved a hand in the air. "Oh, I know what you're thinking, Detective—all these international criminals hide behind a maze of offshore and foreign shell corporations. True. But the Bonitas go one better. They own nothing. Instead, they set other people up to be the manipulators behind the maze of shell corporations. They give a good deal of autonomy to these men as they become movers and shakers. As long as you perform you're left pretty much alone with your operation, your bottom line, and your monthly payments—sixty-five percent of profit. Another thirty or so percent is plowed back into the business. Which leaves three percent, five if you're very clever, left over at the day's end."

"I assume," Croaker said, "you're speaking about yourself."

"The thing is," the slim man continued, not quite ignoring the statement, "their scheme is insidious. I mean, the more successful you are at running what they've set up for you, the more you're left alone and the stronger the illusion becomes that you're actually in control. But it's all a lie, you see. In reality, you're nothing more than a patsy. You're there to make money for the Bonitas. If you do that, well and good. You go home with your pittance. If you stumble and the bottom line falls, they come and cripple you and spend a damned long time at it. In the meantime, you take all the risk—and if the operation blows up in your face, if, one black day the *federales* come pouring through your back door, you take the fall. There's nothing whatsoever to link the Bonitas to the laws you've broken. And, if you're stupid enough to rat them out, they'll hunt you down and make you die in any one of a variety of very unpleasant ways."

"Like, for instance, decapitating you."

The amber-eyed man hefted his empty glass. "Is there any more of this?"

"On the kitchen counter."

In a moment, he returned with the bottle and a full glass. He set the tequila on the coffee table between them like a signpost.

The sun had dropped below the horizon, and Carlito's face was wreathed in shadow. He appeared even more handsome, a magnet for vulnerable girls. But in this twilight, the sinister aspect he cultivated like a pet croc had become pronounced. Croaker could imagine him as a gunrunner or a drug dealer for the Bonitas, moving like a dancer through glittering circles of money and power, gorging on the role, becoming one with it. It was difficult, if not impossible, to leave the orbit of a supernova without incurring profound and permanent damage. Croaker wondered what form of damage Carlito had suffered.

Despite the open windows, it seemed abruptly stifling in the small house. Croaker got up, stood looking out into the street. The sky was orange and purple, but below the treetops sharp shadows had crept across the lawns and parked cars, making of them inky shapes that held unfathomable secrets.

"What did you do for Heitor and Antonio Bonita?"

"I ran guns and munitions. The usual stuff."

He said it too quickly and Croaker knew he was lying. There was nothing usual about this man.

Croaker said, "How did it end?"

"Badly." The amber-eyed man had come, silent as a cat, to stand beside him.

In unspoken consent, perhaps, they had neglected to turn on any lights inside the house. What illumination existed came from the streetlights. To a passerby—if there had been one—they might very well have been mistaken for ghosts, disembodied faces peering out the plate glass window of a newly deserted house.

"I was in love once," Carlito said from close beside Croaker. His voice was thin, almost reedy, barely above a whisper. "It seems so long ago. Five years; an eternity." He lapsed into a brooding silence from which Croaker was reluctant to rouse him. Croaker knew from hard experience that painful memories needed their own time to work themselves loose.

The amber-eyed man cleared his throat, as if he were getting rid of excess emotion. "Anyway, I asked her to marry me. She was a good girl, this woman. Pure in heart and spirit. She saw something in me . . ." He waved his glass and tequila sloshed around its sides. "No matter. She didn't know what I did, not precisely, but she didn't like it. She said she could smell a stink on me, and when I said to her, 'What stink? I'm no damned river fisherman,' she held me very close and whispered in my ear. 'The stink I smell is not on your body, it comes from your soul.' "

The slim man downed the last of his tequila. For a moment, he seemed inclined to fetch the bottle, but then he changed his mind. "Stupid girl, I thought. What does she know? But then, lying beside her at night, I would fall into bad dreams and I would awake in the morning with the stink of burning flesh in my nose. This went on for weeks. And finally, I realized I was dreaming of my own flesh burning." He turned to Croaker. "That's when I knew she was no stupid girl. She was very, very special. She smelled the corruption on me, and I thought, She must hate this smell. Why does she stay with me? How can she love me? Because, *señor*, sex is easy. It's like breathing, what could be more natural? But love is hard. Love does things to you you have no hope of understanding. Love changes you even when you have no intention of being changed."

He glanced down at his empty glass and away again, into the anonymity of the shadowed street. "And then, finally, I understood. She was waiting. Waiting for me to come to hate the stink as much as she did."

The amber-eyed man had put aside his now useless glass. His hands had turned into fists and he pressed them onto the window-sill as he leaned against it. "I wanted to change, I really did." Tension corded his ramrod-straight arms, distorting the expensive fabric of his suit. "But everything in life has a price. Some things in life you think you must have, but the price, if you knew it beforehand, you'd never, ever pay."

He took a deep breath. "God or something like Him—Fate, per-haps—took this woman away from me."

Croaker watched as he turned and walked away from the illumi-nation of the streetlights into the darkness of his sister's house. He wanted to ask a question that burned in the back of his throat, but the air was still too charged with the agony of memories. A great evil was entangled here like a web that crossed time to damage lives beyond any hope of repair.

"You're welcome to this place," Carlito said in a strangled voice. "I want no part of it. If you feel Sonia's spirit here, all the better. It seems good that she can speak to you in this manner."

Croaker knew he was thinking of the way in which this woman—who had died five years ago—had spoken to him. At last, he came away from the window and, his eyes adjusted to the gloom, found

Carlito withdrawn to a corner, as if needing to fend off all the bad karma he'd stirred up.

"Do you believe in spirits?" Croaker asked him.

"I'd like to think so." Those lambent amber eyes focused on him. "Yes."

Of course he would, Croaker thought. He'd give anything to hear this woman's voice again, even in his dreams.

"They're both waiting, aren't they," Carlito whispered. "Rosa and now Sonia. They're joined somehow."

Croaker felt a coil of electricity at the answer to the question that was burning the back of his throat. "Did you say her name was Rosa?"

"*Si*. Rosa Milagros."

Christ, Croaker thought. *That's how he knew Bennie. He fell in love with his sister and she was decapitated by the Bonitas.* Maybe this explained the subtle strangeness of his earlier reactions: he'd been living Rosa's murder all over again.

Carlito's eyes were wide and staring. It was as if he was talking to himself, as if Croaker were not there at all. "I'm damned now, I know that. Rosa could have saved me. I have done things . . . I continue to do things. . . ."

He turned his face away and, crossing the room in three huge strides, flung open the door and was gone.

As Croaker drove north on I-95 he flicked on a tape of Jan & Dean's greatest hits. Surf music from the glorious 1960s. What better songs to think by? On either side of him thrill seekers in Camaros and Firebirds wove in and out of the multiple-lane traffic, passing on the right whenever they saw an opening. They had a habit of cutting back in inches from the trailing car's front grille. If you traveled I-95 regularly it didn't pay to think of the highway's accident ratio.

He wanted to turn over in his mind the startling revelation that Sonia's brother had been in love with Bennie's sister, Rosa. What role did he play in this widening web? It was clear to Croaker that he knew more about Antonio and Heitor than he had revealed.

One thing was for sure: the moment Carlito went out the door, Croaker felt as if a dark and dangerous cloud had vanished.

He got off the highway at Atlantic Boulevard and went west. Jan & Dean had segued from "Surf City" into "New Girl in School." Before his dinner date with Jenny Marsh in West Palm Beach, he had another stop to make. He turned into the strip mall off Highway 441 and ejected the cassette of Jan & Dean.

He dug out his computer and checked on the status of the request for information on the private phone number Majeur had given him.

The database had spewed out a paragraph's worth of information. First off, it was a cellular number. No surprise there. But the strange thing was it was not listed in Majeur's name. The individual the number was billed to was one Benito Milagros.

Bennie. And his mysterious, secretive midnight run tomorrow. Was it a coincidence that Juan Garcia Barbacena was coming into Miami at precisely midnight tomorrow?

Croaker sat for a long time in the strip mall while traffic whizzed by in either direction. Black palms danced against an indigo sky. Illumination from overhead sodium lights threw the hoods of parked cars into sharp relief. At night, the blacked-out windows of the Margate Gun & Racquet Club reflected the next-door granite monuments with their maudlin sentiments carved for all eternity. Croaker was unpleasantly reminded of his meeting with Majeur in the cemetery, and that brought back into focus what he was going to have to do in order to save Rachel's life.

He punched in Bennie's number.

"*Hola!*"

"Bennie, it's me."

"*Amigo*, what's up? Any news on your niece?"

"Status quo." Croaker noticed he was gripping his cell phone too tightly. "Bennie, you know a lawyer named Majeur?"

"No."

"Marcellus Rojas Diego Majeur."

"Lewis, I think with a name like that I'd remember him if I knew him. Which I don't."

"Rafe had heard of him."

"Roubinnet?" Was that a wary note Croaker detected in Bennie's voice? "What're you doing hanging out with him?"

"I ran into him is all," Croaker said. "But he told me this Majeur's wired into heavy-duty drug people."

"Then he must be." Bennie's voice sounded abruptly distant. "If Roubinnet says so."

"You two on the outs? Didn't you want to back him for a second term as mayor?"

"That was a while ago, Lewis. Times change. People, too."

"Listen, Bennie—"

"I gotta go. Sorry. The Colombian delegation I'm expecting's at the door. Later, *amigo*. And watch who you hang with."

"Bennie, I don't know whether I can make that run we spoke of yesterday."

Silence on the other end of the line. But Bennie had not hung up.

"Hey, what's up with you, *amigo?*" Croaker heard the brittle tone to the voice. "I'm counting on you."

"I know, Bennie. But something's come up and I—"

"Now, listen. You gave your word. This is too damn important. What the fuck's changed since yesterday, huh? I think—know what I think, *amigo?* You been listenin' to evil little bees buzzin' in your ear."

"You wouldn't mean Rafe."

"Face-to-face," Bennie snapped. "You an' me. I can, like, blow these fuckin' Colombians off for a couple hours. All they seem to be interested in anyway is yapping like dogs among themselves."

"Okay. Meet me in the lobby of the Royal Poinciana Hospital. That's in Palm Beach."

"Good enough. Take me, what, ninety minutes? An' don't, like, be talking to anyone in the meantime."

"What, like Rafe?" But Bennie had already broken the connection.

Croaker put down the phone. Friction between Bennie and Rafe? What the hell was going on? Bennie said he didn't know Majeur, yet phone company records clearly showed Majeur's cell phone billed to Bennie. Why was Bennie lying? And what the hell was so important about his midnight run? This was a Bennie he hadn't seen before.

He struggled to remind himself that there were many aspects of Bennie's life he knew nothing about. As close as he might have become to Bennie, how well did he really know him? Surprises were popping up daily. Suddenly the world seemed to have been turned on its head with the possibility that his friendship with Bennie held some dark and sinister hidden agenda.

He got out of the car and stowed the computer in his trunk. From the same hidden bay, he began stuffing his pockets with small metallic and plastic items. He needed to deal with the job at hand, and so he cleared his mind of all the questions for which he had, as yet, no answers.

It was just after seven. Gold Coast Exotic Auto Rentals was closed for the day. Vonda had been right on the money.

He strolled around to the back of the mall, where the deliveries and garbage pickups for the complex were made. He located Gold Coast's rear door and checked it out. A nearby sodium streetlight would point an unmistakable finger at anyone in the immediate vicinity. He had a cure for that. He worked on the base of the light for three or four minutes with his stainless-steel nails, using them as pick and wire cutters. The light winked out. Shadows closed in as if starved by the stark glare.

As expected, the rear door was alarmed. Croaker had a cure for that, as well. When he had located the Bell South junction box for the rental company, he pried open the metal door. After verifying the alarm system was hardwired into the phone lines, he cut the telephone cables.

Quickly, using a stainless-steel nail, he picked the lock on the rear door and slipped silently inside. The rental office was dark, the street and traffic lights from out front the only illumination. It smelled dankly of mildew and the musty electronic charge of machinery.

He kept his head down and crept behind the counter. He saw a small Miami Hurricanes pennant, perhaps Vonda's, in a dusty jam jar, along with some other miscellaneous souvenirs. A woman's sweater, old and moth-eaten, lay folded on the shelf beneath, along with a well-used nail buffer, bottles of spectacularly colored nail polish, and one of those small, collapsible umbrellas.

Farther on, he came to the computer terminal. He was about to turn it on when he felt something. A faint but discernible aura of heat was emanating from the back of the computer. He squinted at his watch. Eighteen minutes after seven. Vonda had told him she closed at six-thirty, sharp. Even allowing for a few minutes of over-time, the computer should have been cold by now.

He fired up the computer and right away he knew there was a problem. The software the company was using booted up well enough, but if it was to be believed, there were no files, no directories, no lists of names. The software was virgin, as clear of data as it had been the day it had been installed. Someone had purged the hard drive of memory, and judging by the temperature of the machine, it had been done within the last fifteen minutes.

He searched the nearby area for a tape backup or floppy disks, knowing full well he wouldn't find them. Anyone clever enough to purge a hard drive would take or destroy the tape and floppies as well.

It was on his hunt for the backups that he came upon Vonda. Or, more accurately, all that remained of her. Her head, severed as neatly and expertly as Sonia's, was lying in wait for him. Covered in shadows, it stared at him from a shelf as if it were another of her own souvenirs. Blood ran along the rim of the shelf, looking for an indentation off which to drip.

Croaker felt as if he had been kicked in the stomach. He sat back on his heels, trying to breathe deeply. He needed to get back his equilibrium. He closed his eyes for a moment. Immersed in darkness, he could hear the low wash of the traffic going by outside. Not a voice, not a dog bark disturbed the almost absolute silence.

He stared at Vonda's head and his breath caught in his throat. He had to blink to make sure it wasn't a trick of the shadows, that he wasn't hallucinating, but there it was. A black three-inch floppy disk was wedged between her clamped jaws. As Croaker moved closer, he saw the floppy had a label. Something was written on it and he moved slightly to read it:

LOOKING FOR THIS, DETECTIVE?

He raised his hand, trying to pry the floppy from between Vonda's lips. He pulled hard and the entire head dropped into his lap. He should have laughed at the absurdity of the situation, but it was too sad.

The moment was positively surreal. Vonda's head in his lap, the eyes staring up at him, looking blankly for help. And above them, in the center of her forhead, a symbol drawn in blood: a dot within a square.

The Bonitas.

With an effort, he maintained his grip on reality and peered down at her mouth. It looked as if someone had Krazy Glued her teeth to the floppy. Curiouser and curiouser. *This cannot be happening,* he thought. *Next thing you know, I'll see the White Rabbit racing past me, muttering "I'm late, I'm late for a very important date! No time to say Hello, Good-bye! I'm late, I'm late, I'm late!"*

Carefully, he extruded his stainless-steel nails, chipped the floppy free of the glue. He pocketed the floppy, took Vonda's head by the steellike tendrils of her permed hair and replaced it on the shelf. Then he froze. He'd heard something—a soft footfall, perhaps, or the furtive movement of a body. *Someone was here!* Not a creature with white furry legs and a pocket watch. Someone with a dark and dangerous psyche.

Antonio or Heitor?

He listened beyond the throb of blood pulsing in his veins. Nothing. *Wait,* he cautioned himself. *Just wait and listen.*

Ghostly images of exotic cars appeared and just as quickly vanished off the tacky walls in the headlights of the traffic outside. Dust motes floated through the air as if dislodged by restless spirits. Voices drifted in from out front. A car door slammed, an engine coughed to life, and headlights swung across his field of vision.

At precisely that moment, he heard the noise again. He turned his head away from the lights, but he could see nothing in the deep gloom that, a moment later, returned to the interior. He heard a slow drip and thought that perhaps Vonda's seeping blood had found its way off the shelf. Out of the corner of his eyes, he saw a flash, as of something metallic. It was at the far end of the office, moving from left to right, toward the rear. Someone *was* in here with him. Someone who, having murdered Vonda, had then purged the computer's hard drive, and left him the ballsy note. Someone who knew him, knew he'd be here.

Which one? Antonio or Heitor? He wondered whether it mattered.

It was just about then he heard a sharp crack as of glass shattering and knew he'd run out of time. He risked a glance above the top of the counter, heard and saw nothing in response. Still crouching, he crab-walked as fast as he was able behind the counter until he came to the other end.

There, he could see a windowpane had been smashed out, leaving only shards hanging from the edges of the frame. From outside, he heard something that sounded like a heavy-duty car engine. And beneath it, another noise, deep and pulsing . . . a generator!

He levered himself through the jagged opening, out into a section of the rear of the strip mall hidden from the area near Gold Coast's back door. He emerged just in time to see a white panel truck jouncing away from him toward the far entrance to the highway. Maneuvering between the glass fragments strewn all over the concrete apron, he began running very hard, all the while trying to read the rear tag.

He was gaining on the panel truck, and now he struck out at an angle, anticipating its turn onto 441. The truck slowed for an instant to better take a speed bump just before the exit, and Croaker left his feet, leaping with his left arm extended. His biomechanical fingers struck the rear bumper, flaying paint and plastic until they grasped and took hold.

He tried to regain his feet but the truck lurched forward over the speed bump and his hip and knee struck the blacktop with a sickening jolt. His right hand fumbled for a hold on the plastic bumper but could find none. The panel truck had reached the exit and he had only an instant to gain a less tentative purchase. He struggled to pull himself up onto the rear bumper.

He had one foot and the opposite knee on the bumper, but right then the panel truck screeched as the brakes came off and it slewed in a screaming right-hand turn out into traffic.

Centrifugal force hit Croaker like a mule kick in the small of his back, and his arm was almost wrenched clean out of its socket. His foot slid along the slick bumper top and gave out onto whistling air. It dragged along the blacktop, sparks flying from his shoe sole, and he just missed having his kneecap smashed. If he didn't get himself up onto the back of the truck, he'd be flayed alive. But he was not about to let go, not when he was this close to the murderers.

The truck was weaving dangerously in and out of traffic. Horns blared angrily, and behind him, Croaker could hear the protesting squeal of jammed-on brakes.

He heaved himself upward, swinging his legs with all the force he could muster, and hooked his biomechanical hand over the left-hand door handle. A moment later, he got his feet planted on the bumper. He clung there for a moment, shivering, as if he were on a sheer rock face. Wind buffeted him, and his upper body rattled painfully against the metal of the rear doors as the truck continued to weave back and forth between lanes. He did not want to look down at the blurred road. That was when he saw the mystic symbol—a triangle within a circle—just as Mr. Leyes had described it.

The panel truck must have been doing seventy. Croaker braced himself against the left-hand door. His biomechanical fingers were wrapped securely around the handle. He reached up and grasped the handle of the right-hand door, jerked it down, and pulled hard.

It slammed all the way open, taken by the back-rush of wind. At that moment, the panel truck swerved into the next lane and Croaker almost lost his balance. One foot slipped off the plastic bumper and only the strength of his biomechanical hand kept him from being pitched headlong onto the fast receding road.

He had to use all his concentration to haul himself back up onto his precarious perch. That was when the panel truck screeched to a jarring halt. Gravity and momentum warred with each other for a split second and he felt as if he were in free fall. Then gravity won out and he was slammed with tremendous force into the left-hand door.

Almost immediately, the truck lurched into gear and accelerated hard again, putting more strain on his biomechanical fingers to hold him fast as he slammed into the rear. Half-dazed, he felt himself being jerked sideways as a fist grabbed his shirtfront. His head came around and he found himself staring into a pair of amber eyes, as familiar as they were baleful. The face was as handsome and predatory as a fox's. Hair the color of burnt caramel sprouted from atop a high forehead with the wildness of a cockscomb. It was Carlito!

Wide lips pursed as the amber-eyed man said, "So this is the detective!"

A white-knuckled fist slammed into Croaker's face. Stars exploded behind his eyes, and if it wasn't for the passing streetlights flickering off the arced blade of a scalpel, he might have missed it. The scalpel, held in the amber-eyed man's right fist, was coming right at his throat. He shook his head, trying to clear it. The amber-eyed man smiled grimly and Croaker caught a glimpse of another face just behind him in the truck's interior. Another pair of amber eyes blinked at him out of a face identical to the first one.

My God, Croaker thought with the sudden impact of revelation. *Twins!*

"Not Carlito, he's dead," the second amber-eyed twin said as if reading his mind. "I myself had a hand in his demise. His history had a sadder end than I told you." His eyes blazed with a feral intensity. "So swiftly we meet again, Detective! Who would have thought? *Madre de mentiras,* I had fun at our first encounter! How about you?"

The first amber-eyed twin brandished his scalpel. "Antonio!" he cried over the wail of the wind and the screech of the tires. "He's like a tick on our backside. What shall we do with him?"

It wasn't Sonia's brother he'd met at her house, Croaker thought wildly. It was Antonio Bonita!

Croaker managed to get his right arm into position to deliver a blow, but the amber-eyed twin who was Heitor Bonita slammed the heel of his shoe into Croaker's ribs. Pain electrified him as he tried to catch his breath. Heitor kicked viciously again, and Croaker's tentative footing failed him. He slid to his knees, hanging by the death grip he maintained on the door handle with his biomechanical fingers as Antonio watched with the utter detachment of a god.

Heitor leaned out of the open doorway. As he did so, his gaze was caught by reflected light spinning off Croaker's biomechanical hand.

"Now what is this?" Heitor said. The wind plucked his words away but not before Croaker marked the particular timbre of the voice.

"The hand," Antonio said. "I told you."

"So you did," Heitor said. "I want it." The scalpel arced in a blur, and Croaker could see what was about to happen. Heitor seemed fascinated by the biomechanical hand. Like a lepidopterist on a field trip who discovers a new species of butterfly, he was not going to let it get away. He was going to cut it off Croaker's hand at the wrist.

Croaker tried to clear his head, to gather his strength, but with each passing instant his perch was becoming more difficult to maintain. He looked up into Heitor's face—Antonio's face, there was no difference—and his blood ran cold.

For that moment, he had the eerie sensation of being pinned to a dissecting table. Four eyes peered at him avidly. Two sets of nostrils flared as if at the scent of fresh blood. Two mouths curled in the same beatific smile, as if the men were embarking on a sacred mission.

Croaker, with no other option left him, let go of the door handle. It was that or lose his biomechanical hand.

With no warning at all, Antonio had lunged for him, the fingers grasping him in an iron grip. Saved from the scarifying fall to the ribboning highway just below him, Croaker scrabbled desperately for purchase on the rear bumper.

Fear was thick in his throat. It was purely instinctive; it came from the dark and lonely place in the mind where no thought existed. He was not afraid of many things. He had, in fact, come across many diseased minds. But these twins were different. They exuded a single terrifying aura that made his stomach clench. Seeing them was like looking at two boys delightedly playing at the bottom of a grave. A joy wreathed them, so pure it was almost holy.

Two sets of amber eyes bored into him and he felt a gust of wind billow through him like an evil premonition. Antonio's grip on him tightened and Heitor maneuvered in the gaping doorway of the truck as he prepared for his bit of impromptu surgery. As he did so, Croaker got an almost hallucinatory glimpse inside the truck. He saw a metal and porcelain machine with tubes running from it. It looked familiar. Where had he seen something like it before? But there was no time to think. His perch on the rear bumper gave way, whipping him out over the highway. He glanced down. The panel truck was running at such high speed the pavement was one long blur. Fall the wrong way and he could easily shatter his ribs or, worse, his neck.

And he would have fallen, but Antonio, braced against the side of the door opening, held him steady in his viselike grip. For an instant he peered up into Antonio's predatory face and something like sheet lightning, mysterious and potent, passed between them.

"Not now . . . not yet . . ." Antonio stayed the arc of his twin's scalpel with his other hand. *"Paciencia."*

"No!" Heitor cried. "I want it! I'll have it *now!*" And he wrestled his arm from his twin's grasp. The scalpel flashed evilly in the passing streetlights. It was coming again and there was nothing Croaker could do. Heitor would have his trophy.

Then Antonio did a very odd thing. He smiled down at Croaker in an almost benign manner. "The dark stones know." The howling wind clawed his words to shreds as his fingers opened and he relinquished his grip.

In that frozen moment when the razor edge of the scalpel passed within a hair's breadth of his left wrist, Croaker choked back violent nausea and did the only thing he could do. He tucked his head into his chest and willed his body to relax as it was flung off the back of the speeding truck and plummeted to the pavement of the highway.

He bounced and bounced again, then rolled as he had been taught, keeping his body relaxed and letting the momentum take him freely. He tumbled head over heels along oily concrete and cinders, amid a welter of screeching brakes and shouted curses. The only thing that saved him from being run over was that traffic had stayed well back of the white panel truck that had been driving so erratically.

As it sped away in a cloud of diesel fumes, he managed to gain the side of the highway. Not long after, a young surfer in a beat-up pickup stopped and asked if he was hurt.

Croaker, fighting nausea and fierce aches in shoulder and ribs, said no, but a lift would be just fine. But on the jouncy ride back up the highway, with rap music blaring in his ears, he was haunted by the sight of those avid faces, twisted in greed and lust. His teeth gritted in pain and he closed his eyes against the fierce glare of oncoming headlights. A flare of remembrance: a stainless-steel and porcelain machine in the white panel truck's interior, tubes going into and out of it. He was sure he'd seen it before. Where? Then the sound of the compressor welled up inside him. The compressor that Mr. Leyes had heard when Sonia was killed, the compressor he'd heard, later, outside Gold Coast Exotic Car Rentals where Vonda had died. The compressor that was used to power . . .

With a cry that startled the surfer out of his music-induced reverie, Croaker sat up straight. He had it now! The Bonitas were using a perfusion machine. That's what he had seen in the back of their panel truck. The compressor made it portable. Now he had his proof. Antonio and Heitor had taken a panel truck, a perfusion machine powered by a compressor, and made their organ harvesting operation both portable and mobile.

The scalpel Heitor had brandished flashed through his mind like the arc of a shooting star in the night sky.

Croaker had the surfer drop him far enough away from the strip mall so he wouldn't be traced back to Vonda's murder site. As he walked, could not stop himself from picturing Sonia's headless body—and Vonda's—opened up, the organs plucked out like ripe fruit by the reavers. Right now, the perfusion machine might be pumping Belzer solution through Vonda's kidneys, perhaps Sonia's as well. It was ironic and terribly unfair. They had access to kidneys and he had none—save through Majeur. But where was that kidney coming from?

Abruptly, he put his hand to his throbbing temple. There was that pernicious thought again, undermining the very fabric on which he'd built his life. These were organs from people he knew— people who had been cold-bloodedly murdered. What kind of monsters were the Bonitas? He didn't yet know, but he had to find out.

Croaker shuddered. Unbidden, he saw Antonio's and Heitor's faces again. He was struck by their amber eyes, lambent as moons, cold, cruel, pitiless. Estrella Leyes was right. Never had he witnessed two people so estranged from God or the rest of the human race.

4

An hour and fifteen minutes later, Croaker parked in the lot outside the Royal Poinciana Hospital. The vintage Mustang Majeur's client had given him was right where he'd left it. It sure looked beautiful. He found himself thinking about buying a cover for it. The ferocious Florida sun would otherwise burn away the finish, fade the upholstery, and dry up all the exposed rubber parts. That he already considered it his own car was disturbing. One way or another, he'd have to decide what to do with it.

With a rag from the glove compartment, he wiped down the steering wheel and the leather seat of the T-bird that had been spotted with blood from his cuts and abrasions. It was almost eight-thirty. All his heroics, it seemed, had gone for nothing; the license tag he'd gotten off the rear of the Bonitas' panel van was a dead end. His uplink to the Motor Vehicle database informed him the number was off a seven-year-old Honda Civic registered in Dade County. Tags got stolen so often, he knew, the cops didn't bother looking for them anymore.

Not surprising that the panel truck had stolen tags. The Bonitas were thorough professionals. He was beginning to get the measure of them. Their evil, like urban spoor, was unmistakable. Despite that, Croaker found himself ruminating on curious aspects of his two encounters with Antonio. How to figure Antonio saying, *Love does things to you you have no hope of understanding. Love changes you even when you have no intention of being changed.* Was this true? Had Antonio truly loved Rosa Milagros? Impossible. He'd killed her; he and Heitor had lopped off her head as if she had been some water buffalo ripe for the slaughter. *God or something like Him—Fate, perhaps—took this woman away from me,* Antonio had confessed. Meaning what? He and Heitor were men who felt nothing. And yet he seemed stigmatized by Rosa's murder. *They're both waiting, aren't they? Rosa and now Sonia. They're joined somehow.* Why confess anything to Croaker? What was Croaker to Antonio? He recalled with electrifying intensity the look Antonio had given him, that had penetrated like a virus deep into the marrow of his bones. *Both Bennie and Estrella Leyes seem convinced that Humaitá Milagros's spirit lives on inside me,* Croaker thought. *Is this what Antonio saw in me?* Is that why he'd said, *I'm damned now, I know that. Rosa could have saved me. I have done things . . . I continue to do things . . .*

Then he remembered Estrella's warning to him, that Humaitá had thought he'd detected a spark of humanity in Antonio and Heitor and they had killed him for it. She'd told him not to make the same mistake. Unconsciously, he curled his hand around the spirit-stone. He felt as he had at Sonia's funeral: as if he was vulnerable to dark spirits.

Action was the only way to snap himself out of these disquieting thoughts. He grabbed his Gap bag out of the trunk and headed directly into the men's room to wash off the rest of the blood and change his soiled and shredded clothes. Because he went through the Emergency Room, no one gave him a second look.

But when he entered the main lobby to get to the elevator bank that would take him to the CCD unit, he ran right into Bennie.

"Jesus Christ, *amigo*, where the hell've you been?" Bennie was clearly fuming and it was an intimidating sight. He grasped Croaker's elbow with fingers that felt like steel pincers, steering him into a corner. "Listen, I want to know what the hell's going on."

Croaker did not appreciate Bennie's grip. "What are you talking about?"

"We had a deal, clean and simple, right? The boat thing. Then, you call and, like, clear out of the blue you're talking with Roubinnet and in almost the same breath you're, you know, bailing. I want to know why. What did that sonuvabitch say about me?"

"First, take your hand off me."

"When you answer my question." Bennie's fingers tightened their grip. "Hey, *amigo,* wake up. This is no fuckin' joke. I make a deal with someone I expect it to happen, period."

"What is that?" Croaker was angry now. "A threat?"

"Play it like it lays, *amigo.*"

"Bennie, I thought we were friends."

Bennie spat onto the marble floor. "Friends don't back out on their word."

"They don't lie, either," Croaker said. "What are you and Majeur up to?"

"Who?"

Croaker glared at his friend. "I told you. Marcellus Rojas Diego Majeur, the attorney."

"An' I told *you.* I don't know any Majeur."

Croaker wrapped his biomechanical fingers around Bennie's wrist. "You don't know the top Latin American drug lords, Bennie? You don't know who reps them over here? Is that what you expect me to believe?" For a moment, they faced each other—friends once, perhaps; now nothing more than two stags clashing antlers.

"Let go." Croaker felt his blood rushing in his ears. "Don't make me do this."

"*Amigo,* consider any action before you take it."

Slowly and deliberately, Croaker exerted pressure until Bennie was forced to let him go. "I don't know what the hell is up with you. But if you keep on lying, I'm quits." He punched the elevator button.

Bennie took a threatening step toward him. "Fuck that. I've still got plenty to say. A deal's a deal. No one bails on Bennie Milagros. No one, *comprende?* I'm gonna hold you to that midnight run—"

"How are you going to do that?" The elevator doors opened and Croaker stepped in. "Have your Colombian buddies talk me to death?"

Bennie made a sudden lunge at him. The doors were closing, but Bennie was quick as a sprinter. He slammed the rubber bumpers with his shoulders and the doors ricocheted back. He stepped into the elevator and Croaker smashed the back of his biomechanical hand into his chest. Bennie staggered back and the doors slid shut in his face.

Upstairs, Croaker took a moment to allow the excess adrenaline to drain away. The meeting with Bennie had been profoundly disturbing. What had happened between them? It was as if they were talking at cross-purposes, each of them locked in his own little world. Worse, at the heart of it all was a terrible inarticulateness, as if they had nothing to communicate but threats. Their time on the *Captain Sumo,* only days ago, seemed like months, the camaraderie that had sprung up between them an illusion. What if it was an illusion, he asked himself, spun by Bennie to rope Croaker into this midnight run? What the hell was so damn important about it?

Once, on a back country fishing trip, Croaker had been bitten by a pygmy rattlesnake. *"I feel your tension,"* Stone Tree had said as he had cut open the wound. *"The toxin will be neutralized within minutes. Why do you worry?"* When Croaker had told him it was because there were so many questions in life that had no answers, Stone Tree had replied: *"If you find this is so, you are asking the wrong questions."*

Before trying to find Jenny Marsh, Croaker looked in on Rachel. Dr. Stansky stood beside her bed, his hands clasped behind his back. He glanced up sharply as Croaker came in, then nodded in cool recognition.

Croaker stooped to kiss Rachel's forehead. It felt as if she were burning up, and he experienced a quick stab of panic. "What's happened?"

Dr. Stansky's Olympian ego was mollified by the anxiety in Croaker's tone. Here was a human emotion with which he could deal. "There's no good news. They're having trouble controlling the sepsis. No doubt Rachel's severely weakened condition is a contributing factor." His voice modulated, adding soothing overtones. "But the staff here is doing everything they can." He pointed to two new IV tubes going into her. "They've switched to more powerful antibiotics. It's a waiting game now. That's why I urged Mrs. Duke to take a break. She'd been here just about all day and her nerves were worn thin." Then he noticed Croaker's condition. "You certainly look the worse for wear."

Croaker grimaced. "I fell off a truck."

"Everyone's a comedian." He peered reprovingly from beneath humorless brows. "Let me take a look at you." He unbuttoned Croaker's shirt and began his examination. "Some nasty truck."

"Any luck finding a kidney?" Croaker asked. Maybe he could still get off the hook with Majeur and his despicable deal.

Dr. Stansky shook his head as he snapped on latex gloves, then plucked several items off a countertop. "I'm afraid it's useless." He used a tweezers with curved tines to extract several small pebbles out of the reddish abrasion on Croaker's right shoulder. "There's nothing I can do for her, you see. Nothing at all." He applied a topical disinfectant and an antibiotic cream to all the cuts and scrapes with a gauze pad. "I've pulled in every favor, twisted every arm." He dropped the soiled gauze into a disposal canister marked DANGER-BIOHAZARD. "No one can help. I thought they'd be able to, but they simply can't." He stripped off the gloves and threw them after the gauze. "It's a matter of ethics, you see. These medical people, these organ handlers, ethics is what defines them." His gaze alit on Rachel's comatose face. "She's in God's hands now, that's all there is to it."

Croaker thanked Dr. Stansky and left the cubicle. He was dispirited, in pain and hungry. It was only now he remembered that he hadn't eaten all day.

He saw Jenny Marsh coming toward him from the lounge area where she'd first told him in confidence about the American organ harvesting. The Bonitas' activities lent a whole new aspect to it that made her input all the more important.

He stopped in his tracks. Dressed in black cotton pants and a sueded silk jacket over a blue-green blouse she looked startlingly beautiful. Her catlike face had touches of makeup on it, not much but enough to give her an entirely new dimension. And what had she done to her hair? It hung loose and full and gleaming so that it just touched her shoulders.

"Dr. Stansky told me you're having a helluva time with my niece," he said as he drank her in.

She nodded grimly. "I don't understand it. The sepsis just doesn't want to give up."

"Dr. Stansky says the infection's taking advantage of her weakened condition."

"Undoubtedly." Jenny frowned. "But I still find it odd. You'd think with the course of treatment we're giving her, she'd be able to fight it off. She's weak, but she isn't eighty years old." She shook her head. "Still, it's there and it's killing her. If she's to have any chance at all, we've got to have that kidney."

He held up the documentation Majeur had given him. "Then I've got good news. I hope."

As he moved into the light, Jenny got a full look at the scrapes and bruises still visible. "My God," she said, "what happened to you?"

He put a hand to his jaw with its day's rough stubble and an ache still throbbing from the punch Antonio had delivered. "I seem to be suffering from an overexposure to the vicious undercurrents of life. Not to worry. Stansky patched me up while he was talking down to me. With his attitude, I'm surprised he didn't charge me."

He handed over the documents and said, "Jenny, I want you to tell me if this is Rachel's ticket to life." Their gazes locked for a moment. "No medical doubletalk, okay?"

She hesitated a moment and he could see her considering what he was asking of her. Doctors worked long and hard to gain the status of demigods. Asking one to give up that privilege, even for a moment, required a leap of trust for both parties.

At length, she nodded. "I'll straight-shoot it, no matter the cost."

"I appreciate that."

"You damn well better." Her gaze dropped to the papers she held.

In a moment, she said, "Lew, you aren't seriously considering using this unregistered organ, are you?"

"That depends," he said. "Is it real?"

"The documentation appears authentic, but—"

"Then I'm doing it."

"But—" Jenny's gaze flicked up, her eyes flashing emerald in the overhead lights.

"No buts. If Rachel's life can be saved that's all that matters."

Jenny's words rode harshly over his. "But the bottom line is you don't know where this kidney's coming from."

He tapped the top sheet of paper. "According to this, from the same place you or anyone else gets organs: the United Network Organ Sharing."

"Right." Some emotion was stuck in her eyes. What was it? "But, see, it can't be because I've been through the UNOS national computer network more times than I care to count, and I swear to you there's no kidney to be had." She held up the papers. "I checked a couple of hours ago, between operations. Updates don't happen that fast. This kidney is unregistered. It's illegal."

Croaker felt a weakness in the backs of his knees, and all the aches he'd amassed during this gruelling day seemed to press in on him at once. "Christ, Jenny, don't do this to Rachie. Earlier, you told me that in her case you might consider using an unregistered kidney."

"A moment of weakness—or madness." There was a confused look on her face. "For her, for you, I don't know which." She shook her head. "Now it doesn't matter, because I've regained the little bit of sanity left me. I won't touch an unregistered kidney."

"Even to save Rachel's life?"

"Yes," she said evenly. "Even for that."

The tension between them flickered and flared. Jenny was strong and she was principled. That was good, but could she understand his predicament? This was not her niece they were talking about.

This was not a girl she had lost a long time ago, only by some miracle to have rediscovered. This was not a second chance for her, a rare and fragile opportunity to atone for past lapses. But it was for him. And the thought that he might lose Rachel again—this time forever—was intolerable.

"Lew, I know you'd move heaven and earth for her," she said, proving him wrong. "I can see it in every move you make around her. But, listen to what I'm saying. If this kidney's unregistered you *cannot* use it. If you do, you're not only condoning a sin so heinous it cannot be named, you've become a part of it."

Her green eyes sparked with the force of her will, and Croaker knew that they were at an impasse. What happened when an irresistible force met an immovable object?

The agony was he knew she was right. He thought of Antonio and Heitor, the reavers, harvesting organs as if they were mushrooms in the forest. He couldn't be a party to that, but if there was even the slimmest hope that the kidney Majeur was offering was as clean as the lawyer claimed, Croaker had to play the string out to its end, even if the end proved too bitter to bear.

"But what if it is legit?" he said.

"Whistling in the dark, Lew."

To give in this much cost her nothing in integrity and she led him over to a computer terminal where she logged on. Surgeons and musicians had the same kinds of fingers, Croaker thought, each one always moving independently in their assigned tasks, as if they had ten hands instead of two.

In sure, swift strokes, Jenny typed in the codes to access the UNOS system in Richmond, Virginia. Lit by the pixels of the screen, her face looked eerie, like that of a fairy queen in a children's story or perhaps a Shakespearean play. He knew she was on-line when she consulted the documentation to get the serial number of Majeur's kidney. She typed it in and pressed the Enter key. A soft sigh escaped her lips.

"What is it?" Croaker said. From his angle, the screen looked like little more than a blur.

"It's impossible," Jenny said as she turned toward him. "The goddamn kidney's registered. It must have come on net while I was in surgery. It's been reserved for Rachel."

Croaker felt the thrill of elation race through him. "It's real," he whispered. "It's real and it's legit." Out of utter darkness had come a single beam, lighting his way. A path had appeared, dangerous, lonely, and all too likely corrosive to his soul. But for Rachel it was the blessed path back to life. "Thank God."

Then he thought of something. "Jenny, if the organ's already in the UNOS data bank, let's see if we can get it released."

Jenny pressed some keys. She shook her head. "No go. All I'm getting is an In Transit message. It's not so unusual. The moment they get a donor's consent, do the blood work up and antigens tests, the organ details go on-line. They're meted out as to need, compatibility, and geographical location, so we have to assume this donor's in the South Florida area. But the kidney itself isn't ready yet."

Damn, Croaker thought. He'd hoped he could outwit Majeur at his own game by getting the organ without having to go through with his end of the deal. But the UNOS system wasn't complying.

Jenny shut down her computer and leaned over the desk on ramrod straight arms. She closed her eyes, and Croaker watched her profile, graceful and strong, limned against the subdued night-lights of the Dialysis Unit.

Then she turned around. "Lew, how did you work this miracle?"

He spread the fingers of his hands. "By definition, miracles aren't explainable."

"Right. But really. How did you do it?"

He stared at her mutely.

Her emerald gaze raked his face. "Okay. The clock's ticking. The sepsis will kill her in a matter of days if we can't get it under control. And the longer it remains unchecked the greater the odds we won't lick it. Tell your donor's people I'll need some time to verify the antigen findings on the documentation. In one way, we're lucky. Usually, I'd have to do a kidney biopsy on Rachel's before the transplant, but in this case we have to forego it. Her condition's too critical to chance two operations. That's turned into a plus now because it'll save time. The moment the organ is released, we go."

"Right," Croaker said. He felt his elation quickly replaced by a vivid sense of a steel door slamming shut behind him. Now he'd have to call Majeur and take his reprehensible deal. For Rachel's sake, he had to have that organ. He was committed to terminating Juan Garcia Barbacena, who would be within striking distance shortly after midnight tomorrow. Surely, the devil had him by the throat. The question was: would the devil ever let him go?

As in a dream or one of Bennie's drug-induced altered states, he observed himself using the phone on the desk to call Majeur's private number. He got the lawyer's recorded voice and he left an urgent message, giving Majeur his cell phone number.

"I have to wait for the call back," he told Jenny.

"Okay. Nothing more we can do here for the moment." She put

a hand to her midsection. "That was my stomach begging for food. Now I'm begging you. Feed me. Please."

By the time they pulled into the restaurant's parking lot, it was teeming. Not just raining, but a tropical downpour that obscured even the far side of the Intracoastal. In South Florida, you were never aware of raindrops as discreet entities. Rather, rain was solid as walls, spit out of a lowering sky.

Harbor Lights was located just east of the Flagler Memorial Bridge. Geographically, it was not far from Matty's place, but ideologically it was on the other side of town, a rare haven for young people in the old money oasis of Palm Beach. The restaurant was named for the Platters hit of 1960; the music in the place came from that decade, which was cool again. Croaker chose a spot in the far left-hand corner of the lot and killed the engine. For some time, he sat looking at the rain-swept parking lot as headlights swung across the sheened tarmac. People hurried in and out of their cars, their backs hunched against the storm.

"You seem very far away just now." He could smell the light citrus fragrance Jenny wore. "What is it you're seeing?"

Croaker stirred. It felt strange and nice to have her beside him. "I was thinking of all the promises I've made and kept. None of them seem as important as the one I made to myself to keep Rachel safe from harm."

Inside, he shivered in the sudden freeze of air-conditioning as a hostess who seemed all browned legs and arms led them through the two-level, wood-trimmed restaurant. Its open kitchen, stainless-steel glinting through gouts of steam, was on his right, the thronged bar off to the left. The Happenings were singing "See You in September," reminding him of the hot summer nights of his youth and even hotter girls in sleeveless blouses and tight capri pants. The smell of the steaming city asphalt in August was like a perfume all the girls wore.

"Would you mind if we sat outside?" Jenny asked. "I find that after surgery I can't stand crowds. It's like my nerves are rubbed raw." To his surprise, her beauty was undimmed by her exhaustion. On the contrary, the slightly ragged edge of vulnerability heightened her allure. "Too much proximity to human flesh and blood, I suppose."

Croaker, whose head ached fiercely, could empathize with her. "Suits me fine. I've had it with air-conditioning." Outside, beneath an enormous blue awning, they had the deck to themselves. The hostess lit candles for them. The flames immediately flickered in the wind gusts, sending shadows skittering nervously along the wall.

Jenny asked for a Scotch and he ordered a club soda with two limes and a double espresso from a dark-eyed young waitress. As he sank into the seat beside Jenny, he noticed the green of her eyes was made translucent in the candle-filled semidarkness.

The rain thrummed a heavy tattoo against the fabric of the awning, threw up a fine spray against the concrete of the dock. The waitress came with their drinks and a couple of menus.

Croaker drank his club soda in two long swallows, then turned his attention to the espresso. "Now that the possibility has passed us by, I need to know one thing," he said. "Do you have personal knowledge of this illegal organ harvesting?"

Jenny seemed to study him with the rapt attention she no doubt reserved for the opened-up sites of her operations. "Has this become some kind of obsession for you because of Rachel?"

"Because of her," he admitted. "And other things."

Her voice was peculiarly expressive. "Cop things, Detective?"

"You haven't answered my question."

"No, I have no personal knowledge of it. I've already told you how I feel about illegal organ harvesting. It's anathema to me."

The waitress returned to ask if they'd like to order. Jenny said she'd have a Tex-Mex salad, grilled pompano, and a side of pasta; Croaker said he'd have the same.

When they were alone again, Croaker said, "And yet in that one moment earlier today you were prepared to transplant a kidney no matter its source."

"I thought about it, yes." Jenny sipped her Scotch. "I was reminded of medical school." She looked at him over the rim of her glass. "There were times there when I felt as if I were a novitiate in a nunnery daydreaming of sex. My professors would discuss certain protocols and I'd find myself questioning them. Is this right? Isn't there another way? A better method?" Her front teeth chinked softly against the glass. "These heretical thoughts surfaced only at certain times, when the protocols being discussed were ones for which no explanation was readily available. They just worked, no one knew why. But all these protocols—for cancers, for instance—had serious side effects for the patient. And I'd think, Are we doing more harm than good? More often than not, the patient was saved, that much was true. But he or she was changed—weakened, damaged. Like sand through an hourglass, our magic protocols had drained away years along with the disease."

A gust of wind moaned through the dockside, fluttering the candle flames. A couple of candles at nearby tables went out.

"All this came back to me in that instant with you. The kidney.

166

I had another heretical thought, but it's gone now. My life is restored to its proper order."

Croaker tasted his espresso, patient now that he saw what was happening. He sensed that she'd told him the truth. Also, that her analogy about the novitiate was on the mark. For her, medicine was like religion: it made sense out of the unexplainable. It carved order out of chaos. Playing with its rules, then, was, to use her own words, anathema, heretical, because those rules were all that stood between her and the endless night of eternity. In that regard, they were very much alike: both sentinels on guard against evil.

With these thoughts came a certain knowledge that some gulf that had separated them had vanished, leaving them in startling and vulnerable proximity to one another.

The downpour drummed unceasingly on the awning and thunder rumbled ominously. A moment later, lightning unstitched the darkness in a blue-white flash. A brown pelican, disturbed out of slumber from its perch beneath the bridge, flapped its wings, made a shallow arc across the Intracoastal. Its long bill thrust forward, it glided through the rain on a mission unknown.

Their food and the call on Coaker's cell phone came all at once. As the dark-eyed waitress set down their plates, Croaker went off into a corner untouched by the fluttering candlelight. He was near the water, at the edge of the blue awning. Rain spattered his shoulders, seeping down the back of his neck.

In darkness, he did the dirty deed and spoke to Marcellus Rojas Diego Majeur. The tiny numbers on his cell phone glowed green, like phosphors on the ocean. They seemed to squirm before his eyes like tiny evil eels about to insinuate themselves beneath his skin.

He heard Majeur's voice in his ear and he immediately felt invaded. He kept his eye on Jenny, her face floating in soft light, as if the sight of her would keep him safe from Majeur's spellcraft. This close to the final edge, he felt a certain dread creeping through him.

"It's a done deal." Croaker's toes curled in hard reflex as the rain beaded his shoe tips. "I'm all yours."

"Excellent," Majeur said. He seemed to have had no doubts the kidney he was offering would pass muster. "All that remains is the transfer of information on the subject." He meant Juan Garcia Barbacena, the victim. He was being circumspect because he knew Croaker was on a cell phone. "His schedule has not altered. Midnight tomorrow."

"Where?" Croaker stole another glance at Jenny, willing a part of him to weld itself to her. This he needed above all else so that when, as inevitably would happen, he was stained by sin, he might hold out hope of salvation through this link to her.

"Not over the phone," Majeur said. "But south, *señor*. It will be south."

The Miami area. "I'll need the kidney before then."

"Kiss him first on the back of the neck and send him down." Majeur could not deny himself a chuckle, perhaps at his clever turn of phrase. "Then your niece will have what she requires."

Croaker wanted to argue, but what with? He had no leverage. "I need the information on our friend."

"We're compiling the last of the details," Majeur told him. "He does everything last minute—the security's better that way."

"I can't afford to wait," Croaker said. "My niece's condition has worsened."

"Patience is required, Mr. Croaker. My client leaves nothing to chance, neither should you." Majeur clucked his tongue in sympathy. "Believe me, the information will simplify a difficult and perilous task. For Rachel's sake, you don't want anything to go amiss— and neither do we."

No, I need to kill Juan Garcia Barbacena the first time going in, Croaker thought. *But what will be left of me when I'm finished? Will I be able to live with myself?*

"What if she dies while I'm waiting for you to get your act together?"

"What if the sky falls and we are all washed into the sea?" Croaker could hear Majeur's even breathing on the other end of the line. "Have faith, sir. We will come out the other side of this whole."

Where did a lawyer like Majeur get faith like that? Croaker wondered. "Meet me at ten-thirty this morning. That's as long as I'm prepared to wait," he said. "On the boardwalk in SoBe opposite the News Cafe."

"That's cutting it close, but I can be there."

"Be sure you are," Croaker said. "The clock's ticking and I need all the time I can get."

Croaker pocketed the phone as he walked back to the table.

"I had them take our plates back," Jenny said. "The food would have gotten cold." But there were questions, silent as fish, swimming in her eyes.

He nodded in thanks as he sat down. That small gesture of sending his food back with hers felt like a tender kiss on the cheek. He tried to stop his mind from racing. Whatever lay ahead for him didn't matter, he knew. It was Rachel's life that needed saving. He could worry about his own later.

"Is everything all right?" She could not keep the anxiety out of her voice. "We *are* going to get the kidney?"

"As soon as I pay for it."

"They want money?"

Their food came. The waitress asked if she could get them anything else and he said no, thanks very much.

"That's all right." Jenny took up slivers of her grilled pompano. "I had no business asking."

Mist had sprung up across the plucked skin of the water, drifting in soft tangles that reminded him of a lover's hair spread across a rumpled pillowcase.

He looked at Jenny. A fine net of droplets sparkled like diamonds in her wind-tousled hair, and the candlelight shone in her eyes like the sun. He found himself regretting that he'd set up this rendezvous to elicit her professional advice. He liked her; more, he was attracted to her.

She very deftly twirled some pasta on the tines of her fork. "See, while you were on the phone I was thinking . . . The thing is, I'd like it to be my business."

Antonio and Heitor were summoned into his mind like genii, their amber eyes glowing with cold passion. He said, "I don't think that's such a good idea." He ate the fish without tasting it, uncomfortable with the hurt look on her face. "The truth is I'd like it, too, Jenny."

She tilted her head, curious. "Well, then . . . ?"

"I'm falling down some kind of well, blind as a bat in sunlight, and I don't want to take you with me."

"Even if I choose to go?"

"That's not a choice you can make. You don't have enough to go by."

"By all means." She spread her hands. "You'll find I'm a very good listener."

He waved his fork. "Forget it."

"Well, that's a laugh. I finally get up the nerve to take a positive step and you won't let me."

"Jenny—"

"No, no. I've come this far. It's a matter of trust, isn't it? I want you to hear this." There was an expression on her face that seemed to him to be somewhere between sad and rueful. "As successful as I've been professionally, I've managed to royally screw up my personal life. I drove away my husband. At the time, he and I were both convinced it was my overriding dedication to medicine that did us in." She stared out at the rain-spattered night. "But, I know the truth and it's quite a bit more bitter. He was a decent guy."

Thunder ruled the sky. Across the Intracoastal, a fishing boat bounced and rolled at its mooring, its decks white with rain.

Jenny shrugged. "Who knows, maybe, deep down, I don't think I deserve a decent guy. I mean, look who I've picked since then. Dino, my last boyfriend, is typical. Big, macho type. Drove a Ferrari, dressed real well. A real hunk, proud of his sexual stamina. 'Jen, I'm gonna screw you 'til you scream.' He actually said that and, worse, I was actually intrigued." She watched his expression, for disapproval perhaps. "So what happened? We did it for ninety minutes straight. Instead of an orgasm, he gave me a bladder infection."

They both laughed quietly, almost politely, but the mood didn't last. Too much electricity in the air.

He was silent for a moment, and she went on in a softer tone. "You see how it is, don't you? How I surprised myself by being attracted to you. Because you're a decent guy. I knew it the moment we met. Then I saw you with Rachel and it pierced my heart."

Though he couldn't say how, he knew there was more she had to say. But she didn't go on. Sometimes, as now, Croaker had come upon a moment with a woman when some unspoken message passed through the air and hung suspended and invisible, a kind of primitive recognition that stirred the cauldron of the universe out of its set pattern. It was raw and sweaty, a jungle thing, no doubt about it.

Jenny's breath caught in her throat. "I'm not good at this," she whispered. "Really, I'm not."

"It's comforting to know that you're not good at something."

"I'm not good at skiing, either," she said.

He took her hand as he rose. "We're not going skiing."

Tim Buckley was singing his sad songs of grace and dreamed encounters in a voice so fragile it made you want to cry. Jenny had infused her apartment with his music as if it were incense, and by this act alone Croaker knew she was revealing a hitherto hidden part of herself.

For Croaker, one of the most wonderful moments in life was when he first touched a woman with intimate intent. The sense of anticipation, the perception of what boundaries were about to flower open was so impassioned it made his blood seethe.

They stood in the middle of her living room, barefoot on a thick carpet of swirling shapes and colors, hands moving on each other. She smelled of lemon and sandalwood, and when her hair swung against his cheek, he could feel it all the way down to his groin.

"I love the way you feel," he said softly.

She curled her head against his shoulder. Then she did something quite extraordinary. "Tell me how," she whispered in response. "Tell me everything."

So he did. Every place he touched her, he described. And her body quickened in response, her thighs trembling, her breath rushing out of her in tiny perfumed exhalations. With the forefinger of his right hand he touched the side of her neck, feeling the triphammer pulse of blood, then trailed it into the hollow of her throat, where another pulse beckoned him, then down over the swell of a breast until he found her nipple, swollen with desire. He described all of this into the whorl of her ear and she clutched him tightly to her. She was turned on, he suspected, not only because of the heightened sense of the sex it gave her—the down and dirtiness of it—but because it gave her tangible evidence that he was thinking of *her*, that there was more to this for him than mere lust. There was nothing a woman hated more than to be left alone by her partner during sex.

He put his arms lower on her and she climbed him like a tree trunk, locking her ankles over the top of his buttocks. The pains he'd received from beatings from Antonio and the highway pavement receded into the background. He pulled her to him, telling her how it made him feel. She shuddered hard against him and began to tell him how he was making her feel. She was hot and wet and open, and when he entered her there was no resistance at all. With every move he made she spoke to him, murmuring thrilling incantatory phrases that incited them both. She came so fast it took him completely by surprise. And by the time he had recovered, she was climbing that mountain again, shuddering and moaning between her gasped-out narrative.

This was a Jenny Marsh so far removed from the cool physician-surgeon commanding the corridors of Royal Poinciana Hospital she might as well never have been exposed to civilization. Who had seen Jenny Marsh like this before him? Her husband? Perhaps. Not Dino, the stud, or any of her other boyfriends. The moment held all the rare and breathless magic of glimpsing a unicorn prancing in moonlight. In gasped-out delight, she let go of everything she held rigid in her professional life.

He drove into her one last time, throbbing uncontrollably as she urged him on with the throaty sound of her voice, the scrape of her nails along his sweat-ribboned flesh, the beat of her bare heels on the small of his back.

Later, twined in her bed in the darkness of the night, she turned her face to his. Lights from outside filtered through the vertical blinds, figuring her face with pale curls and crescents like aboriginal tattoos. Her eyes were in deep shadow and he could not read her.

With extraordinary delicacy, she traced the asymmetrical scrapes and bruises beneath their gauze wrapping, as if she needed to assure herself of Dr. Stansky's competence. "You have that faraway look in your eyes," she whispered. "Tell me what you're thinking."

It's a matter of trust, isn't it? she had said. And she was right. Trust between two people was all that mattered. If you could trust someone with your heart, with the secret history of your life, then even if the rest of the world went to hell it wouldn't matter so much. For what he was committed to do now in order to save Rachel felt like a living hell, and more than anything now he needed solace if not absolution.

He told her about Antonio and Heitor, the hideous organ harvesting they'd brought to South Florida, about Sonia and Vonda, and about Bennie and his Guarani healer grandfather.

"Oh, Lew, tell me this is some kind of terribly sick joke."

"Believe me, I wish it was." He took out the soul-catcher stone. It gleamed dully, its dark green turned to pitch black by the shadows.

"What's that?"

He held it between the tips of his fingers. "Remember when Rachel woke up? Not only woke from her coma but spoke rationally to me. Remember you said you couldn't figure it, that there was no medical explanation?"

"Lew, in my business there's often no medical explanation. That's something I wouldn't admit to just anybody."

"This is what I did just before she woke." He pressed the dark stone between her bare breasts.

Staring down at it, she shook her head. "I don't feel anything."

"Perhaps you won't. But Rachel did."

Jenny sighed. "The fact is cancers go into remission, patients recover when we've privately given up on them. The human body is a miraculous engine of life."

"This time it had help."

He could hear her breathing, feel her soft breath like puffs of air keeping a balloon aloft over summer fields.

"Dear God!"

A sharply indrawn breath. Her hands closed tightly over his where he held the soul-catcher to her chest. Her eyes fluttered closed and he could see her eyeballs beneath moving like some-one dreaming.

Streetlight entered the room as slowly as syrup. With each beat of his heart time seemed to accumulate like gemstones at their feet.

Her eyes flew open and in a voice hoarse with shock, she said, "I saw something." She looked down at his hand pressed against her. "Take it away." A violent shudder passed through her. "Please."

Croaker twisted, put the dark stone on her bedside table. "What did you see?"

"What is it you have to do to get this kidney?" Her voice was like a taloned ghost, eviscerating the small pocket of serenity they had built to insulate themselves against the outside world. He knew she had struggled against asking this dreadful question, sensing that his answer would be even more dreadful.

Holding her tight, with her legs around him, the naked core of her fast against him, he didn't answer her. He didn't have to; all too soon he could feel the scald of her tears against his flesh.

"Lew, oh, my God, oh, my God, I saw you. You were floating in the water. Shallow water. Green and gold. You were facedown, one arm is gone, torn away by—I don't know what. Floating into mangrove. Bump. Bump. Bump. Against roots like the black legs of a great spider." Her forehead burrowed into his shoulder. "And there was blood. So much blood that none could be left inside you."

She didn't want to let him go, but she was smart enough not to argue. He had promises to keep and miles to go before he slept. Outside her building, he got into the T-bird. The storm had ended as abruptly as it had begun, leaving the air humid and still and smelling of jasmine, decomposing leaves, and loamy earth. An almost full moon rode low in the sky, dulled to burnished copper. The tree frogs' insistent song shrilled the darkness.

He remembered when his father died, shot down in an alley not three blocks from home. He'd relived the moment when he'd been called to the scene over and over as if it were an endless loop. He couldn't think of his father in any other way than the man, suddenly old, crumpled, lifeless. It was as if he'd lost his father *and* all his memories of their life together. Until his father's cop buddies took him out drinking after the funeral. There, half-drunk, he'd absorbed their stories about his father—funny, sad, prideful, embarrassing—but always intimate. And in that way he'd regained his inner balance. Gradually, his father came back to him and he'd felt restored.

Now he thought about Sonia. His intimacy with Jenny had somehow freed him from the nightmare of constantly reliving the moment when he had pulled open her refrigerator door. At last, he could remember her as she should be remembered, her strong lithe body in his arms as they merengued across the Shark Bar's dance floor.

He drove to an all-night gas station. It was lonely, the quiet broken only by the buzzing of the moths and the faint sound of a plaintive country and western song coming from inside the central kiosk. Everything was automated; he didn't have to contact another human soul. That was all right by him. Just now, he felt as Jenny had after her hours in surgery. The oblivion of apartness was all he craved. Like Stone Tree in his comfortable shack in the Everglades.

While the tank was being filled, he tried not to think of the vision the spirit-stone had showed her. *Bump. Bump. Bump.* His own death. With a convulsive gesture, he inserted the floppy disk he'd pulled from Vonda's jaws into his notebook computer. The data had been partially corrupted by saliva, blood, glue, dust, who knew what else. The computer balked but he persisted.

Then his screen was filled with lines of data. Apparently the data had been encrypted, because every so often a gibberish word would appear in the text. What he read sent a chill through his veins.

Here, laid out in admittedly incomplete form, was documentation of a secret life, lived in the shadows carefully constructed by Uncle Sam. According to the spotty data, there was a high-level official running a top-secret operation within Croaker's own Anti-Cartel Task Force. There was a stern warning that all personnel working for something called DICTRIB were to be denied access to this data. DICTRIB, Croaker discovered several pages farther on, was the acronym for the Developing Capital Countries Trade Relations Bureau, secreted away within the U.S. Department of State.

The data showed vast sums of money being moved from the States down to various places in Latin America. Embedded in this data, however, was a frightening nugget: the fund transfers had only destination codes. The State Department was quite fussy about paperwork. All departmental requisition and transfer authorizations were required to have both origin and destination codes in order to be logged in with the dreadful dragons at Finance and Bookkeeping, who were wont to penny-pinch you to death. These ACTF transfers lacked origin codes.

That could mean only one thing: this operation was black-budgeted. Black-budget, a term Croaker had learned in his time with the ACTF, meant the operation was funded without the consent or even knowledge of Congress. In effect, it didn't exist. Blackbudgets were deemed necessary by the bureaucrats because, sometimes, covert operations or even entire divisions were deemed necessary—even vital—to powerful interests, even though their methods would never pass muster on Capitol Hill.

For security reasons, the major players in black-budget operations always used pseudonyms on documentation, whether electronic or hard copy. Often, these pseudonyms had secret meanings known only to those who chose them. This one was using the name Sero.

With a sense of mounting horror, Croaker recalled Estrella Leyes telling him about the special relationship between Bennie and his grandfather: *Humaitá had a secret name for Bennie he always used when they were together. Sero, he called him. Sero, the mountain.*

Here was a secret so foul it sent Croaker's head spinning. Could it be? Could Bennie Milagros be working for the Feds? Was that why he was so vague and secretive about his business dealings?

And what was Sero doing?

On his computer screen, Croaker saw evidence mounting. Not only of movements of cash, but of weapons, tactical command cadres, and strategic deployments of ACTF personnel throughout Latin America. All sanctioned and directed by Sero. By Bennie? Just what in the hell was he up to? Each time Croaker encountered a destination code, he pulled up more evidence of this highly detailed and carefully considered network. So much so, in fact, that at some point he realized that he was looking at the prep work for what must be the final phase of the operation. What the hell was going on down there? With the buildup of agents and arms, it looked like a hot war brewing, so far along that it could boil over at any minute.

And then he came upon one last bit of data. It was partially corrupted—so much so that it resisted all his attempts to copy it onto his hard drive. It showed evidence that Sero was running Juan Garcia Barbacena. Barbacena was Sero's chief agent and informant in the field.

The pain of betrayal was so severe Croaker almost doubled over. Now he knew why that secretive midnight run was so vitally important to Bennie. He was going to meet Barbacena. He needed to find a means of transportation that was totally secure. What better way than with a private charter boat, captained by a friend? That way, only two people knew of the arrangements before he gave them to Barbacena: Bennie and Croaker.

So this is what his friendship with Bennie had been reduced to: it was nothing more than a ruse to get Barbacena into the country under a security blackout.

Croaker pushed on with his work and was able to salvage two

partial invoices detailing shipments of what were designated medical supplies. But when he saw the six-digit numeric of place of loading—where the supposed medical supplies came from—his blood ran cold. He knew that code from his dealings with the ACTF. It was the Federal Arsenal in Arlington.

Sero wasn't sending Barbacena medical supplies; he was sending him government war matériel.

Croaker sat in the T-bird, stunned into immobility. This was a Bennie that Croaker did not know and could barely imagine. And yet, this was the way it was with the best of the masters. They created personas so perfectly realized it was impossible to imagine them any other way. Croaker ran a hand across burning eyes. He felt as if he was having a nightmare of a disaster happening he was powerless to stop—only to wake up to discover that reality was the real nightmare.

Of course, the thought immediately occurred to him that it was the Bonitas who had left this modern-day artifact for him to find. He pulled out the floppy, stared bleakly at the brief, ironic note: LOOKING FOR THIS, DETECTIVE?

Considering the source, the data had to be viewed with a certain degree of skepticism. Could be the Bonitas were trying to put Bennie in a frame. They certainly hated him enough. But it defied logic. How the hell could they have gotten access to a restricted government database?

But there was more evidence that Bennie's life was a lie. According to the Bell South records, he was paying for Majeur's private line. Was he Majeur's mysterious client? But if he was running Barbacena, why would he want his own agent killed?

That led Croaker back to Antonio and Heitor. They knew of Croaker, knew he was a detective. They also knew he'd seen Sonia. Antonio's first question to him rang in his mind: *You the boyfriend?* The Bonitas must know he and Bennie were friends. A sudden chill swept through him. How much more did they know about him? Was Rachel now in jeopardy from them? Was Jenny? His scalp began to crawl.

Majeur was not who he said he was, and now, it seemed, neither was Bennie.

Who was lying and who was telling the truth? Who presented more danger: the Bonitas or Bennie? At this moment, Croaker had to admit he didn't know. But he was sure going to find out. Until he did, he was like a man with a highly infectious disease, passing on deadly danger to everyone with whom he came in contact.

He got slowly out of the car and, walking through a battery of moths fluttering in the bright lights, returned the gas pump nozzle to its bay, closed the gas cap on the T-bird, and got his credit card receipt.

All of a sudden he got a flash of the Bonita brothers in his face as he clung to the back of their panel truck. *"Not now . . . not yet . . ."* Antonio had said, staying Heitor's hand. What did that mean? And why had Antonio allowed him to escape?

Back in the T-bird, he stared at the computer screen. He was at the end of the list of ACTF destination codes. He was about to close down the file when he notcied that the ribbon bar on the left side of the screen showed that he was not, in fact, at the end of the file. He hit the Home key twice, then the Down Arrow key. There, at the very end of the file, were embeds—symbols within seemingly innocuous text. You'd have to be looking for them, to notice they were screen prompts. He called them up and discovered three more destination codes. These, however, had a different prefix than the others. He cleared the screen, punched in the codes. The screen went black. He could see his modem being activated. Then the screen bloomed with color. He was interfacing with the DICTRIB net. Immediately, a security block popped up. All he could think of was to type in his ACTF temporary I.D.

The software accepted it. He entered the DICTRIB requisition codes and pressed Enter. The screen was wiped clear of data, replaced by an ominous message:

CODE RESCINDED. FURTHER ACCESS DENIED PENDING INTERVIEW 0600 TOMORROW FLAMINGO PARK STADIUM. ROSS DARLING.

Who the hell was Ross Darling? Croaker thought. And what the hell was DICTRIB? He worked the keyboard, trying to get an answer, but he was effectively blocked. Worse, when he relogged onto the ACTF net, he got nothing but a blank screen. His temporary access code had been revoked. Something he'd done had woken the hydra.

DAY FOUR

1

```

┌─────┐
│  ·  │
└─────┘
```

The spine of South Beach consisted of three main north-south thoroughfares—Ocean Drive, Washington and Collins Avenue—as they ran from First to Eighteenth Streets. But those boundaries were, of necessity, fluid; each week, it seemed, South Beach was expanding northward and westward.

South Beach had been in a state of decline for so long, residents still seemed stunned by its recent revival. Built in the Art Deco and Moderne styles in the 1930s and 1940s, it had been through the Great Depression when you could get a room at a near-deserted hotel for five dollars a week. Through the 1950s and 1960s it was part of the safe haven for retirees, mainly Jews from New York's garment and dry goods unions shops.

In the late 1970s and early 1980s, the run-down historic buildings attracted speculators with more money than expertise, and again, many people lost money. But only a few crucial years later, by the end of the decade, an influx of European designers, models, and photographers took quick advantage of the bargain-basement prices. They were intrigued by the kitschy architecture and wild Deco colors, but, Croaker suspected, their interest had more to do with resurrecting old-time Hollywood glamour than it did with a renascence of a bygone period of history.

It was just past midnight when Croaker parked the T-bird near the Madonna Club. Less than twenty-four hours until Juan Garcia Barbacena landed in South Florida and became Croaker's prey.

Photos of the lap dancers to be hired inside the club were sheened with colored neon, lending them an unreal edge. The retouched glamour of the photos—artificial and flavorless—served to remind him of Vonda's empty life. Like Sonia, all she'd needed was a chance at life she was not now going to get. Passing a cigar store with salsa music, raw and sweaty, blaring from its interior, his thoughts strayed to Bennie, and then the sick feeling in his stomach surfaced all over again.

He found the Lightning Tube without difficulty. This was the place Gideon's band ManMan was playing. Who was Gideon? Rachel's boyfriend. Her drug connection. All too likely both.

The Lightning Tube had blacked-out windows just like the Margate Gun & Racquet Club. He went around the corner, saw that the club extended all the way back to a narrow alley filled with green Dumpsters and a thin tabby cat that stared at him with eyes like marbles. Above the back door was a security light that buzzed like a nest of angry hornets. In the dirty stucco wall were two filthy windows. He looked in one, saw a urinal and a sink. On the opposite side of the alley was a metal security door bolted and padlocked. There were no windows in this building. He turned around and went back to the front entrance.

Inside, it looked like a garage—concrete floor and walls, a trio of old gasoline pumps from the 1950s. Blowups of pin-up calendar pages from that decade were projected on the ceiling. Steel catwalks crisscrossed the bilevel space. A bar, constructed out of iron and aqua-tinted fused glass, was the current center of activity. Cool cats in polyester sleeveless shirts and shiny slacks rubbed shoulders with model-wannabes with big lips and bigger busts.

A large-screen TV hanging from the ceiling was showing an episode of *The Patty Duke Show,* the great one where she played identical cousins. The sound was off, high-decibel rock music providing a bizarre soundtrack.

Beyond, on the raised dance floor, ManMan was setting up.

Croaker ordered two bottles of Blackened Voodoo, a New Orleans beer with a definite kick. He watched the graceless moves the cool cats were putting on the hot babes. He understood; at their age, he'd done no better. Maybe the only real difference between him and them was that he was a little less scared stiff by life.

Croaker, bottles in hand, strolled over to the band setup, approaching a guitarist.

"Beer?" he said.

She turned. "Do I know you?"

Croaker couldn't help staring. The irises of her eyes were as yellow as a New York City taxi, and the pupils were pitch black vertical crescents. She looked like something out of *Cat People.*

He shoved a bottle into her fist. "You do now."

She grinned, showing a silver blob piercing the center of her tongue. "Here. Take a *real* good look." She stuck the tongue out at him. The blob resolved itself into a tiny sculpted skull. She laughed and downed half the Blackened Voodoo in one ravenous swallow.

"I'm looking for Gideon."

She had a wide, almost pouty mouth, a strong, assertive nose, and glossy blonde hair. In another incarnation she might have been a college homecoming queen. But she wouldn't have been half as interesting.

She smacked her lips. "Gideon isn't here."

She was dressed in a black lace top and silver Lurex skirt so short the lower curve of her buttocks was visible beneath black tights. She wore four black leather belts with assorted studs, one on top of another, an armful of jangling Third World bracelets, and plain black ankle-high boots with chunky Cuban heels.

"You a fan, a groupie, or just looking to get laid?"

"That's some bad-ass attitude you've got there," he said, staring at her. Something about her seemed familiar. Could they have met before?

"Stay awhile; you'll get a load of what crawls through the door."

"I'd just like a word with Gideon."

She finished her beer. "Okay. You said that. So how come?"

"It's a personal matter."

She shoved the empty bottle on top of an amp and snickered. "Yeah, right. They all say that."

Her guitar was one of those solid-body electric instruments, fireball red with black roses on front and back. She slung it on her hip like a cowboy's six-gun. "This isn't about Gideon," she said. "It's about you." She leaned in, gave him a disdainful sniff. "You stink, man. Like you're strapped." She lifted an eyebrow. "Are you? Carrying a gun in that manly armpit?"

Once, as a boy, he had peered inside a burnt-out light switch only to discover the naked end of a loose wire glowing whitely. That hot aura had held him transfixed. He had wondered what would have happened to him had he stuck his finger inside without looking first. This girl reminded him of that light switch: a brittle plastic exterior concealing a white-hot current that could shock.

He lifted his arms. "I'm weaponless."

She rested her arms loosely on the top of her guitar. He noticed that they were well muscled. "Except for that Terminator hand of yours."

He dug out the photo of Rachel his sister had given him, held it in front of the guitarist's face. "You recognize her?"

"No."

But she was lying; Croaker was sure of it. It was a popular misconception that the eyes were an accurate monitor of truth, lies, imminent action. Forget the eyes, Croaker's father had taught him; look to the tiny muscles on either side of the mouth. These were the places where secrets were given up. "Her name's Rachel Duke. She and Gideon have a thing going, right?"

"You say you're not a cop, but I say you're a lying geek."

"Actually, I'm Rachel's uncle."

She fingered the strings of her guitar with studied nonchalance, but something in her expression had changed. Maybe she was Gideon's old girlfriend, jealous of Rachel. That's how things usually went in these bands. Whatever, he knew he had to press his advantage.

"I saw Rachel yesterday," he said. "In the hospital. She's dying."

For the first time she faltered. "Rachel's dying?" Slowly, deliberately she took off the electric guitar.

"You knew she was in the hospital, didn't you?"

"I was with her the night she freaked." Those eerie cat's eyes seemed to glow. "I'm Gideon."

"You're Gideon?" Croaker could not help staring at the peaked breasts that protruded saucily from beneath her black lace top. One thing for sure, he thought in that stunned instant, Gideon was nobody's boyfriend, least of all Rachel's.

A look of disgust crossed Gideon's face. "Fuck you. I knew you'd have that reaction."

Now he recognized her. Put a black wig on her head, dress her up in a see-through vinyl raincoat, and she was the model in the photo in Rachel's room. A sudden rage burned within him. He became aware that with each passing moment the one-ounce bag of coke in his pocket seemed heavier and heavier, until now it had become an insupportable weight. Something inside him egged him on—some spiteful piece so furious at Rachel's helpless situation, the hellish moral box he was in, his own bad assessment of Bennie, at the murders of Sonia and Vonda so close at hand they were like nerves rubbed raw. And now this—confronting his niece's lover, who just happened to be a lesbian feeding Rachel all kinds of drugs. He was unsure whether he wanted to interrogate her or murder her.

He slapped the plastic bag on the black top of the bank of amps, flipped open his federal I.D. and said, "Hey, pal, you're busted."

Gideon's gaze never touched the bag of coke. "What's this shit?"

"Something I found stitched into the lining of Rachel's leather jacket," Croaker said. "You know, the one with 'ManMan' printed on it."

"What were you doing in her closet? Gawking?"

"Looking for her diary."

Gideon pointed the guitar's neck at the bag of coke. "Hey, that shit's got nothing to do with me."

"It's got everything to do with you. You sold it to Rachel, didn't you?"

"I never sold her anything." Gideon's eyes glittered fiercely. Then she put aside her guitar. "Excuse me, I have to go pee."

Croaker watched her make her way through the dancing throng to the toilets in the back of the club. He moved after her. As soon as he saw her disappear into the ladies' room, he went through the kitchen to the rear door. He pushed through it into the Dumpster-filled alley.

He was just in time to see her slim body sliding legs first out the window of the ladies' room. He made enough sound to scare the tabby cat. Gideon, landing in a semicrouch, whirled toward him.

He could see her face, painted in yellow and black by the security light, like jungle camouflage. Her cat's eyes burned in the darkness as she backed up against the filthy wall.

He could feel the coiled tension sparking off her skin. What was she beneath her tribal paraphernalia? She was like some throwback creature, instincts honed to jungle pitch. If she wasn't quite feral, she wasn't domesticated either.

Croaker twirled the ounce bag of coke. "Now you'll tell me about this."

She almost spat out her words. "I do drugs. I make no bones about it. But I don't sell."

"Not here," he said and, taking her by the elbow, led her out of the alley and down Washington to the T-bird. He opened the door for her and they got in.

"Okay." He nodded. "You and Rachel did drugs together."

"Lots of other things, too." That defiant look was back on her face.

"But you provided the dope."

She nodded. "I drummed that one into her head. It was either me or some sleazebag out to rip her off. Too much evil karma floating around."

"Gideon, she O.D.'d on bad shit. And because of her drug dependency she may very well die."

"Look, I . . . Christ, Rachel's got an addictive personality. But I personally scoped out all the stuff we did."

"This time you fucked up."

She pointed a forefinger at him. "You've still got that attitude, don't you?"

"What attitude?"

"The 'You corrupted my pure little innocent niece' attitude!"

They sat, glowering at each other from a close proximity that rankled them both. *We're like wild dogs going at it,* he thought in despair. *What's wrong with us?*

And then he understood what was happening. They were battling over the same bit of territory: Rachel.

"Listen, Gideon, I care for Rachel. I know you do, too. I'm sure you want to help her."

She shook her head. "You have no idea what I want."

"I assume what drives you are the same emotions that touch everyone." It was the wrong thing to say. He knew it even before he'd finished the sentence.

Gideon made the harsh sound of a buzzer. *"Brrrup!* Wrong, uncle cop." Her voice had taken on the slightly condescending lilt of a game show host. "And now you've run out of questions to ask the freak. You're time's up and you've flamed out. We must ask you to get the hell out of our face."

"Gideon, I need your help. I know somewhere Rachel must have a diary. I went through her room and couldn't find it."

In another act of defiance, she reached out and turned on the cassette tape machine. "What're we gonna have here," she sneered, "Barry Manilow?" But her expression changed when she heard Nancy Sinatra singing "These Boots Are Made for Walking."

She gave him a quick look, then opened the glove box. Out tumbled a wall of cassettes: The Everly Brothers, Jan & Dean, Irma Thomas, Lesley Gore, the whole works. Gideon sifted through this veritable history of 1960s pop music as if she were in a treasure trove.

Suddenly she looked at him. And when she spoke, there was a new note in her voice: "You into this music—really?" A hint of conciliation.

"It's a passion."

"Yeah. With me, too." Her head bobbed up and down. "A-fucking-mazing."

The curious and thorny exterior was now dissolving, revealing the true creature beneath. In that moment, his anger was broken like moonlight on water. "For what it's worth, Gideon, I don't think you're a freak."

"Christ, I wish I could believe that."

"You can."

She looked down at the cassettes, turning them over one by one. At last, she said, "I hope so. We both belong to Rachel."

So she had felt it, too, that ferocious animal's imperative over territory.

"Then why did you run away from me?"

" 'Hey, pal, you're busted.' " She mimicked his voice with uncanny accuracy. "I saw the look on your face. I was indicted, tried, and sentenced all within the space of a heartbeat. Right then, you weren't ready to listen to anything—especially what I had to tell you."

He said nothing because she was right. He had been ready, willing, and able to condemn her out of hand. The late nights, the coke, the adrenaline rushes, the kinky sex. The whole sleazy picture had formed in his mind and he knew why. It was because of what she was. He felt the small bulge of the red rubber ball with the silk cords at the bottom of his pocket. She was dead on. In his mind, she'd corrupted Rachel.

"I made a mistake with you," he said. "I won't do it again."

"Is that so?" But her tone was less defiant. She'd gone through that phase, made her stand—and her point. Now a cautious note of curiosity had crept in.

She bent her head down, put her thumb and forefinger into each eye. When she lifted her head, the bizarre cat's eyes were lying on the tips of her fingers. They were contact lenses. Her own eyes were china blue. As she put the lenses away in a plastic case, her eyes lost focus for a moment. He would have given just about anything to know what she was thinking.

"You were right about Rachel. She does have a diary." She looked at him from the side. "Did you happen to see the sachet in her dresser drawer?"

"Sure. It smelled of lilac."

"So does her diary."

She stuffed it inside the sachet, Croaker thought. An ingenious hiding place for a girl with secrets and an inquisitive mother. "Thanks," he said.

Gideon seemed not to have heard him. "Older people have this thing." She stacked the cassettes back in the glove box. "They think it's the wisdom of years that makes their flesh hang from their bones like crepe paper." She looked at him. "Well, here's something for you to chew over. Rachel O.D.'d, but it sure as hell wasn't because the drugs were bad. I was doing the same shit that she was—all fucking night long. *That* I guarantee a hundred percent. Got it?"

Croaker thought about the implications of what Gideon had just told him. He knew he needed to speak to Jenny Marsh as soon as possible. Why had Rachel O.D.'d and not Gideon?

"That night," he said softly, "did Rachel do a lot of drugs?"

"Yeah."

"What kind?"

Cars hissed by. The Nancy Sinatra tape had finished playing, but neither of them made a move to replace it.

"Early in the evening we dropped some acid. We smoked maybe a couple of joints over dinner. Then, later, when we were at the club, we both did coke."

His fingers curled into fists on the steering wheel. "Jesus."

"In retrospect, the whole cocktail thing—you know, the drug mix—was maybe something we shouldn't have done."

"You could say that."

"I'm sorry." Gideon put her head back against the leather seat. "You can't possibly know how sorry." Tears were glittering in her eyes. "I don't want anything to happen to her."

"I know." This was not a young woman you could easily take in your arms to console. So he did the next best thing; he changed the subject "What club?"

She wiped her eyes with a forefinger. "What?"

"You said you were at a club that night. Which one?"

"The Boneyard, up here on Lincoln Road. It's a coffee bar in front. In back, it's got this Internet virtual sex thing. Rachel liked to hook up there a lot."

"You didn't?"

Gideon gave him a dark and unnatural look. "I indulged her."

That remark sank into his consciousness like a fishing lure into deep water.

"Here's the thing," he said. "I need you to tell me about Rachel." He took out the red rubber ball. Its black silk strings fluttered down. "You know what this is." It lay in his hand like an evil eye, plucked from a skull.

"It's a ball gag. S-M shit."

"I found it at the bottom of Rachel's closet. Did you and she—?"

Gideon shook her head. "Not my thing. Not *our* thing."

In her face he saw the truth form like an air bubble rising to the surface of a lake. Croaker took a deep breath, let it all go. "Was she seeing someone else?"

Gideon suddenly seemed disturbed. "Maybe she was. Anyway, I thought so." She sighed. "We argued about it often enough. She always denied it, but . . ."

Croaker held still. Because it seemed to have triggered a response, he didn't want her to lose sight of the ball gag.

"But what?"

"You know everyone's got buttons. You push 'em and wham!, they go off like fireworks. The question of whether she was seeing someone else was one of Rachel's." Gideon put her hands together almost as if she were praying. "I told you that she had an addictive personality. That didn't begin and end with drugs."

"What did it begin with?" he asked softly.

"Sex." Gideon shook her head. "See, for me sex is very straight-forward, always has been. But for Rachel—" She spread her hands. "I don't know, it seemed like she was all tied up in knots about it." She interlaced her fingers tightly. "It was almost like pleasure and guilt were mixed up together, as if she couldn't feel one without the other."

"Which role is she into?" He rolled the red ball around his fingertips. "Dominant or submissive?"

"I don't know. With me, she's neither. We trade off, depending on our moods." She pushed her hair off the side of her face.

"Do you have any idea who else she was seeing?"

"Uh-uh."

He said, "She found someone to do the S-M thing with."

Gideon nodded. "That's my guess."

"Man or woman?"

"I'd say a man. Definitely."

"No suspicions who?"

"Uh-uh."

Croaker continued to roll the ball. "She must have given you clues. People always do, whether they're aware of it or not."

"You'd have to be a psychic to pick up on them," she said. "I mean, the only male I'm aware she's seen has been Ronald what's-his-name. Her doctor."

"Stansky?"

"That's the guy."

"I know about that. My sister said she took Rachel to see him six months ago. That was for Rachel's annual school exam. But you couldn't have been with her all the time. You have your band— you must've been on the road. She could've seen anybody then and you'd never know unless she told you."

Something had come into Gideon's body. A tension that was so pronounced Croaker could feel its reflection, like midday sunlight off pavement. "What is it?"

"Maybe nothing." Gideon toyed with her silver-studded belts. "But it's interesting Rachel's mom thinks she saw Stansky only once."

"Why?"

"Because during that time Rachel saw Dr. Stansky maybe half a dozen times."

"What for?"

Gideon shrugged. "Insomnia. Problems with her period. A sinus infection. Anemia. That sort of thing." She saw the look on his face and responded to it. "But there couldn't have been anything more to it."

"How do you know that?"

"'Cause I drove Rachel every time she went."

"Wait a minute," Croaker said. "What did Rachel need you to drive her for? She could've biked over. Stansky's office is in Palm Beach, not far from where she lives."

"No, it's not," Gideon said. "This Stansky's got a clinic in Margate."

Margate, Croaker thought. *That's where the Gold Coast Exotic Car Rentals is.*

Something began to click in his mind. It was the sound of a sinister engine running in absolute darkness.

Croaker held up the obscene red rubber ball with its silk cords. "I wonder if Dr. Ronald Stansky knows what a ball gag is."

Gideon gazed at it as if it were a dark star. She tapped its curve with a fingertip. "I wonder if the damn thing's his."

Croaker saw her back to the club, then returned to the T-bird.

"I want to see Rachel," Gideon had told him just before he'd left her, "but I don't want to be there with Matty. Rachel doesn't want her to know about us and I don't want to be the one to break it to her."

"Don't worry. She'll think you're just a friend."

"No she won't," Gideon told him. "I'm not just a friend and I won't lie."

Croaker knew enough about her to believe that, so he told her when Matty was least likely to be at the hospital.

He turned the ignition and gunned the engine. It seemed to him curious that he now thought that Rachel was in some ways lucky to have met Gideon. He pulled out in time to touch off the air horn of a semi rolling up Washington right behind him. He sounded his own horn, but the semi wasn't slowing. Its driver seemed confident in his truck's overwhelming size.

Croaker thought, *The hell with it,* and stepped on the gas. The turquoise T-bird shot out into the avenue. In the periphery of his vision, he was aware of the huge chrome grille of the semi filling the rearview mirror. It seemed to overflow it. The driver of the semi, startled out of his cockiness, slammed on his brakes as Croaker roared off.

By the time he had made a left onto Tenth Street, he had a sense he was being followed. A white BMW sedan with heavily smoked windows. To make sure, Croaker made a sudden left onto Pennsylvania with the T-bird's custom engine roaring. The white BMW accelerated into the turn, rocking on its shocks.

Croaker could see the Miami area laid out in front of him as if on a lighted grid. Miami Beach was one of what was essentially a chain of islands separated from the mainland by the Intracoastal Waterway and Biscayne Bay. It was connected to Miami by a series of causeways. Because South Beach was on the extreme southern end, going south from here was a dead end unless you were going to take the MacArthur Causeway, that linked Fifth Street here with Thirteenth Street in Miami.

That was going to be his immediate destination.

Guessing right, the white BMW made up some time and was close on his tail as he wove in and out of the slow-moving traffic on the causeway. It was interesting—and ominous—that the BMW was not interested in hiding its intent. They flew past Star Island on the right, then Palm and Hibiscus Islands, small, exclusive enclaves of houses, each with their own boat slips amid the palm trees and massive Florida rooms giving out onto magnificent million-dollar views of the bay. There was enough money afloat on that small part of the bay to satisfy even the most grandiose ego.

Despite his best efforts, Croaker could not pull away. Flat out, the T-bird's 425-horsepower engine could out-torque the BMW, but when it came to maneuvering between cars the BMW's streamlined shape and superior cornering had a distinct advantage.

All at once they were into another world entirely: downtown Miami, stark and modern, anonymous-looking big businesses vying with tacky tourist shops. Traffic dried up like drizzle in tropical sunlight. When there was a choice, Croaker had been careful each time to take the obvious one. He wanted to make it easy for the driver of the BMW to get so comfortable with them he'd begin to unconsciously anticipate them.

It was the same technique by which you controlled a suspect in an interrogation. You revealed little bits of yourself until he was under the misapprehension that he was in control. That was okay. Your first job was to get him to be in synch with you. Then when you pulled away this security, he was yours.

The T-bird crisscrossed shadows. For moments at a time it was lost to the BMW until the driver caught on and switched his attention from the silhouette of the T-bird to the twin beams of its head-lights, which told him not only where Croaker was but where he was headed.

The sidewalks were as deserted as if a neutron bomb had been detonated. Even the hustlers and streetwalkers had migrated with the tourists and the kids south to Coconut Grove. Blue-white light bounced off high-rises' reflective windows, but in between, the darkness had the stifling impenetrability of the jungle.

Croaker headed south again, along the very end of Biscayne Bou-levard. Soon he would run out of road. At First Street, he cut over to S.E. Second Avenue. Still heading south.

They were alone on the street, arrowing through the unquiet urban night.

Into the city smell of hot, sooty concrete, seeping diesel fumes and stripped rubber tires came another scent: water, slow-moving as sludge.

They were approaching the Miami River, and Croaker's scalp began to itch.

As the driver of the BMW read his moves and reacted to them, as Croaker then responded to the BMW's counters, a kind of invisi-ble cord had sprung up between them. Like knife-wielding adver-saries bound by a short length of rope, they had traversed the city without having lost or gained ground. Their arena was still the space between the T-bird and the BMW.

Now that was about to change.

Up ahead, he could see it, a large hulking presence, part massive steel stanchions, part poured concrete. In the streetlight-studded darkness, it looked like the skeleton of a saurian rising from its tar pit deathbed.

It was the new Brickell Avenue Bridge, and he was headed right for it.

The bridge had been under construction for over a year now, its concrete underbed only half complete. The rest of the span was bare metal girders. The approach road was closed off and barri-caded with wooden sawhorses, banks of blinking amber lights, and a mobile electronic message board that warned: ROAD CLOSED. DANGER!

You bet.

As he approached, he could make out the forms of cranes, bull-dozers, piles of steel piping, iron girders, wooden scaffoldings, bags of cement powder. He was heading straight for the unfinished bridge. It was there in the close shadows that he would engage the BMW. If he didn't plunge at top speed into the river.

Croaker extinguished his headlights. Then he jerked the wheel over hard to the left, pushing the T-bird into a lane that would have been filled with oncoming traffic had it been hours earlier. With a screech of tires, he floored the car, pouring all the horsepower under the hood into a single fireball shot that would bring him through the barriers, onto the unfinished bridge.

He had baited his pursuer with those beams, hiding in the shadows so the driver would be forced to fix his attention on them in order to follow the T-bird. Just when the driver had become used to its beacon lights, he'd switched them off.

On the unfinished span, he drove the T-bird with the concentration of an acrobat venturing out onto a high wire. Beneath his tires, bare iron rails. Between them were gaps that could trap a wheel and instantly disable the T-bird.

He took his foot off the accelerator. The T-bird glided along the iron girders of the bridge like a locomotive. Then he stepped on the brake.

Bursts of yellow from the caution lights illuminated the interior in the rhythmic bursts of fireworks. He got out of the car and found a space between the sawhorses. He edged into the darkened construction site.

It smelled of oiled machinery, wet concrete, and creosote. He paralleled the BMW's headlight beams as if he were skating on moonlight. He could see the glint of metal. Pipes and girders were stacked on either side of him. They were striped by dark shadows thrown from a makeshift ramp of wooden boards and plywood just to his left. From between the gaps, the amber caution lights winked on and off like giant jewels. Beneath his feet, more metallic glints. Water ran in dark rivulets across the rough underbed of the unfinished bridge.

To the west, he could hear the roar of a car engine joining the endless hum of traffic on I-95. But he was far away from that sound, so much like a beehive, on a dark and perilous periphery. He was acutely aware that his work here had as little to do with that traffic stream as it did with the big boats berthed at the nearby island havens. He was all alone in the night, as cut off from everyone and everything as if he were piloting the *Captain Sumo* in uncharted waters miles from shore.

From behind him came a deep-throated roar. He turned in time to see the white BMW airborne. The driver had used a wooden work ramp as a launch. Croaker picked up a length of metal pipe. The BMW overflew the T-bird and was almost upon him when he raised his biomechanical hand. He jammed the end of the pipe between the front axle and the underbed of the car. When it landed, it went into an arcing skid. It tipped up onto its right-side wheels. The pipe created a shower of sparks, trailing behind it like a Roman candle.

Croaker ran into the shadows.

Somewhere behind him a car door slammed. He listened for another door to slam, but none came. There had been only one person in the BMW, and he was now following Croaker onto the bridge.

He worked the construction site scientifically, breaking it down into quarters and methodically searching each one. This far onto the bridge, the beams of the BMW's headlights were fractured into brittle shards by the machinery and materials. The only other illumination came from the blinking hazard lights at the foot of the bridge.

He was almost midway over the river. The iron girders arced like a pair of mastodon's tusks, bare and burnished in the light like patinaed ivory. He looked down at the river, and when he turned back he saw something behind him. Melting back into deep shadow, he circled back the way he had come. It was difficult to make out anything clearly. The blinking lights played tricks, causing him to see movement where there was none. He thought he saw a patch of darkness more distinct than the surrounding shadows. He froze where he was, watching it for some time. It could be the silhouette of a human being, or not. But there seemed to be a quality about it that was somehow unnerving.

A moment later he lost the shape. He blinked. Had it moved or had it merely been a trick of the light? He couldn't say, but in any case he moved cautiously toward where it had been. He was now on the edge of the bridge's skeleton. In front of him, between the bare bones of its steel girders, the river gleamed dully.

It was in that split instant looking down at the water that he sensed the movement behind him. He'd heard nothing, however, but the now familiar background sounds of the city at night. His head came up and he was turning to look behind him when the gun butt crashed into the side of his head.

Croaker collapsed onto the girder. The acrid smell of rust and oiled metal swept over him as he gripped the girder. He grunted as a steel-tipped boot struck his rib cage. It plunged into his side again. In order to get away, he was forced farther out along the span. He crawled painfully along the girder, with the understructure below him and the river below that. His tormentor followed, striking him again and again with the heel of a boot. He could not see beyond that boot, could not even turn his head enough to identify the figure towering above him.

Now the heel smashed into Croaker's side, kicking his body off the girder. With a rush of humid air into his lungs, he swung from the girder, holding on only with his hands. Every time he tried to gather his legs beneath him to try to swing his whole body back up onto the girder, a boot trod hard on hip or knee.

Croaker felt the fear stir deep inside his belly. This man was giving him no chance to counter. The two choices left him were equally bad: he could either continue to grip the girder while he was slowly pummeled into unconsciousness or he could let go now and drop into the black and gunmetal spiderweb of the understructure. Maybe he'd survive all that metal and drop into the river; more likely the metalwork would break his neck or back or legs before hitting the water.

Croaker did the only thing he could do. He waited for the boot to whistle toward him again. Then he shifted his weight to counterbalance himself as he let go with his biomechanical hand. Opening his stainless-steel and titanium fingers he grabbed the boot just before it struck him and shoved it outward.

The man fell to one knee. In almost the same motion, he dropped his left leg downward. The heel of his boot struck Croaker in the forehead.

Croaker almost lost consciousness and his right hand lost its grip on the steel. Seeing Croaker swinging from the fulcrum of one hand, the man grunted in satisfaction. He pulled back his leg to deliver another vicious kick and Croaker let go with his titanium fingers.

He dropped into blackness. But it was no more than two feet. He landed on a diagonal brace and he clung there, half-stunned, staring upward at his adversary. He had a pain-blurred glimpse of a darkened face. Then he was staring into the muzzle of a gun. From the manner in which the man pointed it at him, from the tension coming into his frame, Croaker knew he was going to use it, that he had meant to use it all along.

When he'd been a kid he'd loved model trains. He loved the perfect miniature world they inhabited, stations with tiny painted metal commuters and sidings where they picked up diminutive wooden logs. But mostly, he loved the sound the metal wheels made over the tracks. It had a peculiar metronomic sound that was blissful. Now, hanging by a thread from the unfinished span, he heard that sound again.

His would-be killer heard it, too, because he whirled in time to see a man. Though he was crouched over, Croaker could see that he was tall and lean. He was hurtling toward them from the far side of the span with impossible speed. As if in a dream, Croaker saw his legs moving with the gliding swing of an expert ice skater. Only there was no ice. He glided across the steel girders like a wraith or a demon summoned up from another time and place. Then he passed through a patch of light and Croaker saw he had on a pair of in-line skates.

For a man approaching at speed he held his upper body astonishingly still. It was very odd. The skater held his left arm straight out as a marksman might, but there was no gun in his hand. Instead, Croaker could see the dark glint of a small round object held against the open palm.

The skater launched himself through the air. He was hurtling straight at Croaker's assailant. The man shifted his aim from Croaker's face to the oncoming skater.

The man pulled the trigger. The sound of a gunshot, flat and ugly, smacked against the buildings. It rebounded over the construction site like a flock of startled birds taking flight.

Then the man and the skater both crashed to the concrete, entangled. The skater immediately pressed two fingers against the side of the man's head. The man seemed to freeze, as if every nerve connection in his brain had been temporarily frozen. With the heel of his other hand, the skater slammed the man's head against rough concrete. Then he opened his slender fingers. The dark stone gleamed against the flesh of his palm. Without a word, he pressed it hard against the man's breastbone. The man's mouth gaped open and he arched off the steel girder and the wet concrete.

Croaker clung to the diagonal brace, panting with expended effort, fear, and an excess of adrenaline. Lights blinking in the distance seemed to spin around on mad axes. He felt his muscles begin to spasm and he knew he could not hold on much longer.

It was then he looked up into the face of the skater. It peered down at him, dark and large as a harvest moon.

The skater clucked like a mother hen. *"Madre de mentiras, señor, you are having one shitty day."*

It was Antonio Bonita.

He clambered down until one foot was braced against the steel beam to which Croaker clung. He reached down and gripped Croaker's hand. With surprising ease, he helped him back onto the girder. He sat back on his haunches as Croaker knelt.

Long after he'd shaken off the aftermath of the vertigo, Croaker kept his chin on his chest as if in utter defeat. He concentrated on putting the pain into a confined space while he built back his strength.

Without warning, he lunged at Antonio, his stainless-steel nails extruded to their full length. But the slim man danced away, circling like a vulture on his in-line skates. He shook his head, lifted a warning finger, rocked it back and forth. Then one finger became two, three, four. And between each finger he produced like a magician a dark green stone, smooth as glass.

"Not tonight, *señor*. Not ever."

Croaker stared at the stones, wondering at their power. And though he knew this was precisely what Antonio wanted, he'd been given enough warning by Estrella Leyes and by his own experiences with the soul-catcher Bennie had given him to know that, for the moment at least, Antonio was beyond his control.

Croaker settled back down, willing the tension out of his frame.

Antonio nodded. "This serenity is difficult for you, I know." He seemed pleased, as if Croaker's effort at self-control proved a point he'd been trying to make.

Croaker kept his expression neutral, though he was racked by pain. "Why did you save me?"

Antonio, circling back, shrugged. "I like you."

"You saved me twice." Croaker began to stretch his terribly cramped muscles. He was careful now not to make any sudden moves. "Your brother wanted to kill me."

"Do not presume to know Heitor's mind, *señor*."

"I don't even know your mind. You killed Sonia."

Antonio said nothing. His amber eyes studied Croaker as incuriously as if he were a specimen on a lab table.

"And yet you came to her house pretending to be her brother, Carlito. Why?"

"I wanted to see you for myself, *señor*." Antonio had come to a halt. He was so still it was unnerving. And now Croaker knew the shadow he'd followed out onto the girder had been Antonio. "No. It was more. I wanted to *meet* you."

"So you could lie to me? What was the bullshit with Carlito and Rosa?"

Antonio's amber eyes darkened. In Southeast Asia, Croaker had been taken tiger hunting. These were large, silent beasts, very powerful, very cunning hunting machines. But these attributes were all secondary, he'd been told, to what made the beast so deadly. It was the tiger's unpredictability. You never knew what was in its heart, when it would turn on a dime and claw the flesh from your rib cage. In the darkness and the striped yellow light Antonio looked like such a large jungle cat—sleek, swift, deadly. Unknowable.

"Others lie to you, *señor*. As Carlito, I spoke the truth. Carlito worked for us, just as I told you. The description of our operation is as I described it. We allow the people who work for us much autonomy. In return, they embarrass us with riches. They enjoy an elite lifestyle—they become untouchable. They are, for a time, like demigods."

"And Carlito?"

"He was just as I depicted him—strong willed, vibrant, a player with a capital *P*. But he was also, how shall I say, a bit too independent minded."

"So you killed him."

"In a way, he was responsible for his own demise, *señor*. He knew the rules going in. We have no secrets from our employees on that score. Betrayal on any level simply is not tolerated."

When, as now, Antonio smiled in just that way Croaker could feel a connection that made his bones grow cold.

"Now you understand," Antonio said. "My life's work is to lead people into sin. If I find that weakness in them, I punish them."

Such an enigmatic man. And yet with Croaker, he seemed to ache to be known.

"Did you love Bennie's sister Rosa? Did you ask her to marry you? Was this the truth you told me? It couldn't be, because you killed her."

"But it is the truth, *señor*. Every word."

Croaker shook his head uncomprehendingly. "What could you possibly know about love? Everyone you touch you kill."

"Not everyone." Antonio pursed his lips. "But it is true that people who fall into my orbit are, ultimately, weak. People sin. It is the human condition."

"And, according to you, sins demand to be punished." Croaker stirred. He could find no position in which his body did not ache. "Why? You're not God, to decide such things."

"In Asunción, I *was* a god. People came to me—sick unto death—people without hope. They surrendered everything to me and I healed them."

This was the special knowledge that Bennie's grandfather had taught the Bonitas. This was the mesmerizing quality of his stare that caught you unguarded. "That man who was about to kill me," Croaker asked. "What did you do to him?"

Antonio grinned. He offered his left hand. In it flashed a dark green stone.

" 'The dark stones know,' " Croaker said. "That's what you said on the back of the truck. This is *Hetá I*."

Now the grin disappeared. "Who has told you this?" The stone vanished as well. "Whatever you think you know of *Hetá I*, forget. This is sound advice, *señor*. It is given out of friendship."

"We're not friends, Antonio."

Antonio rose silent, majestic as a crane unfolding itself in marsh grass. *"Escuchame, señor."* Listen to me. "In this life, friends are not friends."

As he disappeared into the darkness, Croaker called after him: "Antonio, how did you find me here? How did you know I'd be at Sonia's?" There was no answer, and Croaker stood on cramped legs and raised his voice. "I'm going to track you down, Antonio. For what you did to Sonia and Vonda."

The known landscape consisted of the urban susurrus of cars speeding by far away, the steady blinking of the yellow caution lights at the foot of the bridge, the soft purling of the sluggish river far below.

From out of this darkness came Antonio's voice: "You are already in my orbit, *señor*. But as of yet you are another exception. You have not sinned."

A seagull cried, the lorn sound no less explosive than the sound of a gunshot. Croaker shook himself back into awareness of the immediate environment. It was not so easy; Antonio Bonita had a way of holding you spellbound.

Croaker went to where the unknown gunman lay in the shadows. He was young, not more than thirty—and he was large. He must have weighed well over two hundred pounds. He wore black cotton clothes. Lightweight, functional. The kind of clothes you went out in at night when you wanted to blend into dark backgrounds. There was blood all over the lower part of his face. Above, his cheeks and forehead were smeared with lampblack. Even in moderate light, his face wouldn't show up.

In the impossible instant his gray eyes opened, Croaker felt paralyzed with shock.

The man's left hand curled into a modified fist. The knuckles, ugly with calluses and scars, canted forward at a precise angle. Croaker, familiar with many forms of hand-to-hand combat, recognized the preliminary movements of karate. The fist smashed into Croaker's ribs, making him grunt in pain. Then he kneed Croaker and went after him in earnest.

In combat, a skilled assailant has two choices: immobilize the victim or kill him. It was clear this man wanted to kill Croaker. He was going for the throat.

Croaker rolled and the strike glanced off a collarbone. It was still powerful enough to make him see stars. The man gave Croaker a vicious kick in the shin, then drove his deadly fist inward for the killing stroke. Croaker, gasping in pain, had only one option and he took it. He wrapped his biomechanical fingers around the man's throat and pressed inward with his thumb. The cricoid cartilage broke apart and within seconds the man was dead.

It was never an easy thing to kill a man. Even when you had no other choice, the act made you sick in your soul. No matter what anyone told you to the contrary, once you killed a man you were changed forever. There was a scar inside you that no amount of time could heal.

Croaker used his biomechanical hand to search through the dead man's pockets. He found a wad of ten hundred-dollar bills, a handful of extra ammunition, and a Snickers bar. Sugar for a quick burst of energy. He stripped off the corpse's belt and steel-tipped boots, checked inside.

No I.D. No keys. Had he left them in the BMW? A short walk to the white car revealed keys still in the ignition. Croaker searched the car, found nothing. He glanced at the vehicle tag, saw it was one of those reserved for a car dealer. Stolen. No way to trace it. This man was a professional.

On the way back he found the gun. It was a modified Colt .38 Special. One of the modifications was black sticky tape wound very tightly around the grip. The other was that the serial number had been filed off. The mob used weapons like that. So did field agents of the ACTF.

Who was this man? Croaker didn't know, but with a premonitory shiver he rolled the bullets around his palm. He needed to get them into better light to make sure.

Croaker stared down at the corpse. What had Antonio done to immobilize him? Just two fingers to the temple. Then he'd pressed a spirit-catcher to his breastbone. Why? He needed to speak to someone with an expertise in Guarani *Hetá I. Estrella Leyes.*

He picked his way back to where the dark T-bird hulked and, reaching in, turned the key in the ignition.

Square in the beam from the headlights, he took another look at the bullets. Dark Stars. They were custom made. They had heads that acted like shrapnel, exploding inside a body. Lots of damage—usually fatal, even if you missed a vital organ. Also, there was nothing but unidentifiable bits of twisted metal for a ballistics expert to find.

He felt as if he were in an elevator plunging from a height of a hundred stories up. He had seen bullets like these before. In fact, he had had occasion to use them. They were standard issue for certain field personnel in the Anti-Cartel Task Force.

With due deliberation he sat behind the wheel of the T-bird. He looked at his face in the rearview mirror. His skin was as pale as if he'd just seen a ghost. He dropped the bullets into his pocket.

Still lost in thought, he sped off, heading north.

What kind of hydra had he wakened? He'd tried to penetrate something sacrosanct. The Developing Capital Countries Trade Relations Bureau. Was that why the ACTF, the bureau he had once freelanced for, now had him marked for death? Maybe Ross Darling, the man who had cut off Croaker's computer access, would provide the answers. If Darling didn't himself try to finish the job the gunman had been given.

He rolled into SoBe and parked on a quiet, leafy street three blocks from Ocean Drive. It was 3:30 A.M. and he needed some sleep. Only hours before his meeting with Ross Darling.

He hauled himself out of the T-bird and went up the steps of a small stucco building. Its exterior had been recently renovated. Painted deep blue and purple, Art Deco colors to fit in with the surrounding gentrification. He was not surprised to find the front door open. It was always left open.

This was St. Francis of the Palms Church, but everyone in the neighborhood called it the Surfers' Church. Sixteen months ago, the new priest had begun an outreach program to gather the lost kids, already half-dead on coke and heroin, who drifted like a red tide of algae through SoBe. How successful he had been remained yet another religious mystery.

There was something about the interiors of churches, a kind of hush that spoke directly to the soul. You didn't have to be a practicing Catholic to feel it: the particular density of liturgy and extirpated sins. The atmosphere felt as if it hadn't changed in centuries, which was of course the point. You were meant to feel that no matter where you were born, when you passed through the sacred portal you had come home.

Croaker was not hypocrite enough to go through attendant rituals he did not believe in. Nevertheless, he felt the last of the adrenaline leach out of him as he sat in a wooden pew and drank in the place.

The arches in the cream-colored stucco interior were studded with dark wooden beams, stark iron nails whose heads were as big around as his thumbnail. The carved wood altar was covered by a holy cloth. Against the rear wall rose an image of the crucified Christ. On either side were painted plaster statues of the Virgin

Mary and of St. Francis. The interior smelled of candle wax, age, and the sea.

Croaker put his forearms across the back of the pew in front, lowered his head to the impromptu pillow. The moment he closed his eyes, his mind slipped away.

Mercifully, he could no longer recall the instant he had pulled the trigger on his first kill—Ajucar Martinez. Later, people would call Martinez a madman, but Croaker knew better. Martinez wasn't nuts, he was demonically evil. He knew just what he was doing all the way down the line as he had slashed his way through five hookers. Croaker hadn't told Majeur the whole story regarding Martinez. He'd not only tattooed their faces with his razor; he'd not only cut off their breasts. He'd made them eat the organs before he slit their throats. Somewhere in the universe, there might be a word to adequately describe this man, but if so Croaker didn't know it.

Croaker had caught up with him, and when Martinez had come after him with the razor he'd wielded so expertly, Croaker had shot him in the knee. Not nearly enough to stop a man like Martinez, whose extraordinary will to kill and to keep on killing was like a potent intoxicant. It wasn't even enough to shut his mouth. His impromptu oration was horrifying—a vivid description of his work on the whores he'd murdered. It was, Croaker supposed, why he'd shot Martinez in the face. Twice.

The split instant between life and death was now as opaque to him as winter ice in the Adirondacks. But the look on Ajucar Martinez's face was not. Below a shattered forehead, above an all but obliterated jaw and throat, the man's eyes were open in a fixed stare. In them, Croaker could see not only the realization of Martinez's death but a piece of his own life. This shocked him so much that for a moment he'd felt as if his heart had ceased to pump.

Like an animal with a battle-scarred face, something of Croaker had been irrevocably expended in his effort to stay alive. It was no longer his, and he would never get it back. It was this, not the sight of all the blood, that made him turn away and vomit.

That night he had been pursued over the terrain of his dreams. The relentless presence was behind him no matter which way he ran, which turns and twists he took, no matter where he hid.

In the gray light of dawn when he had awakened, he'd quickly dressed. Without shaving or showering, without breakfast in a stomach clenched tight with apprehension, he'd entered the cool echoey apse of S. Maria Gloriosa. He had not been to his neighborhood church in many years, but now it had become a place of ultimate sanctuary. Beneath the great stained-glass windows where, years before, he and Matty had been confirmed, he knelt. He spoke to no one, not even when Father Michael had walked by and Croaker knew he had been recognized.

That afternoon, he'd cancelled his date with his girlfriend. He could no more talk to Angela than he could talk to Father Michael. He had awakened from his nightmare with the sure knowledge of who was pursuing him over the dreamscapes of his own imagining. It was God.

Croaker stirred. There was an art to sleeping in hard, awkward places. If you didn't know what you were doing, you'd wake up with your neck so stiff you couldn't turn it without pain lancing up into your skull. He slid down in the pew and looked out a side window. He watched the movement of the leaves beneath the streetlights. In the way in which they refracted the light, they transformed plain plate glass into the stained-glass windows of S. Maria Gloriosa.

After a time, he closed his eyes. He dreamed he was in a calm and peaceful place. Blue-green light glowed like clouded sunlight on a faceted jewel. He drifted on a diffuse and syrupy bed. Then, with a start that jolted his heart, he realized he was lying facedown in water. His arms were flung wide and his lungs were burning. He longed to take a breath but he knew if he did he'd drown. At last, he couldn't hold out any longer and he opened his mouth to breathe. . . .

Stone Tree had once told him of the giant lying out of sight just below the horizon. Opening eyes full of pearls after a long night's sleep, this giant sent reflected light into the sky in advance of the sun.

Croaker woke up to find the sky was no longer dark.

2

At six in the morning, Flamingo Park Stadium was not quite as deserted as one might expect. On the western fringe of SoBe, it was surrounded by low- and mid-rise buildings from the 1940s and 1950s. A felicitous gentrification was infiltrating the neighborhood—renovations, repainting, and restoring apartments to a state surpassing their original glory. Now "CONDOS FOR SALE" signs hung in front of these complexes even while workmen moved in and out of open doorways.

At this early hour, the tradespeople had not yet arrived, but across Meridian Avenue, kids were tossing hardball around the baseball diamond or skateboarding on the pavement just outside the stadium. Dogs barked joyously as they ran, chasing one another across the playing fields. From somewhere nearby, the scent of freshly brewing coffee entwined with the jacaranda and jasmine.

Croaker, his shirtsleeves rolled up, was giving an impromptu lesson in bunting to a nine-year-old. As Phil Rizutto liked to say, bunting had become a lost art. Croaker was just doing his bit. He felt oddly clearheaded for someone with only a couple of hours of sleep and this was why:

Moments ago, he'd spoken to Rafe Roubinnet on his cell phone. Rafe never slept; he liked to watch the dying of the night from the deck of his sixty-five-foot catamaran. After the incident on the Brickell Bridge Croaker knew he'd need a safe haven. His sister's place was out of the question and Sonia's was already known by the Bonitas. Rafe was the obvious choice: he was a friend who owed Croaker a great deal. The ex-politician's contacts and shrewd mind were priceless assets now. Rafe agreed to meet him at the Miami Yacht Club at one that afternoon.

"Here's the key," Croaker said to a freckle-faced nine-year-old named Ricky. "You want to hit it hard enough to get past the catcher but not hard enough so the first or third baseman will get it in time to tag you out."

"Swinging away, I'm a champ," Ricky said. "I can place the ball anywhere. You think I'm kidding? Watch." He swung the bat in a practice swing. "Right field," he said and promptly hit it there. "Center," he said and drove a line drive up the middle. He put the bat on his shoulder and grinned. "It's a kinda trick, really. Julio—he's the pitcher—sends me the right pitch for wherever I want to hit it." He shrugged. "But with bunting, I don't know. It's not so easy."

"Let's give it a try." Croaker watched the kid put too much pressure on the bat and mistime the bunt.

"Don't hold the bat," he counseled Ricky. "Cradle it. Like this."

He didn't look up, even when a tall, stoop-shouldered man detached himself from the last of the shadows of the wide Meridian Avenue entrance. The man had prematurely white hair and such a red-cheeked face he looked like he'd just come back from a cold-weather run. He had pale blue eyes the color of shallow water and his hair was cropped detention short. He was not a young man but this haircut made him seem older. He had the kind of face you rarely saw anymore—one that had once presided over traveling carnivals. His was a face made up of equal parts sheriff and judge. Perhaps he had seen one too many marvels of human oddity because there was something in his demeanor that made it clear he could no longer be surprised.

The man walked methodically to the backstop. He had the heavy, even tread of a veteran boxer entering the ring: one part wariness, two parts resignation.

He wore one of those traveler's raincoats you could fold away in a pocket. It was tissue-thin and was as wrinkled as an elephant's hide. Beneath it, he wore an old-fashioned charcoal suit with narrow lapels and a pair of Cole-Haan tasseled loafers. Maybe he was an early bird on his way to work.

When the man was positioned directly behind Croaker, he said, "Time to talk."

Croaker spoke softly to Ricky one more time as he repositioned his hands on the bat. When Ricky nodded, he turned around and began to walk down the first baseline in foul territory. The white-haired man was forced to hurry to catch up.

"Ross Darling, I presume?"

"Don't be cute." Darling must be sweating in that raincoat; it was one of those awful man-made fabrics that didn't breathe.

Croaker kept walking at a brisk pace. "You the honcho who eighty-sixed my ACTF code?"

"What was your code doing in Dicktribe territory?"

"Is that how you pronounce DICTRIB?"

"Speak softly and carry a real big dick." Ross Darling pulled his raincoat closer around him, as if he felt a sudden chill. "What did you think you were doing? Fooling around with Mommy's cookie jar?"

This was going to be fun, Croaker thought. Two grown men throwing questions at each other without much hope of getting a single answer. But there was no harm in trying.

"I assume since you closed me down that the distribution numbers I fed into the computer are from the DICTRIB database."

"If they were real I'd want to know real fast what a guy like you is doing with them. I'd request a rendezvous with a guy like you and I'd put a stop to your poaching, pronto."

Croaker sighed. "I suppose this is where you pull a gun and threaten me." He stood so that he was straddling the white first baseline.

"It's true I don't trust you worth a damn," Darling said. "But I don't happen to believe in guns. They're loud and they're gross and, worst of all, they make you lazy. When you're holding a gun you don't have to think, do you?"

His right arm extended and in a flash he'd manacled Croaker's biomechanical hand with a ring of black metal. "A titanium and molybdenum alloy even you can't break. I had it made especially." He said this matter-of-factly, with no particular hubris.

The band held Croaker's hand fast. He was unable to move his fingers, even to flex them. "So you're a thinker, Darling." Croaker kicked in what appeared to be annoyance and frustration at the lime of the first baseline.

There was a sharp crack of a bat. Then Darling quickly ducked as a baseball went whizzing by him.

As he was doing so, Croaker wedged himself against him. "Let me go," Croaker whispered in his ear.

"What?" Darling froze at the feel of metal pressed to the side of his jaw.

"This," Croaker said, "is a modified Colt .38 Special."

Darling did nothing for a moment. He breathed evenly, in and out. Croaker could almost hear him turning over the probabilities in his mind. At length, he carefully snapped open the titanium and molybdenum cuff.

Croaker moved the .38 to where Darling could see it. As Darling examined it, he waved at Ricky, who gave Darling the finger, then waved back at Croaker. Kicking the first baseline had been the signal for the kid to hit a ball at Darling. "It's got black tape wound around the grip and the serial number has been professionally defaced. Sound familiar?"

"Should it?" Darling said blandly. He'd already recovered from this small reversal of fortune.

Croaker dug in his pocket. "It's loaded with these." He held up one of the handmade bullets. "I remember what we call these, Darling. Dark Stars. Because when they hit that's all they leave. A big black fucking hole in the target."

"You sound pissed."

"Being set up for target practice does that to me." Croaker waggled the .38 Colt Special. "Last night, someone tried to take my head off with this."

"Christ. The situation's worse than I thought," Darling said.

"Just what the hell does that mean?"

"You've been officially sanctioned for termination," Darling said. "How does that particular bureaucratic euphemism grab you?"

The sun had crept above the low lying clouds on the eastern

horizon. It sent its light flooding over the top of the bleachers. A shadow, a dark crescent made by the top tier of the bleachers, ringed the field.

"All of a sudden, the fog's clearing," Croaker said. "Un-huh. I can see how you'd want me killed, pronto."

"It doesn't track," Darling said. "Think about it. Why would I set up a meet with you and in the interim order your termination?"

"You tell me."

"I wouldn't," Darling said. "I didn't. Moeover, I know who did."

He was awfully cool for a man with a gun to his head. As Croaker wondered about this, his eye was caught by an almost phantom movement. The shadow cast by the bleachers had changed shape. A little piece stuck up above the symmetrical curve and this interested Croaker. It was in a place directly behind Darling's left shoulder. Croaker was more or less facing it. If he looked up he might see what was causing it. Or maybe not. He'd be looking directly into the sun.

"Okay, I'll bite," Croaker said. "If you didn't order the termination, who did?"

Darling said archly, "Hey, I have an idea. Let's have a piss-off. You're hot because you've been sanctioned. I'm hot because I don't know what the fuck an ACTF freelancer is doing with classified Dicktribe code numbers."

Croaker ground the muzzle of the .38 deeper into the other man's temple. "Listen, you little shit. I know there's a specific ACTF directive against computer access by any and all DICTRIB personnel. It's clear DICTRIB and the ACTF are enemies. I've done work for the ACTF. Last night I almost get my head blown off by a Fed stalking me. His weapon of choice is ACTF issue. I think you know all about the attack."

"I do. But you're dead wrong, Croaker, if you think I had anything to do with it."

"At least I'm not dead."

Out of the corner of his eye, Croaker saw the slight movement in the edge of the bleachers shadow and knew what that meant. Without warning, he grabbed a fistful of Darling's raincoat with his biomechanical hand and jerked him clean off his feet. Darling stumbled and Croaker half-dragged him into the shadows of the bleachers.

They crouched under the seats. It smelled of rotting wood and decayed plant matter. Soft light, laced through with sawdust, filtered down from above. It felt cool and protected.

"What the hell is this all about?" Darling whispered.

"Only one reason why a man with a gun to his head stays so calm," Croaker told him. "He's not alone." He jerked again on Darling. "Isn't that right? Someone's at the top of the bleachers—I saw his shadow on the field. Get him down here where I can see him," Croaker growled.

"You don't get it. My man is a lookout and a sentinel. He's armed with a high-powered rifle but I guarantee he won't shoot you." Darling's gaze did not leave Croaker's face. "On the other hand, he'll make damn sure no one else does."

The sudden crack of the hickory bat against the ball was amplified by the close quarters they were in. There were shouts of encouragement. Someone had hit a long ball.

"Like who?"

"Why don't you ask Spaulding Gunn, the director of your own ACTF? He's the one who ordered the sanction." He looked at the expression on Croaker's face. "Poor bastard. You don't believe me, do you?"

"Why should I?"

Croaker, looking out at the playing field, could see Ricky running as hard as he could toward first base. The ball he'd just bunted was bouncing between the catcher and the first baseman. Right now Croaker felt like that carefully placed ball, ricocheting between a rock and a hard place. Who was lying and who was telling the truth?

"Okay, answer me this," Croaker said. "I've seen compelling evidence that there's a highly classified and volatile ACTF operation under way. It's black-budgeted and it involves pouring agents and arms into Mexico. Is this the truth?"

"It is."

Croaker took a breath. Now for the question he did not want to ask. "I caught a glimpse of what appears to be an agent code-named Sero operating under ACTF aegis. Who is Sero?"

"Sero is the name of Gunn's second-in-command, that much is confirmed. We don't know his real name. Yet."

Darling was about to say something more when his cell phone rang like the call of doom. He looked at Croaker, who nodded his permission. He listened for a moment, said into the phone, "You know the drill," and hung up. "That was my sentinel," he told Croaker. "We have to move. Now." His eyes were very pale. "Gunn's people have found us."

"Gunn wants you dead, on this you can rely." Darling crouched in the darkness, his elbows on his thighs. People, typically, have one of two reactions to confined quarters. Either they are uncomfortable in them or they affect a studied indifference to them. Darling's reaction was neither. In the way he held himself in this dark, cramped space was the certain knowledge that he had served time overseas. In Southeast Asia you learned to embrace close quarters smelling of dampness and urine because they were often the only thing standing between you and being caught by the enemy. You also learned to use weapons of silence. Croaker remembered Darling's speech against guns. It had been short and to-the-point. It had also been correct.

Croaker and Darling were in an aluminum air conduit that hung from the ceiling of the basement of the White House, a gay club on the north side of Lincoln Road. It was not far from the Boneyard, the Internet sex club Gideon and Rachel frequented.

The White House was where Darling had taken them when he'd got the signal that Gunn's people were on the way. Half a dozen of them—young men in lightweight suits and Versace T-shirts. They could have passed for models, except for the .38 guns in quick-release holsters at the small of their backs.

Croaker knew ACTF field personnel when he saw them.

Two were gone now, diverted by Darling's rifle-toting Boy Scout on the top tier of the Flamingo Park Stadium. The rest had gotten the scent and, like bloodhounds, were not to be deterred.

"What the hell is going on?" Croaker said. "I *work* for the ACTF."

Darling cocked his head, listening to the rhythm of the industrial silence. The metered thump of the massive compressor that controlled the central air-conditioning unit and the generator that had come on when Darling had cut the main power. He said, "Gunn wants you dead because you've contracted to assassinate Juan Garcia Barbacena."

There was no point in asking how Gunn had found out. Croaker had worked inside the ACTF long enough to know they could ferret out just about any secret if they put their resources behind the effort. But there was another, more pressing question he needed to ask. He needed confirmation of the intelligence he'd found embedded in the floppy disc. "I want to know if Spaulding Gunn and the ACTF is running Juan Garcia Barbacena as an agent in place in Latin America."

"Why do you think he wants you terminated," Darling said. "Barbacena is Gunn's point man south of the border. Gunn and the man named Sero."

Croaker felt his heart hammering in his chest. "What if I were to tell you that Sero is the secret nickname Bennie Milagros's grandfather called him?"

Darling's eyes widened. "Is this true?"

Croaker nodded.

"Christ, we've caught a break at last!"

Darling broke off abruptly. Croaker strained his ears. Nothing.

Croaker shook his head. "This doesn't sound anything like the ACTF I was mustered into."

"There's a good reason for that," Darling said. "It's not." With his head cocked like that, he had the appearance of a hunting dog. He seemed satisfied that they were alone. "Within ten months of Spaulding Gunn's appointment as director, he had eviscerated the ACTF of all key personnel and had installed his own people. How did he manage that? He had been given the unprecedented clout to cut through all the governmental red tape. Somebody had an agenda that just couldn't wait. And that somebody, we subsequently discovered, was a group composed of canny, old-line Senators and some of the top people at the Department of Commerce who were aggrieved that much of their power had been taken away in the most recent governmental budget shake-up."

"How did DICTRIB come into being?" Croaker asked.

Darling gestured. "Where did all the former ACTF people end up? We could have become desk jockeys at some other bureau within State. Or we could have taken early retirement. We did neither. Instead, we banded together, formed a nucleus, called in every favor that was due us, and were duly set up in a bureau of our own. Three years ago the Developing Capital Countries Trade Relations Bureau was a sleepy little bureau inhabited mostly by worldview economists with thick glasses and egg on their ties. In the back rooms, where Gunn can't see or hear, we made it into a full-fledged operations bureau, just like the ACTF. It was a modest setup, to be sure. But it was ours. We were determined to make it an outpost to keep track of Spaulding Gunn, find out his agenda, and throw a very heavy wrench into it."

Darling was listening again.

"This sounds like war," Croaker said. "Only it can't be because it's between two factions of the U.S. Government. It's nuts. The people who let you take over DICTRIB can't know what you're up to. They'd never sanction a hot war between bureaus."

"Our people are cabinet level," Darling said. "They can and they have."

"But why?"

"Latin America, bud. It's the next economic miracle about to take off like the space shuttle. Only this time, it isn't on the other side of the Pacific. It's right on our doorstep because the key to all of Latin America is Mexico. And the profit potential is nothing short of mind altering." Darling looked at Croaker. "The situation's like this: Gunn's gone into orbit on this. Even his own people know it. But they're either too greedy or too damn scared of him to reign him in. That's where Dicktribe comes in. We edge in, take over Gunn's game, keep it under control."

"Install your own people, you mean," Croaker said.

"Better ours than Gunn's, bud. Believe it."

"But first Barbacena has to be taken out."

Darling nodded. "With his priceless south-of-the-border contacts, he's the key. Without him, Gunn's plan is dead in the water." He paused, tense. He seemed to be sounding all of their environment at once. "The name of the game is control," he said. "And in this game, there's only one rule: he who controls the most, reaps all the profits. And, believe me, profits are where it's at these days. Especially for politicians. It's a whole new world for them out there and they don't like what they see. They're running scared. People are turning them off just like they turn off the networks for cable channels. It's the time of the independents and that makes everybody nervous. D'you think the speaker of the house or minority whip like knowing they're being zapped in mid-oration? Not damn likely."

"Okay. I can see that. But what exactly is Gunn up to with Barbacena?"

Darling stiffened. Now Croaker could hear them. Arrhythmic sounds intermittently beneath the drone of the compressors: Gunn's people, searching for him.

Croaker could tell their pursuers were close. Three armed men. Three blind mice.

Another sound from behind them caused him to turn his head. Not blind, then. They'd sprung their trap and were closing in from both front and back. Now Croaker understood why they'd been making so much noise. It was the theory of the hunt: they had become "beaters," driving their prey to the killing ground.

"They must be using heat seekers," he whispered into Darling's ear, who nodded. Heat seekers used infrared beams to pick up the body heat of a human being. Even absolute darkness wasn't a deterrent.

"Keep very still," Darling had whispered back. "There's plenty of metal and concrete to deflect the beams."

Before Darling had a chance to stop him, Croaker slithered farther along the conduit to a large removable grill. Peering through the latticework, Croaker could see a vertical ladder bolted to the concrete wall that led down into the basement proper. There, the darkness was leavened by a series of ancient yellow-bulbed emergency lights that had come on when Darling had cut the power. They spread their weak glow in foot-wide circles over rough concrete walls blue with mildew. No matter what Darling thought, he'd be damned if he was going to be caught in a confined space where he had no room to maneuver. He took out the .38 and loaded it with Dark Stars.

He pushed aside the metal grate and let himself down through it. He grasped the top rung of the ladder and began to descend. The place smelled unpleasant and musty, and the rungs were gritty with rust and oily dirt, accumulated over who knew how many years.

He was less than halfway down when the rung beneath his left foot gave way. He swung out wildly, came crashing back against the metal ladder. The back of his right hand smashed against a rung and the gun went spinning out of his grasp. It landed, bounced, and skittered into darkness on the rock hard concrete floor below.

Cursing under his breath, Croaker steadied himself and went on, descending more cautiously now.

Behind him, he could hear Darling's soft breathing. He was coming.

So were the mice.

Good. They'd have to figure they'd flushed their prey.

He reached the floor of the basement and immediately knew he'd have no chance of finding the gun in this ill-lighted maze. Besides, there was no time.

Once, Croaker had gone hunting for alligators in the back country of the Everglades. Stone Tree had given him the drill. The alligator, he had said, is a predator. He attacks with speed, and if you turn tail and run in a straight line he'll catch you for sure.

In the most primitive part of his brain man is also a predator.

One of the mice was very close now, his powerful legs pumping in long strides, taking full advantage of the heat seeker he held in one hand. In the darkness, he believed it gave him an absolute advantage. That belief often made people overconfident, and this is what Croaker was counting on.

There was no way to outrun him so Croaker didn't try. Predators count on their prey turning tail and running. So Croaker did the one thing this predator wouldn't imagine. He held his ground and, as the man bore down on him, swung his left arm up and out. He grabbed the man in midflight, wound his arm around the assailant's waist, and pulled him down sharply in the direction of his own momentum.

But even as the assailant crashed to the concrete floor, he slashed upward with a knife. Croaker felt the blade slice through the material of his shirt. He chopped at the man's wrist and the knife went flying, but he had left himself open and the man sent a short, vicious chop to his kidneys.

Croaker went down on all fours, and the man brought the edge of his hand down sharply between his shoulder blades. Croaker collapsed, all breath driven out of him.

The man scrambled after his knife. Just as his hand closed around it, Darling dropped from the conduit and kicked out. The man was very fast and Darling managed to connect with his shoulder instead of his throat. The man spun around and Darling came after him. That was a mistake.

The man deflected Darling's punch, jammed his fist into Darling's stomach. Darling doubled over, gagging, and the man slammed a knee into the side of Darling's face.

As Darling dropped to the floor, Croaker drove a stainless-steel nail into the man's side. He gasped, tried to use the heel of his hand as a club. But Croaker grabbed it, began to twist it away. The man tried to knee him in the groin, struck bone instead. Croaker chopped down very hard with the edge of his hand, striking the side of the man's neck. He collapsed in a heap.

Croaker heard shouts from the other end of the basement. Scooping up the heat seeker, he ran to where Darling was gasping on all fours, braced against an iron pillar.

"Shit," Darling said as Croaker helped him up. "I've got to get out on the street more." He gingerly touched his cheek. "The bastard almost broke my jaw."

"Come on." Croaker hefted the heat seeker. "Now we have a chance."

In a series of storerooms, he found everything he needed: aluminum foil, wire cutters, electrician's tape, an extension cord. He took off his jacket and wound sheets of aluminum foil around his chest.

He whispered to Darling as he worked. "When they demonstrated the heat seekers to us, they warned us to be careful around kitchens—foil, the microwave if it was on, would play havoc with the infrared beams." He tucked the last piece of foil into his armpit. "This ought to be enough to fool them." Then he gestured. "You're going to be the bait, okay?"

Darling nodded.

They went back out into the basement proper. Croaker kept track of their pursuers with the heat seeker. "They're coming," he said. "If we're lucky, they're only reading you."

When he found an outlet in the wall, he went to work on the extension cord with the wire cutters. When he was finished, he plugged in the cord. He directed Darling farther down the basement so that the extension was between him and their pursuers. Then he stretched the cord out until it was taut. He taped the other end to the wall against which he crouched. It was just above ankle height.

He could hear the pursuers coming at a run, and he took one last glance at the heat seeker to make sure of the trajectory of the source. He had just enough time to register the conflicting data when someone ran right into the center section of the extension cord. The part from which Croaker had stripped away the insulation. A welter of sparks shot into the air and he could smell the singe of burning cloth and flesh. He saw two figures on the bare concrete floor spasming with the aftermath of the electric current.

He was just getting up from where he was crouching when he felt the muzzle of a gun press against the back of his head.

"Okay, smart boy, stay right where you are and call your buddy over." The muzzle jammed painfully against his skull. No wonder the heat seeker had given him confused readings. At some point as they had been running, this man had separated from the others in a flanking maneuver. "Nice and easy now. Let's not alarm him, okay?"

Croaker did as he was told, and Darling came toward them from the spot where he'd been standing. Sparks still flew and juddered in the darkness, throwing a fitful illumination over the scene.

Croaker, looking down, could see that the lower part of his legs were made visible in the arcing light. The man, standing to one side of him and slightly behind, might be visible, too, if you knew where to look or what was happening.

"Stop right there," the man said from right beside Croaker's ear.

But Darling didn't seem to hear him; he kept on coming.

"I said"—the man gripped the back of Croaker's neck, his thumb pressed hard in the carotid as he swung his gun around toward Darling—"stop right there."

There was a movement from the shadows—no more than a blur, really—and Croaker felt a swift current of air. Then the man pulled the trigger. The flash of light, the harsh sound of the report, seemed contained and magnified by the concrete walls.

Croaker slammed his elbow into the man's side, but he was already falling. A knife blade was buried in his throat. Croaker let him fall.

"Darling?"

"Just a flesh wound." Ross Darling came toward him clutching his right shoulder. Blood was dribbling between his white fingers. He gave Croaker a small smile as he kicked the dead man who'd been holding Croaker at gunpoint. "No so good with my fists but I still know how to throw the knife."

"Barbacena's mission has been to destabilize Mexico." Darling looked like an albino. The overhead fluorescent lights drained all color from his face. "He is doing this quite cleverly. You see, he saw in the ragtag Chiapas dissidents a perfect cat's-paw—people with a cause who he could indoctrinate and arm. A force he could make mighty and manifest themselves at just the right time. Who he could use to attain his own ends. With Gunn's help and money, he has done just that. Even more importantly, he has given them a power base. He has brought in professional soldiers to train farmers how to kill. He has given them what every dissident the world over dreams of: legitimacy."

Darling swung his head abruptly around, said in a sharp tone, "Doctor, enough already. Get this done and over with. I have important work to do."

They were in the White House basement, but now the power had been restored, the lights were on, and the area was crawling with DICTRIB agents, including a doctor who was tending to Darling.

"The wound has to be properly cleaned to prevent infection." The doctor was a dark-skinned Hispanic with oiled hair and the unflappable manner of a M.A.S.H. surgeon. It was clear he was used to plying his trade on the fly. "Don't move." He coated a cotton swab with a yellowish liquid. When he applied it to the wound Darling winced and bit his lip.

"Just give me a shot of penicillin or whatever it is and slap the damn bandage on," Darling said with watering eyes.

He turned back to Croaker. "At this meeting, Gunn himself will give Barbacena his final orders. If Barbacena is allowed to return to Chiapas, he will sell the dissidents arms which Gunn is providing—advanced weaponry from our own military arsenals. This superior firepower along with key intelligence will allow the dissidents to gain complete control of the south of Mexico. The Mexican Government will be in complete disarray.

"In a matter of hours they will have lost control of the reins of power. The Bolsa—the Mexican stock market—will plunge. It will be like 1929 on Wall Street. We are so closely tied to Mexico that our own equity and bond markets will plunge in sympathy. In desperation, the Mexican government will plead with Washington for help, and ironically, Wall Street will be clamoring for exactly the same thing: intervention of a semipermanent sort."

Young men in shirtsleeves and holstered 9mm Brownings came and went wordlessly, cleaning up the remains of the human carnage. The smell of industrial-strength cleaners and disinfectants clogged the recycled air. When they were finished, Croaker was certain there would be no trace of this mortal encounter.

"Then and only then Gunn and his people in the government will step in," Darling went on, "and, with Barbacena's help, dismantle the dissidents piece by piece, once and for all. In their wake, they'll leave in place a new government made up of their hand-picked people. A puppet government, eternally in debt to certain elements in Washington. Then these elements will be able to manipulate both the manufacturing and the financial markets in Mexico. And you know the saying: as Mexico goes so goes South America."

"But how are they going to find these people so quickly?" Croaker asked.

Darling smiled as he rubbed the white patch of gauze the doctor had taped over the wound. "Spaulding Gunn has already recruited them, indoctrinated them, and set them in place in positions of business prominence in Mexico City. They're like sleepers awaiting their call to action."

Croaker thought for a moment. "So if, during the course of this rendezvous with Gunn, Barbacena was to be terminated you would feel . . . what?"

"I'd kiss your goddamned feet!" Darling nodded. "That's right. If our presence inside Justice has proved anything it's this: Spaulding Gunn is a dangerous madman. The power he's been given has warped him. His ambitions override the specific mandate he's been given. He's planning to take ultimate control over the economic pipeline he's helped establish with Latin America." Darling waved the doctor away. "I'll be brutally honest, Croaker. Terminating Barbacena is the only answer. It's a move we'd dearly love to make, but for us it's too radical. Even if we succeeded in terminating him, even if we were as careful as we could be, we'd leave a trail behind that someone like Gunn is expert enough to ferret out."

He got up and they walked through the labyrinthine basement.

"I want to be perfectly candid with you," Darling said. "Here's what's bothering me. More than anything, I need a way to terminate Barbacena." He snapped his fingers. "And, just like that, you appear." His pale gaze bored hard into Croaker's eyes. "How is that, do you think?"

"The same thought has occurred to me," Croaker said. "But I was approached by a man named Marcellus Rojas Diego Majeur."

"Majeur . . . Majeur." Darling rolled the name around. "He's a hotshot lawyer for some of the elite South American drug lords."

"Right. Here's the deal. Juan Garcia Barbacena had a wife."

Darling nodded. "Theresa Marquesa."

"She found out he was cheating on her. She threatened him and he killed her. He beat her unconscious and then strangled her with an electrical cord. Because he is protected, he'll never be charged. *This* is why I was hired to terminate Barbacena. It has nothing to do with you or Gunn or your dirty little war. It's strictly personal."

Darling considered this. He nodded. "It makes sense. I've read the file on her death. The police found evidence of a break-in—forced entry, money and jewelry stolen. It was ruled an unsolved homicide and now it's a closed case. In fact, from what I could see only a token investigation was ever done. For instance, where were the bodyguards when Theresa was attacked? I thought it curious that Barbacena himself never objected."

His brow furrowed. "There's still the matter of how you came into possession of classified Dicktribe codes."

"The Bonitas."

"Christ, if the Bonitas are involved . . ." Darling turned, signaled to an agent who hurried over with a notebook computer. Darling snatched it from him and crouched down. He turned it on and his finger spun the trackball mouse.

"This is a classified ACTF file we're looking at," Darling said.

Nothing was sacrosanct these days, Croaker thought as he scanned the information on the screen, not even the most top-secret files. But then he knew firsthand what the government could compile on an average citizen. Just about everything, down to his children's preferences in toys and videos.

"There's a pattern," he said.

"You bet there's a pattern." Darling leaned forward, punched the Page Down key.

Croaker was looking at what the ACTF called a Serial UnSub, a file put together over time with enough similar or identical bits and pieces of murder MOs to designate the case "Serial Murders, Suspect Unknown."

"You see, this one was relatively easy to compile," Darling said. "All the victims were decapitated."

"And none of the bodies were ever found." Croaker ran his gaze down the list. "This file is four years old."

Darling nodded. "The first decapitated head was discovered out-

214

side Tallahassee. Coroner indicated in his report that the murderer knew his business. No cutting and hacking, no jagged wounds. The neck was severed neatly and completely with a scalpel."

Croaker had an immediate flash of Heitor Bonita in the gaping black doorway of the panel truck, wielding a scalpel. "With only a scalpel?" he asked.

"That was the coroner's judgment. There were no metal tooth marks."

Croaker looked up from the screen. "So the murderer didn't use a saw. He severed the spinal column with just the scalpel. That would take a lot of strength."

"It would take a goddamn bull."

Croaker wanted more than anything to take a breath of fresh air, to see the blue sky and feel the sun burning his skin, but he was in the wrong place for that. It would be nice, one day, to feel clean again, but he wondered whether he ever would. "The Bonitas are responsible for all these murders, aren't they?"

"We think so, even though there's no proof." Darling used the trackball and the screen changed. "Take a look at this."

Croaker scanned another confidential ACTF file. It detailed a burgeoning black market for human organs in the Southeast.

"There's something this file doesn't show," Croaker said. "You have very little time to get an organ from one body to another. Except for kidneys, organs can't be kept outside a human body for long. Antigen typing typically takes six to eight hours. How did these people know which bodies to send to which recipients?"

"We have no idea." Darling said it in a voice that led Croaker to believe he had other, more pressing questions to answer. "We've been trying to figure out why Gunn has these files. He's tracking the Bonitas; he's keeping a close eye on the organ harvesting ring. But he's not taking any action against it."

"Evil soul, this Gunn," Croaker said. "Clearly, there's a connection between him and the Bonitas."

"You bet." Darling shut down the computer. "I see they hacked into our system, which, considering our safeguards, is alarming enough. But just what the hell were they up to slipping *you* Dick-tribe codes?"

Croaker sighed. "I think it was accidental. The Bonitas and Bennie Milagros have a history together, and it's not a particularly pleasant one. Bennie pretended to be my friend. He didn't tell me he was working for Gunn. He's involved in your little war up to his eyebrows. That's the material they wanted me to see. The DICTRIB codes just happened to be embedded at the tail end of the file. The Bonitas probably didn't even know they were there."

"Let's hope you're right. In the meantime, I'm changing all the computer security codes." Darling left the computer on the concrete floor while he walked Croaker to the rear stairway that lead up to an alley behind Lincoln Road. "I wish I could give you more tangible help, like backup or tactical support, but it just isn't possible. So far as I've involved myself with your safety, I've already put my bureau at risk."

"Don't worry," Croaker said. "I appreciate the help you have given me."

Darling extended his hand and Croaker took it. "One more bit of advice. Stay as far away from the Bonitas as you can. They're pure poison. And, as you've seen, they're being protected by Gunn." Those eyes that seemed witness to all man's foibles and follies now stared deep into Croaker's soul. "Get to Juan Garcia Barbacena. For the good of everyone, do what needs to be done. And then for God's sake get clear."

3

Croaker listened to Love's 1968 album *Forever Changes* as he sped north to Palm Beach on I-95. Somehow, the band's rococo psychedelia seemed appropriate to the occasion.

American interests inside Latin America. It was business as usual, he thought. We were going south of the border for the same reason we always stick our noses into foreign countries: to protect the interests of a very privileged few. With the Latin economies exploding, we sure as hell wouldn't want insurgents or, worse, socialist-leaning governments in power. We marched into Kuwait for the oil lobby. Which lobby was backing Gunn? The autos? Maybe it's the exporters. It made sense. Mexico is our second largest export market behind Canada. We couldn't afford to let that level of profit be compromised by the rabble-rousers. But that kind of work is plenty dirty. It's got to be kept behind locked doors.

Thoughts of secrets led him, inevitably, to Antonio and Heitor. *They're pure poison,* Ross Darling had said. *And as you've seen, they're being protected by Gunn.* Of course they were protected. According to the files, they were running an organ harvesting operation with ACTF connivance. Is that how Gunn had amassed his enormous power in so short a time? Was it leveraged off the dead bodies of people murdered by the Bonitas? How many elderly senators, congressmen, cabinet members, would be lined up for new parts, assured they could get any organ their aging bodies needed? Croaker didn't care to speculate on numbers. When it came to survival, human beings were the cleverest of species. Stone Tree had told him that. He said it was because they were so damned good at rationalizing. Even the most evil of men fervently believed they were acting out of right and good.

Except maybe the Bonitas. Croaker had spent enough time around Antonio to understand that there was a difference in these twins, they were something "other." There was a terrible, pale fire in their souls that was inextinguishable. It would be easy to mistake that fire for *Hetá I.* They were people who knew good from evil; they had simply chosen evil.

He exited the highway and went east on Okeechobee Boulevard, to Olive, which was U.S. 1. There he went north.

What was bothering him the most was Rachel. It was just too coincidental her getting ill at just the time Barbacena was coming into Miami. The moment Gideon had told him the drugs she and Rachel had taken were clean, he'd become convinced that Rachel's collapse and condition had somehow been engineered. But how? And by whom? He had one suspect in mind, but he needed some kind of proof.

He pulled into the parking lot of the Royal Poinciana Hospital.

The true hell of his situation was now staring him in the face. Even if his suspicions about Rachel being set up proved true, there was nothing he could do about it. She was still dying. Without the kidney being offered by Majeur's client she wouldn't last the week. He was sinking deeper and deeper into a wide-ranging conspiracy. But his path was set. Kill Juan Garcia Barbacena and Rachel would live. There were no alternatives. The fact that Majeur and now Darling had given him any number of reasons to detest Barbacena did not help much. Killing someone in defense of your own life was one thing. Coldly and calculatingly planning a murder from afar was quite another. Croaker had met a good number of paid assassins and mercenaries in his time. One thing they all shared that Croaker did not was they had hearts of stone.

Croaker got out of the T-bird and wanted to run across the concrete. It was not yet eleven and the day was already swelteringly hot.

The hospital was as cool and hushed as the mechanism of a Swiss clock. There was something about hospitals that made you tired the moment you walked in. Maybe they fed gaseous tranquilizers into the recycled air to keep everyone calm.

In CCD, Croaker tiptoed into Rachel's cubical. She looked white as milk and so thin she might have floated away if not for the blanket and sheets. Blue veins pulsed slowly beneath skin turned thin and waxy. The digital readouts told him she still had a fever. They hadn't yet beaten the sepsis infection.

As he kissed her warm forehead, he whispered, "I found Gideon. She'll be here soon, honey." Then he took her limp hand in his and squeezed. "Hold on, Rachie. You've come this far. Just hold on a little longer."

Matty, returning from the bathroom, saw him and flew into his arms.

"Lew, where have you been? Where did you sleep last night?" She had been weeping, he saw. The sight of him made her begin all over again.

"Hush." He stroked the side of her face. "By tomorrow she'll have a new kidney."

"Oh, Lew!"

He gently disengaged himself from her arms. "Matty, do you have that extra key to your apartment?"

She nodded, rummaging through her handbag. As she handed it to him, she said, "You found Gideon, didn't you? What's he like?"

"Not at all what I expected."

"I'd like to see him." She drew out a Kleenex and wiped beneath her eyes. "In a way I feel I know him. He's a kind of link now to her."

Croaker led her to a chair and made her sit down. "Have you seen Dr. Stansky?" He did not want to continue talking about Gideon. His sister already had enough on her mind without having to deal with Rachel's sexual orientation.

Matty shook her head. She looked very tired. "Usually, he comes in late in the day. Do you want me to give him a message when I see him?"

"No. In fact, don't even mention I asked." He leaned down and kissed her cheek. It was as cool as Rachel's was warm. "Are you okay, Matty?"

"I'm fine."

"You don't look it. When was the last time you ate?"

She gave him a wan smile. "I'm not hungry."

"Force yourself. Honey, this will be over soon. Everything will be all right, I promise you. In the meantime, you're no good to Rachie in this state."

She forced a wider smile and nodded. He left her there, at her vigil. There was nothing more he could say. But he went down to the commissary and bought some food, which he asked a floor nurse to give her.

He found Jenny Marsh in her Drug Abuse Study laboratory down the hall from CCD. She looked up from her position bent over a microscope. Beyond, two young assistants glanced at him, then went back to their work at the bank of centrifuges. She put down the pen with which she'd been jotting notes on a yellow lined pad. She smiled. It was a cool smile, detached, almost impersonal. It was not the smile he wanted.

"I hope you can catch up on your sleep this afternoon," he said. "Sometime after midnight the kidney will be released."

"Excellent." She nodded, still all-business. "I'd already planned on staying right here. There are a couple of cots in the next room. I'll call you the moment I get word it's on its way. You can watch the operation if you wish."

"That may not be possible." Who knows where he'd be. Maybe floating face down in shallow water. He lowered his voice as he came closer. "There's something else I learned. It might be significant. The drugs Rachel was taking the night of her collapse were pure."

Surprise registered on Jenny Marsh's face. "That can't be right. It's highly unlikely she'd have gone into coma from the amounts she was taking unless the stuff had been cut with something bad."

"I thought that, too. But I spoke to the person she was with that night. This person took the same drugs—the whole cocktail—acid, joints, coke, and she was fine. On the other hand, she presumably has two kidneys, unlike Rachel."

"Wouldn't matter." Jenny was frowning. "There's something odd here but I'll be damned if I know what it is."

"Jenny, I saw Rachel a few minutes ago. Why isn't the infection clearing up?"

"I've been wondering about that myself." She tapped a finger on the lab counter. "It's probable that in her weakened condition she's having a difficult time fighting off an infection a healthy person would get rid of in hours."

He was watching her expression carefully. "You don't seem convinced."

She looked up into his face, and he could clearly see the weariness and worry there. "To tell you the truth, I'm not." She indicated the slide she had been viewing when he'd come in. "I've got nothing tangible to go on. In fact, from a strictly medical point of view it would be surprising if she had thrown the infection off easily. And yet the fact that she's made no progress at all is bugging the hell out of me. It's as if every time we take one step forward Rachel takes two steps back."

He waited in vain for her to finish her thought. When he saw that she wasn't going to, he said, "What about the transplant? Can you do it if the fever isn't down?"

"That wouldn't be advisable," Jenny said.

Croaker didn't like the sound of that. "You've got to get the infection under control before I give you the kidney."

She nodded. "We're doing our best, Lew, believe me."

"I know you are." He put a hand briefly over hers and squeezed. She pulled her hand gently but firmly away.

One of the assistants extracted a test tube from the centrifuge, held it up to the light. She said something to the other assistant, who nodded. They went into the adjacent room.

"Jenny, what's the matter?" he asked. "You're acting like last night never happened."

"When I was in high school—before I hit all those college courses that turned my desire to be a doctor into an obsession—I was a different person. All I thought about then was boys. What sweater, what skirt to wear to show off what I had. It was a carefree time of life."

He looked down at her. "Sounds good to me."

She nodded. "It was lovely. But I've got too many responsibilities now to let my eyes go out of focus." She got up and went over to the windows. He stood a little apart from her. From this position, he could see a pulse beating in the hollow of her throat. "The truth is, I've missed you. Already. This is a very bad sign."

He cocked his head. "Bad in what way?"

She turned to face him. "Because when I woke up this morning the first thing that entered my mind was 'What am I going to wear today? I want to look good for Lew.'"

He smiled. "That doesn't sound so dire."

"It does to me. I've built my whole world to work along certain lines. Now—with you—it's being blown to pieces."

He drew her into his arms. "Be strong, Dr. Marsh. Let your eyes go out of focus an hour a day." He looked into her green eyes. "Surely you can spare me that much out of your hectic life."

"Oh, Lew—"

Her lips opened against his and he felt the heat coming off her. Her body was trembling with repressed desire. He stroked her back and her body began to melt against his. She tore herself away at the sound of her returning assistants. He wondered if her heart was pounding as hard as his was, but one look in her eyes told him it must be.

With an effort, she got her breathing back to normal. She set limits for her behavior and kept to them. He liked that in her. "Listen, do me a favor. If Stansky makes rounds early today, make up some excuse but keep him away from Rachel."

"Why?"

He squeezed her hand. "I'm not sure yet. I'm working on a theory. I know how you doctors like to band together so I don't want to go around accusing people without backup."

"But if you suspect Stansky's some kind of threat to her . . . My God, I've got to know that."

"Believe me, when I have something, I'll call you. I have your beeper number. Okay?"

For a moment she held on to his hand. Her eyes searched his face, as if she was trying to memorize every line and feature of it. "I was wrong before. It's a good feeling to miss you and then have you walk into my lab, but . . ." For an instant her eyes clouded over and he thought she was going to cry. Her voice was a hoarse whisper. "Come back, Lew. Promise me."

He smiled at her. "I promise."

But a dark and evil presentiment gripped his heart. He knew she was thinking of the vision the soul-catcher had shown her of him lying facedown in shallow water. The scene of his death.

The flamingo T-bird was waiting patiently for him in the hospital parking lot. He unlocked the car, turned on the ignition. It was as hot as Hades in there and he stood outside for a time with the door open and the air conditioner going full blast. Then he got in and drove it slowly over to Matty's place. He luxuriated in the feel of the heavy engine, the solid bodywork, the smell of the lovingly conditioned leather seats. For an instant, time rolled back to when he was eighteen, when all he could think of was girls and cars, maybe in that order, maybe not, depending on his mood. Could be that was as close as he had come to being carefree. But unlike Jenny Marsh, he'd grown up in Hell's Kitchen, where nothing worth having came without a serious price. Every day created another battleground, another fight over territory, bragging rights, a girl.

And always there was some hothead eager to bounce your brains off the sidewalk. As he pulled into the Harbour Pointe visitors' parking lot he wondered what it would be like being a part of Jenny's carefree high-school days. He found he couldn't imagine it.

Even though he had the key, the concierge stopped him, consulting a list owners compiled with the names of people who had keys. Matty, hoping he would stay with her, had put his name on the list the night he'd slept over.

Upstairs, he went directly into Rachel's room. Everything was the same as the last time he was here. He went to the dresser, opened the bottom drawer. There was the large sachet. Carefully, he untied the ribbon that held the cloth together and pulled a small diary from the fragrant crumbles of dried flowers and spiced herbs. Just as Gideon had told him.

He sat on Rachel's bed and ran his hand over the surface. It was dark blue paperboard with tan corners of simulated leather. He opened it and, with a heavily beating heart, began to read.

The first entry was dated January 1 of this year. Croaker quickly riffled through the pages. Rather than making an entry for every day, Rachel had written only about key events during the year. Obviously, she was not a girl to scribble "Woke up, had a fight with Mom, went to school, met Gideon, got stoned."

In fact, as he began to read in earnest, he saw this was less a diary than the stream-of-consciousness inner workings of his niece's mind. It was not an easy read. There are places in the human soul so intimate to bare them is shocking. In them dwell deformed things: strange wishes, bizarre desires, obsessions even—all the demons that drive us but should never see the light of day. Rachel had felt a need to give these shadows life, and now Croaker was poring over them like a shaman studying the thrown bones of a sacred animal.

Halfway through, he set aside the diary and looked up. He saw Rachel standing on the far side of the bedroom. She was looking at him just as if she were really there. She didn't look like the dying girl he had just left in the hospital; instead, she appeared very much like the girl in the prom dress photo—solemn but healthy. This illusion opened its mouth and spoke to him in the words he had just read:

"Today something snapped. When Mom told me Donald was dead I could hear a sound like a clap of thunder. Mom was watching my face real hard to see what I'd do. So I did nothing, just sat there and stared at my corn flakes. And then I thought about how cruel Donald and I had been to each other for two years. Pretending it was over when obviously it wasn't. That thought defeated me. I can't explain it, but I had this weird urge to take a carving knife and slit my wrists to the bone. I might have done it, too, if I didn't think of how sad it would make Gideon. I spent about ten minutes imagining her face, imagining my blood all over the floor. Her face, my blood. I just couldn't do that to her.

"But I wanted to. I could feel the ache like a magnetic pull. I want to rush headfirst into that California mountainside. I wanted so much to join him. What was I going to do without him? I can't imagine . . ."

"The thing is Donald loved me. I know he did. In fact, I'm sure now he loved me more than he ever loved Mom. I hate him for that; for other things, too. But none of that stops me from loving him. Just the opposite, really. It's as if many of the things he did bound us closer together. It's odd. Mom came to hate him because of his cruelty. She never got it. I think that's what enslaved me to him. That's the right word, too, enslavement. I'd do anything he asked of me. Anything. And that was the secret—that was the bond between us. He could have asked me to plunge a knife into my breast and I would have done it without a second thought. Not that he would have, though. He was too busy using his penis like a weapon . . .

"Those sessions hurt me. But the pain was so sweet. I would come with tears in my eyes, with my body shaking. Sometimes, there was blood. Just a little bit, a drop, a crimson eye. This, too, would bind us, like an oath. On our hands and knees, we'd wipe it up together. And, afterwards, he was so tender . . .

"When he told me he'd started training me when I was so young, I immediately thought of *The Story of O*, which he gave me to read when I was ten. I read it over and over until I had memorized whole passages of it. I'd recite it during some of our sessions and that seemed to turn him on like nothing else. At first, I thought it was the words, because sometimes we'd act out the scene I was reciting. But then I came to understand. He loved the fact I'd learned his lesson so completely . . .

"When he asked me if I thought what we were doing was wrong, I remember looking into his face and saw something I'd never before seen there: fear. It was then I understood that he was as much enslaved as I was. We both existed here, apart from the world. It seemed to me that the sessions were the only time we were alive. Outside this circle of secrets, we were just letting hours pass, going through the motions of living. But it wasn't living at all. The longing for each other, the denials, then, after all that holding back, the rush of joyous pain . . . and that single crimson drop of blood—that was living.''

Croaker took a deep breath, and the vision of Rachel vanished. He put a hand to his forehead, found that he was sweating. He had spent most of his adult life picking through the twisted labyrinth of the criminal psyche. You tried to enure yourself, to find ways to detach yourself so you wouldn't be swept under by the garbage. But it wasn't possible. Because you were sticking your nose into a place that was, essentially, the only true sanctuary left.

Over the years, Croaker had learned not to be shocked by these revelations. But this was different. Rachel was no criminal, no psychopath. She was just a girl in desperate need of help. And she was his niece.

This terrible peek into her soul chilled him to the bone. If it was true that you never really knew what people were thinking, it was also true that, most times, you didn't want to find out.

This was why homicide cops burned out. The better they were, the faster the burn. Because there was only so much close exposure to psychosis you could take. Then it was time to close your eyes and turn away from a sun that burned too bright and had come too close.

He wiped his face clean of sweat, took up the diary again and read the second half.

At length, his vision of Rachel as she had been reappeared in the bedroom. This time, she was sitting cross-legged in the center of the floor. ''It must have been fate,'' his vision of her said. ''When Ronald put his hand on my naked breast during a physical exam, my nipple rose against his palm and he twisted it until tears came to my eyes. Then I knew, and I was his. I asked him after that first session how he knew. He said he could see it in my eyes. I asked him what he saw, and he told me, 'You were naked and when you looked at me I saw there was no barrier between us.' I wonder if that's the definition of submission? Then he asked me the question I'll always remember: 'I've seen you naked before, many times. But there was always the wall, the defense of the inner castle. What changed today?'

''Of course I knew. It was Donald's death. That's what's changed me. And then I saw how I could go on. Being with Gideon is nice. I can even say I love her. But, for me, love isn't enough. There's this *thing* inside me for which I have no name. It's the thing Donald tapped into. It's the same thing that Ronald saw in my eyes. I need it. I have to have it. Now I know I can go on. The sessions will continue. I will survive . . .''

So the sessions—as Rachel called the S-M sexual trysts—continued with Dr. Ronald Stansky standing in for her father, Donald Duke. It was a sick story, getting sicker all the time. How damaged must Rachel be in order to cling to this way of life? So severely damaged that she was misunderstood by everyone. There was something about that damage that set her apart—made her unknowable, even to Gideon. Croaker wanted to gather her up in his arms and protect her. His heart broke for Rachel, who craved only one thing: love. If only she knew it.

If she survived this trial, he'd have to see she began a whole new life. And that meant telling Matty everything.

But not now. Not yet.

He was so caught up in these thoughts that he almost missed it. But something had caught in the net of his memory and he flipped back to the next-to-last page. It was dated three days before Rachel's collapse.

"This last session was strange," she said. "I mean all sessions are strange. Donald once told me that's where their power lies, in opening yourself up to all the dark forces inside yourself, surrendering to them. But this was stranger than most.

"I guess it was because we weren't alone. I mean, often we weren't alone in the beginning. During the medical tests, of course, Ronald's nurse would be bustling around to draw blood or set the X-ray machine in place or take the specimen cup from me. I guess he had to do these tests to make it okay for me to be at the clinic so often. But after the tests, the nurse would leave and Ronald and I would be alone to begin our journey. It was odd but exciting, doing it in the examination room—all that clinical stuff and here we were banging away. I think that's why Ronald never took me to a motel or anywhere else. Also, in a motel room that doctor-patient thing wouldn't be there.

"This time, there was someone with him. A man, tall and lean and dark. He looked like a shadow. Ronald asked if I would mind. The man wanted to watch. He wouldn't touch me, wouldn't say a word. Just watch. Somehow, I liked that. It reminded me of how I sometimes felt with Donald. I wanted Mom to see us together, even though I knew it would hurt her terribly. But it was the only way she would ever get to know me, and I knew she never would.

"So I said okay. I let the man watch. He did it like he'd done it before, like he knew what it meant to *watch*. Not just seeing things, but *observing*. I knew everything Ronald and I did meant something to him, and that made our pleasure so much more intense.

"Afterward, when Ronald was cleaning up, the man came over

to me. We looked at each other for such a long time it felt as if my lungs would burst. 'I didn't know,' he said. It was such a mysterious thing to say, a little thrill went through me. And he had this voice, not much more than a hoarse whisper. I wanted to ask him what he meant, but I thought I'd look like an idiot. For some reason, I knew this was someone I didn't want to embarrass myself with. 'I didn't know anything about you,' he said. I was so startled I felt my heart leap just as if it was a football kicked between the goalposts. Blood rushed in my temples and I couldn't say a thing.

"Later, when he and Ronald sat talking, I drifted into the other room. They didn't notice. When talk gets serious, men have no use for girls or women. His suit jacket was hanging on this old-fashioned wood coat rack Ronald has at the clinic. I was drawn to the jacket as if it was magnetized. For a long time I didn't do anything. I was content to let it brush against my cheek. It smelled strongly of him and I liked that. Then I slipped my hand inside and found his wallet. It was one of those European-style wallets like Donald used to carry—slim and so long you can't stuff it into your back pocket. It's a rich man's wallet because you have to put it in the inside pocket of a suit jacket. It was made out of crocodile skin, dyed a blue so dark it looked black. I loved that color. I opened it up, not knowing why, and then I saw his name embossed in gold: Trey Merli. Could anyone really have that name? If you drop the *y*, *'tre merli'* means three blackbirds, in Italian. I read it over and over again, until it took on a kind of magical quality. Trey Merli."

There, the entry seemed to end. However, in the two blank lines left before the end of the page, Rachel had scribbled something hastily in pencil. It was an address. Trey Merli's?

Croaker looked up from Rachel's diary, the blood singing in his veins. According to Vonda Shepherd, Trey Merli owned Gold Coast Exotic Auto Rentals in Margate. Gold Coast was the place Majeur had rented the grape-colored Lincoln. Now it turned out that Merli knew Dr. Ronald Stansky. What could that mean? Croaker didn't yet know. But it was clear that the evil engine in Margate that he had glimpsed was about to deliver up its black and ugly secrets.

The address Rachel had scribbled in her diary was on Hibiscus Island. The island was out in the middle of Biscayne Bay. You got there by crossing the bay on the MacArthur Causeway, taking the Fountain Street turnoff onto Palm Island, then continuing onto Hibiscus.

The island was small, no more than ten blocks long and just two blocks wide, but it was home to large, stucco houses, each with their own boat mooring. Croaker eased the T-bird into the curb in front of a white house in the middle of the block. It looked similar to its neighbors, except for the dark blue awnings and the matching trim. He got out. The brutal heat felt good on all his aches and pains.

He went up the driveway paving and rang the doorbell. There was no response, so he walked around the side of the house, past orange bougainvillea and pink hibiscus. In the back was the Florida room and a screened-in pool area. Eight white chaise lounges with blue Textilene cushions were arranged in two rows so perfectly one would think there was a photo shoot going on. The area, however, was deserted. The pool filters burbled like a just fed infant; a palm tree's fronds brushed against the top of the screen. On a cart sat a pile of freshly laundered towels in candy-colored stripes. Below, were three different kinds of sunscreens.

Beyond the screened-in pool was the bulkheaded dock. There was no boat in the slip, but when Croaker came around the back he saw that the screen door was not entirely shut. He opened it and stepped inside. Through the windows straight ahead he could see a large living room. To the right were the windows of the master suite; to the left, the windows of the two-bedroom guest wing. The only movement he saw was of a green plastic alligator float drifting in the pool. It eyed him incuriously as he crossed the patio. The slider to the living room was unlocked and he stepped into the air-conditioned interior.

He was met by a sea of beige and off-white furniture. It was expensive, spotless, and uncreased. Five place-settings were arrayed on the Travertine marble dining room table around a high spray of fresh flowers. But there was no smell of food. Neither was there a hint of perfume or cigarette smoke.

In the kitchen, Croaker went through the pantry and cabinet drawers. All were well stocked with food, gadgets, and utensils. He left the refrigerator until last. Ever since Sonia's death that common-place utility item had taken on an eerie aura. He could never again open a refrigerator door without thinking of her head staring at him from inside.

With his grip tight on the handle, he thought, What if Trey Merli's head is in there? Then, his teeth gritted, he jerked the door open. Inside, were the normal contents of a normal refrigerator, nothing more.

He waited a moment for his accelerated pulse to slow a bit. The door shut with a small sigh.

More beige and off-white in the luxurious master suite: a king-size bed, an antique French Provincial armoire that had been stripped and bleached, a wall mirror framed in gilt. Croaker looked through the armoire without finding anything of interest beside the fact that Trey Merli had good taste in clothes and a good deal of money. His fashion colors ran to dark blue suits and white shirts, something Croaker could have guessed from the exterior of the house.

At the foot of the bed was a large sand-colored lacquer box approximately thirty inches deep and almost as long as the width of the bed. Beside one night table was a remote. Croaker picked this up and pressed the Open button. The box at the foot of the bed opened soundlessly and equipment rose out of its depths. There was a twenty-four inch TV, a VCR, a laser-disc player and a welter of software. Croaker counted more than a dozen videotapes and about ten laser discs in slip cases like those old-fashioned LP records used to come in.

On the bed was a neat stack of three white dress shirts. They were freshly laundered, folded around cardboard sheets, held in place by paper ribbons. Taped to the opened sheet of brown paper on which they lay was taped the cleaner's pink copy of the receipt. The shirts were the same style and brand that were inside the armoire.

But now Croaker could see something odd. It wasn't about the shirts but about the cardboard around which they were folded. They looked doubled over. He held on to the top shirt and, using his biomechanical fingers, slid the cardboard out. Only to discover a manila folder.

As he looked at it he felt his heart give a lurch. The name typed on the tab was Sonia Villa-Lobos.

He opened the file. It was a record of Sonia's medical history as recorded by Dr. Ronald Stansky. He saw, with a glance to the top of the page, that this file came from Stansky's clinic in Margate, not from his private practice office in West Palm Beach. Sonia was Stansky's patient?

Quickly, he withdrew the second file, looked at the name typed on the tab. To his horror, he saw that it was Vonda Shepherd's file. He flipped it open. She was Stansky's patient as well? Even if he believed in coincidences—which he didn't—he'd never buy this as one. He saw many of the same tests being performed in the same order. Maybe that was medical protocol, maybe not. But they all ended with one specific test that made his blood run cold.

He drew out the third file. His mind refused to register the name on it. Rachel Duke. His right hand shook as he leafed through the file with an increasing sense of alarm. His mind began to spin in a certain direction that, quite frankly, scared the hell out of him. If he was correct . . .

He folded down the brown paper wrapping, took a look at the name of the cleaners on the receipt: Jiffy Tyme Dry Cleaners, it read. The address was on Biscayne Boulevard. Why did that sound familiar?

Croaker froze. He'd heard something—a small sound coming from the living room. He silently moved to another spot in the bedroom, one that had a better view of the open doorway into the hall.

The hall was empty as far as the first turn. Beyond that, he was blind.

He went out of the bedroom and down the hall. Just before the turn, he paused.

"I can't see you," a voice said. "But I can see your shadow."

The voice sounded very familiar.

Croaker went slowly and deliberately into the living room. The slim, amber-eyed man was sitting cross-legged in an overstuffed off-white chair.

"I see we're fated to keep running into one another, Antonio," he said.

"And at the oddest moments." His arms rested lightly on the upholstered chair. "And may I inquire as to your purpose here?"

Croaker watched him with fixed intent. "You mean you don't know?"

"I want to hear it from your mouth." His amber gaze flicked from the windows, to the paintings on the walls, to the perfectly set dinner table, before fixing Croaker. *"Que hermosa tu boca!"* How beautiful is your mouth.

"You never answered my question," Croaker said.

The narrow, handsome head never moved. "Which question?"

"About Rosa. You told me you loved her, Antonio. But you couldn't have loved her. You killed her. You lopped off her head as if she were an animal."

For a long time the amber-eyed man said nothing. But there was something building inside him. It was like the pressure drop your ears registered in the quiet just before the onset of a terrible thunderstorm.

"No," he said quite suddenly. *"I killed Rosa."*

He rose, unfolding from the chair, and came slowly and casually toward Croaker. *This is how you recognize a man,* Stone Tree had once told Croaker. *He can change his name, he can change his I.D., he can even change his face. But his gait will always give him away. Just as fingerprints can identify a man out of a million similar men, so can a man's gait. That never changes. Even if he breaks a bone, his body adapts and the peculiarities of the old gait reemerge.*

This wasn't Antonio. It was Heitor. Croaker knew Antonio's rolling, liquid gait; this man's was altogether different. It was angular, full of small, impatient motions.

"I wondered what my brother was up to," Heitor said. "Telling tales out of school is not his style, is it? No." This close, Croaker could smell his animal scent. This man held no respect for the restraints of civilization. "And the death of Rosa Milagros is the tale that should be told least of all." He spoke quietly, slowly, as if he were on Valium. "It disturbs me greatly that he thinks of Rosa still. He loved her, he said. To you."

"He told me he was damned," Croaker said with some effort. "Now I think you're both damned."

He turned and headed across the living room toward the slider. Through the glass he could see sunlight spin off the pool. He could just see the head of the plastic alligator, floating without a care in the world. Good thing it could not know that with each moment sunlight was degrading its skin. All too soon it would begin losing air and then it would be tossed in the garbage.

Croaker felt Heitor's presence just behind him. Good. He did not want Heitor anywhere near the master suite.

"Once, I dreamt I was damned." Heitor said this as if he and Croaker were in the middle of a conversation.

Croaker stopped in front of the slider. In its glass, he could see Heitor's reflection as he spoke.

"In this dream, I trod upon the flaming heads of the damned. As I neared them, they bent their heads, presenting their necks so that a flat path appeared for me. At the end of the path was the Devil." Heitor crossed his arms over his chest. "How would you imagine him, *señor*? As a man in a red suit with horns, a tail and a pitchfork? *Madre de mentiras*, no. The Devil was as my mother had described him to me when I was little: he had a shark's head and the body of a beautiful naked woman." He smiled. "My mother warned me to beware the Devil. Because he is ugly? No, *señor*. Because he is beautiful. It is this beauty that makes him powerful."

Croaker felt the edge to this man. What was beneath his almost unnatural calm? "What happened in this dream when you met the Devil?"

"I ate him." Heitor's amber eyes twinkled with delight. "Without a moment's hesitation, *señor*, I took out my scalpel and carved his flesh into bite-size chunks. I thought it would stink of death and putrefaction, but all I tasted was roses." He pursed his lips. "It was raw, just like my mother taught me to eat my meat. She said all the power in a dead thing vanishes with heat. Keep it cool, keep it raw. *Muy bueno.*"

Heitor timed the last word to his action. He spun Croaker around. The heel of his hand was jammed just beneath Croaker's chin. Two fingers of Heitor's other hand pressed against his temple. It was just what Antonio had done with the gunman to subdue him. It was *Hetá I.* Croaker could do nothing more than slip his right hand in his pocket.

Now he felt a chill invading him. It was as if he were encased in a block of ice. He tried to move but he couldn't. The two fingers held him immobile while Heitor's amber gaze bore into him.

Heitor's face hovered in front of Croaker's. "Who are you to hear Antonio's confessions? You are a messenger, nothing more. And when your message is delivered . . ." He drew back and laughed. "I'll keep you guessing as to what happens then." Abruptly, his face darkened again. "But my brother, perhaps he has illusions. Perhaps he sees you as more than a messenger. I should kill you now."

"Then the message will never be delivered." There was a riddle here that needed solving, Croaker knew. But in his current state, he couldn't think clearly.

"I'll do it myself!" Heitor spat this out. "That's what I've wanted all along. I am not one to stand by like a potbellied man in middle age and watch others hunt."

Croaker had spent the last several moments focusing his energies on getting the fingers of his right hand to move. One by one, they closed around the spirit-stone. He felt the familiar warmth, a tingling radiating out that was like the heat of a sun. And as that heat spread, the paralysis dissipated.

A canny look suffused Heitor's face. "Perhaps my brother wants to tell you your fate. This is not allowed in *Hetá I.* Perhaps, though, he wishes you to know how you will be betrayed by those closest to you. We have seen these things; we are privy to many, many secrets of the human heart. And, *señor*, let me tell you they are all dark."

Croaker squeezed the spirit-stone harder.

"Antonio says that we know too much, that it is unnatural. He says knowing these secrets that should not be known has made us what we are. I say, So fucking what? *Madre de mentiras,* life is one big game to us. Play it or die. Lose and die. Win and survive to play another day. These are our only laws. And now, *señor*, you exist under those laws. *Comprende?*"

"Sure, Heitor. I *comprende* just fine." He pressed his right palm with the spirit-stone in it against Heitor's flat, muscle-ridged stomach.

Heitor's amber eyes opened wide. His lips opened, but no sound emerged. With a sweep of his left arm, Croaker broke the other man's hold. He chopped down hard on Heitor's clavicle, thrust his sinking body away from him, and pulled on the slider handle.

That was a mistake.

Heitor slammed into his waist and the two of them hit the glass slider with such force that it shattered and they hurtled through out onto the patio paving. Rolling over and over, they went over the concrete coping into the pool.

Croaker went under. The water was shallow, pale as air. He had a quick flash of Jenny's vision of him floating facedown in shallow water. Was he approaching the moment of his death?

He saw the underbelly of the plastic alligator, pushed it out of the way as he broke the surface. Heitor pulled him back under, shook him like a disobedient dog until Croaker was overcome by vertigo. In desperation, Croaker slammed the heel of his biomechanical hand underneath Heitor's jaw. He broke free and pushed upward, gasping for air.

"*Maricone,* where did you get that spirit-stone?" Heitor was smart. "I want it!" With his free hand, he produced the scalpel. Light spun off the wicked-looking stainless-steel blade. "No single stone should have stopped me like that."

Croaker recalled his recent conversation with Ross Darling when they were looking at the UnSub file: *So the murderer didn't use a saw,* Croaker had said. *He severed the spinal column with just the scalpel. That would take a lot of strength.*

It would take a goddamn bull, Darling had said.

He was so right.

The blade swept in a shallow arc. "It doesn't belong to you. Give it to me or I'll cut your other hand off." The blade hovered, poised. "One quick flick of the wrist is all it will take."

"The dark stones know," Croaker said, calculating each word. "You can't have it. It belonged to Humaitá."

Croaker had that single moment of shock in which to act. He slammed his forehead into the bridge of Heitor's nose. Blood gushed and Heitor reared back in convulsive reaction. He made tiny gasping sounds like fish flopping out of water.

Croaker rolled away and scrambled up. Heitor reached out for him blindly and Croaker drove a well-placed kick into his rib cage. Heitor grunted and his face went under. Croaker put the plastic alligator between him and Heitor as he swam toward the edge of the pool.

He turned back in time to see Heitor swimming toward him underwater in quick, powerful strokes.

Heitor ignored his swollen nose, which streamed blood behind him in lovely patterns. He brandished the scalpel. He appeared to be grinning as he slashed out with the blade. Croaker grabbed the alligator, jammed it down. With a loud hiss, the point of the scalpel punctured the plastic and the alligator deflated.

Heitor rose to the surface. Water pink with his blood sluiced off him. *"Escuchame, señor.* Now you have given me what I crave. This is the kind of hunt I can savor."

"Does it hurt, Heitor? The broken nose."

Heitor spat blood into the pool. "We worship pain, *señor.* We welcome it. It is the validation of the hunt." He raised the scalpel, balancing it in his palm. "When we feel pain we *know* we are alive."

He waded through the water. "Do you think you can stop me from taking your hand?"

Croaker held the spirit-stone in front of him. "Finish it, Heitor. Now. Do it if you can."

Inches away, Heitor paused. He stared into Croaker's eyes. His right hand came up, weaving the scalpel back and forth in a lazy pattern.

Croaker moved the spirit-stone and Heitor retreated a pace. An expression of pure hatred turned his handsome face ugly.

"I'll remember," he whispered as he backed away through the water. "Not now, not yet. But soon." It was almost the lilting croon of a lullaby. He slipped silently to the gunite steps, quickly crossed the screened-in patio, and was gone.

Croaker let out a long pent-up breath. He collapsed back into the water. He was sick to his stomach from the excess adrenaline and his throat was dry. He could see Heitor's blood drifting through the pool in strands that parted and thinned to a light stain.

With a groan, he pulled himself out of the pool and lay on his back on the patio tiles. His head fell against the coping, and he closed his eyes. Each encounter with the Bonitas seemed to take more and more out of him. What would happen the next time they met? He didn't want to think about that now, so he thought about Jenny. At length, he took a couple of large beach towels and went back to the T-bird. After spreading the towels over the seat, he got in. His shoes squooshed.

He took out his cell phone and dialed Jenny's number. He prayed that she wasn't in surgery.

"Hello?"

He let out an audible sigh when he heard her voice. "Jenny, it's Lew. Look, I don't have a lot of time so don't ask questions, but I've got some interesting evidence regarding the Stansky situation."

"Tell me."

"I saw a copy of his medical file on Rachel—"

"How did you—?"

"Doesn't matter. The point is, he knew she had one kidney. He X-rayed her in September of last year and made a notation of it. And, Jenny, he's also the doctor of record for two murder victims who I suspect were used for organ harvesting."

He could hear Jenny's sharply indrawn breath. "But that alone—"

"Isn't enough. I know. But get this. Stansky screened both of them for Human Lymphocitic Antigens. These were healthy young women. Nobody does antigen typing unless—"

"Unless there's a need to match up their organs with a compatible host," Jenny finished in a hushed voice.

"You see the logic of it, don't you?" he asked. "Imagine yourself running an organ harvesting business. What's your main problem?"

"Getting healthy bodies."

"Suppose that's already been taken care of."

He could almost hear her shudder. "Then, time. You'd have to get the antigen typing down ASAP so you know which patient is compatible with which organ."

"Right. What if you had that information *before* the victim was killed?"

"Oh, Lew. Tell me this isn't what's happening here."

"I'm very much afraid it is. Our friend Dr. Stansky is hip-deep in an organ harvesting operation. He's the scout. He matches his patients up with the harvesters' needs. As in everything logical, it's as neat as a pin."

There was a pause on the line. He could hear her rapid breathing. "Lew, did Stansky do HLA testing on Rachel?"

"A1: 52; A2: 26; B1: 30 . . ." He recited all eight readings from memory.

"Oh, God, that's Rachel's HLA profile," she said. "Why would Stansky have done the test? He couldn't have known Rachel would be in need of a kidney when he saw her."

That's the whole point, Croaker thought. "Jenny, listen to me. I want you to move Rachel. Is she too sick for that?"

"No, but—"

"A good hospital—the best."

"Jackson Memorial, in Miami. I'm affiliated—"

"Okay, do it. Now. But, Jenny, don't tell Stansky where she's being taken."

"But he's her doctor. I—"

"Talk to Matty. Get her to change physicians. You can do it—"

"But, Lew—"

"Jenny, what happens if sepsis is being regularly reintroduced to Rachel's system?"

"She wouldn't be able to fight it off no matter how much antibiotics we could give her."

"Isn't that what's happening? Call me when Rachel's been moved," he said and put the cell phone away.

There was something else on his mind. He'd found Stansky's files in Trey Merli's shirts. These shirts had just returned from the Jiffy Tyme Dry Cleaners on Biscayne Boulevard.

Where had he heard that name before? He considered the address on Biscayne, but he couldn't recall where that number was.

He drove to a gas station. Inside the kiosk, he found a wire rack of local maps. He bought one and, along with a pair of cheap beach towels, took it out to the car. He stood there for a moment, letting the sun bake him for a moment. He could still feel the residue of the unnatural chill Heitor had laid on him.

He opened up the map, traced Biscayne Boulevard north from where he was. That's when it clicked in his mind. Pablo Leyes had told him that his wife, Estrella, worked on Biscayne Boulevard. At a dry cleaners named Jiffy Tyme.

The News Cafe was open twenty-four hours. Croaker stood in the shadows beneath the green awning, looking out at the pinkish oyster-shell light over the beach across Ocean Drive. It was 11:10, less than thirteen hours before Croaker would have to put Barbacena in the gun sight. Even though it was before lunchtime, the restaurant was far from empty. Models with long legs and sunglasses coming off early morning fashion shoots were busy chain-smoking while they attacked high-cholesterol breakfasts. In between mouthfuls, they dished other models.

Croaker was wearing olive trousers, a pale green short-sleeve shirt of nubby linen, and thin socks with white diamonds on them. New clothes he had bought at a nearby boutique. His shoes still squeaked when he walked, though. They'd need a couple of days to dry out.

Majeur arrived without fanfare. As he parked the grape-colored Lincoln and got out, Croaker went across the street.

Majeur was dressed in a stylized dark-blue Versace tuxedo. A white rose was pinned to his satin lapel. Its bruised petals were stained with what appeared to be lipstick. It was as dark as dried blood. He swung his pencil-thin attaché case against his thigh with a kind of insouciance, as if he were prodding a favorite horse to show its best moves.

His hatchet face had lost none of its rich mahogany glow but tendrils of his slick, gunmetal hair curled damply against his forehead. Obviously, Croaker wasn't the only one sleep-deprived. But this was not an outfit befitting a man burning the midnight oil as he collated intelligence on Juan Garcia Barbacena and his amazing Technicolor security machine.

Glancing at his gold Patek Philippe watch, Majeur said, "Punctuality says much about a man's more private habits. Good morning, sir."

"Not much of a morning yet," Croaker said.

"But it will be," Majeur said. "I promise you that." His eyes had that slightly watery look people get when they've had too much to drink.

They strolled slowly along the beach as the heat spread upward from the baking sand. It was like an oven.

Croaker said, "You look like you've had quite a night."

"Some people you just have to dress up for." Majeur offered Croaker a chocolate-covered mint, then popped one into his mouth. "Sadly, I believe I am approaching an age when too much champagne sours the stomach."

"It always did. But when you're young you just don't care."

Majeur seemed to roll that thought around with the mint. "That is true. The destruction occurs early. The body, morals—they both suffer beneath the onslaught of life."

With a small frisson Croaker realized the lawyer was talking about himself. "The body has gravity to contend with," he said. "But as for morals—"

"As for morals," Majeur continued, "they suffer from each roll of the dice. Life is a gamble, sir, a discordant dance against the odds. No lasting good ever came from that."

Croaker had an intuition that life for Majeur had been reduced to a relationship with one person: his client. "Is that where you were last night? Visiting the gambler?"

"I am never far from him. He and I have become like Siamese twins."

"In that event, when one dies what do you think will happen to the other?"

Majeur slipped off the gold marriage band from the third finger of his left hand. He turned it around contemplatively on the tips of his slender fingers. "When one takes the first step on a path, *señor*, one often fails to grasp what may lie at the end. This, I think, is a state necessary to impel one onward." Light shone off the gold band as he slowly turned it. "Sacrifice is the essential building block of life, sir. Small ones, large ones and—occasionally—one so profound that one cannot possibly be aware of its consequences." He held the gold band up. "You see this ring, *señor*. It represents nine years of my life. A life imagined, it seems now, by someone unknown to me." He lofted the ring. Flying through the glistening morning, it joined the white-green breakers sinking into the sand. "Now, like those waves, that dream has gone and another one has taken its place."

"I'll tell you something, Majeur," Croaker said. "It's damn hard to work up sympathy for the man who's extorting me."

The lawyer laughed, that high-pitched curiously feminine sound. "I agree. Besides giving me a sour stomach, too much champagne makes me maudlin. I detest people who are maudlin, don't you?" Majeur gave him a crooked smile. "But my maundering highlights an oddity." He took out a cigar in a metal sheath, looked at it for a moment, then, apparently reconsidering, put it back inside his tuxedo jacket. "You see, unlike you, I understand that a relationship has sprung up between us."

"Sort of like the rapport between torturer and the tortured."

Majeur laughed again. "I will say, considering you aren't an attorney, you certainly have a way with words, *señor*." He rubbed at the place on his finger where the wedding band had been. "But who is to say who is the torturer and who is the tortured?"

Croaker paused, aware that Majeur had just told him something important.

"Majeur—"

"I think, sir, that time makes fools of us all." Majeur shook his head as if trying to clear out the excess of champagne he'd consumed. "To work, *señor*. We have promises to keep." The pause had been fatal. The tenuous thread that had, a moment before, seemed to connect them, had vanished. "And a subject to send down before we sleep."

Majeur unsnapped his attaché, extracted a small manila envelope, two folded blueprints, and a sheaf of onionskin papers held together with a white paper clip. He handed them over.

The papers were filled with single-spaced typewritten paragraphs of text; the envelope contained a dozen black-and-white photos, each with a name on the back. The photos bore the mark of the surveillance camera. They were grainy, the subjects unposed, on the run.

"It is all there, *señor*. Everything you need."

Croaker studied the top photo. He saw a remarkably young man with thick, pitch black hair, a disarmingly dimpled smile, and eyes as sharp as a falcon's. Not a handsome man, but in this case it made no difference. The face was virile, strong in every sense of the word. This was Juan Garcia Barbacena.

"The subject has a fascination for exotic food, spices, two-wheeled vehicles, and sex. In this country, he travels in convoy." Ever security conscious, Majeur would not utter Barbacena's name in public. "He is driven in a bulletproof gray Rolls-Royce. Two black Mercedes sedans in front, two behind. He has nine men with him at all times—professional bodyguards. Four drive the Mercs, four ride shotgun, one drives the Rolls. Also, there's a woman who's a food taster." Majeur's nicotine-stained teeth shone like buttered kernels of corn as he smiled. "He's like a Roman Caesar, you see. He has paid for his absolute power with paranoia."

"In this case," Croaker said, flipping through the sheets of onionskin, "his paranoia seems all too justified."

"An accurate observation, sir." Majeur snapped his attaché shut. "Which is why we have chosen you to kiss him down." He shot the cuffs of his white tuxedo shirt, subtly adjusting the gold and lapis cufflinks. "The bodyguards run in four six-hour shifts. That way, they're always fresh and alert."

"What about the food taster?"

"She's Thai," Majeur observed. "She sleeps curled like a cat at his side when he has no need of her."

"Sex?"

"Her talents lie elsewhere." Majeur looked out across the beach to where a beautiful golden lab leapt to catch a Frisbee tossed by his master. Majeur stopped, apparently not wanting to get too close. They sat on a bench, like the old men who, later in the day, would be hunched, chins on their canes, watching with rheumy eyes the topless girls, dreaming of being nineteen again.

"For him, business invariably comes first. But sex is an imperative." Majeur smelled of tequila and a floral scent that did not belong to him. "He travels with three girls. Like a harem. It's a crap shoot as to which one he will choose. Sometimes it's more than one at once."

"Lucky man," Croaker said.

Majeur put his head back to observe a sky rich in color. "Not today."

Croaker consulted the written material. "I see he stays at unconventional places."

"No hotels, that's right. He owns a building here in Miami Beach and another in Miami. Warehouses. At least, that's what they appear to be. On the inside, they have been completely remodeled to his specifications—opulent bedroom suites, conference rooms, and business lounges with all the latest high-tech computer gear and satellite uplinks. This way, he can have the run of the place, position his bodyguards for maximum security, and no one knows about it."

"I see you have the building plans here." Croaker unfolded the blueprints. "They're accurate?"

"Absolutely up-to-date."

Croaker looked down the beach to where the golden lab was leaping in an expression of absolute joy through the surf. "There's only one thing remaining."

Majeur nodded. "Whatever you need, sir, I can get."

Croaker put a hand in his pocket. "A long gun. A Steyr—"

"Just a moment." Majeur held up his hand. He reached into his breast pocket and took out his wallet and an ultraslim gold pen. He flipped open the wallet, turned over a business card, and prepared to jot down Croaker's specifications.

But Croaker was aware of these small movements only peripherally. His gaze was caught by the wallet. It was long and slim—a European-style wallet made of crocodile hide. In low light it might have passed for black, but in the morning's bright sun Croaker could see it was a very dark blue. It was the wallet Rachel had described in her diary. The wallet owned by the man Dr. Ronald Stansky had brought to their last S-M session, who had watched them perform. Majeur was Trey Merli.

"Go on, señor. I'm waiting."

Croaker cleared his throat and focused his mind. All sorts of thoughts were running rampant through his head. What the hell kind of conspiracy had he stumbled into? He made himself go on. "I want a Steyr SSG .308 with a Swarsky scope and a Harris Bipod. Tape-wrapped stock, serial number filed off."

"Done. Ammunition?"

"One box will be sufficient."

"Is there anything else?"

"Binoculars. Zeiss ten by fifty-six Night Owl." But in truth Croaker had only half his mind on these details.

Majeur nodded. "Delivery of the equipment, *señor*." The edge of his Versace tux jacket was flapping against his thigh. "Eight-thirty tonight at—"

"No. I'll tell you where, Majeur."

The lawyer inclined his head. "As you wish, sir."

"The bar of the Raleigh Hotel."

"A delightful place." A thin smile wrinkled his lips. "I applaud your choice." Then, like ice splintering under a heavy footstep, his expression changed. "*Señor*, I sound a single note of warning. Do not mistake our rapport for a weakness on my part. I know what you tried to do on the UNOS system. You are locked out of the kidney until such time as I am satisfied you have fulfilled your end of the bargain. You cannot get it, you *will* not get it, until the subject's heart has ceased to beat."

"And how will you know it's been done?"

Majeur tilted back his head. "Oh, *señor*, I will know. I'm paid to know."

Croaker watched the lawyer walk back to his car and drive off. Sand rattled against his shoes. He thought about the crocodile hide wallet. He thought of Majeur watching Rachel and Stansky go through their sexual catechism.

He might be Marcellus Rojas Diego Majeur, attorney-at-law. But he was also Trey Merli, owner of Gold Coast Exotic Auto Rental in Margate.

When the grape-colored Lincoln had disappeared, Croaker walked slowly back beneath the green awning of the News Cafe and ordered a fresh orange juice with a large squeeze of lime, two eggs over easy with salsa, and a double order of bacon.

Heitor had called him a messenger. What had he meant by that? What message did Croaker have and who was he delivering it to? Croaker took his juice and sat at a table. His aches and pains were now too numerous to keep track of so he turned his mind elsewhere. He sipped his juice and let the vibrance of SoBe wash over him.

While he was otherwise engaged, life had begun to creep into Ocean Drive. Professionals—camera- and sound-men—swung into the restaurant for Cokes and muffins, burly boys in string tops off-loaded sparkling fresh produce from trucks, tourists took pictures of one another with the trademark awning behind them. The air smelled of root vegetables, cilantro, and makeup. A jaunty Jack Russell terrier trotted by, followed by a woman in a bikini and in-line skates. The day was, at last, in full swing.

4

The manta moved through the green water as languidly as a sun worshipper. So big it seemed as unreal as a cloud, it sucked plankton up into its wide mouth like some alien vacuum cleaner. Seen from above, it was black as pitch, its long horned fins extending in front, its whiplike tail undulating behind.

Following it, Croaker and Rafe Roubinnet, in scuba gear, swam in wide ellipses. They rose and fell as if on columns of air, but really, they were riding the same current as the fish.

The Spanish *manto* meant cloak, and that was what this beast most resembled. Gold flecks glittered on its rough skin as the edges of its wings rippled. But when Croaker sank down, diving deeper into the water, he could see that its belly was as pale as ice shining in dawn light. Bennie and Majeur were just like this ray, pulling a *manto* around them to hide what lay beneath.

Rafe touched Croaker's arm, pointed to his watch, then gestured upward. The speargun, attached to his wrist by a short nylon cord, fluttered through the water in concert like an admonishing finger. Time to leave. Croaker nodded, waggled his clear fins, and began his ascent to the surface.

Long before he got there, he could see the dark shadow of Rafe's catamaran. Glancing back down through the green water, Croaker could see the manta, dwindling into its dark, unfathomable world. Part of him longed to be taken by it, down and down into another realm. And with it, all the obligations that weighed upon his soul like a lead casing. Vanished in the darkness of another place.

Croaker breached the surface. Bright sunlight bounced off the water, almost blinding him. They handed up their tanks, weight belts, fins, and spearguns to a waiting crewman.

They climbed up the rope ladder, slippery with salt and seaweed. The polished, sun-washed foredeck felt good beneath Croaker's bare feet. The dive had somehow renewed him, as Rafe had promised it would.

They stripped off their masks and shorties—neoprene wet suits with short sleeves and legs. All they wore were bathing suits. Rafe clucked like a mother hen over the deep purple and green bruises that spotted Croaker's skin.

"Christ, you need a good long vacation." He threw Croaker an oversize towel.

Croaker dabbed gingerly at his body. "Hell, this *is* my vacation."

Rafe Roubinnet's boat was a beautiful sixty-five-foot handmade cat. Made of carbon fiber, the same strong but lightweight material as Dennis Conner's America's Cup boat, it was sloop-rigged, which meant it had a single mast. There was a cabin—or house—mounted on aluminum struts above the water and between the two huge pontoons. The foredeck was made of a thin sheet of West System epoxy resin, painted glistening white with gold piping like the rest of the boat. Aft of the house was a nylon webbing for the crew of four to cross from pontoon to pontoon. The wheels were set into cockpits scooped out of the aft section of the pontoons. There were two wheels because the cat had twin screws—a pair of mammoth gas engines, five hundred horsepower Chevy hemis, typically seen beneath the hoods of racing cars—for use when Rafe wanted to motor-sail or needed to outrun a storm. The twin screws gave the cat another advantage: they made it highly maneuverable. It was the kind of boat you would feel comfortable in even if you went all the way up to Newport, Rhode Island.

A small folding table had been set up on the foredeck. It was covered with a homey blue-and-white checkered cloth. The cloth had pockets on the corners, each filled with a small lead weight to keep it battened down. Croaker could see that the ends of the table legs fit into specially made depressions in the deck so it wouldn't shift in the swells. They sat on canvas captain's chairs with gold anchors silk-screened on the backs, drying and warming, eating fresh stone crabs, Caesar salad, and warm garlic bread. There was beer and champagne in a large metal cooler, but Croaker opted for club soda.

They ate in companionable silence for some time. When he thought enough time had passed, Croaker said, "When did you and Bennie part company?"

It was obviously a delicate subject so he was not particularly surprised when Rafe said: "I'd rather not talk about Bennie."

"But I would," Croaker pressed.

Rafe gave Croaker a long look while he munched on a forkful of salad. "Always the detective, eh, *compadre?*" He nodded. "Okay, you're right."

"He got pissed you wouldn't run for mayor again."

"Pissed?" Rafe snorted. "Hell, *compadre,* he went ballistic. He had big plans, which is why he'd offered to help finance my campaign in a major way." Rafe shrugged. "Maybe he wanted Miami to become a safe haven for his clients; maybe he had something grander in mind. With Bennie it's always something grander. But, really it didn't matter because I cut the discussion short. It was simple. I was quits with politics. Bennie, apparently, didn't agree."

"But it's more than that," Croaker said. "You told me you don't like the company he keeps."

"By and large, that's true." Rafe threw down some shell and sighed. He leaned back, his captain's chair tipped on its rear legs. "The truth is Bennie's a user, *compadre*. He makes friends for a reason, and that reason is to benefit Benito Milagros. He has this amoral streak. It's what makes him irresistible to a great many women. And I can understand that. There's a certain rush in watching somebody cleverly circumvent the law."

Croaker pushed his plate away. "Rafe, I need some straight talk. Where I'm going tonight, I'd say it's downright vital."

"I don't like the sound of that, *compadre*." A certain tension had come into the tall man's frame. "Does this have something to do with Juan Garcia Barbacena?"

Croaker hitched his chair forward. "It has everything to do with Barbacena. At midnight I'm going to put my head beneath the guillotine."

Rafe's chair came crashing down onto all four legs. "That's when Barbacena's landing in Miami."

The two men looked at each other for a long time. Sunlight spangled the ocean. A pair of cormorants flew by, heading for land. For his part, Croaker wanted to go the other way. Down and down, following the manta, until the thought of the city and what he had to do tonight vanished. But Rachel wouldn't let him. His tail—the electrical cord—was plugged into her hospital monitors. He couldn't let her life signs flatline.

"You said you'd help me, Rafe."

Roubinnet nodded gravely. "Count on it. Whatever you need, *compadre*. Nothing in life frightens me."

"Not even helping to plot Juan Garcia Barbacena's death?"

Rafe shook his head. "Barbacena's a hardened criminal. I've got no qualms on that score. No, the world will be a far better place without him. I'll help you. Even though I know his death will make Bennie one very happy *hombre*."

In the ensuing silence, Croaker could hear the blood coursing through his veins. The pounding of his heart was almost painful. The boat rocked a little on gathering swells.

Very softly, Croaker said, "Did you know that Bennie works for the U.S. Government? He's running Barbacena in a sanctioned operation in Mexico."

"It doesn't surprise me to hear this. He's in the company of thieves, *compadre.*"

"Quite a bit worse," Croaker said. "But if Barbacena's working for him why would Bennie want him dead?"

Rafe stood up. "Let's take a stroll." They went forward. The boat had lifted anchor after they'd come back on board. It was running lightly before the wind, more or less paralleling the coast. They stood looking out at the green-blue water, dotted with fishing and pleasure boats. "*Compadre,* you must have had a mentor. A rabbi, I think they call it in New York, no?"

Croaker nodded.

"Of course," Rafe said. "If he's smart, every man, when he is young, finds a rabbi to learn from. I am no exception. And neither is Bennie." He clamped his hands together. "After a time, the ties that bind you to your rabbi run very deep. You understand. It's an intimate relationship unlike any other; you and your rabbi come to share strengths—and fears. Now think of your rabbi. Imagine he has a daughter. She is a beautiful creature, very strong in many ways, weak in others. Like all women, she is enigmatic."

Rafe was staring out at the creamy wake. "All right, then. This young woman meets a man and falls in love with him. He is strong, clever, charismatic. But he is the wrong man for her. Your rabbi knows this; you know this. But nothing can convince her. 'Love conquers all,' she insists. 'I know him. I will change him.' "

Rafe stirred, as if in a dream. "Tragic words. But, then, love can be terribly tragic, *compadre. Verdad?*"

"Yes," Croaker said. "It's the truth."

Rafe folded his arms over his browned chest. "Well, then, events transpire with the chilling inevitability of fate. They marry. The man loves her for a time. He abuses her, as well. But hope persists inside her. More time passes. He ignores her, cheats on her. One could say she takes the abuse and the indifference with a degree of stoicism. It is also possible that she mistakes fear for hope. Then everything changes. When she finds out about the mistress, something snaps inside her. Her strength comes to the fore, and rashly, she confronts him. And for her efforts she is murdered."

"He beats her, then strangles her with an electrical cord," Croaker said. Long before Rafe had come to the end of this morality tale, Croaker had known that he was speaking about Juan Garcia and Theresa Marquesa Barbacena.

"So you already knew Theresa's fate," Rafe said. "Now you know the rest. Bennie's mentor—his rabbi, in your parlance—was Javier Marquesa. Theresa's father." He meant Juan Garcia Barbacena's dead wife. Who, according to Majeur, Barbacena had savagely murdered.

When they returned to the table, they found the dishes had been cleared. They had been replaced by bowls of watermelon chunks, mango slices, and papaya halves. A silver thermos of coffee stood in the center, next to a plate of lime wedges.

Rafe leaned over the table, squeezed the juice from several wedges onto the fresh fruit. The gaily colored table was between them.

"Rafe, I found out that Bennie's paying the bill for Majeur's cell phone."

"I'm sure that's not all he's paying for." Rafe dished out the fruit.

"But I know Majeur is working for the Bonitas," Croaker said. "It doesn't make sense that Bennie hired him to coerce me into settling his score with Barbacena. It's the Bonitas who have access to the kidney Rachel needs."

Rafe steepled his fingers. "Unless Majeur is working for Bennie *and* the Bonitas without any of them knowing." He grunted. "That would be just like Bennie. Devious to a fault. And don't forget, they all come from the same region in Asunción. They know one another well."

Croaker thought about this for some time. "So it's possible Bennie put my niece's life at risk."

"A sad day, *compadre*." Rafe handed a plate to Croaker. "Disillusionment is a barbed little pill that sticks in your throat." He poured steaming black coffee into sea mugs, weighted at their wide bottoms. "But life must go on, isn't it so?"

Croaker nodded, his eyes hooded. "One thing bothers me, though. Bennie has a large and complex operation going. Barbacena is the spearhead. Why would Bennie contract to have him eliminated now? Why not wait until the operation has been completed?"

"I can think of several reasons." Rafe tapped his fingertips together. "With Barbacena coming here to Miami, he's at his most vulnerable now. Afterward, who knows, he might vanish back into some South American jungle. Then again, word is Barbacena's taken some dubious risks recently. In the process he's made enemies in high places. That would be a grave liability to someone in Bennie's position."

Croaker considered these things as he ate some fruit. It was cool and sweet and tart all at the same time. He thought about Bennie.

What was the real motivation for his actions? Who knew what a man with such a restless spirit really wanted?

"Who d'you think Bennie would pick as Barbacena's replacement?" he asked.

Rafe shrugged. "I'm unfamiliar with the new players. The benefits of retirement, *compadre*. But you can bet there's someone. It's only good business. You never fire an employee without having already hired his replacement."

The same crewman who served lunch emerged from the cabin with Croaker's cell phone.

"Call for you, Mr. Croaker," the young man said, handing over the phone.

"Lew?" He heard Jenny Marsh's voice in his ear and he walked to the far rail.

"Hi," he said. "How are you making out?" The wind whistling around him made it impossible to hear. He told her to hold on while he went into the house.

"Are you okay?" Jenny said as he closed the door behind him. "The way you cut off the last call—"

"It couldn't be helped." His heart constricted at the anxiety in her voice. "I was calling from a place I shouldn't have been in. I'm fine now." He was alone in the main salon, and he sat on a built-in sofa. "What about Rachel?"

"Rachel and I are at Jackson Memorial," she said.

"That was quick."

"I used a medevac helicopter. It was the only way. The ambulance ride would have done her no good at all. What do you mean you're fine *now*."

Nothing could get past this woman, he thought. "I tripped and fell into a pool, is all. It was nothing, believe me."

"Damn you, I *don't* believe you."

He knew she was thinking of the spirit-stone vision. He cut her short. "Stansky?"

"In the dark and he'll stay that way," Jenny said. "I gave explicit instructions at the Royal Poinciana Dialysis unit. He won't be told anything. Anyway, he doesn't come in until about six in the evening."

He stared out at a tanker moving slowly along the horizon. He didn't want to tell her that with Stansky's connections, the doctor could easily find out where Jenny had taken Rachel. That wasn't the immediate problem he was facing, however. Everything seemed to be coming down to a matter of timing. "And Matty?"

"Your sister's okay. I told her we lacked equipment that Rachel now needed. That got her anxious, of course, but I managed to settle her down. I told her Jackson's better able to handle the transplant."

"As long as she's calm. The last thing we need is for her to be calling Stansky now."

"She won't. She trusts me. Rachel's now my patient."

"Great."

"Now do you mind telling me what the hell is going on?"

"No problem. Just as soon as I get there. Until then, I want you to keep a close eye on the infection."

"Already being done hour by hour. I could read you that far."

"You're a whiz." He looked at his watch. It was just after three. "I'll be there by five. Until then, no one gets in to see Rachel except you and Matty. Okay?"

"Of course." There was a brief hesitation. "Lew, you're scaring the hell out of me. I'm going to get hospital security up here right now."

"A sensible precaution," he said. "Sit tight. And try not to worry."

"Oh, right. That will be a breeze."

He did his best to ignore her sarcasm. "One more thing, Jenny. Sometime in the next couple of hours I'm going to give you a call. I'm going to say, Go. That's it: Go. When I do, I want you to have Matty call Stansky. Have her tell him where Rachel's been moved."

"Are you nuts?"

"You'll understand when I get there. Just do it, Jenny. Okay?"

"No, it's not okay. You're going to have to do a lot better than that."

Through a window, he watched Rafe speaking to one of the crew. Croaker could imagine other crewmen scrambling in the aft netting, rerigging the sail as the boat came about. "I need him to verify this theory. Your monitoring the infection level will hopefully do part of it, but only Stansky can provide the other half. I need my hands on him, but at the time and place of my choosing."

"Right. Okay. I can understand that. I have the same suspicions about him you have. When you get here we'll compare notes." She sounded at least partially mollified.

"Sounds good. Jenny, I'm glad you're with Rachel."

"Me, too." She hesitated a moment. "Lew, will you swear to me you're all right?"

"Except for a couple of more scrapes and bruises I'm fine. Really. See you soon."

The house was divided into a number of cabins, some separated by bulkheads. To one side of the main salon was a half-bulkhead—

a serving counter behind which was the compact but highly efficient galley gleaming with stainless steel and copper. At the far end of the salon was a head. One of two doors led to the master stateroom with its own head, the other to a short corridor ending in two other cabins that could be used as offices during the day and as guest bedrooms at night. The crew was quartered in berths within the pontoons.

A crewman entered, bringing a tray back to the galley. Because the bulkheads were thin, Croaker went all the way back into the head off Rafe's stateroom.

Inside the cramped space, he dialed Ronald Stansky's West Palm Beach office. The receptionist told him in her crisp, indifferent voice that the doctor was at clinic today and did he need the number. Croaker said he did. He broke the connection and dialed it.

He identified himself to Stansky as Juan Hidalgo. He spoke in a combination of Spanish and badly fractured English; a man like Stansky would disdain having to learn Spanish even though he worked part-time at a clinic. Something to do with a pain in his lower abdomen, he told the doctor. Stansky finally got it. Continuing in Juan Hidalgo's laborious manner, Croaker told Stansky that he was at work and it might take him an hour to get there. The doctor assured him he'd wait.

With the knowledge that Stansky was firmly in place for the next couple of hours, he called Jenny and gave her Stansky's clinic number. He put the cell phone away.

Just as he reached for the door to the head, the cat lurched in a swell and he slid sideways. He was stopped from falling against a bulkhead because the circular rag rug on the floor did not give. Curious, he knelt down. Peeling back an edge, he saw that it was quite cleverly "tacked" down with Velcro strips. He was about to replace the section of rug when he noticed something beneath it on the floor.

Peeling back more, he discovered a circular cover cut into the floor surrounded by a thick rubber gasket seal. In its center was a small metal wheel. Had it been open, the circle was just large enough for a hefty man to fit through. After a moment's thought, Croaker flattened the rug back onto its Velcro mounts and emerged from the head.

He fetched the plans of Barbacena's converted warehouses Majeur had given him and went back out onto the foredeck. He spread the plans on the table, placing bowls and sea mugs on the corners to keep the wind from ripping them.

"This top one is the Miami residence," he said.

Rafe took a good look at it. "You're kidding, right? This is locked up like Fort Knox. I don't see any way in."

"But I do," Croaker said. His forefinger stabbed out. "You see here, where the electrical conduit comes through the basement from the street. Normally, there's no egress. But when Barbacena renovated he needed an army of lines for his computers, satellite feeds, what have you. That's way over what had been intended when the building was built. They had to put in several relay boosters. And that means access."

"I don't see any boosters here. I see a freezer and a prefab wine cellar."

"Take another look."

Rafe peered more closely at the plan.

"See the erasure marks?"

Rafe traced his finger over the spot. "I see 'em."

"What was erased were three letters: FPL."

Rafe looked up at him. "Florida Power and Light."

Croaker nodded.

"I know everybody there," Rafe said. "All it will take is one call to verify the access." But he made no move toward the house. Instead, he rolled up the top sheet, revealing the plan for the Miami Beach warehouse. He scanned it briefly. "Same layout here, basically. Both these places are death traps. Even if you get in undetected, even if you get to Barbacena without being caught or killed, you'll never get out alive. See, my first week in office I got a crash course in assassinations and security. One of those subjects that's fascinating and terrifying at the same time."

Croaker nodded. "So what we're looking at here is a suicide mission."

"If you try to do it this way, there's no doubt of it." Rafe glanced from the plans to Croaker. "Maybe that's what Bennie wants."

"That's occurred to me."

Rafe sat back down in a captain's chair. "Then we've got to come up with an alternative." He steepled his fingers. "When I was mayor, I drove my security handlers crazy. Why? Because I was outside so much. Snipers, they kept moaning. A sniper is how they got to JFK, they complained. It's how they got to King and Bobby Kennedy. The outdoors is their worst nightmare." He looked at Croaker. "I may have made these guys nuts, but I took everything they said very damn seriously. They knew their business." He leaned forward, tapped the plans emphatically. "Forget this stuff. Unless you're one of the Mario Brothers, you'll never get through to him. It's outdoors where you've got to make your move."

"Great minds think alike," Croaker said. "As it happens, Barbacena's a vegetarian. Very strict about it. Also, traveling makes him hungry. According to my information, the first thing he does when he disembarks is eat."

"Hmm. There are damn few vegetarian restaurants in the area."

"Even fewer that are still serving at midnight," Croaker said, thinking of the short list provided in the material Majeur had given him.

Rafe's expression broke into a smile. *"Ay de mi.* If we can pin down where Barbacena will have his midnight snack, you can take him."

Rafe's words were like a beacon in the night. It was reassuring to know that he agreed with Croaker's own assessment of the situation. Croaker recited the list of vegetarian restaurants he'd memorized.

"There's only one that serves after midnight," Rafe said with a wolfish grin. "An Chay. Asian food in a rain forest setting. Very trendy. It's on Ninth and Washington in SoBe."

"That's where Barbacena will be," Croaker said. He turned abruptly away, almost stumbling to the far rail. There he stood, his back to Rafe and the crew, staring down at his biomechanical hand. *I'm racing toward midnight,* he thought. *I have no more time to evade the inevitable.* He wrapped his flesh-and-blood fingers around the cool metal at the base of his artificial hand.

A moment later he felt a presence behind him. *"Compadre,* it's always like this." Rafe's voice was soft on the sea breeze. "At the eleventh hour is when all the old doubts and fears start piling up. They'll cripple you if you give into them."

Rafe stopped. He was close enough to Croaker now to see what Croaker was doing. Slowly and deliberately, Croaker pressed a series of five small buttons on the inside of his left wrist. He waited three seconds, then pressed them again in another order. Then he gave the biomechanical hand a sharp twist to the left. It came off. He cradled it in his right hand.

"You know, when I was in Southeast Asia I saw an old man display a krait just this way." Croaker looked at Rafe. "Do you know about kraits, Rafe? No? They're snakes of the genus *Bungarus,* the most highly venomous in the world. This old man handled them every day of his life. I often wondered whether it occurred to him that all it would take was one misstep, one bite, and he'd be dead."

Croaker turned his biomechanical hand over so that it was palm up, the fingers, curled, seemingly at rest. "In the old man's grip, the krait seemed as harmless as this hand." He held up the hand so the sunlight fired the metallic blue. "And beautiful. They're banded in fantastic colors. But it would be a mistake to think that kraits were anything other than deadly."

A kind of sadness touched Rafe's handsome face. "*Compadre,* those Jap techno-surgeons sure knew what they were doing when they gave you that hand. The things it can do!"

Neither of them cared to look at the stub of his wrist with its stainless-steel collar, its grooves and whorls, micromotors, calibrated rods and fibers. This was too intimate a sight, like another man's genitals.

"I wonder," Rafe said. "Do you feel naked—you know, naked—without it?"

"A bit. It's as much a part of me as my flesh-and-blood hand." Croaker looked away. "Each moment it becomes more concrete. I'm shown Barbacena's photo. Now he's a real person instead of a name in a file. You and I work on penetration and now I know exactly where he'll be in the first few minutes past midnight." He jerked his head in disgust. "It's hit me, Rafe. Up until this moment I've been finding more and more elaborate ways of fooling myself. I'd split myself into two distinct people. Out of self-preservation. It wouldn't be me who looked through the sniper scope, I kept telling myself. It wouldn't be me who centered Juan Garcia Barbacena in the crosshairs. It would be someone else who pulled the trigger and blew his head off. But now the self-deception has cracked like so many mirrors. Behind it all, there's only me."

He stared bleakly into the sun-dazzle on the water. "Come midnight it will be *my* eye in the sight, *my* finger on the Steyr's hair trigger. *My* decision to exert that last bit of pressure. Until I hear the familiar percussion in my ears, feel the recoil absorbed by my right pectoral muscle."

He was gripping his biomechanical hand so tightly his fingers seemed white and bloodless. "Yes. Barbacena will die. Rachel will have her kidney. And I will have to wake up tomorrow morning and realize the terrible price I've paid to be the master of life and death."

"This pain you feel now, I admit it can't be minimized. But the deed is worth doing, *compadre.* Deep down, you know that. This is an evil man. For what he has done, for what he will do, he deserves to die." Rafe gripped his shoulder. "And when you see your niece recovered, when you see the smile on her lovely face, whatever doubts still linger will disappear like so much rain."

Would they? Croaker wondered. He wished he was as sure of that as Rafe was.

Nevertheless, Rafe was right about one thing. He reattached the hand, swinging it onto the stainless-steel grooves on the outer circumference of his wrist stub. Working the buttons, he realigned his nerves and tendons with the conduits running through the biomechanical interior. He flexed the titanium and polycarbonate fingers, extruded the stainless-steel nails, retracted them. The truth he was stuck with was this: curse or gift, he didn't feel complete without this appendage.

He stared at the skyline of Miami looming ever larger as they headed into shore. Sunlight emblazoned the high-rises, turning them the color of brass. Like brass, they had been beaten into shape by the society of man. Just as he had, forged on the anvil of venality and betrayal.

He realized it wasn't only for the murder of his would-be killer he'd sought sanctuary at the Surfers' church last night. It was for the deliberate act of cold-blooded murder he was bound to commit tonight.

Croaker was in the T-bird on his way to Jackson Memorial when he noticed the flashing lights of a Metro-Dade patrol car behind him. He glanced at the speedometer even though he knew he hadn't been exceeding the limit. The last thing he needed was to be pulled over by an overzealous cop. But that was just what was happening.

He rolled to a stop at the curb and waited while the patrol car nosed in behind him. There was a space of maybe fifteen feet between the tail of the T-bird and the nose of Chevy patrol car. Lights revolved, flashing; traffic passed. Nothing happened.

That was okay. The cop was on the phone, checking the registration of the T-bird. Standard operating procedure.

Croaker was looking at the windshield of the cop car in his rearview mirror when his cell phone rang. Probably Jenny, telling him that hospital security was in place. But it wasn't Jenny.

"Lew, am I glad I got hold of you." Rocky Saguas's voice buzzed in his ear. He was one of Croaker's contacts, a detective lieutenant in charge of a squad at the Metro-Dade Police.

"Not as glad as I am to hear from you. I got one of your flyswatters sitting on my tail."

"Now?"

Croaker kept his eyes on the rearview mirror. "Even as we speak."

"This is not good," Saguas fretted. "Not any fucking good at all."

Croaker sat up straighter in his seat. "What's up, Rock?"

"I don't know what the fuck is going on but I sure don't like it. I just got back to the office and I find this priority bulletin come across the wire. From the FBI. It's a request to pick you up and hold you in isolation for transfer to fed authority."

An icy ball was forming in the pit of Croaker's stomach. Feds. The ACTF must be desperate. Opening up their search for him to local law enforcement would inevitably cause questions to be asked. Questions they'd rather not answer. Which was why the order included the "iso" designation. They wanted him in strict isolation until they got their hands on him.

"They give you cause?" Croaker asked.

"Says here you're wanted for questioning concerning the death of Vonda Shepherd. Bullshit, I say," Saguas went on. "I pulled the file. This Shepherd girl, she was blonde, Cauc, twenty-six. Worked at Gold Coast Exotic Auto Rentals in Margate. I made some calls, reached out to the uniform who caught the B and E squeal. Said he found her head. Like off the fucking body, man. It was a goddamn horror movie. He barfed his lunch all over his nice shiny shoes."

As Croaker watched, the door of the patrol car opened and a pair of shiny boots emerged.

"It wasn't me, Rock. I didn't whack her."

"Of course you didn't. But you musta done something. There's a shit storm of activity around here and it's all aimed at you."

A heavyset young cop was attached to those shiny boots. He had a grim, lantern jaw and short blond hair sparkling with sweat in the heat. His right hand was on the butt of his service revolver. It was impossible to look behind his reflective aviator sunglasses to guess his intent. Which was the point. In any case, he was heading toward Croaker with the determination of a tank.

"Lew?"

Croaker said nothing. He was watching the attitude of the cop and thinking how his options were rapidly shrinking. He was like a spelunker exploring a cave. The deeper he went, the narrower the next cavern became until now he found himself wedged in on all sides by solid rock.

"Lew?" It was Rocky's voice. "You still there?"

"Yeah."

"Well, don't be. I mean to say, get the hell out of my jurisdiction and do it pronto. This bulletin has highest priority. No choice here, buddy. I gotta put every man I can spare on it. Get me?"

"Sure," Croaker said. "But what about this flycatcher stuck to me?"

"Maybe he hasn't gotten this info yet. Gimme the tag number of his vehicle."

Croaker strained in his seat to read the plate in the mirror. From his days in the NYPD, he was used to reading reversed images. "Three-johnson-caroline-nine-forty-four," he read off.

"Hold on."

Sunlight spun crazily off the young cop's wire-rimmed sunglasses, making him look like a robot, intimidating, inhuman. Cops cultivated an edge like that. You needed whatever advantage you could get when at any moment a semiautomatic might be shoved in your face. Anything that might make the perp say, *Not this one, he's too tough. Let's move on.* The young cop was taking his time, sizing up the situation, just like they taught you in the academy.

In the mirror, Croaker watched the cop put his hand on the trunk of the T-bird. Maybe he thought Vonda's dead body was in there. Croaker kept himself very still, but his heart rate was already elevated. "Rock, I think he's made me. I've run out of time."

The cop's two-way radio squawked. Croaker could hear the word "Urgent!" The cop paused, turned his head. He hesitated a moment, bending down to peer through the T-bird's window at Croaker. "You," he ordered, "stay put!" Then he trotted back to his car and leaned in.

"I got him on the two-way," Saguas said. "Burn rubber."

"Thanks, Rock. I owe you."

"Yeah. You do," Saguas said. "But that'll be another story." He hesitated just an instant. "Lew, take care, okay?"

Croaker took one last look at the cop. He was standing beside the patrol car, speaking into the mike while he stared at the back of the T-bird. Croaker slammed the T-bird in gear, jammed his foot on the accelerator, and took off down the street.

He had to will himself not to look in the rearview mirror. It was all he could do to maneuver through the traffic at high speed. Down here, nearer the hospital complex, there was a very high percentage of elderly drivers. No one was going fast.

Except him.

A siren screamed behind him. The patrol car was coming fast, its revolving lights panicking the Q-Tips behind the wheels of the intervening cars. Croaker turned right, then right again. The patrol car came on. Croaker pushed the T-bird through a narrow gap between a red Toyota and a refrigerated truck. Using the truck as camouflage, he made a sharp left. Turning left again, he was back on NW Seventh Avenue. The patrol car was coming, but he had a moment's respite. Enough to formulate an emergency plan.

He cruised to a stop at a red light and took a long look at the oncoming traffic along the cross street. Once he got a sense of the traffic flow he saw it was going to be uncomfortably close.

Behind him, the patrol car appeared, siren screaming, lights flashing. Croaker glanced in the rearview mirror. For this to work, he needed the patrol car so close there was room only for reflex response. He returned his attention ahead. The light was still red. He prayed for it to hold. If it turned to green now . . .

Here came the patrol car. To his left, a large truck lumbered along the cross street. The young officer in the patrol car was using his loudspeaker ordering Croaker to pull over. Croaker floored the accelerator, swinging left, crossing the path of the oncoming truck. The startled trucker blew his air horn and Croaker just missed crushing his rear bumper on the truck's grille.

The patrol car, speeding after him, was not so fortunate. It rammed the truck almost head-on. The entire front end accordioned in on the young cop. His head came flying forward but before it could slam into the steering wheel, the air bag deployed.

That was as much as Croaker glimpsed as he sped away. His right hand shook a little. When he pulled up in front of the West Wing pavilion, he noticed a crack in the steering wheel where he'd been gripping it with his biomechanical hand.

Like a fine Florida restaurant or nightclub, Jackson Memorial Hospital had valet parking. Considering the area of Miami it was in, it was a smart move. Croaker looked at his watch. It was now forty-five minutes since he'd called Jenny and told her "Go!" Stansky would be arriving any minute, if he wasn't here already.

He glanced up at the pavilion's brick facade, then trotted up the steps into the cool, hushed lobby. He took the elevator up to the fifteenth floor, went quickly along a wide hallway. He passed a nurses' station, then turned a corner. The Dialysis unit was across the street at Jackson Memorial Towers, but Jenny had decided to bring Rachel directly to West Wing 15, where the transplant operating theaters were housed.

He saw Jenny at the far end of the corridor. She had just come out of Rachel's room. As if sensing his approach, she turned. Seeing him, she smiled, then quickly shook her head. Stansky hadn't shown up yet.

"How is she?" he asked. They were still some ways apart, but the corridor was clear and the nurses' station more than a hundred feet behind him around the corner. Between them were only two patient rooms and a bathroom. Jenny had wisely picked a quiet little backwater section of the floor to keep Rachel safe.

"Better," Jenny said.

"It was Stansky, wasn't it?"

She nodded, only briefly distracted by a tall, slim technician in a white coat pushing a man in a wheelchair out of a room between them. "Your instinct was right. No wonder we were making no headway with the infection. Stansky was reintroducing the sepsis into Rachel's intravenous tube every day."

"He was poisoning her," Croaker said. "Why?"

The technician turned the wheelchair in Croaker's direction. "Why don't you ask him yourself?" the technician said as he kicked off the wheelchair's brakes and hurled it directly at Croaker.

Even though the "patient" was partially slumped over, Croaker recognized him. It was Stansky. The doctor's wrists and ankles were bound cruelly to the wheelchair with wire and his suit looked dark with sweat and blood. Croaker snared one arm of the wheelchair with his biomechanical hand. It swung around on two wheels, almost pitching over on its side before he had it under control. By that time, he'd already determined that Dr. Ronald Stansky was quite dead.

Croaker looked past Stansky to see the man in the white coat. He was standing just behind Jenny. One arm was locked across her throat.

"You see how ridiculously easy this is, *señor*? Finding the vulnerable spot is my forte. That is because it is a distinct pleasure."

Croaker looked into Jenny's green eyes. There was concern there, to be sure. But no panic. He returned his attention to the man in the technician's coat. It was Antonio, not Heitor; his nose wasn't broken.

"You once told me that others lied to me," Croaker said. "Stansky was one of the worst offenders, wasn't he?"

"Oh, there are worse, I assure you."

Croaker held out his hands, palms up. "Antonio, this is between you and me," he said. "There's no need to involve anyone else."

"No man is an island, *señor*. Surely you know that." Those amber eyes scrutinized Croaker as he walked slowly down the corridor. "It is by his private and business connections with the world that a man may be influenced."

"Manipulated, you mean."

Antonio smiled. "My English is not so fine as yours, *señor. Perdoname.*"

"Cut the crap, Antonio. What do you want?"

"*Madre de mentiras.* You have the patience of a moth."

"You and Heitor have worn my patience thin," Croaker said. "But it's your time that's limited. Hospital security is crawling all over this floor."

"Unfortunately for you, no." Antonio's eyes blazed briefly. "That's far enough, *señor*." For emphasis, he tightened his grip on Jenny's throat, making her gag. "Hospital security—laughable though it is—has been neutralized. We're here now, *señor*, the three of us. And, of course, your niece. Until I say otherwise."

"Tell me," Croaker said. "How much did Stansky know about your organ harvesting operation? That's why you murdered him, isn't it? So he couldn't talk."

"Stansky had become more trouble than he was worth. Perhaps you know something of his sexual peccadilloes."

"So much for your English being 'not so fine.' " Every few seconds, his gaze flicked to Jenny's face, monitoring her like a doctor checks on a patient in critical condition. He didn't know how she would handle herself in a crisis.

Antonio smiled. "*Peccadillo*"—he rolled the *ll*s, Spanish style— "comes from the Spanish. *Pecado*. It means 'little sin.' " He sighed as if he were truly saddened. "Stansky's sins weren't so little anymore. Pity. He had his uses."

"Like pimping for you and Heitor." In interrogations, it was wise to tell your subject several dark and dirty things about himself. This put the two of you on a different plane. An intimacy evolved, and that's what you wanted. Also, it put the subject off guard, softened him up for the questions you inevitably wanted answered. "Stansky culled the live bodies for you to plunder from among the patients in his Margate clinic. What I want to know is what's your connection with Trey Merli?"

"Hmm." Antonio's eyes were hooded. "What's a trey merli?"

"Here's what's been bothering me, Antonio." Croaker went on as if Antonio hadn't spoken. "I break into Gold Coast Exotic Auto Rentals and what do I find?"

Antonio broke into a beatific smile. "A young woman's head. *¡Que linda muchacha!*" Such a beautiful girl!

Croaker's hands curled into fists. He saw in Antonio's face how the other man delighted in baiting him. With effort, he refocused on what he needed to do. "You're already inside. Yet you didn't trip the alarm. When I follow you out, it's through a broken rear window. Only the glass shards are all on the *outside*."

Antonio shrugged. "So?"

"You broke the window getting out. Which means there was only one way for you to have gotten in. You had a key *and* the alarm

257

code." Croaker cocked his head. "Now who could have given you those things except the owner? A man named Trey Merli. But maybe you know him as Marcellus Rojas Diego Majeur."

"Curious, isn't it?" There was a smile on Antonio's face not unlike the one on the *Mona Lisa*.

At that moment, the door to the bathroom opened and Matty stepped out into the corridor. Several things happened at once. Matty gave a little "oh!" at what she saw; Antonio moved his head sightly to see what was happening; Jenny smashed the heel of her shoe against Antonio's instep, and Croaker went into action. He had seen in Jenny's eyes what she had meant to do a split second before she did it and he was prepared.

He raced past Matty, spinning her out of harm's way. He had just an instant while Antonio was reacting to the sharp and unexpected pain in his foot. He locked his biomechanical fingers around Antonio's wrist, pulled the muscular arm away from Jenny's throat. She ducked down, gasping in air.

Croaker extruded the stainless-steel nail of his forefinger. It slid across Antonio's throat.

"Don't make another move, *señor*."

It was an odd order for Antonio to give. He was the man with the weapon at his throat. Then Croaker saw that Jenny's face was white and pinched. He looked down to see the stiletto blade of a gravity knife pressed against her side. Antonio was gripping it with his free hand.

"What do they call this, *señor*? A Mexican standoff, no?"

Antonio seemed inordinately pleased with himself. As if he'd planned this all along. Croaker was furious. To have one of the Bonita twins so near to the three women he cared most about in life was intolerable. With his face very close to Antonio's, he said, "What is it you want?"

"*This, señor*," Antonio hissed. "To push you, to prod you, to become your own personal devil."

"*Why?*"

"To see when and where you will fail, *señor*. To see what kind of man you really are."

"You want to see if I measure up, isn't that right, Antonio? If I've got what it takes to go head-to-head with you."

"*Mano a mano*." There was an almost wistful tone to Antonio's voice. "Truly, that would be something."

With an animal grunt, he slammed his knee into the small of Jenny's back, sending her stumbling into Croaker. As Croaker moved to catch her, Antonio slithered away.

Croaker, turning Jenny away to protect her, looked at Antonio. "This isn't finished."

"*Es verdad, señor.* I would die first." Antonio flicked his wrist and the blade of the gravity knife disappeared into its handle. Pocketing the knife, he vanished around the corner of the corridor.

"Jenny—" Croaker began.

"I'm all right." She had already regained her balance and was rubbing the sore spot in her back. "Who in God's name was that?"

"Antonio Bonita." Together, they walked toward where Matty was standing near Rachel's room. "He's part of my problem."

Croaker turned to his sister and she nodded. She, too, was okay, just shaken. Then she saw Stansky, slumped over, tied to the wheelchair.

"Oh, my God!"

Croaker took her in his arms, guided her back down the hall and into Rachel's room. "Honey, stay with Rachie, now. Dr. Marsh says the infection's finally under control."

"I know, she told me," Matty said. "I've been praying." She looked at Croaker. "But, Lew, I called Dr. Stansky. You told me to, right? I told him we were here. And now—" She turned, as if she could look through the door to where Stansky's corpse still sat, cooling by the moment.

"Don't think about that," he soothed. "Stansky was corrupt. He was hurting Rachie." He sat her in a chair by the bedside. "You just concentrate on Rachel. Pray, if you want to. By tomorrow, I promise she'll have her kidney."

He squeezed her hand and left her there. Outside, in the corridor, Jenny was coming out of an unoccupied room. "I put Stansky out of public view for the time being. It's enough he scared the daylights out of your sister."

She went to a wall phone and lifted the receiver.

In two strides, Croaker was at her side. "What are you doing?"

"Calling the cops, what else?" she whispered with her hand cupped over the mouthpiece. "After what's just happened it's obvious hospital security won't cut it."

Croaker reached across her, depressed the pips, severing the connection. "Listen to me, Jenny. There've been some unexpected complications. The people who're involved with the organ harvesting are putting me under the gun. They've got the cops looking for me on a trumped-up charge of murder."

"Oh, Christ." Now she did look scared. "But Lew. I have no choice. There's a dead man in that room. I have a duty to call the cops."

"Of course you do. I won't stop you." He took the receiver out of her hand and hung it up. "Listen to me. I'm in such deep water I can't see the surface." He pointed. "Antonio killed Stansky to stop him from talking about the organ harvesting operation. But why bring the body here? Why rattle my cage further by threatening you?"

"You heard him. It was a macho thing." Jenny seemed to be conjuring up Antonio's image in her head. "Christ, I've met so many guys like that."

Croaker nodded. "In a way, it *was* a show of power. Believe me, I was impressed. But don't for a minute think you've met anyone like Antonio Bonita." He studied her face, trying to judge her level of anxiety. "See, he wasn't lying. He wants to test my mettle."

Jenny closed her eyes for a moment. When she opened them, he could see that they were clouded with worry but free of tears.

"Don't you see," he pressed on, "the moment you call the police I have to be out of here. Within minutes of you telling them what's happened, they'll be buzzing around here like bees on flowers. They won't let you alone. That means I can't get to you until it's all over."

"Oh, Lew." She put her head against his chest for a moment. "Now I know what it's like when I give a patient's family bad news. I feel like something irrevocable has happened." She looked at him. "Isn't there some way out? There must be. I can't believe it will all end in tears."

"It won't." He gripped her shoulders. "These people have given me a role to play. For the moment, at least, I've got to stick to it. I can't—I won't—take a chance with Rachel's life."

"But isn't that just what they're counting on?"

Of course she was right. What did it matter that he had caught a glimpse of the daring conspiracy among ACTF director Spaulding Gunn, Bennie, and Barbacena to use the Mexican Chiapas rebels as pawns to destabilize Mexico and install a new government that would make a handful of Americans rich beyond anyone's wildest dreams? They still had him firmly in their vise. As long as Rachel's life hung in the balance, he'd have to do what was required of him.

"Damnit, Lew, I'm not the kind of person to sit on my hands and wait around for something to happen. All right. Maybe you can't do anything except be a rat in their maze. But not me." Her eyes were alight. "Look, they got to her. Some way, somehow they caused her to need this kidney. If I could find out how they did it—"

"It was Stansky. I know it." Croaker shook his head. "But, Jenny, even if you find out how they got to Rachel, what good would it do? She still needs that kidney and I have to pay their price for it."

"Jesus." She slammed the flat of her hand against the wall. "There's got to be *something*."

"If you find it, let me know."

"Don't." She'd heard the defeat in his tone and she glared at him. "Don't you dare give up hope."

His lips brushed hers. "You're a remarkable person, Jenny. I'm sorry as hell I got you into this."

She put a hand behind his neck and kissed him fiercely. She opened his lips with hers and her tongue twined with his. He put his arms around her. He did not want to let her go. The force of her will lent him strength. It was so heady that for an instant he was dizzied. Grudgingly, he finally released her. She didn't cling and she wasn't going to cry.

"Take care of Rachel." He handed her the phone. "In the next twelve hours she's going to need the kind of care only you can give her."

Jenny looked at the receiver as if it were a black widow spider.

"Take it." He curled her fingers around it. "Make the call."

Jenny looked deep into his eyes. "I won't say good-bye. I won't even think it."

He left as Antonio had, swiftly and silently, disappearing around the corner.

Jenny watched that corner of the corridor as if by will alone she could bring him back. She counted silently to sixty. Then she turned and dialed 911.

5

Given a choice, Croaker would not have used the T-bird. He didn't have that luxury; he couldn't afford to have it found at the hospital. So he took the chance, and drove it. The drive to Miami International airport was nerve-racking. Every time he spotted a Metro-Dade patrol car, he made a detour. That put him in neighborhoods best avoided. There was a positive side to that. The cops tended to avoid them as well.

At the airport, he put the T-bird in the long-term parking lot. As he walked to the domestic airline terminals, he made a call on his cell phone.

"Yeah?" a male voice said in his ear.

"Hey, Felix."

"Lew, what the hell."

Felix Pinkwater worked for the Florida Department of Revenue. They'd worked together on several ACTF cases.

"I need a favor," Croaker said. Among other matters, the FDR was in charge of collecting the state corporate taxes.

"How about first thing tomorrow morning. I'm late for my tennis game."

"Felix, I have no leeway. I need this now."

Felix sighed. "What is it, Lew?"

"A club on Lincoln in SoBe called the Boneyard. I need a rundown on the owners."

"Jesus, Lew. What else can I get you?"

"A starring role beside Jodie Foster would be nice. But right now I'll settle for this."

Felix snorted in his ear. "Hold on. Let me get the old computer fired up. This time of the day it's one tired puppy."

Croaker stood outside the terminal. People rushed to make their flights. Others, just deplaning, sauntered out.

"Got it," Felix said in his ear. "The Boneyard is owned by a corporation: Los Mirlos Encantados, Inc."

The Enchanted Blackbirds, Croaker thought, his mind racing. *Tre merli.*

"Los Mirlos Encantados is a subsidiary," Felix was saying. "The parent company is Mineral Imports, S.A."

"And Mineral Imports is owned by?"

"Some Bahamian corporation called Juego Holdings. And don't ask me who owns Juego Holdings. With these offshore shell companies it's impossible to know for sure." Felix sounded aggrieved. Like all bureaucrats, his power resided in his facts and figures.

Croaker's pulse had accelerated. *Juego* meant game in Spanish. And the Game was all-important to the Bonitas.

Croaker laughed. "Toddle on off to your tennis game, Felix. I owe you."

"Big time," Felix said. *"Hasta luego, muchacho."*

In the terminal Croaker did a slow cruise of the airline ticket counters. As he passed the Delta desk, he overheard the attendant saying, "I'm sorry, but the six-ten to Los Angeles is completely sold out. There are no standby seats available and that's our last flight tonight."

She was speaking to a college kid in a denim jacket, jeans, and Reeboks. He had a duffel bag over one broad shoulder.

"There's gotta be something," he said. "I gotta get home. It's my sister's wedding."

"You could try another airline."

The kid shook his head. "I got a discount standby ticket with Delta. I can't afford anything else."

The Delta attendant looked sympathetic. "I'm sorry, but there's nothing I can do."

The kid shook his head and drifted away.

Croaker stepped up to the counter and the attendant greeted him with a pair of bright eyes and a generic smile.

"Yes, sir?"

He asked for a round-trip ticket to L.A. and she gave him the sold-out spiel. She looked at him brightly. "I could get you on the five-fifty tomorrow morning."

"No good," Croaker said. "I've got to get there tonight." He thought for a moment. "What about another airline?"

The attendant nodded. "Let me check."

While she did, Croaker kept his eye on the kid. He was staring at the Delta departure board as if he could manufacture another flight out of hope. Youth could do that to you.

"Sir, American has a flight to Los Angeles leaving at seven-ten. It's the last flight out of the airport." She squinted at the monitor. "I see one seat remaining."

Croaker told her to hold it for him. He gave her a name he made up on the spot.

She nodded. "This is Concourse H. American is in Concourse D, sir. You'd better hurry."

Croaker thanked her and sauntered over to the kid.

"Can you beat that?" he said conversationally. "The flight to L.A. is sold out."

"I know," the kid said. "I tried to get on. I'm flying standby."

"Tough luck," Croaker said. "Well, my buddy and I'll just have to wait until tomorrow. You, too, I guess. You need a lift?"

"No thanks." The kid looked morose. "The thing is, I've got to get there tonight. My sister's getting married."

"Hey, you know there's one seat left on the American flight. It leaves in just about an hour and a half."

The kid shook his head. "Doesn't matter. I don't have the bucks."

"C'mon," Croaker said. "Let's see what we can do."

The kid looked skeptical. "This a joke or what?"

"You want to get home tonight," Croaker said, "right?"

At the American counter, he paid cash for the ticket. He used the fictitious name he'd given the Delta attendant. When he handed over the money, he used his biomechanical hand, displaying it prominently so the American attendant would remember him. Then he went back to the kid and handed him the ticket.

The kid eyed it suspiciously. "Okay. What's the catch?"

Croaker showed him his federal I.D. "Official business. You get the ticket. You travel under the name on the ticket. Then you forget all about it."

"That's it?"

Croaker nodded. "You need my help and I need yours. It's as simple as that."

The kid grinned and pumped Croaker's hand. "Hey, cool. Thanks a lot."

"Give my congratulations to your sister."

Outside, as he waited for a shuttle bus, Croaker felt satisfied. He'd given the cops a trail to follow. The more time they wasted on trying to track him down in L.A., the more leeway he had here in Miami.

He looked around. Everything seemed different: sharp, acutely focused, saturated with color. He was aware of everything. It was always like this at the end of a case, when, at long last, the perp was in sight. Now every decision made, every action undertaken was crucial. Latinos had the best phrase for it: *Bailar en la cuerda floja*. That was what he was doing now: dancing on the slack rope. Balancing on the razor's edge.

He took the shuttle to the Fontainbleu Hotel, then grabbed a cab up to Palm Beach. It was an expensive ride but worth every penny. It was near 8 P.M. when he walked across the concrete parking lot. He took the tag off a Buick Riviera, switched it with the one on the turquoise Mustang. Then he climbed behind the Mustang's wheel. The facade of the Royal Poinciana Hospital loomed cool as an ice cube in the gathering darkness. He got in and turned on the ignition. The engine thrummed happily. He put it in gear and pulled out of the lot. If he kept to the speed limits he had just enough time to make one stop before his eight-thirty appointment with Majeur.

The lobby of the Raleigh Hotel was tall and stately, as evocative of the 1930s as the salon of an old ocean liner. Some years ago, it had been lovingly restored. The terrazzo floor was beautifully patterned and polished. Beyond, up a short flight of stairs, was the open restaurant, which looked out on a garden filled with palm trees and a spectacular pool that had made the cover of *Life* when the hotel first opened.

The bar was justly famous. Tucked away in the left corner of the lobby, its dark terrazzo floor had embedded in it a stylized outline of a martini glass, complete with olive garnish. The place was small and intimate, with a burnished wood bar and a mirror-clad wall of glass shelves filled with liquor bottles of every description. It was an authentic haunt, meant for adults, celebrations, and laughter that burst like the bubbles in fine champagne.

Majeur was already at the bar. A martini glass was in front of him. By his left knee was the kind of hard-sided aluminum case photographers use to carry their delicate equipment.

"A martini for my friend," Majeur told the bartender as Croaker took the stool next to him. "And make it just like this one. Dry as the Kalahari."

He was dressed in the sort of deliberately casual suit that cost $1,600. If it was wrinkled—and it was—it was meant to be. He wore a band-collar shirt of subtly striped silk and Bruno Magli loafers. His eyes were slightly glassy, as if he'd been drinking for a very long time. Maybe he'd been celebrating but he didn't look like he'd be laughing any time soon.

"You picked a fine spot," he said as the bartender set the martini in front of Croaker. "The drinks are first rate."

"That's beside the point," Croaker said.

Majeur took up his glass. "Not to me."

"It's getting late." Croaker slipped off his stool. "Let's get this over with."

Majeur's hand covered his for a moment. "Don't be rude, sir. Enjoy your drink."

Croaker sat back down. With the cops beating the bushes for him, he was uneasy in public places. But maybe this would turn out for the best. Something was eating at Majeur.

Majeur swallowed half his martini. "Do you know anything about the Kalahari, *señor?*"

Because he knew it would calm Majeur, Croaker took a sip of his martini. "Just that it's a desert in Africa."

"It covers a hundred thousand square miles in southern Botswana, eastern Nambia, and western South Africa, to be exact. I once flew over it. Do you know that it's pockmarked with lake beds? Cracked and parched now. Dry as a bone. But once there was water. *¡Y la vida!*" And life!

Croaker had once interrogated a serial bomber who was so antsy the other cops on the squad were sure he was a stone junkie. Croaker knew better. The man simply had to tell them just how smart he'd been. It was an imperative inside himself over which he had lost control. There comes a time in every perp's life when he needs to unburden himself. It might come in the form of bragging or confession or anywhere in between. Like the sun coming up each day, it always showed itself. You just had to be clever enough to recognize it.

"I know you've met my niece," Croaker said. "I know you watched her and Stansky do their thing."

Majeur flicked a hand for another martini. Nothing changed in his face. "I don't want anything to happen to Rachel."

And in that one simple sentence Croaker understood everything. "The question I kept asking myself is why a man like you should be renting a car? You have a lot of money; you probably own more than one car. So why the Lincoln? Now I see. You knew I'd do a run on the tag, that I'd find out you'd rented it from Gold Coast. And you wanted me to go there."

Majeur's martini came and he sampled it. For all his outward reaction, they might have been comparing golf scores.

"At Gold Coast, I meet Vonda," Croaker continued, "who tells me a man named Trey Merli owns it. Also, she's prepared for me. She even knows what a real warrant looks like. Because, she tells me, Trey Merli has shown one to her. The second time I'm there, Antonio Bonita is inside the office, armed with the keys and the alarm code. From Rachel's diary I discover that Trey Merli knows Dr. Ronald Stansky, her physician. She'd scribbled down an address on Hibiscus. When I go there, everything is placed just so. Including a load of shirts from the Jiffy Tyme Dry Cleaners. But instead of cardboard between the folded shirts, I find certain medical files. This place isn't a home, it's a stage set, I assume for my benefit." Croaker took another sip of his martini. "Then there's the matter of the grave."

Majeur's dark gaze met Croaker's in the mirror at the back of the bar. "Which grave, sir?"

"Theresa Marquesa Barbacena's. Barbacena himself is almost never in the States. What on earth would his wife's grave be doing in South Florida?"

Majeur nodded his head. "So it's true what they say, that you're one fine detective. Of course that was not her grave, just a stage set. Yes, I set clues for you: the false grave, the rental car—this was a trail back to Trey Merli. And at Trey Merli's house I was able to leave for you the files on Sonia, Vonda, and your niece."

"But why? You work for the Bonitas."

Majeur stared into the clear depths of his martini. Then, he quickly downed it and threw some money on the table. "It's getting close in here."

They went out into the lobby, up the stairs, through a glass door out into air sticky with humidity. The velvet evening hung in the palm fronds like spiderwebs. Lights twinkled around the perimeter of the pool. A couple of kids, waist deep in water, splashed each other while a youngish woman in a bandeau bathing suit looked on indulgently. Otherwise, the pool area was deserted.

The two men walked slowly until they heard the rhythmic sounds of the surf.

Majeur carried the aluminum case as if he were a replacement window salesman. Near the seawall he put the case down between them. "Now I will tell you something, *señor*. As they say, *Yo hablo con el corazón en la mano.*" I speak from the heart. "You grow up, you gain a profession, you make career choices. For good or ill, they're yours. You meet a woman, fall in love, get married. In other words, there is a routine, a rhythm. This is life."

He took out a cigar. "But then, *señor*, something happens." He slipped it out of its case, clipped off the end, and lighted it. "This something is as unexplainable as it is unexpected. You see someone and a door opens to a place inside you that was there all along. Only you didn't know it. *Señor*, this person, without even knowing it, leads you to a new place. Your old life fades like a photograph in the fire. And another life, as it seems, magically and mysteriously begins."

Croaker thought of Majeur slipping off his wedding ring and throwing it into the South Beach surf.

"*Señor*, this is what happened when I saw Rachel. I saw her with that pig, Stansky, and my heart stopped." He turned to look at Croaker directly. "*Escúchame, señor.* This was not a matter of lust. Lust is a thing of the surface, of the moment. Like smoke, it disappears on the first gust of wind. No, I am speaking of something permanent, profound. This was a matter of finding myself. When I saw her, when I saw what she was doing, what Stansky was doing to her, I saw how lost and alone a human being could be. And in that moment, I recognized myself. In her. I saw how alone I was in my marriage. I woke up in bed the next morning and looked at the person next to me. I saw a woman from a prominent family, a woman of significant pedigree, a women for whom I had no feeling whatsoever. I had married her simply to please my father. And I thought of Rachel. She became a mirror in which I saw my own soul. I knew, then, that I had to do something to save her. In a sense, it was the first step in saving myself. *Comprende?*"

Of course Croaker understood. He had felt something remarkably similar as he'd been reading Rachel's diary—the urgent necessity to save her. From men like the late Donald Duke and Stansky and all the others who marched in their footsteps.

"So you decided to play both sides of the fence. You'd betray the Bonitas while continuing to carrying out their orders."

Majeur nodded. "The morning after I saw Rachel and Stansky together I knew I had to do something to try and thwart the Bonitas. But what? They are very clever men; I could not give myself away." Majeur stared at the children climbing out of the pool. "They used Rachel to get to you. They need Barbacena dead. At the same time, they have to maintain reasonable deniability. They chose you— someone with skill and training; someone who could not be traced back to them should he be caught."

"Majeur, how did they get to Rachel?"

"I do not know, *señor.* Truly." He shrugged. "You cannot change what has already happened. She still needs the kidney."

Croaker believed him; Majeur looked miserable.

"I did some digging recently," Croaker said. "Does the name Juego Holdings sound familiar to you?"

"But of course. I have done some paperwork for that entity. It is one of Antonio and Heitor's shell corporations."

So it was as Croaker had suspected. The Bonitas owned the Bone-yard, the club on Lincoln Road where Rachel had collapsed in an apparent drug overdose. Another link between Antonio, Heitor, and Rachel. But what did it really prove? Why had she collapsed at just that moment? What had they done to her?

"Now that I know you've betrayed the Bonitas," Croaker said, turning his thoughts back to the present, "I want to know how you became involved in the first place."

Majeur's shoulders slumped. His dapper clothes seemed to fall in listless folds, as if in the last few minutes he'd shriveled physi-cally. "It certainly wasn't my idea." He placed the cigar very pre-cisely on the sea wall, letting it smoulder like a dormant volcano. "A year ago, maybe a little more, I was contacted by Antionio Bonita. He was already working for your government. He showed me reams of records. They were offical—government documenta-tion. The *federales* knew everything—who I represented, the deals I'd brokered, the drugs that had passed from hand to hand. They had me by the throat."

"So they co-opted you."

Majeur nodded. "I kept on with my practice. This is what they wanted. Antonio told me that from time to time I would be contacted. My role would be given to me in detail. All that was required of me was to follow the script."

"Which is what you did in this case. Until you saw Rachel with Stansky."

"Correct, *señor*." Majeur watched cigar smoke taken by the wind. "This morning, I told you that life was a gamble. By betraying the Bonitas—by allowing you to see it was they who damaged your niece to coerce you into murdering Juan Garcia Barbacena—I am gambling that you will be the one to stop these monsters."

But it wasn't merely justice Majeur wanted. Croaker had seen that look in many a man's eye and he knew what it meant. "Listen to me, Majeur, I won't kill the Bonitas for you or for anyone else."

"I know it. But there may come a time soon when you are given no other choice." Majeur picked up his cigar. "I have no illusions, sir. We have entered into a most deadly game. My actions have already left me in mortal peril. The Bonitas knew you would show up at Gold Coast and they took precautions. *Ouizás ellos se le ponérmos la mosca detrás de la oreja.*" I think they already suspect me. "With the twins, who can say?"

He was standing straighter now. A modicum of the old Majeur was reasserting itself. "If they do, it does not matter. Not now. Tonight, I have declared myself. I reject them and it is a feeling *muy bueno.*"

Croaker listened to the surf. In its constancy, it reminded him of the rise of life over death. More than anything now, he needed that reassurance. It seemed clear now that Bennie could not be involved with the ACTF. The Bonitas must have set him up. But there was still a nagging doubt and Croaker knew he needed factual confirmation of what he'd learned. He needed to get his hands on Majeur's phone bills to see if they jibed with the Southern Bell computer records that showed Bennie was paying for Majeur's cell phone line.

"Listen to me," Majeur said. "The Bonitas run this organ harvesting ring, but in this they are not independent. Your government is involved. In what manner, I do not know. But it is clear that they have made some kind of lunatic deal with the Bonitas." He took the cigar out of his mouth. "One does not make deals with a pair of rabid dogs."

"But you've never met the Fed who made the deal with the Bonitas—the man who calls the shots."

"No. Just Antonio." Majeur picked up his cigar. "And now I must be going. But I will meet you at midnight."

"How do you know where I'll be?"

Majeur smiled. "I know where the target will be. We both read the same material; it's a sure bet we came to the same conclusion. You are not going to penetrate those two fortresses. With his entourage, I will gamble you are not going to make the attempt anywhere indoors."

"How d'you know?"

"The odds, sir. At heart I am a gambler. You know." He waited a moment, trying to read Croaker's expression. "You have been to the restaurant already, haven't you?"

Croaker nodded. "Don't take this the wrong way, Majeur, but I don't want your help. It's too dangerous for both of us. As you say, the Bonitas have an uncanny ability of finding out everything."

Majeur gave him a fierce grin. He reached down, moved the aluminum case next to Croaker. "This is something I must do. For myself, *señor.* Call it the rehabilitation of a soul."

Croaker took possession of the tools of the assassin's trade. "There's a building." He gave Majeur an address on Washington Avenue. "It's directly across from An Chay. Three stories high. Access to the rooftop is gained in the rear. From there, I'll have a clear vantage point to the front of the restaurant. The angle is ideal."

"You have made a wise choice. With all of the target's vaunted security, it is prudent for you to have a lookout. And in the moments just before and after impact, someone to watch your back. Besides, the quicker the kill is confirmed, the quicker Rachel gets her kidney."

"Thanks, Majeur."

"*De nada.* There is a way you can show my gratitude to Rachel when she recovers her health. Tell her a little about me."

"You'll do that yourself," Croaker said. "You'll see her at Jackson Memorial when this is all over."

Majeur's gesture was curiously formal. "That would give me pleasure, sir."

As he began to turn away, Croaker said: "Majeur—"

"*Señor?*"

"There's another reason why you'll come armed tonight, isn't there?"

Majeur smoked his cigar for some time, his gaze drifting.

"You're thinking of Heitor and Antonio," Croaker prompted. "After I hit the target, they have no more use for me. Heitor is obsessed with this—" He raised his biomechanical hand. "And as for Antonio—I don't yet quite know what he's obsessed with. But he's drawn to me."

"No matter, sir. They will kill you." There seemed no doubt in Majeur's mind. "They have no other choice. You know too much; you are too dangerous to them."

"I know." Croaker discovered they were alone in the lighted pool area. "Just one more thing."

"I have told you everything."

"Not quite everything. What's your involvement with Estrella Leyes?" It was not so much a stab in the dark as a foray into the shadows. The medical files at Trey Merli's house had been slipped between shirts just back from Jiffy Tyme Dry Cleaners, where Estrella worked.

"So. You have traveled farther than I had anticipated," Majeur said. "Estrella and I grew up together. In those days, she was like my older sister. But where my interests lie in the business world, hers lie in the larger universe that surrounds us all."

"You mean *Hetá I.*"

Majeur nodded. "After I stole the files from Stansky I needed a place to stash them. Estrella volunteered."

"I've met her," Croaker said. "It's clear the Bonitas frighten her."

"Terrify is more the word." Croaker could see the concern for Estrella on Majeur's face. "She has seen firsthand the kind of terrible rituals they perform on humans. It is said—she has told me this—that the twins are not born of human womb. As the story goes, they were left on a dying woman's doorstep. Even then, as infants, they were capable of terrible things. They ate her child. So she tried to kill them, the woman. But they would not die. Instead, they clung to her, crying in their hunger and their desperate need. By their constant suckling, they healed her. In a kind of hideous symbiosis they strengthened one another. Soon, she forgot about her own child. They made her forget. She took them in. She became their mother."

Croaker almost laughed. "Jesus, you don't believe that crap, do you? I mean, there are stories of bogeymen, vampires, all sorts of demons the world over. But that's all they are. Stories."

Majeur shrugged. "On this subject I am neutral, *señor.* The law is what I know." He gave a little smile that seemed somehow sad. "The law and how to circumvent it."

"What power the Bonitas have they learned from Humaitá Milagros. Then they perverted that knowledge to their own ends."

"That is one history. But listen to me carefully. In Guarani, *history* and *legend* are expressed by the same word." Majeur looked down at the aluminum case, perhaps thinking of its contents. "One thing I do know: Estrella Leyes is not an ignorant woman."

"Trey Merli" 's house on Hibiscus Island was just as Croaker had left it after his encounter with Heitor. Wherever Majeur had needed to go, it wasn't back here. Croaker slipped in through the screened porch. He went swiftly and silently through the darkened house. The perfectly set table looked eerie—a tableau awaiting stage directions to come alive.

There was a den, but after twenty minutes of searching, he was convinced it contained no household records. He went into the master bedroom. The shirts were still on the bed, the TV and video equipment still risen from their lacquer coffin at the foot of the bed.

Something was bothering him about the whole situation with the Bonitas, the ACTF, and Bennie, but he couldn't put his finger on just what. He didn't believe Majeur had lied to him. On the other hand, he was convinced Majeur didn't know the whole truth.

He turned on a lamp and his eye wandered over the details of the room. *More often than not, it isn't what's hidden you're looking for,* his father had once told him. *It's what's right in front of your nose.*

Croaker stared at the stack of laser discs: *Casablanca, Blade Runner, Last Tango in Paris.* Beneath, something metallic gleamed. He reached over, pushed the laser discs aside. His finger hooked around a latch and lifted. Out rolled a deep drawer. Inside, were hanging file folders. Tax returns, bills, receipts, investment records. He looked through those but found nothing unusual, except that Majeur was a good deal wealthier than he had imagined. His gaze fell on a tab on which was written: PHONE RECEIPTS. Just what he was looking for.

Croaker took out the folder and leafed through it. The house had three phone lines. Nothing surprising in that, given its owner's profession. Then, he saw the current bill for the private cell number Majeur had given him. It was sent to Majeur and contained a notation that it had been paid by check. The notation gave the check number and the date it had been paid. Croaker looked at the month's previous bill and the one before that. They were the same— billed to and paid for by Marcellus Rojas Diego Majeur.

There was a ghost in the machine. On one point, at least, Antonio had got it right: everyone was lying to Croaker. Even computers. But then computers were dispassionate. They merely displayed data programmed by humans. And data could be altered.

Croaker felt almost light-headed. According to the records he'd found, Bennie wasn't paying Majeur's cell phone bill as the Bell South records showed. That meant Bennie hadn't lied to him about knowing Majeur. Everything Croaker had learned about Bennie from the computer floppy disk was now suspect. But if his involvement in the ACTF was a lie—if all the documentation about "Sero" had been planted by Antonio and Heitor—what was Bennie planning to do at midnight tonight at precisely the same moment that Juan Garcia Barbacena was arriving in Miami? Why did he need the *Captain Sumo?*

It was almost 10 P.M. when Croaker pulled up to Estrella Leyes's house in El Portal. Through the front windows he could see the blue flicker of the TV set: Pablo Leyes watching ESPN.

Next door, Sonia's house was dark and still. For a time, Croaker stood beside the night-blooming jasmine. The sensuous perfume wafted in waves from the white, starlike blossoms. In the gathered shadows, he seemed part of the street, as essential to this block as the big old lemon tree that shaded the east side of Sonia's house. He listened to the palm fronds clatter in the night wind and imagined it was the sound of Sonia's voice. He wanted to hear her laughter, to see the bright glint of her eyes in candlelight. He wanted to punish the men who had denied her a chance at life. That they were the same men who had injured Rachel seemed cruel beyond any compromise. He knew there would come a time when he would meet Antonio and Heitor for the final time. He could feel it like an ache deep in his bones. There would be no half measures, no question of surrender. There could only be vengeance and death.

Goaded into motion by such turbulent emotion, he strode through the glow of a streetlight. Coming home should never involve so much pain and suffering, he thought.

The Leyes's front door was wide open so that what little breeze blew across the block could cool the house through the screen door. The noise from inside drowned out even the most industrious insects' drone. According to the hyperbolic announcer, the vaunted Argentine soccer team was on the march. A blade of glimmering blue light, brilliant as a spark from an arc welder's torch, spilled across the porch like a beckoning finger.

A large moth was stuck on the screen door as if with a dab of mortar. Illuminated by an irregular patch of moonlight, its pale, speckled wings seemed made of the same powder women applied to their cheeks. The moth hung absolutely motionless, as if suspended between moonlight and the void. Croaker, moving, cast his shadow, and the moth, a spectral shape like two hearts touching, hurtled into the night. Croaker opened the screen door and stepped inside.

He saw squadrons of chanting fans as players kicked a soccer ball back and forth across the TV screen. Someone was sitting in a big upholstered chair glued to the action. From where Croaker stood, he could just see the top of a man's head over the chairback. It looked like Pablo Leyes's bald dome.

There was a strong smell of herbs and spices, and Croaker was reminded of Estrella's healing work with Nestor, Sonia's dancer friend. A shadow fell on a section of countertop past the open arch into the kitchen. It darkened a photo of a young girl amid tropical foliage. No doubt Estrella Leyes in the jungle outside Asunción. This beautiful girl stared at the observer with an uncanny prescience—as if she had already anticipated this moment in the future, when she would be scrutinized by a stranger.

At that moment, Croaker would have called out, but something was wrong. The open front door, the loudness of the TV, exaggerated by the quietude of the street outside. The ghostly shadow in the kitchen. Croaker was struck by the eerie sense that the flickering images on the screen were spewing their high-tension energy into a static room. He stared at the back of the chair.

He recalled the first time he had seen *Psycho*. There was a scene near the end where Marion Crane goes up to the attic of the Bates house and turns the rocking chair around, revealing the mummified corpse of Norman Bates's mother. Up until then, you were sure Mrs. Bates was alive because Norman periodically talked to her. In that moment, everything was revealed: her death and Norman's madness.

After finding human heads in refrigerators and office shelves, it took little imagination to picture another corpse watching soccer with filmed-over eyes. But if Pablo Leyes was dead, whose shadow ebbed and flowed in the kitchen?

Croaker touched the soul-catcher at the bottom of his pocket. He made his decision to move, and in that moment, a voice said, "Mr. Croaker. An unexpected pleasure."

The chair swiveled around and Pablo Leyes smiled. "Don't be startled, son." He hooked an enormous spatulate thumb back over his shoulder. "I saw your reflection in the TV screen." His bald head distorted the hectic TV images into strange bursts of light, like constellations on a planetarium's ceiling.

Croaker relaxed, dropping his hand to his side. "I hope you don't mind the intrusion but it's important I see you."

Leyes beamed. "Hell, son, with a request like that you're welcome day or night." He stroked the meat of his arm. "Seems it's been forever since I was important enough for someone to come see me after hours." He gestured. "You want a drink—anything? There's some of Estrella's killer paella she can heat up. Just take a minute."

"Thank you, but no. I have very little time."

"Time enough to sit, though." He waited while Croaker perched on the arm of a tatty sofa. "Now, what's so pressing, son?"

"I remembered you'd worked for Southern Bell."

Leyes nodded. "That's right. Lineman. Those were the days, let me tell you. Like a damn cowboy. Ride them poles. Yahoo!"

"But you worked as a supervisor, as well."

Leyes's watery eyes clouded over. "For as long as I could stand it. Which wasn't all that long. I'm no damn paper pusher, make book on it."

Croaker hunched forward. "I need some info on how someone could break into the Southern Bell computer system."

"Hack it, you mean?" Leyes' face twisted up. "Hell, son, I could do it from here with my notebook computer." He squinted up at Croaker. "That what you want to do, make a little mischief at my old alma mater?" He seemed intrigued by the idea, excited even.

"I'd like to get in," Croaker said. "Several days ago, I logged on using a police access code."

"Couldn't hack it with that, let me tell you."

"No, I know. That's why I'm here." Croaker had to raise his voice over the frenzied soundtrack from the TV. Someone had scored a goal. "I got some info from the Southern Bell system that I now suspect is false. I'd like you to check it out, if you would."

Leyes grinned. "Hell, son, nothing would give me greater pleasure." He pulled his wheelchair into view and Croaker got the wheelchair into position. "That's right. Now, give me a lift into the saddle." He lifted himself out of the upholstered chair with his massive arms. Croaker took hold of him under his armpits and he flopped into the leather wheelchair seat with the solid *thwack* of a deepwater fish landing on a boat deck.

"Make yourself to home," he called as he propelled himself out of the living room and down the hall to the rear of the house. "Estrella's in the kitchen. I'll be back with the hardware in a couple minutes."

In the kitchen, a large iron skillet was on the stove. It was filled with vegetables and herbs, slowly sautéing. Next to it, a wooden chopping board was covered with salad—romaine lettuce, cucumbers, coriander. Croaker didn't see Estrella.

The back door was open. She must have taken the garbage out.

He pushed through the screen door, stood on the small concrete stoop, waiting for his eyes to adjust to the dark. Thick swaths of black-green tree hibiscus blotted out the moon and bougainvillea draped like bunting. Crickets and tree frogs chirruped in the still, soupy air.

"Mrs. Leyes?"

A sound from the rank of three galvanized steel garbage cans drew him down off the stoop. His footsteps were silent in the grass and loamy mulch beneath the trees.

He found her crouched with her back against the middle garbage can. Her elbows were on her drawn-up knees, her wrists crossed one over the other. It was a kind of meditative pose, a serene state, but altogether too fixed.

When he knelt down beside her he saw that her lips had been sewn shut. Her eyes were open, staring at the swaths of bougainvillea. By dawn tomorrow they would be reborn in all their magnificent colors. Estrella Leyes would never see it.

He placed two fingers on her carotid artery. No pulse. He took out a pocket knife and carefully slipped the blade between her lips. This close, he could see the neat sutures applied through her flesh with a surgeon's artful precision. No beads of blood oozed around the punctures, which meant her mouth had been stitched shut after she died.

The moment he cut the sutures, her lower jaw dropped open. Her mouth was filled with small, smooth stones, dark and wet with her saliva. A drool of it dripped onto her chest where a dark stain slowly spread around the black hilt of a chef's knife. What section of blade Croaker could see was mossy with coriander.

Croaker wiped away the sudden sweat on his face with the back of his hand. He launched himself up. In three strides he was back on the stoop and through the screen door.

The cooking smells, once so delicious, now seemed cloying. They followed him down the hall. He walked in absolute silence as Stone Tree had taught him, rolling his soles from heel to toe, his weight evenly balanced on the outside of his feet.

He went into each doorway he passed. To the right was a tiled bath, pristine white, smelling of sandalwood. Across from it, on the left, was a small study with a daybed, a cheap desk, and a sisal rug the color of burnt toffee. Farther along on the left was the master bedroom, decorated in rose and off-white. The last door on the right was closed. He put his ear to the door, heard nothing.

Turning the knob, he unlatched the door. Then, taking a step back, he kicked it open. He found himself in a large room. It was obviously a new addition because it was unfinished. Wallboard, taped at the seams, was still unpainted, the floor was unsanded wood, spattered with dollops of chalk white spackle and black pencil notations as to window measurements. The single piece of furniture was a green metal desk, piled with computers, modems, software packages, and instruction manuals. From a hole in the ceiling a single wire dangled, attached to a brown plastic fixture and a bare bulb. The bulb, however, was not the source of illumination. A small fire flickered in a rough stone vessel that sat on the floor. By its light he saw the crocodile.

It was an evil-looking reptile, horned and scaled, a prehistoric predator that considered man fair game. It crouched in the corner of the room. Its small, amber eyes glowed as it tracked Croaker's movement. Its thickly armored tail flicked in warning. Its black lips pulled back from yellow incisors and it hissed low in its throat as its heavily muscled body tensed.

Croaker saw Pablo Leyes. He lay on his left side, his wheelchair upended and partially on top of him. Someone—or something— had taken an enormous bite out of him. It looked as if his spine had been severed.

Croaker took a step in his direction, and the croc shot forward. Its great gray jaws opened, then snapped shut with the report of a rifle shot. Croaker leapt back.

Someone chuckled.

"*Cuidado, señor.*" Have a care! "He will kill you if you give him half a chance."

Someone stepped out of the shadows cloaking the right side of the room. "Besides, Leyes is dead. Take it from me." A square white bandage covered the center of his face.

"Heitor. Christ, what have you done here?"

"Last night, I dreamt I was all alone," Heitor said. "In a starry sky I floated, tumbling, helpless. I looked at those stars, but they were so far away their light failed to illuminate me, their gravity failed to hold me. Then I awoke. And, *señor*, I knew in my heart I had dreamt about you." Heitor clucked his tongue reprovingly.

"But this isn't your dream. I have the ability to choose." Croaker was in a semicrouch. "And I say to hell with your laws."

As if it were following the conversation, the croc's huge head swiveled around.

"Then you'll die, *señor*, as surely as Estrella and Pablo died."

There was something obscene about Heitor referring to his victims by their Christian names. It suggested an unspeakable intimacy.

"But you won't kill me now, Heitor. Not yet. You'll wait until I put a bullet through Juan Garcia Barbacena's brain."

Barbacena's name seemed to send Heitor into a frenzy. "I should be the one to kill him!" His eyes blazed as he thumped his chest. "It isn't right. I've known that from the beginning! *Madre de mentiras*, this way is too damned civilized. Time and again, I told Antonio. A shit like Barbacena doesn't deserve a clean death. He should be allowed to see oblivion approaching slowly"—he pointed with two fingers "—here, in my eyes. And it should be done in accordance with *Hetá I*."

"Don't try that with me," Croaker said. "*Hetá I* is a healing art. You and Antonio twisted it, perverted it into something bestial and evil." He swept his arm in an arc. "Just look around you. Estrella was the healer and you killed her. There's no healing here; only sickness and death."

Heitor's extreme agitation had brought blood to his face. A red stain seeped through the bandage over his nose. He crouched down next to the croc. "See what becomes of your plans to *civilize* us."

Croaker felt his heart skip a beat. Either Heitor was mad or he was talking to the crocodile. The croc grinned simply by dint of keeping its jaws shut. Its amber eyes glowed with singular malevolence as its mailed tail slammed against the wall. Wallboard shattered and dried spackle rose in the air in a miniature mushroom cloud.

"Heitor—"

"Don't talk to me!" Heitor cried. "Tell it to Antonio."

"Antonio isn't here, Heitor." Patience was required now, Croaker knew. "It's just us chickens and the ghosts of the people you've murdered."

Heitor put his hand over the flames that rose from the stone vessel. "Sorcerers are capable of many things, *señor*. If you were born in Asunción you would know. If your veins flowed with Guarani blood, you would understand." He lowered his hand. As he did so, the crocodile's eyes turned to slits. "Transformation is one of the foundations of *Hetá I*. The sorcerer is consumed by fire and remains unmarked."

His hand plunged into the fire. The cuff of his shirt blazed, the smells of burning cotton and crisped human hair were suddenly strong in the room. Heitor made a fist as the flames spread up his arm. The spark and crackle of the burning fabric seemed as loud as a forest fire. His lips curled back from his teeth and now Croaker heard an eerie sound. It seemed like chanting.

Heitor stood as the flames curled across his chest and back like a living serpent. His shirt, turning black, disappearing in small tufts of smoke, broke apart at the shoulders, hanging down in sparking tatters.

Then, Heitor opened his clenched fist. In it were three dark stones. The crocodile's eyes opened. The flames glimmered and died, as if doused by wind and rain.

Heitor smiled. He pointed to the crocodile. "The sorcerer becomes an animal in order to drink the blood of his enemies and remain strong and virile so that even the passing years cannot touch him. *Señor*, these are truths I tell you." He tore off what remained of his ruined shirt and threw it on the floor. "Here you see the truth but your mind won't accept it."

Heitor was not entirely correct. Croaker was thinking of Humaitá Milagros, who Bennie was sure had been reincarnated as a tiger shark. "Bennie Milagros isn't paying for Majeur's cell phone; Majeur himself is," Croaker said. "But you wanted me to think otherwise. You wanted to pit me against Bennie, to cut me off from everyone and everything. Why?"

"For the same reason I killed Pablo and Estrella," Heitor said. "Man is a social creature; daily he draws on the resources around him," Heitor said. "In crises, he will seek the assistance of those closest to him." It was astonishing. There wasn't a mark on him. "It never fails, this part of human nature. Like a vine seeking the rough bole of a tree." The fire might have seared off his hair, but it had left his flesh unmarked. "You see, *señor*, a man is understood only when he stands alone. Finally, the last layers of civilization are stripped away. What is revealed is the *essence*. This is a commodity most rare, precious, and beautiful. It is to be savored like a magnificent cigar."

Heitor laughed. As he did so, the croc's jaws gaped open. For a mad instant, it appeared as if the laughter were emanating from the reptile. "You do not understand, *señor*? The Leyes, they would have helped you. They did before. Now we are in a new phase of the game. You are alone."

Even before he had finished speaking, Croaker was on the move. With his biomechanical hand, he ripped the wire from the ceiling. At the same time, he slammed his left foot down on the top of the crocodile's snout. The teeth clashed together with a ferocious clang. He whipped the wire around the jaws, lashing them tightly and securely together with a thief's knot. The beast thrashed beneath Croaker's shoe but could do no damage.

With an incoherent roar, Heitor rushed Croaker. Without seeming to move at all, Croaker slammed the heel of his biomechanical hand into Heitor's broken nose.

Heitor screamed and fell to the floor as if poleaxed. Blood spurted from the ruptured wound. Croaker kicked him hard in the soft spot just beneath the lowest rib and Heitor fetched up against the corner where the crocodile had first crouched. He was out cold.

Bending down, Croaker took hold of Heitor by his hair and dragged him back down the hall and into the kitchen. The smell of burnt food greeted him and he took the skillet off the burner as he passed the stove. Dropping Heitor in the center of the floor, Croaker went to the refrigerator and took out a tray full of ice. He stripped Heitor's trousers to his knees, then applied the ice to his testicles. Heitor awoke with a start and a little scream.

Croaker knelt, putting all his weight on the knee that pressed against Heitor's sternum. *"Hola,* Heitor," he said. Then he reached up, turned up the flame on the burner. He extruded a stainless steel nail from the end of one biomechanical finger and let it heat up in the gas flame.

Looking into Heitor's amber eyes, Croaker said, "I knew a guy once. Called himself Charcoal Man. Charcoal Man worked the city—Coney Island, the East Village, Forty-second Street, wherever tourists hung out and the cops wouldn't bother him. He would eat fire. He'd run a burning torch up and down his bare arm. Then he'd set himself on fire. That's the kind of thing, you've got to admit, really gets a crowd going." Croaker's nail glowed red and he studied it meditatively. "So I guess by your standards, this guy was a sorcerer." Croaker smiled without warmth. "Only I knew his tricks, Heitor. How he coated his mouth and throat, how he rubbed his arms with a Vaseline-based ointment, how he prepared his whole body so he wouldn't be roasted alive." The glowing nail made a curved shadow over Heitor's face. "Sorcerer, trickster. I guess it's just a matter of semantics."

Croaker moved the red-hot fingernail so Heitor could feel its heat like the sole plate of an iron. "Now here is what I want to know, Heitor. I want the truth about Bennie's sister Rosa. What were the circumstances of her death?"

Heitor's amber eyes looked beyond the nail to Croaker's face. There was blood all over his puffy cheeks and lips and ugly bruises were forming beneath his eyes. "What do you imagine, *maricone?* That I will shudder in fear and vomit up my soul to you merely because you order it?"

"No, Heitor. I expect nothing from you." From his pocket Croaker extracted Humaitá's spirit-stone. He saw Heitor's eyes open wide as he pressed it into the hollow of the slim man's throat.

"Ack!" Heitor's jaws worked spastically. "Acckkk!"

"Now," Croaker said softly. "Tell me what I want to know. Tell me about Rosa Milagros."

For a moment nothing happened. Then, it seemed as if the amber color drained from Heitor's eyes. They appeared as transparent as windows.

"I spit on the woman," Heitor hissed. "I curse her in whatever hell she finds herself."

"Why?" Croaker asked. "What did she ever do to you?"

"Before she came, Antonio and I were *mokoi*."

"*Mokoi*," Croaker repeated. "What's that?"

"The bond between twins. It is special. It is sacred. The bitch Rosa ripped us apart like a doctor prematurely drags a fetus from the womb." His face twisted in rage and in his maniacal thrashing he almost unseated Croaker's knee. "It was a violation! An abomination! I could not allow it."

Illumination flooded Croaker. So Antonio had told the truth about his love for Rosa. This revelation was so astonishing that for the moment Croaker did not know what to make of it. "You killed Rosa," he whispered.

"She loved him, she said. She could smell the stink of corruption on him, she said. She could save him, she said." The spirit-stone was leaching the memory out of Heitor like blood from a stone. In his agony he was only peripherally aware of Croaker. "She seduced him, drew him away from *mokoi*. The *us* that had been, the *us* that was our foundation, the basis of life itself, she destroyed. I thought, After I kill her, it will be all right. *Mokoi* will return. It will be as it always had been between Antonio and myself." Droplets of blood flew as he shook his head. "Dead wrong. She reached out from beyond the grave and the gulf between Antonio and me only grew deeper. Antonio knew what I had done. In that first moment when he discovered her body, I believed he was actually going to kill me. I could see it in his eyes. A twin knows. But he couldn't do it.

"We are of the same womb, of the same moment, birth and death. Antonio remembered that in time. But there was punishment to come. Like a woman in a jealous rage, he withheld *mokoi*. The soul of one twin cannot meet the other unless both are willing. From that time, our special bond was severed."

Croaker pressed the spirit-stone more firmly into Heitor's flesh. "Now I want to know about Bennie. What's your connection with him?"

Heitor's eerily transparent eyes seemed fixed on a point not in space, but in time. "It has to do with the bones, of course. We want the bones. Everyone does."

"What bones?"

"That will be enough!" a new voice commanded.

Croaker turned to see Antonio coming down the hallway. He filled the open archway to the kitchen, looked past Croaker to his prone and bloody twin. "There is quite enough of a mess as it is without adding more." His amber eyes flicked back to Croaker. "Get off him, señor. I beg of you." He said this in a soft, almost paternal voice tinged with what could only be called profound sadness.

Croaker did not move. Antonio, dressed in an oyster gray linen suit, held the length of wire Croaker had used to bind the crocodile's snout as a cowboy holds his coiled lasso. There was no sign of the reptile. However, a curious red welt ran across the bridge of Antonio's nose, down both cheeks and beneath his jaw. It was as if he had been bound by the wire. Croaker dismissed the thought as he palmed the spirit-stone so Antonio wouldn't see it.

Antonio's expression hardened and he said, "I do not repeat myself, señor. Do as I have said or suffer the consequences."

With the spirit-stone taken away, color was flooding back into Heitor's eyes. The flux of full consciousness transfigured the pupils.

"I am not afraid, Antonio," Croaker said. "But you and Heitor should be. I've come for you." He placed his glowing nail against Heitor's right cheek.

Antonio jumped at the same instant his twin did. "Señor, you do not know—"

There was a searing hiss, a sickly sweet smell that clung to the back of the throat. Heitor screamed. He thrashed and moaned but he could not dislodge Croaker. So much for sorcery.

"The dark stones know." Croaker sheathed his nail. What remained on Heitor's cheek was a deep red wound that seeped blood. He looked up at Antonio. "Now he carries my mark. It will serve to remind you both—"

There was a sudden fierce gust of wind that took Croaker's breath away. He must have blacked out for a moment because he next found himself against the refrigerator door, three feet from where Heitor lay. His back ached, as if he had slammed into the fridge. Antonio was now standing between him and Heitor.

Antonio stood over Croaker, trembling with barely suppressed rage. "Remember I told you that you were an exception, because you hadn't sinned. Now that has changed. *Pobre.*" Poor soul. "The world is like blood. Always fluid, always changing. Friendships form, dissolve. The only truism in life is that you can hold on to nothing." There was that sadness again, tingeing his face as well as his voice. "You should not have harmed Heitor."

"Look what he's done here. He's like a rabid dog." Croaker struggled to his feet with great difficulty. His legs felt like their bones had turned to liquid. Outrage threatened to close his throat. "For God's sake, he murdered Rosa." He grabbed onto the refrigerator handle to hold himself steady. "Why do you continue to defend him?"

"Why do you think?"

"He's damned you, Antonio. You said it yourself." Croaker was desperately stalling for time while he tried to regain his strength. What the hell had happened to him? *Hetá I.* Something Antonio had done to him had robbed him of energy. "Face it. *Mokoi* is gone. Whatever it was that linked you two, that made you special, no longer exists."

"*Yo tengo la sartén por el mango.*" I'm running the show. "Leave now." Antonio's face was flushed with blood. "If you harbor any hope of saving your niece, *señor,* walk out of here and don't look back."

Stalemate. For now, that's the best he could expect, Croaker knew. With Rachel's life hanging in the balance he had no other choice and Antonio knew it. But as soon as Barbacena was dead, as soon as Majeur confirmed the kill, the kidney would be released and Jenny could do her thing. Then, the rules would change. Then would come the final reckoning.

"*Está terminado del todo.* It is over between us, *señor.* The friendship. Now we are mortal enemies. *Comprende?* After midnight, who can say what will transpire? The *federales* want you and they are abetted by the police. For you, there will be nowhere to hide."

In the living room, the soccer match was over. According to the announcer, something called *The Extreme Games* was about to begin.

Antonio's mocking voice stopped Croaker at the front door. "*Dígame, señor.* Sonia or Vonda. Let's have your best guess. Which one 'donated' her kidney so your niece might survive?"

Accompanied by Antonio's soft laughter, Croaker stumbled blindly outside. At the curb, he hung on to the Mustang. But it did no good. The rich, sweet smell of the night-blooming jasmine made him violently sick.

DAY FIVE

1

An oppressive wind was blowing in off the ocean. It had an evil smell, as if it had churned up all the sins that had been buried for centuries in the ocean floor. Croaker, crouched on the rooftop of the three-story building on Washington and Ninth opposite the vegetarian restaurant An Chay, could feel the pressure drop. Thickening clouds were already so low the aquamarine and marlin blue neon lights of the Deco building facades were hazed in eerie halos.

A storm was on its way. Stone Tree would know how fast it would make landfall and how bad it would be. Meanwhile, the SoBe nightlife wasn't missing a beat. Cool music poured like syrup into the humid air, hot cars paraded by, girls and boys, spangled in tropical colors, mingled every which way. For them, it was a night like any other.

But somewhere, not far from here, Juan Garcia Barbacena was arriving. Was it by private plane that had touched down or maybe by boat outside the three-mile limit. Maybe Bennie was pulling alongside in his midnight blue cigarette.

Which scenario was the right one? Croaker didn't know. Just as he didn't know whether Bennie was friend or foe.

Thirty-three minutes after midnight and counting.

Croaker rechecked the Steyr and the Harris Bipod. He took another look through the Swarsky scope, made some minor adjustments, and got used to looking at the environment in the flat two dimensions of the scope's viewing circle. Satisfied, he put the rifle aside and relaxed. Come what may, he was ready.

He picked up the Zeiss Night Owl, scanned the street below. Using binoculars very quickly taught you the value of patience. With the field of vision so limited, if you panned too quickly, you were sure to miss something significant. Also, there was a rhythm.

Thirty seconds scrutinizing the environment, looking for the target, ten seconds relaxing. Otherwise, eye fatigue would set in, and again, you risked missing an important element.

Croaker watched the young faces coming and going, animated by a couple of beers, a few joints, and the anticipation of sex. He remembered those days, when the summers seemed endless and the word *future* held no meaning. Summers made him think of fishing. Fishing made him think of Bennie. Who was Bennie Milagros, anyway? A pal or a government operative leading a secret life? *Funny,* Croaker thought, *either way, I miss him.*

Instinct drove Croaker to take up the binoculars and scan Washington Avenue in front of An Chay. Like all street scenes, it had changed but stayed the same. Different people, same basic configuration. Except . . .

Except for the young man lounging against the fender of a black Mercedes convertible—the new one, blunt and boxy, ugly as sin. He wore a lightweight Armani suit and Italian loafers. His hair was long, slicked back off his wide forehead. When he crossed his arms across his chest, Croaker could see the muscles stretching the fabric.

Using the young man as a focal point, Croaker tracked slowly in each direction. Just to the left he found two more young musclemen. There were three to the right. They had just emerged from a Mercedes sedan, also black. A second black Mercedes sedan was parked around the corner on Ninth Street. Croaker began looking for the gray Rolls-Royce.

At that moment, he heard a sound behind him. It was a tiny noise, not more than what an old door might make if it was pushed open a crack. He heard it distinctly just the same. Nerves. Heightened tension created greater acuity of the senses. It was instinctive, part of the primitive animal defense mechanism that had survived centuries of increasing civilization.

He swung the Steyr around, half expecting to confront one of Barbacena's security entourage. Instead, he saw Majeur coming toward him in a half-crouch. Someone was with him. His heart almost stopped. It was Jenny.

"Majeur, what the hell d'you think you're doing?" He was furious. "In a couple of minutes this will be a red zone. Get her out of here."

"Lew, please listen!" Jenny said urgently.

"Jenny, what about Rachel? How could you leave her now?"

"Lew, please believe me, she's in good hands. I hand-picked a team to watch over her."

"But she doesn't have *you*." The sharpness in his voice surprised

Croaker. Afraid for Rachel's life and Jenny's safety, he turned to look down at Washington Avenue. Here came the gray Rolls. *Oh, my God,* he thought. *We're all fucked now.* "You promised you'd be there when the kidney arrived."

Majeur inched forward. "Sir, I would not have brought her unless—"

"Lew, for God's sake—"

"Shut up, both of you." The Steyr, balanced against his chest on the Harris Bipod, already felt like an old and trusted friend. "I've got a job to do. Despite what's going on here. Rachel has to be saved. That's the only thing that matters."

"Don't you see, that's why I've come."

Jenny was just behind him. He could feel the heat of her body, the smell of her. The Rolls had blacked-out windows and three stubby antennas. What did he have in there besides cell phones? A portable computer hooked up to the World Wide Web and the Internet? The Rolls'-street-side rear door was opening. Barbacena's men were clustered around the car like the Praetorian Guard. He was coming.

Croaker leveled the Steyr, gaining the angle he wanted. The Steyr was equipped with two triggers, one behind the other. The front trigger required a standard 2¼-pound pull. The one behind was a hair trigger, needing only ¼ pound of pressure to fire the rifle.

Then he heard Jenny whispering in his ear. "Majeur came to see Rachel. That's where I met him. I told him what I'd found because I'd been trying to call you."

Croaker curled his forefinger around the front trigger. "I turned it off. The last thing I need is my cell phone ringing now." A woman was emerging from the Rolls. Tall and slim and Oriental, she was dressed in a sea green shantung silk suit. The Thai food taster.

"I made Majeur bring me. I told you that I wasn't going to stand idly by. I had some ideas of my own. After hearing your evidence against Stansky, I got to thinking. What caused Rachel's acute renal shutdown? Stansky knew her history; he was poisoning her by reintroducing the sepsis into her IVs. And I thought, What if they had poisoned Rachel in the beginning?"

The street was crawling with security. Barbacena's goons had begun to fan out, methodically and systematically sectoring the immediate area. But Jenny had caught Croaker's attention at last. "Poisoned?" It was as if a great ray of light revealed a hidden shape in the shadows. Now he understood the significance of the Bonitas owning the Bonyard. Rachel didn't OD on the drug cocktail. The

Bonitas had poisoned her. But so what? He was still caught in the awful vise. He had to kill Barbacena to save Rachel's life.

Across the street, the Thai taster was talking to one of the security goons. Then, she bent down, apparently delivering a message to someone still inside the Rolls. Barbacena. The Thai taster said something to the goon, and he ordered two men into the restaurant.

The Thai taster stepped away from the Rolls. A figure was emerging. Black elephant-skin loafers, black tropical-weight linen suit, white voile silk band-collared shirt. A flash of gold at his wrist as he put a hand on the roof of the Rolls.

Croaker recognized him immediately: Juan Garcia Barbacena. The target. Croaker pulled the front trigger, cocking the action, then moved his hand backward. He rested his forefinger lightly on the hair trigger. Now only the slightest squeeze was all that stood between the target and oblivion.

He felt Jenny's hand on his back and tried not to react to it. "This is why I had to come. To stop you. Rachel was poisoned. Along with the drugs you'd expect to find, her blood showed traces of ethylene glycol by-products."

With Barbacena's head squarely in the scope's sights, Croaker froze. "Ethylene glycol? That's antifreeze."

"Right," Jenny said. "It's also an almost perfect poison. It's odorless, tasteless, and you only need to ingest three ounces. Put it in a soda or coffee and she'd never know. With Rachel's drug history, plus the fact she only had one kidney, they were betting it would go undetected. And they were right."

The Thai taster was on the sidewalk. Barbacena was turning away from the building where they all crouched. In a moment, he would disappear through the doorway to An Chay and the opportunity would be lost forever.

Barbacena's face hung as large as a full moon in front of him. He steeled his finger against the hair trigger for the last time. He took a deep breath, let it out slowly and evenly. When it was all gone, his finger would tighten against the hair trigger and Barbacena would hit the pavement with half a head.

"What good does knowing this do me," he said, "except to make me hate the Bonitas all the more?"

"I've put her on a treatment protocol," Jenny rushed on urgently. "Ethanol IV, which will slow the formation of glycolic acid. And we're continuing to flush her kidney."

Croaker eased his finger off the hair trigger. "What d'you mean? The breakdown products must've damaged her kidney."

"But they didn't destroy it. There is damage to the renal tubules, but the human body is a marvelous machine. Once we flush the glycolic acid from her system, they'll regenerate in a matter of months. Her kidney will be rehabilitated." She gripped his shoulders. "Do you understand, Lew? Rachel doesn't need the transplant. You don't have to go through with this hellish bargain."

Through the Swarsky scope, Croaker watched the Thai taster precede Juan Garcia Barbacena into the restaurant. They vanished from his view like game fish, briefly seen, plunging into the depths of the ocean.

He put the Steyr aside and sat down on the roof. "So, it's over." He felt as if he weighed a thousand pounds. Coming so close to killing someone in cold blood was like standing at the edge of an abyss—once you took the next step you had no idea how far you would fall. Now, to be able to back away was a relief almost too intense to absorb.

Croaker's head was buzzing with an excess of adrenaline. "Why didn't you discover this poisoning before?"

Jenny, sitting beside him, said softly, "We were going on basic assumptions. Rachel had a great deal of controlled substances in her system. She was a chronic drug abuser. She was in acute renal shutdown. A girl of her age, what else *could* we think?"

She never took her gaze off Croaker's face. "But then I had the blood samples I'd taken from her for my drug abuse study medevaced to me and I took a long hard look at them. There was no reason for us to have done so earlier because we were looking for a drug O.D. and that's exactly what we found. The circumstances and the symptomology were absolutely consistent.

"We would have seen the ethylene glycol in a minute had we done a kidney biopsy, but Rachel's condition was already too critical to even consider such an invasive test. However, when I analyzed the blood I'd drawn from her for my research program I saw it was highly acidic. Ethylene glycol, itself, is more or less harmless. But when the body starts to break it down you get glycolic acid, which is terribly destructive. We were lucky on two counts: because she only has one kidney, they needed to use a minimum dose to cause the renal failure. Also, the dialysis was the best thing we could have done for her because it kept the kidney flushed. If not for the sepsis Stansky introduced, she might have begun to recover by now."

Croaker took her hand. "It was incredibly brave of you to come here."

"And not as foolhardy as you thought." She gave him a smile.

"It was a gamble." Croaker looked past her to where Majeur was standing, a slim silhouette in the misty neon glow.

"It is ten minutes after one," Majeur said as he came across the roof. "I was scheduled to call Antonio by one the latest."

"We've got to get out of here." Croaker left the materials of the assassin's trade where they were. He had no desire to touch them again, and Majeur had never wanted possession of them in the first place.

As they walked to the rear of the roof, Croaker said to Majeur, "I have some bad news. The Leyes are dead."

Majeur stopped in his tracks. A strong gust of wind ruffled his hair and blew open his jacket. "*Ay de mi.* Estrella—?"

Croaker nodded. "Heitor killed them. I got there too late."

A look like flint came into Majeur's eyes. "It was her greatest fear. But she knew one day the Bonitas would come for her." Majeur shook his head, fighting back deep emotion. "Bennie will be sick at heart."

Croaker took a deep breath, tried to still the hammering of his heart.

"Lew," Jenny said, "what's the matter?"

Majeur looked at him. "*Señor,* you appear ill."

Croaker said, "Tell me, Majeur. Do you mean Bennie Milagros?"

Majeur nodded. "We all know each other for years, sir. How could it be otherwise? Bennie, Estrella, Antonio, Heitor, myself. Humaitá was the glue that bound us together, you see. We all grew up in his back pocket. It was tragic when he was killed. We all flew apart like seeds spat from a mouth."

Croaker put a hand to his head to try to stop the sudden throbbing. "Bennie swore to me that he didn't know you. What reason would he have to lie to me?"

Majeur shook his head. "That I cannot say, *señor.*"

Was Bennie friend or foe? Croaker wondered. First he and Croaker were the best of buddies. Then, it seemed as if he had a secret life with the ACTF. It seemed as if he had used Croaker. But the damning information on the floppy disk that linked him to the top-secret ACTF operation in Mexico could have been planted by the Bonitas. Friend, again? And now this. Bennie *had* lied. So what was true and what was false? Croaker had been returned to Majeur's Kalahari, whose shifting dunes brought constantly changing fortunes, where allies became enemies as easily as sand slipped between your fingers.

"Unless it was because of the bones."

Croaker stared into Majeur's face. Heitor had mentioned bones at the Leyeses' just before Antonio had intervened.

"What do you mean, the bones?"

Majeur looked abruptly uneasy. "This is not something one easily tells—*perdoname, señor*—an outsider. You see, Bennie's grandfather was a *sukia*. Among the Guarani, such an extraordinary healer appears perhaps once in a man's lifetime. Often, it is far less. In any case, the *sukia* is venerated beyond any other healer because his powers are so great. When he dies, it is said these extraordinary powers live on. In his healing stones—his spirit-catchers. And in his bones. This is why his corpse is burnt on a pyre—so the bones might be cleansed of flesh and preserved."

Majeur looked at his watch. "Sir, it is very dangerous to remain here. We must leave. Now."

Croaker glanced at Jenny, nodded. In single file, they went down the vertical metal ladder of the fire escape. Majeur went first, then Jenny, with Croaker the last off the roof.

On the street, Croaker turned to Majeur. "What happened to Humaitá's bones?"

"I think you can guess," Majeur said as they trotted toward the Mustang. "Following the funeral pyre, the bones disappeared. They were stolen."

Croaker unlocked the door and they piled inside—Jenny in the front passenger's seat, Majeur in back. "Do you know by whom?"

"I have no proof." Majeur settled himself in the backseat. "But it seemed clear to me that it must have been Heitor and Antonio. They coveted Humaitá's power. They killed him. Why would they do that unless they could take his power and keep it like lightning in a bottle?"

Croaker thought of the extreme secrecy—not to mention urgency—of Bennie's request to made a sea rendezvous at midnight on the *Captain Sumo*. As he fired up the ignition, he said, "Majeur, how did Barbacena arrive in Miami? By plane or by boat?"

"Boat," Majeur said. "A plane would have been too insecure. But the boat would not have landed. Again, too much risk. A launch would have been sent out to get him and his people."

Is that what Bennie had tried to inveigle out of Croaker? A means of transport for Barbacena? But nothing about Bennie and Barbacena made sense. According to Rafe Roubinnet, Bennie wanted Barbacena dead because Barbacena had murdered Theresa Marquesa Barbacena, the daughter of Bennie's mentor. Then why had Bennie allowed Barbacena to gain such an exalted position in Latin America? Why hadn't Bennie sought revenge before this?

Once again, Croaker felt himself enmeshed in a web of lies. Who could he trust? Jenny, surely—and Rafe. Most likely Majeur. But beyond that he could be sure of no one, not even Ross Darling. Government agents invariably had their own agendas, private bureaucratic skirmishes they were bent on winning. Darling was no different. *I'll be damned,* Croaker thought, *if I'll let myself be a pawn in the insane war between him and Spaulding Gunn.*

He turned the corner onto Washington Avenue. Up ahead was An Chay, where Juan Garcia Barbacena was contentedly eating his vegetarian dinner before his meeting with Gunn. Croaker could imagine the scene: the goons stationed at the four corners of the room, the Thai taster in her sea green shantung suit daintily nibbling at each dish as it came steaming from the kitchen. And Barbacena, famished from his journey, digging in with a macho gusto.

Even this far away, the Mustang rocked crazily on its shocks. Croaker slammed on the brakes as the restaurant's windows blew out and debris from its interior hurtled into the street.

"Christ," Majeur cried. "A bomb!"

And Croaker thought, *Heitor! He didn't trust me to get the job done, and he was right. He had his own plan going.*

Jenny was already out the Mustang's door. Croaker shouted after her to stay put, then raced after her, passing the Mercedes convertible. The blast had blown it over on its side. Fortunately, its steel frame had acted like a shield to protect the slow-moving traffic on Washington and the pedestrians across the street. Still, kids sat on the sidewalk or stood dazed, hands to their heads. Smoke streamed from the ripped-open restaurant. As if that was a kind of signal, someone started screaming.

Crowds were forming with alarming speed. Soon, Croaker knew, it would be impossible to get away in the Mustang.

He saw Jenny kneeling beside a young girl who'd been caught in the welter of flying glass and wood shards, and he ran to help her. Jenny was cradling her head, talking to her as she worked to stanch the flow of blood and assess the severity of her wounds. Croaker did as Jenny directed him, ripping clothing into makeshift tourniquets, moving the less severely wounded away from the smoke, fire, and debris. As he and Jenny reached another body, he heard the first sirens. They were coming at speed.

Croaker felt a chill go through him. Even with this kind of chaos, he couldn't afford to be here when the cops arrived.

"Jenny," he said. "Christ, Jenny, we've got to get out of here!"

She turned to him. She was spattered with blood. He opened his mouth to say something but her expression stopped him.

"Lew, I know you can't stay." The sirens were louder now. "The cops are coming and I know they're looking for you. But I'm a doctor and there are people here who need me. I have a duty."

He looked down at the bloody young girl they were tending, and nodded.

"Go on." She pushed him sternly away. But he could see tears glittering in the corners of her eyes.

"Jenn, I—"

She brushed past him, continuing to tend to the wounded. The siren was drawing closer.

Majeur had wormed his way past them. He was now standing quite near the gaping entrance to the burnt-out restaurant.

Croaker called to him. "Majeur, what the hell are you doing? Get away from there!"

"Not yet, *señor*. I must find out what happened in there."

Flames licked and curled and the oily smoke had thickened. There was a terrible sweetish stink in the air that could only come from one source: incinerated human beings.

"What happened?" Croaker shouted. "I'll tell you what happened. Barbacena and his entire cast of characters are dead. Look at it in there, Majeur. It's like a blast furnace. No one could have survived."

Majeur, one hand shielding his face, moved closer, peering into the smoke and flame-filled interior. "There is a back entrance. Perhaps they had some forewarning. Perhaps some of them escaped."

"You're insane." Croaker moved to go after Majeur. More sirens screamed in the night. To Croaker they sounded like the howling of hunting dogs who'd caught the scent of their prey.

At the edge of the blistered interior, Majeur paused and looked back at Croaker. *"Madre de Dios, señor. ¡Vamos!* The cops are only seconds away!"

"I'm not going to let you get caught in there," Croaker said.

"All right." Majeur nodded. "But to be safe wait for me in the car. Give me three minutes. *Señor*, I beg of you. I must do this." His gaze shifted as the first of the police patrol cars screeched to a halt at the edge of the growing throng. *"Por favor, señor. La pelota está aún en el tejado."* The game isn't over yet.

Croaker watched Jenny talking to the wounded and dazed victims while she worked on them with tenderness and efficiency. She had the true gift of the healer. It was as if there was an aura around her that eased people's pain and stilled their terror.

He made his way through the thickening crowd toward the Mustang. He had to fight like a salmon swimming upstream; everyone else was pushing relentlessly toward the locus of the bomb blast.

Back inside the Mustang he turned the ignition. To make sure he wasn't wedged in by traffic, he had to drive up onto the sidewalk facing away from the site of the disaster.

He turned around, staring through the rear window at the chaos. More patrol cars, their lights flashing, had drawn up. Uniformed cops were making their way to the scene, others were working crowd control. Still others were assisting the first of the emergency medical people who had arrived in ambulances. Croaker could see Jenny hard at work. An EMS paramedic knelt beside her. She spoke to him, gesturing, and he nodded. They rose and she took him on a brief tour of her makeshift triage area. He called for the folding gurneys to take the most seriously wounded away.

Fire engines screamed their entrance, and now more of the cops were needed to clear a path for the firefighters lugging hoses. Connections were made to hydrants, and the water was turned on. Soon the bomb squad would arrive.

Where the hell was Majeur? Croaker wondered. He had less than a minute to get out of the interior before he was caught by the first contingent of firefighters in fire-retardant gear and the vanguard of police. In response to all this heightened activity, the crowd surged forward.

Now, at its periphery, near the blackened front of An Chay, Croaker saw Majeur emerge. He looked past the oncoming rescue teams, trying to pick out the turquoise Mustang. Croaker opened the door, stood on the floor rim, and lifted his biomechanical hand. It reflected the revolving lights back at Majeur.

Majeur's face lit up when he saw Croaker and he began to make his way out of the interior. It was then that Croaker saw Heitor emerge like a wraith from the crowd. His twice-broken nose was still bandaged, but the laceration Croaker had made in his cheek was bare—a clean red steak, glistening with unguent.

Croaker shouted and pointed at Heitor.

Majeur, unaware, waved back. Then Heitor was beside him.

"Got you, *maricone!*" Croaker could read Heitor's lips.

Majeur started, turned, and Heitor's right arm moved. From a distance, it seemed as innocent a gesture as one man shaking another's hand. But then Croaker caught a quick metallic flash as the scalpel blade buried itself in Majeur's side.

Croaker was off and running toward the bombed-out restaurant. Majeur's eyes opened wide and his lips pulled back from his teeth as if he had eaten something very sweet. He staggered, but Heitor, ever helpful, kept him on his feet.

Croaker hit the outer shell of the crowd and was slowed to a crawl. No avid onlooker seemed inclined to let him through. He was obliged to claw and muscle people aside, to ignore curses, wild punches, and kicks in order to make any progress at all.

Up ahead, Heitor, acting like a Good Samaritan, hustled Majeur away from the rescue crew. They raced by him, spreading out into the interior as the hoses were brought up. Heitor brought Majeur to the periphery of this activity and gently, almost lovingly, lay Majeur onto the sidewalk.

Helplessly, Croaker watched him twist the scalpel trying to get through the intercostal cartilage between Majeur's ribs and find the heart.

Croaker was close enough to gain a better view of Heitor, but still too far away to be able to intervene. As he continued to squirm his way through the melee, he watched Heitor's head swivel like a dog on point. Heitor rose and began to move through the triage area as if he were invisible. No one noticed him or asked his business there. Either they were all too busy or he'd worked some *Hetá I* spell.

He moved slowly, methodically, as if he were in no hurry. At last, he came to where Jenny was working on a young girl with bad burns. He stood behind her, gazing down at her meditatively. Then, he turned. As if with uncanny knowledge he looked right at Croaker. For a split instant the whole world ceased to exist. An enigmatic smile transformed Heitor's lips and he turned back to the work at hand.

Croaker, frantic, did everything but hurl people from his path. But he was trapped in the terrible surge of the crowd. Dense, sweaty, keyed to the excitement of the moment, they had merged into a solid body that gave but did not break.

He saw Heitor standing over Jenny. Backlit by the smoke and fire Heitor's curling copper-colored hair appeared to be made of flames. Croaker shouted but to no avail. He clawed and elbowed his way forward in time to see Heitor's hands closing around the back of Jenny's neck. Didn't anyone notice? Couldn't they see what was going to happen? This was Heitor's revenge: to murder Jenny in front of Croaker's eyes.

Heitor's right hand touched the side of Jenny's neck. His left hand seemed to stroke her hair. Jenny's head turned to look up. She saw Heitor's battered face, which was what he wanted. He stared down at her. She stiffened as his grip strengthened. Croaker struggled in his agonizing trap. She was going to die and there wasn't anything he could do about it.

"No!" he screamed. *"No!"*

Antonio, at Heitor's side, took hold of his brother's wrists. Antonio, like Heitor before him, had appeared like smoke out of nowhere. Heitor's head whipped around, and he screamed. Antonio shook his head firmly. His whole body stiffened, and Heitor released Jenny.

Croaker broke through the inner ring at last, racing past a fat man and a pair of bodybuilders. But the Bonitas were gone, swallowed up in the chaos of the surging throng.

Croaker took three steps toward Jenny before his way was blocked by two uniformed cops.

"Sorry, bud," one said. "You're off limits."

"Step back, sir," the other uniform said. "Professional personnel are taking care of everyone."

Croaker took a step forward and the second uniform put his hand out. "I said step back, sir." His other hand had gone to the butt of his holstered service revolver.

Croaker paused, gazing over the uniforms' shoulder. He saw Jenny tending to an open wound in a victim on a folding gurney. He craned his neck, saw that it was Majeur. Accompanied by one of the EMS paramedics guiding the gurney, she passed within the protective semicircle of cops on crowd control. Still tending to Majeur, she climbed into the back of an ambulance as the driver slid it inside. The paramedic jumped in after her, the driver climbed behind the wheel, and the ambulance took off.

Croaker relaxed. At least she was safe from Heitor. He began to back off. The last thing he needed now was a confrontation with the police.

"Hey, wait a minute!" the first uniform said. "I think I seen this guy. Ray, didn't his photo come over the APB wire couple hours ago?"

"You think?" Ray, suspicious, unsnapped the guard strap on his holster.

As he drew his service revolver, Croaker ducked away, eeling into the crowd.

"Hey!" he heard the first uniform shout. "Hey, you! Stop!"

It was easier to move away from the locus of interest because every spot he vacated allowed someone to step closer. People were happy to let him through. He took a circuitous route back to the Mustang. He fired the ignition, slammed it in gear, and drove off down the sidewalk until he was clear of the traffic tie-up. Then he floored the accelerator.

As he headed away from the An Chay bombing, he plucked out his cell phone, punched in a number. When he heard the familiar voice in his ear, he felt his heart skip a beat. Stone Tree had said to him, *"When it comes to people, you must stand aside from anger, antipathy, and fear. These emotions clog the senses. When you feel them you cannot experience the rightness of the situation. On the contrary, everything seems wrong, and you take action from that false reading."*

"Hey, Bennie. I've missed the hell outa you."

"Lewis?"

"Listen, about what happened in the hospital—we have to talk about that," Croaker said as he zipped around a Ford sedan. He reaccelerated.

"Something's changed, you wanta talk about it now?"

"Lots," Croaker said. "For one thing, there's an APB out for me."

"Say what?"

Croaker, listening carefully, heard the sharp note of surprise in Bennie's voice. But was it genuine? There was a gamble he was going to have to take. "Also, I know why you wanted me and the *Captain Sumo.*" He ran a light on the amber, turned west. "Bennie, did you get them?"

"Get what?" A certain wariness had slipped into Bennie's tone.

"The bones, Bennie."

"Bones? What the hell you talking about?"

"Don't bullshit me. Your grandfather's bones. That's what it's all about, isn't it, this bad blood between you and the Bonitas? They murdered Humaitá, then stole his bones after he was cremated. You've been trying to get them back from Heitor and Antonio, right?"

"You must be cracked. Why would I care about a pile of bones?"

"Because all your grandfather's *Hetá I* power—all that's left of him—his entire legacy—is in them like living marrow."

Silence on the line. Croaker crossed the MacArthur Causeway, gaining the mainland. The highrise skyline of Miami loomed in front of him. And memories of his near-fatal encounter at the Brickell Bridge.

At length, Bennie said, "Who the hell've you been talking to?"

"People you apparently didn't want me speaking to."

Croaker could hear Bennie take an audible breath. "You know, *amigo,* you're right. We *do* have to talk. Right fucking now. Where are you?"

Croaker told him.

"Good," Bennie said. "I'm in the 'Glades, not so far away. Get your Anglo ass over to Flamingo pronto. And, *amigo*, make damn sure you aren't followed."

"Don't worry," Croaker said. "With the police APB I'm not likely to make a mistake."

"See that you don't," Bennie said. "Both our lives depend on it."

2

Croaker took the Dolphin Expressway west to Florida's Turn-pike. From there he headed south to Florida City, a small cluster of seedy family-style restaurants tricked out with neon and flashing lights to attract tourists heading for the Keys or Everglades National Park. After filling the Mustang's gas tank, he hung a right, heading into the inky blackness.

Within half a mile it seemed as if he'd left all vestiges of civilization behind. There were few lights and fewer structures. Just solitary clusters of tin shacks for migrant workers tending the crops. He passed the State Corrections facility. Three bleak miles on, he was in the Everglades.

Flamingo was in the heart of the southern Everglades. It was just southeast of Cape Sable, on the southern tip of the Florida mainland. From there, fishermen, naturalists, and houseboaters alike had access to more than two hundred square miles of backcountry waterways, mangrove swamps, and buoy-marked channels clear out to the Keys.

All the way down Croaker watched his rearview mirror. Through Florida City there was plenty of traffic behind him. But no cops. He changed lanes frequently just the same, if only out of habit. He was not by nature paranoid.

Once outside Florida City the vehicles behind him were as scarce as oases in a desert. Their headlights shone a long way on the flat, wet stretch of road. He'd been watching the same pair of headlights behind him for some time when he decided to pull off to the side of the road. He killed the engine and the Mustang's lights. The vehicle was a dark-colored Dodge Ram truck, covered with the alkali dust and pale mud of the fields. It slowed as it came abreast of the Mustang, then pulled over just in front.

Croaker tensed. He watched the driver's door swing open. A rangy man in jeans, dusty boots, and a weather-stained cowboy hat walked slowly over to him. He was carrying a shotgun casually at his side. He came up to the Mustang and leaned down to the open window.

"Howdy."

"Evening." There was a small, uncomfortable silence while the man worked a chaw of tobacco around his mouth. He peered into the Mustang's interior as if looking for contraband. "Need any help? Car okay?"

"Everything's fine," Croaker said. "I've been driving all day. I got a little tired and decided to pull over for a while."

The man nodded. "Wise move. Don't wanna fall asleep behind the wheel. 'Specially down here. Nobody to come fetch ya after the car flips over. You got far t'go?"

"Just to the park visitors' center. Picking up my girlfriend." Croaker put a sheepish look on his face. "We had a kind of set-to couple of days back. You know how it is."

There was another uncomfortable silence while the man's flinty eyes searched Croaker's face for answers to questions Croaker could only guess at.

"Better git on over there." The man spat a dark blob onto the ground. "She were my gal I wouldn't care for her bein' out here at night alone."

"Just about to do that," Croaker said. "Thanks."

The man nodded and sauntered back to his truck. Croaker kept track of it as he drove away. About a half mile on, it made a right down a side road.

Croaker continued on to Flamingo without further incident. Sporadic spits of rain greeted him as he drove into the National Park Visitors Center. He drove past the lodge—a row of attached cabins, looking very 1950s, then the restaurant, now long closed for the night. He rolled through the deserted parking lot onto the marina's concrete apron.

One light was on at the side of the activities shack. Behind it, lights at the dock's edge picked out the boats used for backcountry tours and cruises on Florida and Whitewater Bays. They lay to, tied securely in their slips. They were, by necessity, shallow-draft boats, since the water rarely went deeper than five feet and was often no more than a foot or so. It was a scene both serene and bucolic. It reminded Croaker all over again why Stone Tree preferred to live down here in the backcountry.

As he got out of the Mustang, a figure detached itself from the shadows of the activities shack. The light illuminated Bennie's face. He was dressed in black, just like the ACTF agent on Brickell Bridge had been. From his left hand dangled a pair of infrared binoculars for seeing in the dark. "Well, *amigo*, I could hardly have anticipated this."

"Shut up."

"*Muy bien.* I count to ten." Bennie took out a cigar, although it was improbable he'd be able to get it lighted in this wind and rain. "I take into account the state of your, like, agitation an' I, you know, don't take offense."

"What is that?" Croaker asked. "A warning or a testimonial?"

Bennie gave an explosive laugh. He rolled the unlit cigar around his mouth like it was a Snickers bar. "You're one pissed-off *hombre*, you know that? You sure you're not Latino? You definitely got the temper, *muy caliente.*"

"Cut the entertainment. It's skin deep. I've worked out enough of what's going on underneath. Bastard." Rain dribbled down Croaker's collar, running like sweat down his spine. "You knew Majeur. You knew he'd extorted me into killing Barbacena and you did nothing to stop it. Because you wanted Barbacena dead."

"Why would I want that?"

"Javier Marquesa. He was your mentor in Asunción. Barbacena married his daughter and then murdered her."

"Knowledge is power, eh, *amigo*?" Bennie seemed unsurprised that Croaker knew this. "True. Juan Garcia's death has been a dream of mine. But I could never, you know, find the means. He very quickly made himself invulnerable."

"That ended tonight. Barbacena's dead. He was sitting at ground zero, eating his rice and tofu, when Heitor's bomb went off."

Bennie's eyes were dreamy. "At last." He seemed to have relaxed slightly, as if a chronic ache had receded. "I thank God you came through this okay."

"Spare me." Croaker turned up his collar. The rain tasted salty, like tears. "Did you set me up, Bennie? Do you work for the U.S. government?"

The sadness returned to Bennie's face. "I'd never, like, do that to you. We're *amigos*."

"Jesus. You must have a very fucking twisted idea of friendship."

"Maybe. I wouldn't know. To be honest, I've never had a friend before."

The two men stood facing each other. Beside them, the Mustang's engine ticked slowly over. Croaker searched Bennie's face, but he could find nothing of significance there. No signpost, no hint of what was going on in this enigmatic man's mind.

"I saw documentation that a certain agent is ramrodding a top-secret Mexican operation, arming and training the insurgents in the south for a political coup. He's code-named Sero." Croaker saw Bennie's eyes open wide and he nodded. "Yeah. Estrella Leyes told me about the nickname your grandfather called you. Sero. The mountain."

"She shouldn't have done that." Bennie seemed genuinely sad. "That was something sacred between Humaitá and me."

Croaker ignored the melancholia. "Exactly. Now you know how I feel. We saved each other from the tiger shark; we buried Sonia together. I gave you my trust. That's sacred, Bennie. It's a secret between two people. But you lied to me, used our friendship. And now, what do you expect me to believe?"

"You still have my trust, Lewis."

"What the hell d'you mean by that? Is that you in the government computer, Bennie? Are you the ghost in the machine? Right now, I wouldn't bet against it. This operation, it's like a well-oiled machine, running day and night, bringing us closer to the moment when elements within the U.S. government and their big business partners will be running Mexico for their own economic gains. That kind of thing takes a load of planning, not to mention big-time bucks. But we're talking Latin America here. Money and schemes are useless without a great deal of know-how. You understand what I mean by know-how, don't you, Bennie? Connections, connections, connections. Nothing gets done in Latin America without crawling into bed with the corrupt honchos down there. That's your stock-in-trade."

"Maybe so, *amigo*. But do you think I'm the only one?"

The rising wind whistled through the marina, set the boats to rocking. A sudden burst of rain rattled the rigging.

Since Croaker had made no reply Bennie decided to try another tack. "About these people, Lewis—Estrella and Majeur, the ones I never told you—"

"They're dead, Bennie. All of them, except maybe Majeur who, if he isn't dead probably wishes he was." Croaker's balled fist struck Bennie full on the jaw. Croaker was an expert and Bennie never saw the punch coming. The cigar went flying and he went down hard, his backside hitting the concrete apron.

"Dios mio!" Bennie sat there, one hand to his jaw. He seemed genuinely stunned.

Croaker looked down at him. "You stupid bastard. Look what your blood-game with the Bonitas has done. First Sonia, then Vonda Shepherd. Now Estrella, Pablo Leyes, and Majeur. All dead." Bennie sucked meditatively on a tooth. Croaker hoped it was broken. "But what the hell would you care? By your own admission, you never had a friend in your life."

"Except you, *amigo.*"

"Stop calling me that." Croaker dug the soul-catcher out of his pocket, held it in his palm. "I'll tell you the truth, Bennie. I was touched when you gave me your grandfather's spirit-stone. Now, I honestly don't know why you did it. Maybe it was some kind of goddamn bribe to get me out on the boat at midnight. What did you need me for, Bennie? Did you want me to transport you to the backcountry rendezvous point so you could pick up the bones?" He held the spirit-stone for Bennie's to take. "Where are they, Humaitá's bones?"

Bennie stood up. "Don't be waving that around. If it should, like, fall into the wrong hands . . ." He refused Croaker's offer. "You an' I, we've got no healing powers. But Antonio and Heitor could, like, get every secret my grandfather put into it. That stone is, like, a storehouse of his spells, chants, an' healing."

Croaker rolled the smooth soul-catcher around his fingertips. He recalled how it had drawn Rachel out of her coma, how it had drawn the truth from Heitor. "Take it, Bennie. I don't want it."

But Bennie just shook his head. "A gift should never be returned. Otherwise, it becomes an instrument of evil."

"You stubborn sonuvabitch."

Bennie started and Croaker whirled around. A pair of headlights had entered the compound.

"God hear me, Lewis, I warned you our lives would be forfeit if you were followed here."

"But I wasn't," Croaker said. "I can guarantee it."

The headlights were coming straight for them.

"Yeah?" Bennie thrust the binoculars into Croaker's hand. "Tell me what you see."

Croaker, focusing the lenses, saw a pale panel truck pop into view in the infrared lenses. "Sonuvabitch! The Bonitas! How did they know—"

He shoved the binoculars back at Bennie, got down on his hands and knees. Shining his pocket flashlight beneath the Mustang, he let out another oath.

301

"What is it, *amigo?*"

Croaker stood up. "Miniature homing device. On the underside of the car."

"Nice touch," Bennie said. "Those fucking Bonitas."

The panel truck raced around the last turn on its way to the marina.

"Shit!" Croaker said, and they both began to run toward the boats rocking at their berths.

"This one!" Bennie pointed to a dark-green twenty-five-footer as he untied the bow line. "I was just out on it."

Croaker leapt onto the deck, got behind the wheel. The keys were in the ignition and he started up the engine. The white panel truck careened through the parking lot as Bennie flipped off the aft line.

"Ready!" Bennie shouted as the truck screeched to a halt beside the Mustang. Antonio swung out while the truck was still rocking on its shocks. He hit the concrete running. Heitor was just behind him.

Croaker had the boat in gear and was steering it clear of the dock. He spun the wheel around as the boat cleared the far pilings. White wake churned up as he increased speed.

"Nowhere to hide now." Antonio stood on the end of the dock staring balefully after them. "Sero, do you hear me?"

Croaker risked a glance back. So the Bonitas knew Humaitá called Bennie Sero. This was nuts. One minute he was sure Bennie was the ACTF operation mastermind, the next he was equally certain that Antonio and Heitor had set Bennie up. Was "Sero" a true ghost in the machine, a figment of the Bonitas' warped game?

Heitor was running down the length of the dock, paralleling them. He ran full tilt, keeping them in sight as he neared the far end of the dock.

"Crazy bastard!" Bennie said. "What the fuck's he up to?"

Croaker saw Antonio hold his right arm out toward the boat. He looked like Moses about to part the Red Sea. "Christ, Heitor's going to make a run at us," Croaker said.

The boat was in a narrow channel; there wasn't much room to maneuver. He turned the wheel to starboard just as Heitor made his running leap off the end of the pier.

As he did so, Antonio opened his hand. In it, a black stain no larger than a quarter. A soul-catcher. Antonio began to chant, the words swept away by the foul weather.

Heitor opened his arms wide. He looked as if he were flying across the water, propelled by the rising wind. Surely, it couldn't be Antonio's magic.

Against all odds, he made the front of the boat. His shoes skidded and he rolled heavily onto the deck.

Bennie hurried forward. "You're one sorry-looking fucker." Then he kicked Heitor in the ribs.

Croaker, keeping one eye on the narrow channel overhung with mangrove and vines and the other on the dock, saw Antonio raise his arm higher and pick up the pace of his chanting.

Croaker took out Humaitá's spirit-stone. "Bennie, watch out!" he warned. "Stay away from Heitor."

But Bennie was past hearing. *"Hijo de putana!"* He spat on Heitor and kicked him again.

Something—a particularly strong gust of wind—rocked the boat. It caught Bennie by surprise. He lurched and Heitor, reaching up, punched him in the groin.

Bennie went to his knees, gasping. Croaker saw the glint of Heitor's scalpel and he shouted, "Bennie! Catch!"

As Bennie turned, he threw the soul-catcher. Bennie reached up for it, but Heitor was quicker. His left hand darted out and intercepted the throw. There was an instant's flash of heat and light and Heitor began to laugh.

He easily parried Bennie's thrown punch. His hand with the stone in it pressed against the side of Bennie's neck. Bennie went down as if poleaxed. Heitor straddled him, and the scalpel glittered as it moved down toward Bennie's throat.

Croaker threw the boat into neutral, turned off the ignition, and ran forward. In his mind, he saw Heitor stabbing Majeur. He'd been too late to save the lawyer; would he be too late again?

He hit Heitor with such force that the blade missed its mark. It penetrated Bennie's chest, slicing through the heavy muscle as if it were butter. Bennie screamed. Croaker's momentum drove Heitor sideways, into the side of the boat. He grunted, spun, and buckled as Croaker smashed his elbow into the side of his head.

The spirit-stone skittered along the deck and Croaker dove for it. That was a mistake. He knew it the moment he was fully extended and vulnerable. He should have taken care of Heitor first. Heitor drove a knee into the small of his back. Lights exploded behind Croaker's eyes, and he rolled an instant before the point of the scalpel embedded itself in the deck where he'd just been. He struck out, but he had no power behind it, and Heitor brushed it aside.

Heitor grabbed the spirit-stone and, in almost the same motion, smashed the back of his hand into Croaker's face. Dazed, Croaker felt himself engulfed in a kind of eerie lethargy. Years ago, he'd gone elk hunting in the mountains of Montana and had almost frozen to death. This was much the same feeling. A kind of detachment, a sense of slipping into a twilight world where nothing mattered and any movement was unimaginable.

He watched with unblinking eyes as Heitor slowly opened the hand with which he'd struck Croaker. There, embedded in the center of the palm, was Humaitá's spirit stone.

Heitor's bandaged face leered down at him. "See how it works? I have your soul. In here. You're mine, *maricone.* Fight it all you wish, it was meant to be." He crouched down in front of Croaker. "I had a dream that foretold this moment. In the dream I smelled the mangrove. I felt the rain against my face. I felt as clearly as one sees a beacon in the night the pain you have inflicted on me. I used my scalpel—and I discovered the mystery of life and death." He was grinning like a jack-o'-lantern. "I held your bloody head in my hands."

He placed the spirit-stone almost reverently against the center of Croaker's forehead. With his other hand, he plucked the scalpel from the deck. "I want you to feel it all," he said. "I want you to see your death coming. It was foretold in the dark stone. It is in my eyes. Soon it will be all you know." He moved the scalpel to a position level with Croaker's throat. "It's coming closer, *señor.* You see? Yes." The scalpel moved. "Here it is."

Heitor was flung sideways as the loud report echoed through the mangrove swamps. Croaker's gaze swept from the blood leaking from Heitor's shoulder to Bennie, prone on the deck, aiming a snub-nosed .22. Wood chips flew as Bennie got off another shot, but Heitor was no longer there. He'd flung himself over the side, into the channel.

Bennie, clearly exhausted, dropped his arm. The .22 clattered against the deck. *"Amigo?"* His voice was soft and hoarse.

Croaker blinked several times. Blood coursed back into him. The unnatural lethargy was lifting. He levered himself up, staggered to where Bennie lay. Inspecting the wound, he saw that it was deep. Bennie lay in a widening pool of blood.

"Not so good, huh, Lewis?"

"Don't worry." Croaker began to work on him as best he could. He stripped off his own shirt, cut it up with one stainless-steel fingernail. Then, he began to bind up Bennie's wound. The main thing now was to stop the heavy bleeding.

"Worry?" Bennie tried to laugh, then gasped as the pain threatened to overwhelm him. "Why should I worry? I've got a mortal wound and we're out in the middle of nowhere."

"Shut up."

"Once again, I'll ignore your insult. Under . . . under the circum-stances, it's, like, the least I can do." Bennie grimaced as Croaker bound the wound ever more tightly. "No, I won't worry. We can't, like, go back to the dock because Antonio's waiting for us. And somewhere in the water Heitor is swimming like a shark."

"Forget Heitor." Croaker was just about finished. It wasn't much, but for the time being it'd have to do. "He's bleeding like a stuck pig. He'll attract every croc within a five-mile radius."

"You still don't get it, do you, *amigo*? These are the Bonitas. They *eat* crocodiles for tea." Bennie's gaze held Croaker's. "Plus, he's got the soul-catcher."

Croaker shone his pocket flashlight around the deck. No sign of the spirit-stone. He got up. No time to worry about it now. He went aft. The boat had drifted into an outcropping of mangrove. He started up the engine, backed off, then headed around a sweep-ing curve.

Beyond that, the channel straightened out and he was able to put on more speed. Soon they were alone with the mangroves, the purl-ing water, and the nocturnal predators. They were on the Wilder-ness Waterway, heading due north toward Coot Bay.

Bennie tried to sit up. Groaning, he flopped back down into his own blood. "Where we goin', *amigo*? Even if you know a place, no use in, like, hidin' out. I'll be dead by morning."

"Keep still. You're losing blood."

"Can't, Lewis. If I stop talking I'll think about what's going to, you know, happen to me."

"Nothing's going to happen to you," Croaker said angrily. "You're too big a bastard."

"Bastards die," Bennie said, "just like mere mortals." He tried to laugh but it turned into a phlegmy cough.

Croaker didn't like the heavy sound of it. He hoped to God the scalpel hadn't pierced a lung. He forced himself to concentrate on the channel. It was difficult to navigate at night, especially at speed. But with Bennie pumping blood with each beat of his heart, he dared not slow down.

"Hey, *amigo*, you hear 'bout the big-city ambulance chaser goes out to a potential client's house?" Bennie was breathing as hard as if he'd just run a marathon in ninety-plus heat. "It's in the sticks, see? Real backwoods stuff. Seems this farmer, he got run over by his neighbor's tractor an' broke his back. The neighbor's loaded, and you know, the ambulance chaser smells a jackpot." Bennie paused to breathe some. He sounded like a grandfather clock in need of an overhaul. "So anyway, he pulls up in the farm's front yard, steps outa his Porsche and into this, like, big pile of shit. He looks down and goes, 'Jesus God, I'm melting!' "

Croaker laughed. For his efforts, Bennie began a whole new round of coughing. When at last he stopped, Croaker heard him say in a subdued voice, "Shit, it's blood."

Just then Croaker saw the uprooted buttonwood. It was shaped like a manatee, overhanging the waterway. Just past it, Croaker eased the boat down a narrow channel. The air was heavy with the rank aroma of mangrove.

Bennie looked around. "What is this place?"

Croaker cut the engine, let the boat drift down to the end of the channel. "Home," he said, leaping onto shore and hauling on the bow line, "if you happen to be a Seminole who talks to birds and fish."

"Sounds like a fucking Disney character," Bennie grumbled as Croaker scrambled around and tied off the aft line.

Croaker took a deep breath of the world he knew so well and went back into the boat to gather Bennie up in his arms.

3

It was said that Stone Tree walked with the spirits. This was repeated by Keys fishermen and backcountry guides—people not normally susceptible to flights of fancy. He had settled here because it was the center of the world. This is what he had said when Croaker had first sought him out.

"At the center of the world I listen," he had told Croaker.

"What do you hear?" Croaker had asked.

And Stone Tree had said: *"Everything."*

It was at that moment that Croaker knew he wanted Stone Tree to be his guide. Only gradually, as the days and nights passed in languid concentration, melting one into the other, did he realize that he was here for more than instruction on fishing.

People were afraid of Stone Tree in the same way they are afraid of being alone in the night. It was something they could not quite explain. As a consequence, he was pretty much left alone. This was just the way he liked it. It had occurred to Croaker that he let their fear stand guard over him.

Stone Tree lived in a rough wood and tin shack on a spit of land almost wholly surrounded by red mangrove. You couldn't walk on the red mangrove because they grew in the water. The groves were like a moat protecting a medieval castle. Only a small neck of solid land connected the spit to the "mainland."

Bennie's body was growing heavier with each step. As Croaker picked his way across the narrow neck, he was as bent over as an octogenarian with spinal arthritis. As always, he passed close by the manzanilla tree. This time of year, it was laden with small green applelike fruit. They looked tasty, but even the sap was as caustic as lye. Ponce del Rey, a Spanish explorer, had eaten one and had died in agony. As a small child, Stone Tree had done the same. He'd grown ill but, mysteriously, hadn't died. Afterward, his father had named him, declaring him as strong as a stone tree.

Ahead, Croaker saw movement and he froze. Joe came slithering out of the sawgrass and white mangrove, eager to see who was invading its territory. Joe was an eight-foot indigo snake that lived with Stone Tree.

Croaker went to his knees, held out his biomechanical hand for Joe to smell. The constrictor did this by flicking its tongue over the man-made substances. Then it curled itself around the hand and slithered up Croaker's arm. Its head touched Croaker's cheek, and again, its forked tongue flicked out. This time it tasted salt sweat.

"Bennie," Croaker said. "It's okay. We're here."

But there was no reply. Bennie had passed out as Croaker had transported him off the boat.

Croaker whistled softly as he rose and went up the moss-encrusted wooden steps to the shack. The door opened and a towering figure was silhouetted by the flickering light of myriad candles and a single Coleman lantern. Stone Tree was thin as a reed at the edge of the water where he lived.

"You are expected," Stone Tree said. "All is in readiness."

Croaker was unsurprised. Stone Tree knew things others did not. As Croaker put Bennie gently down in the center of the room, Stone Tree said, "Joe remembers adventures past. As always, he is partial to friends." This was the nature of Stone Tree's greeting.

"It feels right to be back," Croaker replied.

Stone Tree nodded. "It was time, Walking Ibis."

Croaker had earned his coming-of-age name the first time Stone Tree had seen him extrude a stainless-steel nail from the tip of his biomechanical finger. Stone Tree said it looked like an ibis's needle-like bill stabbing for fish.

Croaker watched Stone Tree's gaunt, lined face as he went to work. He was as tall as the first Indians here, the Calusa, whose men were almost seven feet in height, with cool, watchful eyes the color of a misty backcountry dawn. He wore his white hair long, pulled back from his wide forehead by a beaded deerskin head-band. It hung in a ponytail, the end of which was tied in a thick knot that bumped against his back like a pendulum whenever he moved. He possessed a wry sense of humor dry as a perfect martini. For all his isolation, Stone Tree had a worldly, inquisitive mind. Where he got his detailed knowledge of the planet Croaker hadn't a clue. Perhaps the kites and cormorants, crested herons and frigate birds that passed by overhead delivered the daily news.

He pressed his withered left hand against Bennie's forehead. He hadn't been born with that hand; he'd come by it unnaturally. A young man had come to him with terminal cancer. Stone Tree had healed him. But in doing so Stone Tree had taken the cancer inside himself. Now it was encapsulated, like a cyst.

"I could see it withering as the healing progressed," he had told Croaker. *"There are all kinds of pain. This is surprising to most people. But why should it not be so? Aren't there all kinds of love? Of course! This was a good pain. I was privileged to experience it."*

With his right hand Stone Tree broke off a large piece of sage, placed it in a shallow bowl in which several coals burned white-hot. Instantly, the sage smoldered, producing a chalky gray-green smoke. Stone Tree used his hands to scoop the smoke as if it were a liquid. In this way he wafted it over every part of Bennie's body, starting with his head and ending with his feet. He did this until all the sage had turned to ash. Then, with two long, slender fingers he plucked the bottom-most coal from the bowl and placed it over the makeshift bandage that Croaker had wrapped around the knife wound.

Croaker had seen Stone Tree handle coals with his bare hands before, so he wasn't surprised. The heat was so intense Croaker started to sweat. When Stone Tree noticed this, he smiled. "You have felt this heat before."

And instantly Croaker recalled the snakebite that Stone Tree had treated. Like the warmth given off by the Guarani spirit-stones, this heat had a healing effect that was difficult to categorize.

The coal burned through the layers of bloody cotton until it lay against the open wound. Bennie didn't thrash or cry out. Neither did his eyes open The heat increased until Croaker felt as if he were inside an oven.

In the meantime, Stone Tree had taken up three panther claws. Large and wickedly curved, they were black as obsidian, as if stained by long use. One by one, he inserted them into Bennie's flesh—one into each cheek, the third beside the place where the white-hot coal rested.

Stone Tree was ready when the black liquid began to ooze out of the incisions he'd made. He used the small bowl with the coals to catch the fluid. When the coals were completely covered and cooled, the liquid stopped its flow. Stone Tree handed the bowl to Croaker.

"Go outside and find a clear area. Dig with only your hands and bury this. Be sure not to get any of its contents on your skin."

Croaker did as Stone Tree bade him. When he returned, Bennie had stopped bleeding. There was a peaceful look on his face; his beathing was deep and even. Stone Tree was stirring an iron pot that hung over a pit filled with glowing coals. An aromatic soup brewed of rootstock and herbs infused the shack with pungent aromas.

"Your friend sleeps," Stone Tree said. "Now we take care of ourselves."

The two of them sat beside the coals eating grilled fish, mashed vegetables, and dried fruit. Stone Tree ate so little that Croaker suspected he'd already had dinner, but it would have been impolite to let Croaker eat alone. In silence, they listened to the sounds of the backcountry. The tree frogs bleeping. The insects whirring. The haunted calls of small predators. The lapping of the nearby water. The soughing of the wind through the buttonwood and Jamaican dogwood. All drowned out, now and again, by wild deluges of rain.

Croaker ate slowly. Meals were a ritual of concentration punctuated by animated conversation. This time, however, Stone Tree had no amusing stories to tell. "You come into my home tonight, Walking Ibis. You bring a wounded friend. Death stalks you. And yet there is something beyond these circumstances that is different. Change is working itself inside you." He reached out his withered hand and pressed it against Croaker's forehead as he had done before with Bennie. The hand was dry and cool as old wood.

"Do you know what is meant when people say I walk with the spirits?"

"You know things," Croaker said. "Which way the winds will blow, when the storms will come and how bad they'll be. You know

I was coming and why. You speak to the animals. You're open to the cycles of nature."

Stone Tree nodded, but there was a wry look to his face. "All these things are true, as far as they go. But what's really meant is that I talk to those who have passed beyond the world you and I know." Stone Tree put down his food bowl. "Tonight I see you on my porch. From the blood, I divine the nature of the storm that has followed you here. But in your eyes I see the change working itself through you. I see the healer's mark on you, as if by a tattooer's needle."

Croaker felt his stomach constrict. "My friend's grandfather was a great Guarani healer. A *sukia*."

"Yes," Stone Tree said. "I have heard of them. They use stones to gather power and to store it."

"Soul-catchers." Croaker thought of Humaitá's spirit-stone in Heitor's possession and he was filled with sudden dread. He remembered Estrella's fear when he'd shown her Humaitá's dark stone. "Do you know something about the spirit-stones?"

Stone Tree shook his head. "Very little. And what I do know is legend, rumor, call it what you will. It is said that under proper circumstances the *sukia* swallowed these stones. Then they became like gods."

"What does that mean?"

Stone Tree shrugged. "With a single touch of their hand they could heal the sick and infirm . . . or they could destroy their enemies. It is the most terrible of the *sukia*'s transformations because it is permanent. The stone stays inside. But because great power is gained, something of equal value must be lost. This is the nature of the universe."

"It didn't happen with this *sukia*," Croaker said. "He was killed many years ago—murdered by the brothers who've followed us here. Before he died he told my friend that he would return as a shark. Five days ago, we encountered a tiger shark. It was very large, very fierce. My friend was sure—"

"That it was Humaitá."

Croaker stared, dumbfounded. "How did you know his name?"

Stone Tree smiled and lightly tapped Croaker's forehead with his withered hand. "He told me, Walking Ibis." It scribed a circle on Croaker's forehead. "He is here. Inside you. Tonight you also walk with the spirits."

Croaker felt a sudden chill. "Stone Tree, it can't be. I don't believe."

Stone Tree used a small shard of buttonwood charcoal to draw something on the floorboards between them. Croaker stared at it. It was an eye with a double iris.

"Here he is," Stone Tree said. "Isn't it so, Walking Ibis?"

Croaker nodded. "That's Humaitá's symbol."

"Your friend awakes." Stone Tree turned, ladled soup into a gourd bowl. "Feed him." He gave Croaker the bowl. "Give him life."

He walked silently outside.

Croaker arranged himself with Bennie's head in his lap. Slowly and laboriously, he fed him the rootstock and herb soup. Bennie drank without protest. His eyes were red rimmed and he seemed thoroughly dazed. Croaker didn't blame him. He looked at the wound. It was raw and red and caked with dried blood. But it was closed just as if it had been sutured by a surgeon.

The wind rose outside; mangrove branches scratched against the thin frame of the shack and rain drummed intermittently against the tin roof. The tree frogs remained, bleeping incessantly. But the insects had ceased to whir. Croaker continued to feed Bennie while Joe dozed on his shoulders.

In time, the gourd was empty. Croaker put it aside, looked down at Bennie. He thought about Humaitá. He thought about spirit possession. Chills crawled like worms through his insides, then dissipated. He didn't believe in spirit possession. It didn't exist.

Bennie's eyes moved. He stared up at Joe comfortably curled on Croaker's shoulders. *"Amigo,* am I dreaming?" he said in a dry and crusty voice. "What the hell's that?"

"Joe. He's an indigo constrictor. Friendly as hell."

"Nuts, the both of you."

"Not in the least. Besides having a personality, he's convenient to have around. He hunts other snakes, including the pygmy rattler, which could give you a pretty nasty bite."

"He get the water moccasins, too? I fuckin' hate water moccasins."

"None here," Croaker said. "No water snakes at all. The back-country's too salty."

Bennie closed his eyes. *"Dios."*

Croaker listened to the storm. It was approaching quickly. He could feel the pressure drop, like popping in his ears. As if in confirmation, thunder rolled ominously. He looked down at the man in his arms. Survivors of earthquakes or bomb blasts had that look of blankness, as if their souls had been blasted into the background.

"Bennie, how do you feel?"

Bennie's eyes snapped open. "Not dead, not alive. Not yet." He seemed unnaturally subdued, rueful even. "Listen, *amigo*. I have some things to say."

"Not now," Croaker said. "Rest."

"If not now, when?" Croaker's silence spurred him on: "I won't deny I lied to you. *Pero esto es agua pasada no mueve molino.*" That's all in the past. "See, I had to. My grandfather's bones—they're all I have left of him. I had to make sure they didn't fall into the wrong hands."

"Like Antonio and Heitor."

"That would be a disaster," Bennie acknowledged. "All my grandfather's powers would be theirs."

"Then they didn't have them."

"Are you for real? They'd, like, never agree to sell them back to me. They'd never even let on they had 'em."

Croaker watched the flicker of the candle flames. They seemed symbols of the storm, and of the uncertain future. "So who had them? Who did you have to meet at midnight?"

"Roubinnet."

"Rafe? Come on. You can do better than that."

Bennie sighed. "I'm, like, you know, unsurprised you don't believe me. Disappointed, but unsurprised. I brought this on myself. But God hear me it's the truth."

"Why should I believe you?"

Bennie tried unsuccessfully to laugh. "I can think of no good reason at all." He closed his eyes briefly. He seemed to be summoning up some hidden wellspring of strength. "*Mira, amigo.* I made a mistake. I didn't trust you. What will you do now? Will you condemn me for, like, life? Is there no way I can redeem myself? For good or ill, I'm in your hands, Lewis."

Croaker was silent for some time. He stared at nothing, listened to everything. Just as Stone Tree had taught him. "Tell me about you and Rafe," he said at length.

Bennie sighed, as if he'd been holding his breath for Croaker's decision. "While he was still mayor of Miami Roubinnet went into business with a Colombian named Gabriella. Gabriella was a real wise guy, got in over his head an' he went to jail."

"What happened?" Croaker asked.

"Shit happened, that's what." Bennie was clearly disgusted. "The idiot decided to use Rafe's money an' get into the drug trade. Why not? He imagined tons of money, the high, flashy life, buckets of power. He got sucked into the whole damn thing." Bennie shook his head. "Anyway, Gabriella, he buys this big German shepherd, see, an' he takes him to a boyhood pal of his—a vet. The vet slits open the dog's abdomen, and Gabriella, like, gives him a dozen plastic bags of coke, which the vet sews into the abdominal cavity. Then, Gabriella ships him off to the States."

"Okay. Then what?"

"So Gabriella, he's a novice at this kind a thing and the vet—he's nervous an' he forgets to sterilize the plastic bags. The shepherd gets infected and customs, they see a sick animal and turn him over to the Stateside vets, who take X-rays and find the bags of coke. Wham-o, they nail Gabriella to the fuckin' wall."

Bennie was silent for a moment, resting. "Rafe knows nothing—or at least he says he knows nothing," he continued. "But he calls me an', like, asks me to get in the middle of the mess. To, you know, extricate him from his partnership, like, after the fact, because the fallout could kill him politically. But the Gabriella case gets messy—too messy for me to deal with. The Colombian authorities alluva sudden, they don't wanna deal—they don't wanna talk to me—period. Which, I gotta say, considering who I know there, is very fucking weird. I even get a death threat. So I back off. Rafe gets pissed, hangs up on me, then reappears coupla days later offering me a deal: I get him off the hook with this hot potato and he'll get me my grandfather's bones."

Croaker glanced down at Bennie. "That sounds like a bribe."

"Yeah. It did to me, too." Bennie looked away for a moment. "But the temptation was too great. I got him free. I chewed up a coupla favors *muy precioso*." Very precious. "I fixed it so nobody knew; nobody could ever link him to Gabriella and that stinking drug deal."

"But that wasn't the end of it."

"Fuck no." Bennie bit his lower lip at the memory. "I come to Rafe for payment an' he says the deal for the bones fell through. *Que lastima!*" What a pity! "But all the while, I'm looking in his eyes an' I, like, see the truth. An' it isn't pretty. The truth is the fucker's changed his mind. He's got my grandfather's bones but he doesn't want to give them up. Offered to pay me for my time. A generous amount, no doubt there. Didn't matter what the amount was, though. He'd fucked me good. I showed him what to do with that money, and let me tell you, he didn't like it one bit." Bennie looked up at Croaker. "God hear me, that gent has one hairy ass."

The two of them laughed, and to Croaker it felt very good.

"Yeah, but, Bennie, how'd you know Rafe was lying?"

"I called the sonuvabitch on it. And guess what? He admits that, yeah, maybe he can still get the bones. But it's, like, gonna cost me.

Can you fuckin' picture this. I've just done him this, like, humongous service, an' he's fucked me. An' on top of that now I gotta do some more shit for him. *Then* I get my grandfather's bones. Tonight was to be the payoff. I was supposed to meet him at midnight, but this fuckin' storm blew up. Because I wasn't in a, like, proper boat to ride out the storm in the bay I had to get back to shore."

"What did Rafe ask you to do?"

"Mediate, what else? It's my specialty, no? But talk about a small world. One of the principals is Juan Garcia Barbacena. Roubinnet is aware of my history with this bastard, but he like asks me anyway. What the hell does he care if it puts acid in my belly."

"So you agreed?"

"So I agreed. What else could I do? It seems Barbacena had finally gotten too high-handed. He'd become power mad, dangerously independent, and contrary. The people who hired him want a final arbitration with him—one last try at getting him back under their control. I mean, Lewis, my impression: these people were ready to chop him if he wouldn't knuckle under."

Croaker's pulse quickened. "Let me guess. Barbacena wouldn't budge."

"Yeah. You could say that." Bennie got a little smile on his face. "He as much as told them to fuck off. Seemed to me when he walked out of the meeting he'd, like, signed his own death warrant."

"When was this?"

"Beginning of the year."

Now it all began to make sense. Gunn had needed time to work out a way of terminating Barbacena so that the ACTF's hands were absolutely clean. "Let me take another guess," Croaker said. "The people he was working for were Department of Justice. Man named Spaulding Gunn." Gunn must have been desperate to involve a civilian like Bennie, Croaker thought. But what choice did he have? Bennie was *numero uno* at this kind of negotiation. He also had a long history of being absolutely discreet. "So this was the extent of your involvement. If the DOJ swore you to secrecy I can understand why you couldn't tell me."

"It was Department of Justice, *amigo*. I saw the badge. But the man's name wasn't Gunn. At least, the name on the I.D. wasn't Gunn." He shifted slightly, and it seemed to take a lot out of him. "It was Ross Darling."

With his heart in his mouth, Croaker said, "Bennie, this is very important. Can you describe him?"

"Sure." When he'd caught his breath, Bennie said, "He was, like, medium height and build. He had this, you know, heavy, deliberate way of moving. Like a boxer or wrestler. And white hair like an old man, only he wasn't all that old. Had these red cheeks, like you see on mountaineers or veteran drunkards. This man was cold sober, though. Could see it in his eyes—pale blue like ice. God hear me, I've seen this kind of man before, Lewis. Wouldn't hesitate to kill anyone who crossed him. If he ever had a conscience, you can be damn sure he'd strangled it in the darkness of one childhood night."

Croaker's blood ran cold. Bennie's description was right on the money. The only trouble was it wasn't Spaulding Gunn he was talking about. It was Ross Darling.

Everything Darling had told Croaker about the interbureau war between DICTRIB and the ACTF was the truth, only in reverse: Darling and DICTRIB were the ones running Barbacena and the Mexican operation.

Croaker's outfit, the ACTF, was trying to stop it. In a moment of revelation, Croaker could see how the scenario had happened. Alienated agents from the ACTF had left Gunn's aegis and, forming a clandestine alliance with certain senators and businessmen, had re-created DICTRIB in their own image. DICTRIB's sole purpose, then, was to be the think tank and the conduit for the Mexican operation that would eventually put control of the Mexican government in the hands of an elite few Americans.

Darling had cut Croaker off from ever contacting anyone inside the ACTF. Of course. If Croaker had, he'd have found out the truth. And because the ACTF had lost touch with him and could not account for his movements, they had assumed he'd crossed over and joined DICTRIB. Which explained the attempt on his life at the Brickell Bridge.

How ironic, Croaker thought. It was Antonio Bonita who'd told him that everyone was lying to him. Everyone, that is, but Antonio himself.

4

Stone Tree crouched beneath a buttonwood, surrounded by darkness and the rain. Croaker hunkered down beside him. He'd left Joe back in the shack to guard Bennie.

"I've been tracking the storm," Stone Tree said. "From rain and wind you have nothing to fear." He held a forked twig between his knobby fingers. "As for the storm that followed you here, he's hidden in the hammock." *Hammock* was the Indian word for forest. "Real close now."

Croaker nodded. "I'm going to have to find him."

Stone Tree's gaze locked with Croaker's. "Remember. Everything I taught you."

"You'll take care of Bennie until I get back."

"Your friend will be safe."

Croaker was about to get up when Stone Tree put his good hand on his arm. "It's a damned waste of energy to hate the storm. Find the way to its heart."

"The problem is, that's been tried before. These brothers were able to murder the *sukia* because of his compassion."

Stone Tree lifted one fist. "Force." He lifted his other hand. "Only begets more force." He cocked his head. "Listen to everything. Decide for yourself what is truth and what is merely perception."

Croaker almost laughed. "Why not? Ever since I got involved with the Bonitas almost everyone I've met has lied to me."

"Are you surprised, Walking Ibis?" He lifted his hands. "This world is a lie. Beyond it, the truth pulses like light on the ocean floor. The spirits speak when I walk with them. Existence isn't limited to this world we see with our eyes. We're butterflies pinned to a page only if we allow it." His head turned quickly, though Croaker heard nothing but the soughing of the wind through the buttonwood and the sawgrass, the energetic splash of rain. "Go now," Stone Tree said. And as Croaker rose, he added: "You believe this storm is deadly. Do not be deceived, Walking Ibis. For you, it is something else altogether."

Croaker moved silently through the hardwood hammock. Rain

pattered down, every so often gusting through the mangroves. Within thirty yards Stone Tree's encampment had disappeared from view. On either side mangrove rose like spectral fingers. They swayed in the wind like netting over a beehive.

Croaker paused beside the manzanilla, momentarily unsure which way to go. Once again he was overcome by the thought of how at home he felt in the darkness. In New York, he'd worked while others slept. And because of his work they could sleep more soundly. But there was an odd thing that happened when you were at home in the night. You became dislocated.

The normal rhythms of life—waking in the morning, eating breakfast at eight, being at work at nine—were disrupted. As the connections to the world around you were slowly severed you found yourself becoming more self-reliant.

All this he saw as helpful to him. During the day there was a steady buzz—a cacophony of frenzied movement that kept people alert and fixated on their own immediate problems. At night, when sleep overtook them, this static was reduced to a murmur. Then, the rhythms of what Stone Tree called the larger reality rose like spectral sounds in the forest.

In the rain-filled night Croaker could sense Heitor. Heitor was a hunter; this is what he'd been itching for ever since the two of them had met. Predator and prey, together in the wilderness. What was it Heitor had said? *A man is understood only when he stands alone.*

A gust of wind brought him a whiff of ozone. He plucked a small green apple with his biomechanical hand and set off down the spine of the hardwood hammock.

Thunder rumbled, and the sky cracked open in a cool, blue-white glare. The storm made tracking impossible. Not only was the physical spoor obliterated but the rain took all scent out of the air.

Gradually he became aware that he was being watched. Moving cautiously between the strangler figs he was able to pick out a pair of amber eyes in the sawgrass underbrush. He reached the end of the hammock. All around him were mangrove—white on the land, black at the edge of the water, red arching out into the waterway itself. He made a clicking sound and the amber eyes disappeared.

He plunged quickly into the mangrove, following. He was close enough now to partially see the shadow, the tiny movements of leaf and grass stalks as the body brushed by. Gaining ground, he saw that they were paralleling the edge of dry land. Three hundred yards farther on he knew the waterway curved inward, reducing the mangrove islet to a narrow isthmus.

He made his move then, leaping in front of the shadow just as it ran out of land. It turned and, as he came up on it, reared onto its hind legs, its jaws hinging open as it spat and hissed.

He recoiled. Christ! It was a bobcat!

Croaker willed himself to freeze. He watched those lambent amber eyes staring at him as the beast snarled and raked the air with a forepaw. Slowly, never taking his eyes from the bobcat, he began to back away.

That was when Heitor took him. Heitor seemed to fly through the wind and the rain as he leaped from his hiding place within the black mangrove. Landing on Croaker's back, he drove a fist into Croaker's side, and they both pitched into the tangle of arched mangrove roots that made up the shoreline.

Instantly, Heitor plunged a forked stick into the muck, pinioning Croaker's biomechanical hand. With the hand embedded in the black viscous detritus, Croaker was deprived of the leverage he needed to use it effectively. Dimly he was aware of Heitor's lopsided appearance as he favored the shoulder where he'd been shot. He wanted to take advantage of the wound, but Heitor didn't seem in the least bit weakened.

On the contrary, Heitor, astride him, smashed his fist into Croaker's face. "This is for the first time you broke my nose." His fist drove into Croaker face again. "This is for the second time. And this is for the scar you left me."

Croaker tasted his own blood. Consciousness flickered in and out as Heitor pummeled him.

The assault ceased as abruptly as it had begun. Croaker opened eyes caked with blood and muck. Heitor had Humaitá's soul-catcher in one hand, a scalpel in the other. The cut Croaker had made in his right cheek looked raw and angry, as if it pulsed with Heitor's rage.

"Antonio said to wait for him. He said not to tackle you on my own." He sneered. "Cautious one! Foolish one! Not tonight. *Mira, señor*, how Humaitá's secrets heal my shoulder. Tonight belongs to the hunter!" He bent low over Croaker. "Look into my eyes. I want you to recognize your death there."

Croaker did, indeed, see something dark and squirmy in Heitor's eyes and something inside him quailed. Was it real or the power of suggestion? In his present position, he knew he had no chance in a physical struggle. But there must be another way. "Heitor," he said, "tell me how it can be that Antonio is still in love with Rosa?"

"What nonsense is this?" Heitor's scalpel hovered, motionless, above Croaker's face. "Do you think you can sway me with lies?"

Croaker pressed on, giving himself that most precious commodity: time. "Didn't you know? That's where his affinity for me lies.

There's a connection between Rosa and Sonia. Antonio felt it when we met at Sonia's house."

"I didn't know he was there." There was an uncertain flicker behind Heitor's eyes. "He didn't tell me."

"Of course he didn't." Croaker was working his biomechanical hand in the muck, manufacturing room to maneuver. "If he did, you'd want to know why he was there. And he wouldn't dare tell you the truth—that he'd come to revisit Rosa's murder. To confess to me."

Heitor's eyes had clouded over. "Why would he want to do that?"

"Because you were right. Rosa had changed him. She told him he was damned. And the very act of your murdering her proved it to him. For the first time I think he understood the nature of the evil the two of you had created."

A certain amount of relief showed on Heitor's face. "Now I know you're lying. If what you're saying was true, why would Antonio continue?"

"Simple. He couldn't stop himself." Croaker had burrowed his biomechanical hand deep enough to regain some motion. "Your way of life had become an end in itself. It had taken on a life of its own. Isn't that true, Heitor?"

"The game. Yes, yes." Heitor's tone was dismissive. *"Madre de mentiras*, you're just stating the obvious."

"Except that Antonio can no longer live with what you've created." Slowly, in the muck, Croaker turned his biomechanical hand on edge so the thumb was uppermost. "In fact, he never could. Humaitá recognized this spark of humanity in Antonio and tried to play him against you. I'm right, aren't I, Heitor?"

"Humaitá." Heitor's jaw clenched as he hissed out the single world like an epithet. "From the first, he insisted on separating us. He said we were different, individuals. He ignored the bond between us. No, no. The dark stones know that's wrong. He worked to sever our bond. *Hijo de putana!* Why? Didn't he understand that the two of us couldn't survive separately?"

Croaker was beginning to understand. "You mean *you* can't survive on your own, don't you, Heitor?"

"No!" Heitor's face was dark with rage and remembrance. "The two of us! *Everything* is the two of us."

"Not everything." One roll of the dice. Croaker knew this was all that was left him. Life or death depended on the truth of his supposition. "It wasn't the two of you who murdered Humaitá, was it?"

Silence. The wind soughing through the mangrove was like some-one in pain.

"The two of us, yes." Heitor was like a child clinging to a cher-ished belief that had saved him from the hideous truth.

"No," Croaker said. "It was you. You were always the hunter, the one with the insatiable blood lust. You murdered Humaitá on your own."

Heitor was back in Asunción, on that dark night on the Paraguay River. "That night I killed him, it was like this, stormy, filled with an evil rain. I drowned him. I remember the bubbles dribbling from his mouth as the air escaped his lungs. Beautiful! And he was so calm, like he'd known all along what would happen. It made me tremble."

Heitor licked his lips. "Afterward, Antonio said I'd slipped my leash. He used that word deliberately, to show me what an animal I could be. *I've been so careful with you,* he said. And he had. Time and again he'd told me how important Humaitá was to us. But I knew the truth. I could see how the old man was trying to destroy us, to sever our special bond. Though it caused me pain, I hid this truth even from Antonio. The dark stones know he wouldn't have understood. I knew. He'd try to stop me. He'd jerk my leash, make me crouch by him, panting and so angry I would lose my breath. Oh, yes. How many times had he done it before?"

"That night, Antonio could no longer be your keeper," Croaker said. "Rosa was right. When you murdered Humaitá, you damned him. He turned from being your failed conscience to your eventual abettor. That's what's eating him alive."

With a wordless cry, Heitor drove the scalpel toward Croaker's throat. In the same instant, Croaker smashed upward with all his strength. His biomechanical hand splintered the thick hardwood stick. The edge of the scalpel glanced off the polycarbonate shell. But such was Heitor's strength of determination that the scalpel pierced the meat of Croaker's right shoulder.

Heitor screamed. The spurting of Croaker's blood seemed to in-flame him all the more, and he twisted the scalpel in the wound. Pain streaked through Croaker's body, driving him to the edge of unconsciousness. He felt himself slipping away. He was astonished, then terrified at the ease with which he could let go of everything, fall backward into the endless abyss.

Then he saw the dark outline of his biomechanical hand, and he remembered. That tiny spark of memory fueled the terror. Adrena-line surged into his bloodstream. The ripped seams of consciousness stitched themselves together for a few more precious moments.

He ground his fingers against his palm, the pressure crushing the tiny sphere he held there. Then, his biomechanical fingers flowered open, and he jammed the pale paste into Heitor's open mouth. Immediately, he jabbed the knuckles of his right hand into Heitor's Adam's apple.

Heitor swallowed. He couldn't help himself. His eyes watered as he ingested the pulp and sap of the manzanilla apple.

Heitor screamed. It was a blood-curdling sound that terrified even the bobcat, who bounded over them and quickly disappeared into the black maze of the hammock.

Arching up, Heitor flung himself this way and that. He clawed at his throat, then his chest and belly. His eyes were open wide and rolling. The whites were bloodshot, and his mouth worked spastically.

Then he caught sight of Croaker, and with a supreme effort of will, he managed to regain some control over himself. With a trembling hand he produced Humaitá's spirit-stone. He pressed it against the center of his chest.

For a moment, nothing seemed to happen. The squally rain had ceased to fall some time ago. Now even the wind had died. It was as if the night itself was holding its breath.

"There, *señor*. You see?" Heitor sat up. He was no longer trembling. His face had lost that white, pinched look. "*Hetá I* prevents me from being poisoned. You cannot harm me, *señor*. I welcome you to try—"

His voice failed him from one instant to the next. His eyes bugged out as his abdomen started to inflate. Horror crossed his face; sweat broke out on his forehead, ran in rivulets down his cheeks and beside his ears. His contorted expression appeared to mirror a terrible struggle going on inside him.

"I—I . . ." Heitor's eyes rolled up until only the whites shone, lambent as neon. His lower jaw dropped open and a protracted hissing could he heard emanating from deep within him. When eventually it died out, his abdomen was completely deflated.

Croaker approached him with caution. As he knelt over him, he could smell a peculiar odor. It seemed to rise from his open mouth as well as from every pore in his body. Even before he checked Heitor's pulse Croaker knew he was dead. He reached out, took the soul-catcher from Heitor's lax grip.

The pain in his shoulder made him turn away. He needed to find a Jamaican dogwood. He wanted to strip off a section of bark, press the underside against his wound. Decades ago, the Calusa and Seminoles dried and ground this bark, spreading the powder on the water. Its powerful narcotic would stun the fish that ate it. They'd float up to the surface where the fishermen netted them by the dozen.

He set off for the hardwood hammock, certain he'd find the dogwood there. But he'd only taken a pace or two when he had an instant flash of Antonio's face. There'd been no sound at all to warn him. He reacted, but it was too late. A section of buttonwood, thick and long as a cudgel, smashed into the side of his head and he fell to the ground, unconscious.

5

When Croaker had been on the force they'd had an unofficial saying. It was written on the precinct's ready-room wall: YOUR GUN IS YOUR RIGHT ARM AND YOUR RIGHT LEG. DON'T BECOME A CRIPPLE! *"Believe it. We live and die by that commandment,"* he'd been told on his first day. *"For the powers that be, it's a purely fiscal policy. They don't want you to lose the damn thing. For me, it's a matter of face. If you're shot with your own sidearm it goes on my fucking record as well as yours."*

Upon awakening, Croaker had cause to remember this incident. Looking down at his body he saw that he was a cripple all over again.

He wiped the rain out of his eyes and stared in disbelief at the stub of his left forearm. Somehow, Antonio had managed to disengage his biomechanical hand's locking mechanism. Croaker felt as naked as if all his clothes had been stripped off.

He sat up and immediately put a hand to his head. He was groggy and there was a dull throbbing he couldn't stop. He took a couple of deep breaths, then looked around. He was on the boat he and Bennie had used to get to Stone Tree's shack.

With his right hand, he dug into his pocket. His heart sank. Humaíta's spirit-stone was gone. Now Antonio had every advantage.

Croaker hauled himself to his feet. As he made his way aft, he almost stumbled. He brought himself up short. He'd become accustomed to the weight of the biomechanical hand. Without it, he seemed like a ship without a rudder. He stared into the water where an alligator lay, still as death, eyeing him with dispassion.

He moved on, his eyes on the deck. Hadn't Bennie's .22 been left on the deck? Now there was no sign of it.

"The gun has been disappeared, *señor*," Antonio said from behind him.

Antonio stepped from the shadows at the bow of the boat, leveling a Mack-10 machine pistol at Croaker. The Mack-10 was a compact automatic weapon that could spew out bullets at an appalling rate.

"Isn't that a bit of overkill? I'm only one man."

"But such a man," Antonio said quite seriously. "Heitor had Humaitá's soul-catcher yet you killed him." Antonio's face seemed a mask beneath which muscles twitched as if they were emotions long held in check. "What secret weapon did you use, I wonder?"

Croaker lifted his stub. "What weapon? You managed to get my hand off even though it was locked in place."

Antonio didn't appear to hear him. His amber eyes were clouded with a swirl of emotion. "*Señor*, I cried for him. *Verdad*. I had sworn to protect him—and I did. To the best of my abilities. But in the end Heitor had a will of his own."

"And he followed that will, come what may," Croaker said. "He always did."

"You know it all. Detective." Antonio had tried to inject a note of contempt in his voice, but failed. He jerked his head. "Did you wonder why I kept you alive? I need you to navigate through this cursed storm."

"Where are we going?"

Antonio flicked the ugly, blunt muzzle of the Mack-10, indicating Croaker should move aft. "Where do you think?"

Of course. It was obvious. It should have been all along.

"Don't want to tell me? Don't think I know?" Antonio was laughing at him. "We're going to make Bennie's rendezvous. I'm going to get Humaitá's bones. Finally."

"I can imagine how much you covet the bones," Croaker said as he was herded aft. "I understand the power in them makes the soul-catcher insignificant."

"Not insignificant, no." Antonio shrugged. "But together, *señor*, if I had them both, it would almost be as if Humaitá is resurrected." He closed his hand into a fist, pressed it to his chest. "And all his knowledge, all his power would be *here*, inside me."

For Croaker, that possibility was a frightening thought indeed. He knew he'd have to stop Antonio from getting Humaitá's bones at all cost. "What I can't figure out is why you let Heitor do it," he said as he took the wheel. "Humaitá had taught you everything. He believed in you. With him alive, your life was set. And yet you decided to burn all of that on his funeral pyre. You helped Heitor, even forgave him. The two of you hid the truth and went on."

"I had no choice, *señor.*"

"That's nonsense." Croaker started up the engine, threw it into reverse. "In the end, choices are all we have to call our own. They're what define us, Antonio. They've certainly defined you."

Antonio grunted. *"Madre de mentiras,* life is sweet when you have all the answers."

Croaker thought Antonio sounded bitter as he slowly backed the boat through the channel that Stone Tree had hand-dug off the main waterway. He looked at the shallow water and thought of fate. In Southeast Asia, where he had spent much time, fate was a big thing. It ruled a person's life from the moment of birth to the instant of death. The Chinese, for example, believed that it was wrong to struggle against your fate. Acceptance of what would inevitably come was counseled. Croaker could never quite buy that line of thinking. To him it was like lying down like a dog in the street to die. Couldn't do it. Never would.

It wasn't good to think of such things, he knew. He barely understood the concept of fate, let alone whether or not he believed in it. But the alternative to thinking these thoughts was worse. For then he'd have to grapple with the realization that he was going to die here, facedown in two feet of brackish water. Just like in Jenny's spirit-stone vision.

"Such profound silence. *señor,*" Antonio said mockingly. "You must be contemplating your death."

"Actually, I was thinking of yours."

Antonio laughed. "You know, *señor,* despite all the grief you have caused me, I do believe I am going to miss you."

"Don't for a minute think the feeling's mutual." Croaker maneuvered the boat into Wilderness Waterway.

"Head south out of the channel," Antonio ordered with a flick of the Mack-10's stubby barrel. "We'll catch up with Roubinnet in Snake Bight." The bight was a kind of cove to the east that fronted the much larger Florida Bay. Beyond the bay were the Keys, flung off the tip of the mainland in an arc as slim and flexed as a woman's arm in repose.

"You and Rafe friends?"

"Fuck no." Antonio settled himself close enough to Croaker to keep an eye on him, but not so near that Croaker could reach him in a lunge. "But speaking of old friends, is Bennie dead yet?"

"You seem to know everything else. Why don't you know that?"

Antonio cocked his head. "Hit a nerve, yes, *señor*? Oh, I think so." He was wearing a gold-colored Polo shirt and chinos. The wind flipped his collar back and forth. "Bennie's a very clever man. But not so clever as he thinks. Maybe that's because he's sentimental. Yes, Bennie. He has deep sentiments for his grandfather. Curious, considering they never really got along." He grunted. "I bet Bennie never told you this."

"Whatever he told me is confidential."

"So's this. But I'll tell you anyway," Antonio said. "It's fitting in a way, between us. Such intimates, linked by death." He smiled. "The truth is—not that you'll believe me—the truth is that Humaitá was a monster. Oh, yes. He was a perfectionist, a slave driver. With children even more than with adults. And, *Dios mio*, the arrogance of the man! Bennie found him intolerable. I didn't blame him. The old man wanted things from Bennie. So many things. From me as well. But I was clever. I took from Humaitá what I could. He drove me to exhaustion and on my knees I devoured the hints of power he dropped for me.

"Heitor—he couldn't take it. And Bennie—well, Bennie wanted none of it at all."

Croaker took them around the last bend toward the southern mouth of the waterway. Ahead lay the bay—and Snake Bight. "What are you saying? That at one time you and Heitor and Bennie all studied *Hetá I* with Humaitá?"

"Now you've got the picture." They were nearing the mouth of the waterway and Antonio stood. "The rigors caused Bennie to wash out early. They put Heitor under extreme pressure."

"And what did they do to you?"

Antonio shrugged. *"Quien sabe?"* Who knows? He was alert now, peering forward into the night filthy with rain and wind as Croaker swung the boat to the east, heading toward the scimitar edge of Snake Bight.

Now for the big question. "How did you and Heitor get recruited by Ross Darling?"

Antonio turned his head to glance in Croaker's direction. "That peon, *señor*? Let me tell you, my brother and I would not waste our time with Darling."

"If not Darling, then who? He's the director."

Now Antonio seemed interested. "Remember *Sero*? There really *is* a man code-named Sero."

"But it's not Bennie."

"Oh, like all of us, your dear Bennie eventually became involved with Dicktribe."

"He told me he mediated Barbacena's last meeting with the Feds."

Antonio said nothing.

"Who is Sero?" Croaker fairly shouted this question. "Goddamnit, I want an answer!"

Antonio cocked his head. "It's killing you, isn't it? The not knowing?"

Maybe Antonio had spent too long in the company of DICTRIB's rogue agents. He and his brother fit right into this new breed of men who plotted revolutions, not for political or ideological ends, but for economic gain. DICTRIB's plan to fund the Chiapas rebellion in Mexico in order to put their people into place was something Antonio and Heitor could savor. Croaker had to admire all over again how cleverly Darling had switched his black hat for a white one all to keep Croaker walking their side of the moral tightrope they'd set up for him.

Up ahead, in Snake Bight, lights could be dimly seen through the squally weather, evidence of another boat. Antonio stirred. "Now that Juan Garcia Barbacena has gone to his just reward, I will take his place," he went on. "As Sero planned. Except that Heitor was supposed to be with me. You see, Juan Garcia had passed over the line. The power Dicktribe had given him was for him like mainlining heroin. He was an addict for it. As a consequence, he'd become increasingly arrogant, abusive, contrary. He wanted only what was good for Juan Garcia. Then, late last year, we discovered that he'd begun to build his own power base quite apart from us. Fantasy had replaced reality. Gone from his mind entirely was the fact that he was owned body and soul by Dicktribe."

Judging by the space between the running lights, the boat looked to be sixty or so feet long. It could very well be Rafe's fleet catamaran.

An uncharacteristic agitation had come into Antonio's body. He seemed to be vibrating to the rhythm of his anticipation. In this way Croaker could judge the fever pitch of his desire for Humaitá's bones.

"At the beginning of this year, a meeting took place between Dicktribe and Barbacena," Antonio continued. "Barbacena walked out, unwilling to negotiate even the smallest point. He had his power base and he thought that made him invulnerable. Subsequently, a determination was made to terminate him. But how to do it? First, Heitor and I were contracted to take over the operation he was spearheading. Then the planning of his termination got under way in earnest. We wanted it done discreetly: that meant no direct intervention. We couldn't do it because by then we were too deeply involved with the Dicktribe operation. It was essential that there be no hint of Dicktribe's involvement. To do so would bring questions about what the bureau was doing in Latin America. We'd risk exposing the entire Mexican operation."

Antonio smiled sweetly. "We chose you, *señor*. You were the ideal choice. An ex-cop, you had a history of homicide, justifiable or not. When a man has killed, he has taken a life. Period. So you had the credentials, the ability. But best of all you had worked on and off for the ACTF. What could be better? You had the wherewithal to kill Barbacena, and afterward, we could use your part-time affiliation to put the blame on the ACTF."

Croaker was appalled. "But you knew you couldn't just sell me on a cold-blooded murder, even if Barbacena's half as cruel as everyone says he is. So you found out about Rachel. You poisoned her with ethylene glycol."

"*Un poco, señor.*"

"Just a little?" Croaker almost leaped at Antonio. With great effort he calmed himself down. "Then you hired Majeur to offer me the deal—Rachel's life for Barbacena's. It all came down to me. I was the perfect assassin for you. I had the credentials, the skills, and if I was caught, I had tenuous ties to the ACTF. Whatever happened, Dicktribe would be in the clear."

Antonio nodded. "All rather neat, don't you agree? And, as far as we were concerned, clean as a cat's whisker." He frowned. "Except you learned just a little bit more at every turn than we had anticipated."

"So Darling stepped in."

"He had no choice. You became insistent on contacting the ACTF. We couldn't allow that, could we?"

"And you began isolating me."

"We did our best." Antonio pursed his lips. "The less resources, the more difficulties. It is forever to your credit, *señor*, that you did not falter. Not even once. On the contrary. You somehow enticed Majeur into becoming your ally. That was something none of us had anticipated. *Madre de mentiras,* even Heitor was forced to admire your ingenuity."

Croaker didn't think much of the compliment. "In the end, it didn't matter. You had thought of everything, didn't you?" he said. "You even had a plan in place if I failed to kill Barbacena."

"That was Heitor's idea, I must admit. But then the urge to kill burned bright inside him."

"So bright it consumed him."

Antonio nodded. *"Pobre."* Poor one.

"One thing I still don't understand." Through the rain, the first outlines of the catamaran's monstrous pontoons became visible. "You knew once you were employed by Dicktribe they'd own you body and soul. As you said, they'd already done it with Barbacena. Why did you allow yourselves to be recruited?"

"As you have no doubt guessed, Heitor fought against it. In fact, he became somewhat embittered." Antonio shrugged. "But Heitor, he was always more comfortable in the jungle. He had no use for civilization. But I understood that times had changed. We had to move up or step aside for the Juan Garcia Barbacenas of the world, and this I would not tolerate." He smiled. "Besides, *señor*, I am smarter than all of them. Our organ harvesting was our insurance policy. As in Latin America, we supplied some of the most powerful people in your government. They came to rely on us for our unique service. If danger presented itself—if Darling ever got the unjudicious idea to terminate us—they would put pressure on him that surely would alter Dicktribe's outlook."

Joe Kemp Key was a dark and misshapen lump passing along their port side. They crossed Snake Bight Channel, where the water was briefly as deep as a man was tall. Then they were into the bight proper where the depth was only a couple of feet. Despite its mammoth size, Rafe's cat was perfect for sailing here, Croaker realized. It had almost no draft.

The catamaran loomed out of the darkness like a sea monster. Croaker could see that the running lights on the landward side had been turned off. "What's going to happen once we get on board?" he asked.

Antonio leveled the muzzle of the Mack-10. "Hasn't the great detective figured it out yet? No? You are not going on board, *señor.* There is simply no need. You have served your purpose."

"It seems to me, Antonio, that for you at least I've served many purposes."

"Really, *señor?*"

Croaker was slowing the boat. The closer he came to Rafe's cat, the nearer he was to his own death. "The one I can't figure out is confessor. Why tell me about Rosa? Even Heitor was surprised at that."

Antonio jerked the barrel of the Mack-10. *"Andale, señor.* Don't dawdle now. Not when I am so close to the bones." He inhaled deeply. "*Ay,* I can smell them. Even from this distance."

"Yeah? What do they smell like?"

Antonio's eyes opened wide. The pupils were dilated. "Power, *señor.* More than you could ever imagine. All of Humaitá's secrets— the ones he never taught me or anyone—there, just waiting for me to suck them out like marrow."

"Rosa," Croaker prompted. "You were going to tell me—"

"Was I? No, no, *señor.*" He waggled the Mack-10. "Only on the point of my death."

There came a hail from aboard Rafe's cat, and Antonio turned. The curve of his long jaw was dimly outlined by the running lights. In that instant of inattention, Croaker left the wheel and leapt across the deck. Perhaps Antonio had been expecting such a move or per- haps he'd seen the blur of movement out of the corner of his eye. It did not matter.

He pulled the trigger and a spray of bullets arced into the rain. Their bright sparks followed Croaker's shallow dive overboard. Stone Tree had showed him how to move in water that was often so shallow it only came up to your shins. Croaker sped forward, not down. Still, his chest scraped against the muddy bottom as he made for the cat.

He was all too aware that this was Jenny's vision come to sick- ening life. He was facedown in shallow water in mortal fear of his life.

Bullets peppered the water as he made it to the edge of the closest pontoon. It loomed huge as a dirigible on the surface of the water. He edged his way along until he found a handhold, then he climbed over the pontoon, losing himself in the shadows beneath the cat.

For what seemed a long time after that nothing happened. Then he heard the deep roar of the cat's Chevies. As the huge boat picked up speed, he began to slip backward along the slick top. Blown like a leaf in a windstorm he almost fell, caught himself, then slid back- ward at an appalling rate.

In desperation he reached out, hooked his arm around a strut. For a long, painful moment he swung out over the water. Then he scrambled back onto the pontoon.

The cat was gaining speed. At this rate, he'd never stay on. Croaker looked all around him. There was nothing but the strut to hold on to and, given his overall state of fatigue and the injury to his shoulder, he couldn't maintain his grip for much longer. But he had to. In his mind's eye he could see Antonio confronting Rafe. How much damage would Antonio inflict on the restaurateur unless

Croaker could intervene? He remembered Sonia, Vonda, Estrella and Pablo Leyes, Majeur. All victims of the Bonitas. He couldn't let the same thing happen to Rafe. But how to get into the house?

Then he remembered something. He glanced upward. Near the rear of the cat's house he saw the dark, circular rim. It was the outside of the cover he'd noticed when he'd been in the head earlier that afternoon.

It was a myth that catamarans couldn't capsize. They could— and did—under certain adverse conditions. When they did, they wouldn't sink. But you would be trapped inside the house with no way out. Rafe had provided for that possibility. He'd had an escape hatch built into the floor. That way, if the cat ever turned over, he'd just pop that hatch and crawl to safety.

Croaker began to inch up the strut. Rafe's prudence might just provide for Croaker's own escape. At the base of the cat's super-structure, he wrapped his legs around the strut and transferred his handhold to one of the aluminum bars that ran beneath the house. He took a deep breath and let go with his legs.

For a moment he swung beneath the house. Below him, the pon-toons skimmed across black water ruffled by the driving wind. If he fell now, chances were he'd be crushed. He reached up, hooked his left arm around the bar, edging farther along toward the center of the house. In this way, he moved with agonizing slowness, trans-ferring his weight from the crook of one arm to the other. Each time he put pressure on his left shoulder, his teeth ground together with the pain that lanced through him. He felt a heat, then a burn-ing beneath the makeshift bark bandage. He was bleeding again, not a good sign. He didn't yet feel weakened, but that was a false reading that could only end in disaster. The massive amounts of adrenaline his system must be pumping out would mask any such debility until it was too late. He'd need to make a rush at Antonio and he'd be too slow or the energy wouldn't be there at all, and Antonio would cut him down without serious effort or thought.

His teeth began to chatter as the cat, picking up ever more speed, began to hit real waves. He peered out from underneath the house. They had been motoring southeast and had now hit the open, deeper water of Whipray Basin. Dead ahead lay the small chain of the Buttonwood Keys.

Croaker reached the center of the house and looked up. He saw the rubber seal around the hatch, a black halo that seemed to beckon him. Holding on to the aluminum bar with his left arm he reached up. Rain and wind took his breath away. Once, he had to close his eyes momentarily as vertigo swept over him.

He felt around in the darkness, but all he encountered was a smooth fiberglass surface. Where was the mechanism that opened the hatch? Perhaps there was none on this side. He hung his head. If the hatch had no egress from outside he was doomed.

He took several deep breaths and tried again. Still nothing. Then, on the third try his fingertips discovered a seam. He hadn't felt it before because of the heavy chattering of the boat over the waves. His hopes rose.

Digging his fingernails into the seam, he tried to pry it up. He screamed into the wind at the intense pain that lanced through his left shoulder.

With a pop half-muffled by the wind the fiberglass panel came off. Inside, was a shallow well within which was housed a small wheel. Croaker allowed himself an instant's elation as he turned the wheel to the left. When it couldn't go anymore, he lifted the hatch up and, using his elbows, scrambled through.

Inside the head, he propped himself against a bulkhead and shivered. He took the rag rug and wrapped it around himself. He could smell his own blood, feel it warm and sticky running down his side. He wanted to put his head back and go to sleep.

With a start, he roused himself. Panic gripped him. He'd almost passed out. He shucked the rug off his shoulders as he rose. He noted that he was a bit unsteady as he reached for the door. Also, waves of blackness kept lapping at his consciousness. To keep himself awake he began to count backward by the hour to the last time he'd slept.

Mistake.

He started again, finding himself leaning against the door, his head lolling. He slapped himself, hard. Then he turned the knob and slowly and silently opened the door.

No one was in Rafe's stateroom, but through the half-open door he could hear voices drifting in from the main salon. Had to be Rafe and Antonio; the crewmen were all surely on deck manning the cat in this rough weather.

As he crossed Rafe's stateroom, the inflections of the voices came more clearly to him. Yes. Rafe and Antonio were talking in the main salon. From behind the door he could see the two of them. They were at the front of the salon. Limned by the golden teardrops from a single lamp and the galley lights they appeared like figures projected on a screen—both larger than life and unreal in their two-dimensionality. Rafe was on the galley side of the counter, Antonio on the salon side. The half-bulkhead was symbolic of their conversation. Of course, it had to do with Humaitá's bones. From what

Croaker could make out, Rafe had them, all right, but what the hell was he going to do, just hand them over to Antonio?

Antonio was telling Rafe that he had no choice as Croaker stole into the deep shadows at the rear of the salon. He opened a long vertical cabinet inset into the port bulkhead. Inside was stored the scuba gear. Croaker got out a shortie, a neoprene wet suit with short sleeves and legs that came to midthigh. He pulled it on inside Rafe's stateroom. In lieu of a proper tourniquet, the close-fitting neoprene would help stanch the flow of blood from his shoulder wound.

Back at the cabinet, he pushed aside other suits and took out a serrated-blade dagger in its sheath attached to a belt. He strapped this on, using his stump to hold the buckle tight against his belly. Then he removed a speargun from its hook. He slid a bolt into the slot, cocked the action.

By this time the animated conversation between Antonio and Rafe had become acrimonious. Threats were flying back and forth like a hail of needles. As much as Croaker admired Rafe's forceful personality, he was no match for Antonio. Besides, Croaker was determined that no one else would get hurt.

"Give them here." Antonio beckoned with the fingers of one hand as Croaker double-checked the action on the speargun.

"*Escuchame, señor*," Rafe replied, "as I have told you, the bones are a nonnegotiable point. Period."

"Fuck negotiation," Antonio said. "This goes beyond negotiation."

"You don't have your automatic weapon now, *señor*." Rafe spread his hands wide. "You see why I could not let you on board with it?"

"Power, power." Antonio was apparently holding himself in check by an extreme force of will. Or perhaps he was just waiting for the right moment to strike. "Who's got the power?"

"I do, apparently," Rafe said as a wave rattled the glasses and bottles on their shelves. "The bones are power. Don't be dense. It's power I'll never let you have. No need to elaborate further, *verdad?*" He appeared not in the least bit intimidated. But then he didn't know Antonio Bonita. "That should be sufficient warning."

Rafe had overstepped his advantage. As Croaker knew, men like Antonio and Heitor did not react well to verbal warnings.

Antonio was all but climbing over the counter in his zeal to get at Rafe. Croaker had seen that feverish look before in the eyes of hunt dogs that had treed the fox. A tiny *snik!* presaged Antonio's attack with his stiletto-bladed gravity knife.

The bolt Croaker fired from the speargun caught him in mid-lunge. It pierced his side with such force it passed clear through him, embedding itself in the bulkhead behind him. Antonio was flung backward to the foot of the doorway.

"What the hell—!" Rafe, with a stunned expression on his face, watched Croaker emerge from the shadows. *"Compadre, que pasa?* Where did you come from?"

Something was up because the catamaran had abruptly changed course. It was coming about. "Stay away from this bastard," Croaker warned, pointing to Antonio. As he hurried across the salon he bumped into ends of furniture. Was that because the boat was lifting and falling in the swells or because he was close to passing out? "He's still as dangerous as a scorpion's tail."

"Jesus Christ, *compadre.* Don't—"

Croaker lurched away from Rafe's grab because Antonio had pulled himself upright and had jerked the door open. The hoarse voice of the storm invaded the salon. Rain struck their faces in quick spits. Nevertheless, Antonio, with one hand pressed to his side, swung out onto the foredeck.

"Por favor, leave him," Rafe urged.

But Croaker was past hearing. Out on the deck the wind had changed. He could see that the storm had abruptly shifted. It was sheering off to the east, forcing the cat to motor south out of Whip-ray Basin. They were now making directly for the bight.

Behind him, he could see Rafe's tall frame silhouetted by the light streaming from inside the house. Then, Rafe followed him onto the deck.

Antonio was heading aft, around the side of the house. Croaker wondered if he wanted to take control of the cat, but he could already see Antonio climbing across the webbing that spanned the aft space between the pontoons. What was he after? He couldn't be making for one of the wheels. Even if he overpowered the crewman, there was a second wheelman on the other pontoon. The cat could not be driven by one man.

Then Croaker saw the dark shape bucking between the cat's twin wakes. They were towing the boat Croaker and Antonio had used to get to Snake Bight. That was Antonio's immediate destination because that's where he'd left the Mack-10. Croaker knew he couldn't allow Antonio to get it.

Out on the webbing, Croaker was almost blown overboard. He had only one hand to hang on with, and his shoes kept slipping on the wet nylon. He kicked them off. Because he wasn't wearing socks he could dig in with his bare toes.

The wind was lowering as the storm continued to sheer off to the east. It soughed through the cat, twanging rigging bound fast to mast and deck pins. One or two first magnitude stars played peek-a-boo with fast-scudding clouds. The rain had ceased altogether.

"Antonio!" Croaker cried. "Antonio!"

Antonio paused, then turned. He was on all fours, bouncing as he clung to the webbing. Periodically, waves slapped upward, drenching both of them.

A smile wreathed his face. *"Hola, señor!* We have come to our inevitable conclusion." Staring into Croaker's eyes, he took out a dark stone. He held it on the tip of his tongue for a long moment. Maybe he was deciding whether or not to take this final step; but most likely he wanted Croaker to understand the import of what he was about to do.

He swallowed.

"Now it comes!" His shout was so strong that Croaker could hear him clearly over the soughing wind. "Power that burns brighter than a sun!"

Croaker began to scramble aft, but a firm hand on his arm stopped him.

"Rafe! Let go!"

"Not yet, *compadre.*" Rafe's hard gaze locked onto his. "From now on, this is a joint venture. *Comprende?*"

"Rafe, you don't get it—"

"No one threatens me, *compadre. No one.*"

As they watched, Antonio ran crab-wise to the edge of the webbing, then somersaulted over the edge. But he did not fall. Instead, he dropped into the water, striking out in a path parallel to the line that ran between the cat and the trailing boat, which rocked in the cat's churning wake.

"There's a better way," Rafe said in Croaker's ear. He lifted an arm and the crew manning the cat's wheels responded. The cat came about. Behind it, the smaller boat began to curve in an arc away from Antonio.

Now Rafe scrambled aft with Croaker following him onto the starboard pontoon. He grabbed a small electronic winch and began to draw in the line attached to the small boat.

"Here," he said, ceding the controls to Croaker as the boat approached. He climbed to the edge of the webbing, then flipped off it into the smaller boat. Croaker stopped the winch.

Overhead, stars blazed hard as grit. Croaker clambered to the edge of the webbing.

"Compadre!" Rafe lifted one arm in a gesture of victory. Moonlight glinted off articulated metal surfaces. *"Mira!* Look what I found!"

He was holding Croaker's biomechanical hand.

Croaker flipped onto the smaller boat, headed toward him.

Rafe was grinning. "Hey, *compadre,* what did the Buddhist say to the hot dog vendor? Make me one with everything."

"That's quite a joke, Rafe. The only problem is Buddhists don't eat meat."

Rafe frowned. "I didn't think of that. Maybe it should be a *vegetarian* hot dog vendor."

"Not funny."

"Neither is this." Rafe had dropped Croaker's biomechanical hand at his feet. Now he was holding Antonio's Mack-10. "This is some mean mother weapon, eh?" He eyed it curiously. "You would have more experience with something like this than I would." He turned it back and forth in his hand. "Tell me, how many rounds per minute does it shoot?"

"Later." Croaker stopped four paces from Rafe. "Let me have my hand."

"I don't think so." Rafe leveled the muzzle of the Mack-10 at Croaker's head. *"Compadre,* do you realize that if I pull the trigger now there'll be nothing left of your head?"

The short hairs at the base of Croaker's neck stirred. "Do me a favor," he said. "Aim some other place, would you?"

"I think not." Rafe put one foot up on the gunwale as he gazed at Croaker. "Please remove your belt. You're much too dangerous a man. I want to know that you're quite unarmed."

"Christ, Rafe—"

"Do as I fucking say, *compadre."*

Oh, Christ!

All of a sudden, the bottom seemed to fall out of the world.

As he numbly complied with Rafe's barked order, Croaker was possessed with the suprareal clarity of senses that comes with profound revelation. In this moment of insight the last puzzling pieces of the enigma he'd penetrated fell into place at last.

The whole picture stunned him into momentary immobility.

As he stared at Rafe, he was acutely aware of his surroundings: the bottom of the boat, his biomechanical hand lying quiescent at Rafe's feet, the water lapping, the nearby cat, the full moon appearing like a gemstone in the furred darkness of the storm's aftermath.

Rafe was grinning. "What is it, *compadre?* You look as if you'd seen a ghost."

In a way, Rafe was right. At long last Croaker was seeing the ghost in the DICTRIB machine. It wasn't Bennie; it wasn't Antonio; and it certainly wasn't Ross Darling.

Croaker felt a fierce wave of rage take hold of him. Trying to keep his voice from cracking, he said, "Here's the thing, Rafe. Something has been bothering me. The Bonitas put a homing device on the Mustang—that's how they tracked me down here. But before that, when I was driving my own T-bird, how did Antonio know I'd be at Sonia's? I wondered about that for some time."

Rafe shrugged. "A small thing. So small it means nothing."

"On its own, I might have forgotten about it," Croaker admitted. He lifted his left arm. "But then Antonio took my biomechanical hand. He couldn't resist. But he didn't chop it off. He unlocked it while I was unconscious. How do you suppose he did that, Rafe? No way for him to have known the combination—and yet he did."

Rafe stood in the rocking boat, silent.

The rage was like a living thing, beating with its own heart inside Croaker's chest. "Of course you do. You were there when I unlocked it. Yesterday afternoon on the cat. You were so close you could have seen me work the combination if you'd wanted to. And as for Antonio knowing I'd be at Sonia's, there was only one way for him to have found out: you told him. You asked me where I was going that day. I told *you* I'd be there."

"So what?"

Rafe's expression was so bland it made Croaker grind his teeth. "So this. Who were the Bonitas reporting to at Dicktribe? Darling? Despite all his experience, he's an ex-grunt. And even if they're as ambitious as Darling seems to be, all ex-grunts get to be is middle management. If they're as lucky as he was. So Darling has a boss. Who is it?"

Rafe grinned almost distractedly. "Sero."

The rage was consuming Croaker. It was like a beast shaking itself free of all restraints. Croaker recognized this beast. It had raised its head when he'd shot the psycho killer Ajucar Martinez; when he'd killed Don Rodrigo, the man who'd ordered his father murdered. Because these men were like Rafe. They had violated every moral code Croaker held dear.

"You told me you didn't know the Bonitas but that was a lie," Croaker managed to get out. "Jesus Christ, Rafe, how many lies did you tell me? You were a friend of mine. I confided in you. I trusted you. And all the while you were fucking me over the way you fucked Bennie out of his grandfather's bones. How the hell can you live your life like that? What kind of bastard are you?"

"The cleverest bastard I know." Rafe seemed to be enjoying this.

Croaker took a deep breath. The enormity of Rafe's betrayal was so painful it threatened to bury him. *"You* were running the Bonitas. The Mexican operation was *your* brainchild, Rafe. You conceived of it while you were in office. That's why you quit your day job. You would've won re-election hands down, but you refused. Now that decision makes sense. You already had another line of work. How long have you been working for the Feds?"

"Well before we set you up by having that wise guy 'threaten' me," Rafe said. "That Miami 'mobster' you ran down was a Dicktribe undercover agent. As a result, a bond was formed. You and I became friends. What could have been simpler? Or more effective?" He shrugged. "But I'm sure that's not what you meant. As director of Dicktribe I've carved out my own empire. I'm as secure as the bullion inside Fort Knox. The Washington bureaucracy is so enormous it's easy as shit to get yourself lost inside the machine. A few good friends, a number of power contacts, a handful of loyal people—hell, that's all you need. The power feeds on itself. You'd be surprised. It grows and compounds like interest. Until one day you find you're at the top of Everest. And let me tell you, *compadre,* that long look down on everyone and everything is one motherfucking rush."

"You engineered everything, didn't you?" Croaker felt chilled to his marrow. He was shaking with anger. This man who had masqueraded as his friend was a reptile, a cold-blooded mastermind without conscience. A consummate actor, he had fooled even Croaker, who was used to prying up public personas to see what lay underneath. "The moment you determined that Barbacena had to be terminated you came up with the scheme to extort me into doing your dirty work. So your hands would be clean. You ordered Rachel poisoned. Christ almighty, how could you do that to an innocent girl?"

"What you really mean is how could you have so misjudged me?" Rafe was unremorseful; in fact, he appeared contemptuous. "In politics as in life, *compadre,* expediency becomes its own principle. You can't see that, I know. You're a cripple in more ways than one."

Croaker felt the rage like a hot ball of wax in his throat. He wanted to gag, but he kept his cool. He had to. He knew the longer he kept Rafe talking the better chance he'd have of figuring out how to get to him. "How did you come by Humaitá's bones?"

"That was the simplest part," Rafe said. "Thefts of that nature happen all the time. Desperate people will sell anything to stay alive. But because of Humaitá's notoriety these needed special care. They were hidden for some years, then smuggled into Miami along with a boatload of coke. That's where I heard about their existence."

"You paid for them?"

Rafe laughed. "No way, *compadre*. One of the benefits of being the mayor. I had the police engineer a raid. The cops found their drugs and I had what I wanted."

Croaker saw the tension come into Rafe's gun hand and he prayed. As he prayed he imagined his biomechanical hand was still attached and contracted the tendons at the end of his severed wrist.

At Rafe's feet, the biomechanical hand jumped as if struck by lightning. Rafe, already on edge, the adrenaline pumping through him, started as he stared down at the inanimate thing that had suddenly, shockingly, moved.

Croaker strode forward and struck him flush on the nose with his right fist. Rafe arched backward, the Mack-10 flying across the deck as a ropy spurt of his own blood arced through the moonlit night.

Croaker kicked Rafe in the ribs and Rafe groaned. Rafe rolled, smashed his fist into the side of Croaker's knee. Croaker went down and Rafe delivered a tremendous two-handed blow to his temple. Croaker fell back against the gunwale.

Rafe, panting like a laboring engine, crawled toward the Mack-10.

Croaker shook his head to clear it. He reached out, picked his biomechanical hand out of the river of blood at the bottom of the boat, and reattached it. Rafe's fingers closed around the machine-pistol's trigger, and with a grimace of pain, he swung it up toward Croaker.

Croaker's biomechanical fingers clenched into a fist. A fireball had coalesced in his chest. The titanium, polycarbonate, and stainless-steel hand crashed down like the hammer of God. It smashed the Mack-10 out of Rafe's grasp and over the side of the boat. It slammed into Rafe's sternum so that the splintered bone pierced his heart.

Croaker stared into Rafe's pale face while the night buzzed on around him. He slipped to his knees in pain and fatigue. But, after so long in the treacherously shifting sands of Rafe's scheming, his heart felt light and free.

"Goddamnit, *compadre*," he whispered to the dead man. "You fucked with the wrong man."

"*Bravo, señor!*" Antonio called from the aft of the catamaran. "*Que macho, eh!*" He stood, grinning, balancing himself against the swells.

"Now there is only the two of us." He shrugged. "What more could I ask for?" His face suddenly fell. "Unless your prior exertions have left you lifeless. In that event the game is over. I have already won!"

Croaker knew he should ignore Antonio's mocking; that at this final stage he should take the time to think things through. But he couldn't. The response was of one animal for another. He had no choice. He gathered himself and went after Antonio.

He clasped the line connecting the two boats, swinging his legs up and crossing his ankles to hold on. Hand over hand, he inched upward. Below, the water rose up to meet him like an angered friend, slapping his back repeatedly. Once it submerged him entirely.

High overhead in the expanding sky more stars appeared as the storm clouds tumbled away to the east. It was dark as sin there, but here at the southern edge of Whipray Bay the full moon peered down at him with a pearly grace. Its reflection, repeated on each wave, etched a phosphorescent trail that seemed to go on forever.

Croaker could see that Antonio was crouched down on the edge of the webbing. He was laughing as he drew his gravity knife and sawed through the line, severing the small boat from the catamaran.

Croaker plunged into the water. A heartbeat later Antonio followed him.

Moonlight turned the water eerily pellucid. Ghostly fingers penetrated the shallows, turning human skin white as bleached bones.

And it was in these shallows that Antonio caught up with Croaker. The water was barely five feet, and Antonio jerked him upward. The two armed men faced each other, Antonio with his gravity knife, Croaker with his biomechanical hand.

Antonio smiled almost benignly. His arms opened wide and he dropped the gravity knife into the water. "If only we were evenly matched, *señor*. But now that I've swallowed the dark stone it will be a poor showing." He waded toward Croaker. "Perhaps on reflection it is better this way. It will be over quickly. I have much work remaining undone."

With each step Antonio took, Croaker could see blood, dark as pitch in the moonlight, leaking from his side. It spread out in the water like the diaphanous veils of a dancer's costume.

Croaker backed away. "You aren't going to kill me like this, Antonio. Not now. Not yet. There's something you want from me."

"I don't think so, *señor*." Antonio reached out and closed his hand around the extruded nails of Croaker's biomechanical hand. Blood continued to leak from the wound in his side but none spurted from his fingers.

"Don't bother denying it." Croaker could see that the small boat was drifting away from them. In the periphery of his vision he saw Rafe's cat maneuvering to come alongside it. "From the beginning you said we were friends. That wasn't true. Never. But there was *something*. A connection."

Antonio's fingers crept along the ridges of the stainless-steel nails. They were very close to Croaker's flesh-and-blood wrist. What would happen when they touched him? "What kind of connection could there be, *señor* detective?"

That familiar derision had crept into Antonio's voice. Croaker knew he was onto something. But he also knew he'd better get to it before Antonio touched him. In truth, he did not know whether he believed in the spirit-stone's ultimate *sukia* transformation, but he had already seen some of its power. At this time, in this place, he was not inclined to take the chance that the rest was pure fantasy.

Croaker wanted to tug his hand away, but something he could neither explain nor understand stopped him. "You yourself said there was a connection. Between Sonia and Rosa. Now I think there's something more."

Antonio would not let go. "The feeling is inescapable, *señor*."

Through the chill of the storm's aftermath Croaker felt the heat emanating from Antonio's hand. It crawled up Croaker's flesh-and-blood forearm just as Antonio's fingers were crawling over the back of Croaker's titanium and polycarbonate hand.

"So it was all true," Antonio whispered. "Just as Heitor dreamed it."

The heat felt as if it were burning Croaker's flesh. "What did Heitor dream?"

"That Humaitá was returning on the wheel of the sun and the moon. That he had touched the spirit of someone living . . . someone we knew. So he could sow the seeds of his revenge."

Croaker felt an involuntary shiver of recognition shoot through him.

"Something I think you should know." The moonlight picked out each aristocratic feature of Antonio's face, accenting the bone structure so that it seemed possible to recognize other people there—ancestors perhaps powerful in their own day, but long buried. "The answer to your question, *señor*. I could have prevented Rosa's death. But I would have had to kill Heitor."

"What?" Croaker shook his head. "I don't understand."

"Humaitá's *Hetá I* training was too much for Bennie. Forever after, he resented his grandfather. If you ask him he will deny it. Of course. This is Bennie. But, believe me, it is the truth." Antonio's grip on Croaker's hand never relaxed. "In this way his life was changed. But so was Heitor's. The training brought out something sinister in him. Heitor had multiple personalities. One of them was homicidal. It—and the others—existed uneasily inside him. Submerged like lead in water. Until the *Hetá I* training.

"The drugs, the fasting, the near-death experiences, leached the other personalities to the surface. And there they remained, damning Heitor to a kind of hell you and I can never imagine."

The Bonitas. The truth about them was even more horrific than the legend they had created. Antonio had hidden the fact of his twin's personality disorder from everyone—perhaps even from Heitor himself. He'd done his best to try to protect Heitor. But when the killing madness arose and Heitor slipped his leash, Antonio was forced to protect him.

"I could not stop him from killing Rosa," Antonio said as if in a trance of remembrance. "Or Juan Garcia Barbacena. But there was your *guapa*—your woman. He would have killed her too."

In his mind's eye, Croaker could vividly see Antonio pulling Heitor's hands away from Jenny's neck. How could he feel profoundly grateful to this man? And yet, he did. For Antonio, this overwhelming devotion to his twin had had the most profound price: it had meant the death of Bennie's sister Rosa, perhaps the only person who could have saved him, the only person he'd ever loved. And, perhaps worst of all, Antonio had had to become an accomplice after the fact, covering up the evidence of Heitor's crime.

Croaker had no more time to consider the irony of this because his attention was caught by a familiar movement in the water. An unnameable chill swept over him. He watched the certain purling in the wave trough behind Antonio, farther out in Whipray Basin. It was heading directly toward them. His blood ran cold, and for a moment, he forgot all about the Bonitas. He'd seen that signature water movement many times before. He knew they were not alone in the bay.

"*Señor, que pasa?*"

Croaker glanced at the blood spilling into the water from Antonio's side. Under the moonlight glare he followed it outward as the current took it farther into the bay. *Oh Christ*, he thought.

"Antonio, let go of my hand."

"Never, *señor*."

"Then we're both going to die." He ignored Antonio's disbelieving smirk. "There's a very large predator shark coming our way."

"What else would you have me believe, *señor?*" He laughed. "This water is too shallow for sharks."

"Normally, yes," Croaker said. He could see the dorsal fin, the rough crown of the back. It was very long. *Jesus God*, he thought. *How the hell big is it?* "But storms like this one disturb shark hunting patterns. Then there's the ton of blood leaking from your side. Combined with our thrashing the shark's got its own picture of what's going on here. It thinks we're prey in its death throes. Once it gets hold of us it'll make that mistake a reality."

Antonio took a quick glance down, clapped his free hand over the wound.

"Too late," Croaker said. "Now let go." He looked into Antonio's amber eyes. "Both boats are too far away. Swimming will only create more thrashing. My hand is our only chance."

Antonio turned slowly. The beast was almost upon them.

"*Madre de mentiras!*" He let go of Croaker's hand.

As they sank down into the water Antonio said, "This shark is enormous, *señor*. That damned hand of yours won't save us. But I have swallowed the world. *Todo el mundo, comprende?*"

Under the water, the world was striped pearl and black. Moonlight glowed in the depths, reminding Croaker of what Stone Tree had said: *This world is a lie. Beyond it, the truth pulses like light on the ocean floor.*

The shark swam into their view.

Here was their truth. It was a monster. Croaker estimated it must be over a thousand pounds. It had caught the scent of blood all right, and it was nosing forward, accelerating as the blood became fresher.

As it passed through a patch of water-filtered moonlight Croaker saw that it was a tiger shark, in size the twin of the one he and Bennie had encountered five days ago. Something passed through him, a kind of shiver like a lightning strike. A tingling began at the base of his neck, spreading upward into his scalp.

He is here. Inside you, Stone Tree had said, speaking of Humaitá. *Tonight you also walk with the spirits.*

The tiger shark was so close, so huge, it became their world. Sharks were almost all cartilage, one of the reasons they were so difficult to kill. But if you were lucky enough to slit open their belly before they hit, you might be okay. Unfortunately, that was almost an impossibility.

Instead, Croaker smashed the heel of his biomechanical hand against the beast's snout. That should have discouraged it. This shark, however, was different. It shook its body from side to side, veered away from Croaker, and headed directly toward Antonio.

Antonio stood his ground. In an eerie way, he seemed to be eager for this encounter. Perhaps it was only to demonstrate the power of his transformation. But Croaker did not think so. How could he be sure? But it seemed as if Antonio saw in this tiger shark exactly what Croaker did.

So Antonio remained motionless as the living missile came on. He extended his left arm like a healer about to bless a maimed pilgrim, certain that one touch would extinguish its life. The tiger shark's jaws opened, and it was as if the moon had gone into eclipse.

There were few things in the world as terrifying as seeing the triple set of teeth coming head-on. Nevertheless, Antonio did not flinch. No fear showed on his face as the jaws clashed shut, snapping off his arm from fingertips to shoulder.

Croaker, on his knees on the bay bottom, lanced upward with the tips of his stainless-steel fingernails at the perfect angle. He used the beast's own forward momentum, holding firm as the bladelike projections pierced the shark's underside. The razor-sharp nails split open the belly as the beast shot past Antonio. A swirl of blood and entrails muddied the water, and at last Croaker, at the end of his endurance, was pulled off his feet. He jerked the nails free. The shark turned, but with its insides spilling out, it was canted over, drifting in an erratic pattern.

Antonio was floating on the water when Croaker reached him. His amber eyes were half-glazed over in shock. Blood pumped in heavy gouts from where his left arm had been. There was nothing at all Croaker could do for him.

"Antonio."

The lean, predatory head turned. Handsome as a god in the pale moonlight, he smiled as he looked down at his limbless left side. "Now, truly, we are the same, *señor*."

"You're mistaken, Antonio. We're nothing alike."

"No, no. Don't you see? I never lied to you. Because the first time I met you I saw all the way down to your soul. I recognized a man as cut off from his past as I was. Strangers in a strange present, *señor*."

Croaker held him closer, feeling the life spilling out of him with every beat of his heart. The amber eyes stared up at Croaker with the full knowledge of what was to come.

Antonio shivered. "*Señor*, I believe now I was damned in my mother's womb. I embraced evil with full knowledge. But always I tried to save Heitor from himself. My penance for both deeds is forever carrying Rosa's memory in my heart."

Antonio loved Rosa, it was true, Croaker thought. The enormity of the tragedy struck him. Antonio could have been saved by her if only he knew what love was.

Antonio gasped suddenly, and his good hand gripped Croaker's with a fierce strength.

"It feels good to have her there now, doesn't it," Croaker said.

"Yes. I feel calm now," he whispered.

Here, at last, was the end of Antonio's search. Ever since Rosa's death he had been seeking the meaning of his feelings for her. He had connected with her the way a shadow falls across a garden and is gone. He'd been a ghost in her life, nothing more. It was all he'd been capable of. But, afterward, he'd found that she had touched him in a profound way. He longed for that human connection again, in whatever form it might come to him.

The first time I met you I saw all the way down to your soul.

This is the way Rosa had changed Antonio: In severing *mokoi*—his lifeline to Heitor—she had shattered the hermetic seal within which the twins had existed. In consequence, an entire world full of possibilities had flooded in. Unprepared as he was to absorb those possibilities, Antonio had nevertheless been left with her imprint. Rosa had shown him that with time's fleeting passage even the most improbable of human connections was to be cherished. Antonio had told his terrible secret—his and Heitor's secret—to just one person: Croaker. The only one he knew would understand. The only one he felt something for. Croaker felt shaken to his core.

Waves lapped at them, and in the distance, he could hear the cat's mammoth engines rumbling as it slowly brought the smaller boat back to the area where they stood.

A wave of convulsions racked Antonio. He had very little time left, but it didn't matter. There was nothing left to say.

Then Croaker was staring into Antonio's dead eyes.

Antonio's corpse rocked on the waves, floating facedown in the shallow water in its pool of blood. Croaker, remembering Jenny's spirit-stone-induced vision, let him go. He dove back under the water. It seemed important now to retrieve Antonio's gravity knife. As if allowing any trace of him to remain here was a sin.

He recalled Stone Tree telling him that it wasn't death that awaited him in the backcountry; it was something else. Now he knew. Improbably, there were gifts that Antonio and Croaker were destined to bestow upon each other. He had shown Antonio that he could be loved. And what, in return, had Antonio given him?

Antonio had loved his brother unconditionally. That was what it meant to have family. For Croaker, that had been a hard lesson to learn.

A movement out of the corner of his eye made him turn his head. He saw the shark. It was still swimming. Slowly, but less erratically than it had before. It was a miracle that it was still alive. What could be left inside it but its breathing apparatus? But that was its nature. Until the moment of death it needed to move forward so water could flow through its gills.

Keeping one eye on it Croaker searched the moonlit bottom for the gravity knife. He spotted it in a rippled lozenge of moonlight. It lay on the bottom, propped against a rock from which tendrils of seaweed curled like oily smoke. He was obliged to swim closer to the mortally wounded shark in order to get it. This he did as slowly as he could. He held his stainless-steel nails at the ready, though how else he could wound the beast he was at a loss to say.

The shark sensed him. It came forward. Croaker tensed. On it came, through darkness and moonlight. When it was very near him it paused. Then, with a weak flick of its tail, it sheered away from him.

As it turned Croaker caught a glimpse of one eye. A shock ran through him and he felt numbed to his marrow. Maybe he was nuts, but it seemed to him as if that round eye had two pupils.

EPILOGUE

On a sultry, cloudless afternoon six weeks later, Croaker completed his final check of the *Captain Sumo* as it lay tied up at his marina in Islamorada. He was not alone. On board were Bennie, Matty, Jenny, and Rachel. They were all together to celebrate Rachel's first full day out of the house. She'd been home for almost two weeks and had begun to drive Matty crazy because she was itching to get up and around.

By that time DICTRIB was just a memory. Ross Darling, the last remaining operative of rank, had been captured in a sting Croaker had dreamed up. It was based on simple necessity. Darling needed to debrief Croaker to find out what had happened to Antonio and Heitor. Without piecing together the cause of their deaths he could never consolidate his power within the agency.

Croaker had no way of contacting Darling, but that was okay because he knew Darling would come after him at the first possible opportunity. This had happened on a storm-charged afternoon a week after Croaker and Bennie emerged from the Everglades. They had been drinking espressos at the Boneyard, Antonio and Heitor's club on Lincoln Road in SoBe. He'd wanted to see it, Croaker had told Bennie, because it was where Rachel had collapsed. But, inside, he felt oddly nostalgic, as if he was somehow closer to Antonio.

Darling's men had picked them up there and, by black Lincoln, had deposited them in the future car park below a concrete and steel skeleton of a hotel on Collins Avenue. There, they rendezvoused with Ross Darling. It had taken the ACTF, who had been carefully monitoring their movements, five minutes to secure the car park and take Darling and his agents into custody.

That was when Croaker had met Spaulding Gunn, the director of the ACTF, for the first time. He was a man of modest stature.

346

Gray-haired and balding, with steel-rimmed spectacles and a neatly groomed beard, he looked like nothing more than a college professor. But when he spoke that image immediately vanished: *"By God,"* he'd said to Croaker, *"it's good to finally shake your hand."*

As Croaker worked on the boat, he kept one eye on the dock.

"Lew," Matty called, "when are we getting under way?"

Croaker saw she was helping Bennie stow the food for lunch. Rachel was at the other end of the boat. Mother and daughter hadn't said two words to each other since Rachel had decided to tell her about Gideon. "Soon as I finish here."

He turned as Jenny's arms slid around his waist. "What were you thinking just now?"

"Nothing."

"You looked so serious." She cocked her head skeptically. "Was it about Majeur? It was touch-and-go for a while, but he's responding well to rehab."

"Actually, I was thinking about my time in the service of the U.S. Government."

"C'mon, Lew." She hugged him. "No gloomy thoughts. This is supposed to be a coming out party for Rachel."

"Funny you should say that," he said, spotting a slim figure on the dock. Taking Jenny's hand, he led her to the dock side of the boat. "Someone I want you to meet."

Gideon came toward them in her hip-swaying walk. Her hair shone pale gold in the sun. She was wearing a pair of cut-off denim shorts, which she'd dyed black, and an oversize Buffalo Brand T-shirt whose sleeves she had snipped to the shoulders. She was barefoot, and she carried an acoustic guitar on her back, as if she'd hitchhiked down U.S. 1 from Miami.

She saw Croaker and waved. Her stack of beaten-copper and beadwork bracelets jangled happily.

"Hi!" She half ran to the boat. "Thanks for inviting me. That was sweet."

She was wearing Rēvo sunglasses. She took them off, displaying her cat's-eye contacts.

Croaker laughed. "Gideon, this is Jenny."

"Rachie's doctor, I know." Gideon stuck out her hand and Jenny took it. "Pleasure to meet you."

"The pleasure's all mine," Jenny said. "Rachie's told me a lot about you."

It seemed to Croaker almost as if Gideon blushed. As they brought her on board Rachel looked up. She stood. In her huge sunglasses, she looked as thin and pale as Kate Moss.

"How long has it been?" Croaker asked.

"Haven't even smoked pot in—what?—more than a month." Gideon's giving up drugs had been Croaker's one stipulation for her continuing to see Rachel.

"Are you doing okay?" Jenny asked.

Gideon laughed. "Don't look so concerned, doc. Amazing as it is to me, being clean as a cat's whisker has distinct advantages."

While Matty watched, stone-faced, Rachel melted into Gideon's arms. Gideon swung her around in what could only be termed gentle exuberance.

Matty walked over to Croaker, carefully avoiding the two girls. "I suppose this was your idea as well." Croaker had counseled his niece to come out to her mother.

"I thought you were fed up being shut out."

"I am, but *this*—"

"Matty, your daughter has her own life to live. The sooner you accept that, the sooner she'll let you into it."

Matty gestured. "But what kind of life is this? What can she expect from it?"

"Someone to love and cherish her. Right now, that seems to be a good deal more than you have."

Matty walked away, silent and thoughtful.

"What do you think she'll do?" Jenny asked.

He turned to her. "What would you do if Rachel were your daughter?"

Jenny hopped onto the dock and cast off the lines while he started the engine. He'd taken her out a number of times in the past month and found her a quick study. She loved to learn and was justly proud of her sea legs. She jumped on board and Croaker backed the *Captain Sumo* out of her berth.

"I'd want her to be happy," Jenny said as she joined Croaker at the wheel.

"So does Matty. Deep down that's all she's ever wanted." He maneuvered the boat around, took her at slow out of the marina.

Some time later, Matty came aft. Bennie was sitting in a captain's chair smoking a cigar as he chatted with Jenny. He must have been telling her some of his stories because she was laughing a lot. Rachel and Gideon were lying side by side on the bow, deep in conversation.

Matty stared at the two girls. "I don't think I can do it."

"If you can't, you can't."

She looked at him sharply. "That's an attitude I never expected from you."

"What's that?"

"Defeatist."

"Matty, what is it you want?"

"I want you to convince me this is right for Rachel."

He turned *Captain Sumo* to port, heading out to sea. "I can't do that."

"Why not?"

"That's not my job in life, Matty. Even as your brother."

Brilliant sunlight sent dazzling sparks across the wave tops. The breeze was fresh and strong. It made Croaker wish they were on Rafe's big cat with the engines off and the sails full out. It was a spinnaker kind of afternoon, when running before the wind could make you fly.

At last he said, "I can see a lot of self-hatred inside Rachel. You can, too. You're not blind. Maybe Gideon can get through to that walled-off place inside her, I don't know. But look what's happened to the two of you. Donald put the fear of God into you. You stopped talking to Rachel—"

"I talk to her all the time," Matty said defensively. "She simply doesn't want to listen."

"Then you keep trying."

Matty shook her head. "What if that doesn't work?"

"There are no guarantees in life," he said. "But I know this: if you don't talk to each other, you'll have nothing."

When they were far out at sea, Bennie served lunch. It was uncharacteristic of him to be so domestic, but he seemed to be enjoying himself so Croaker refrained from commenting.

During Croaker's first week at the NYPD precinct his commander had addressed the rookies. He'd said, *"You may come to hate your life here; I wouldn't be surprised if at times it angered you. You may even learn to like it. But one thing I can assure you. A year from now you won't be the same man or woman you are today. That's the best and only advice I can give you for what you're about to encounter. Remember it, embrace it, and you'll be okay. Guaranteed."*

It occurred to Croaker now that everyone on the *Captain Sumo* had changed, including himself. While the others talked, Croaker watched Rachel and Gideon. There was an animation to his niece's face that warmed him to the marrow. Perhaps coming out to her mother was part of it. There were enough secrets in the family without having to shoulder another one.

Croaker had spent some time with her. When he'd handed over her diary, mutely, she'd known that he had read it. In her eyes he could see that relief she could not bring herself to articulate. And when he'd said to her, *"This is between you and Matty,"* she'd nodded. *"You have to show her the entries,"* he'd said. *"You have to talk about it openly. There's no longer any room inside you to hold it in."*

That moment hadn't happened yet—it was too soon for both of them. But Croaker knew it would. Next week. Next month. Soon.

Watching her now in the brilliant sunlight, it seemed to him that she had for a long time dwelled in the dark and evil place known as isolation. Having begun to emerge, she had done more than just survive. He could see that transformations were not only for *sukia.*

Matty had seated herself beside Gideon. Midway through the meal they had begun to talk, stiffly at first—an odd combination of wariness and formality. But as the lunch went on, their conversation had become more natural. At some point, Rachel had noticed how hard her mother was trying, and seemed a shade less hostile to her.

For dessert Bennie served a huge triple-layer chocolate cake— Rachel's favorite. It said WELCOME BACK RACH in yellow frosting across the top and was decorated with green and yellow stars. It was so good everybody had two pieces. While Bennie served the second helpings Rachel came up behind Croaker and put her arms around him.

"Thanks, Uncle Lew," she whispered in his ear. "For everything."

When he reached up and kissed her cheek he felt hot tears in his eyes.

After lunch, Bennie went aft to smoke another cigar. Croaker joined him.

"Ever since you gave me the bones you found on Rafe's boat I can't, like, stop thinking about my grandfather." Bennie blew a soft stream of smoke that was borne away on the wind. "Even before that, maybe."

He was silent for a long time, and Croaker thought of what Antonio had said: *Humaitá's* Hetá I *training was too much for Bennie. Forever after, he resented his grandfather.*

At last Croaker said, "A force of nature was waiting for us, isn't that what you said, Bennie?"

"Humaitá was that, all right." Bennie stared at the glowing end of his cigar and shook his head in wonderment. "See, it was an amazing thing what you told me about, you know, the tiger shark in Whipray Bay. I mean, what the hell was it doing there? Could have been following Tin Can Channel, I suppose. Water's deeper there. But still . . . It wasn't, like, a natural occurrence." He sucked on his cigar. "It went after Antonio, that beast. Like it was looking for him. Like it had a debt to settle. Could have, if it wanted to, chewed you down to, like, dog meat. But it didn't."

"The curious thing was I had no fear of it," Croaker said.

"To have no fear of a shark." Bennie took the cigar out of his mouth. "That's fucking something to keep in your mind forever."

"I feel as if your grandfather's spirit has been hovering over my shoulder ever since you and I took on the first tiger shark." A small smile spread across Croaker's face. "He was there with me at the end, Bennie. Crazy as it seems, I know it's true."

"I have no doubt, *amigo*." Bennie held up his hand and Croaker grasped it. " 'Cause, see, he's with me now." They looked at each other for a long moment, and something unseen passed between them, some brilliant spark that transcended speech and memory.

At length, Bennie nodded. "The truth, Lewis. I wish to God I had known him better in those days. He wanted something for me I didn't. For his sake, I tried. But as a healer I was no good. Money and power, that was my meat. I wasn't interested in spiritual things. He knew it and didn't, like, blame me." Bennie took another puff of his cigar. "But, see the thing of it is, I blamed him. He'd been real tough on me and I couldn't, you know, get it. I thought he was one hard-hearted sonuvabitch."

"So did Antonio." Croaker had told Bennie some of what Antonio had said. But not all. Secrets were meant to be kept.

Bennie nodded. "Yeah, I suppose it would seem like that to any boy going through *Hetá I* training. It's only in, like, my memory that I can see what he needed to do with us. Believe me, *amigo*, I rue the day I walked away from him." His expression grew uncharacteristically dark. "You know, I . . . it's as if I've convinced myself that if I'd, like, stayed I'd have prevented his murder."

"You can't know that. More probably, you'd have been killed, too."

Bennie shrugged. "Anything's possible, *amigo*."

But he'd said it in a way that made it clear he still blamed himself.

He pointed with his cigar. "This was a neat idea, you know. All the people you love together."

"Family," Croaker said. He thought of what Antonio had said: *The first time I met you I saw all the way down to your soul. I recognized a man as cut off from his past as I was.*

Transformation was just another word for healing, Croaker thought.

"Speaking of which," Bennie said.

Croaker turned his head. "What?"

"Family." Bennie took the cigar out of his mouth. "Speaking of family I'm going back to Asunción Sunday."

Croaker said, "For how long?"

"The truth? I don't know." He clapped Croaker on the back. "No long faces, *amigo*. You had a hand in my decision. When you gave me Humaitá's bones, I realized what I needed to do with them was return them to the Paraguay."

"You'll bury them in the river?"

Bennie looked out to sea. "At first I thought I would. Then I thought not. They're too great a gift." He turned back to Croaker, smiled. "See, I realized I can no longer, like, do what I've been doing. Too much has happened for me to, like, go back. At first I thought I was just, you know, in need of a rest. But now I know better. I'm not the Bennie I was seven weeks ago. The old things I used to covet . . ."

He shrugged. "What to do now, I asked myself? Then I realized the answer was staring me right in the face."

He beckoned, and together they went into the cabin. Croaker saw an old, scuffed, and scarred leather Gladstone bag. Bennie pulled it out from underneath a bench. He opened it and took out a large bone. It looked like a femur. It was smooth and warm-looking. The buttery sunlight lent it the color of ivory.

"The first time I touched them the bones told me, just as if my grandfather was, you know, still alive."

Reverently he put the bone back inside the bag, fastened the brass hasp. He turned to Croaker. "See, I'm going back to study. The bones will help me. A library of knowledge is stored inside them. I'm going to find a *sukia* and learn *Hetá I*."

"It's what Humaitá always wanted for you."

"No, *amigo*." Bennie ushered Croaker back out on deck. "It's what I want for myself."

Croaker could hear Gideon picking out a tune on her guitar. She began to sing. He recognized a Sarah McLachlan song, "Fumbling Towards Ecstasy."

Croaker looked out the window. To the west was the Everglades. The backcountry. "Before you go," he said, "why don't we pay another visit to Stone Tree. I think he'd appreciate seeing Humaitá's bones."

"One healer to another, eh, *amigo*?" Croaker could see that this suggestion made Bennie happy. "Bueno," Bennie said. "I owe him a great debt."

"We both do," Croaker said.

Jenny stuck her head into the open companionway. "Okay for a little company?" As they came back on deck, she slid her arm around Croaker's waist. "Or is this conversation confidential?"

Croaker, hugging her to him, was looking at Rachel. She was

deep in conversation with her mother. There was something about them, limned by the green water and the bright sun. At this distance they might have been sisters. Or even twins.

"Confidential?" Croaker gazed into Jenny's eyes. They were almost the same astonishing color as the ocean. "I don't think there's much need of that around here anymore."